Compromising Positions

Barbara Cutrera

Published by On My Way Up, LLC

This book is a work of fiction. The names, characters, places, and incidents are the result of the author's imagination or are used fictitiously. Any resemblance to actual events, locales, or persons, living or dead, is coincidental.

ISBN: 978-1-944113-04-9

For Uncle Raymond.

Part One

Chapter One

Josie Hollingsworth had no intention of living through that cold November night. Unable to sleep despite her exhaustion, she left the Driskill Hotel at 2:00 a.m. in order to roam the downtown Austin streets. Shivering, she didn't consider returning to her room for a coat. What she *did* consider was how best to end her life, refusing to be a participant in her family's twisted reality any longer.

In the midst of her troubled, aimless wandering, Josie saw something incongruous ahead of her. She realized that the something was a baby crawling along the sidewalk. For an instant, she questioned her sanity.

Perhaps I'm not just overwhelmed and depressed. Maybe I've already gone crazy. Then, *No. I'm not hallucinating. That's a real baby. How did it get here? Where is its mother or father?*

She hurried over to the child, crouching beside it. The baby, clad in faded, blue footie pajamas, stopped, sat, and then smiled at her. She couldn't help but smile back before glancing up and down the street. It was deserted save for her and the child.

Josie picked up the little boy and jogged towards a liquor store that was obviously open all night. A man holding a cloth bag emerged as she approached. He held the door for her, and she thanked him as she rushed inside.

"Hey, *Barbie!*" a gray-haired man with a paunch cried, leering at her as she hurried towards the register. "I like your pretty pink shirt and those skinny jeans! Is that you and Ken's love child?"

Josie had often been compared to a Barbie doll. With her shapely figure, pretty face, large, blue eyes, and long, blonde hair, she understood the reason behind others' eagerness to identify her with the popular doll. However, people often correlated her beauty with low intelligence. And *that* assumption couldn't be farther from the truth.

"The baby's not mine," she countered defensively. Turning towards the elderly man who was obviously the cashier, she said, "I just found him alone outside. Is there a police station nearby? Maybe you could call 911?"

"I ain't gettin' involved in no freaky bullshit!" he insisted. "You want to do somethin' with the kid then take him to the hospital. Make a right when you walk out the door and keep goin'. You'll wind up there."

Josie eventually arrived at the hospital and located the Emergency Room. As she stood in line, she instinctively swayed her hips from side-to-side in what she hoped was a comforting manner for the boy, who simply stared at his surroundings while she held him in her arms. When she made it to the desk, a tired-looking young woman asked her why she was visiting the E.R. that night. When Josie explained, the woman perked up and asked her to step to one side while she called for someone who could help.

Minutes later, a tall, handsome man with broad shoulders and slightly disheveled brown hair approached Josie and the baby. Noting that he wore dark blue scrubs with a long-sleeved, thermal shirt underneath and had a stethoscope around his neck, she deduced that he was a doctor. His complete attention was on the child in her arms. An attractive, middle-aged woman dressed in a magenta top and skirt walked beside him.

"I'm DawnMarie Brittle, a social worker employed by Child Protective Services," the woman said with a smile. "It's a little crazy around here tonight, which is why I happen to be here at the hospital. Would you follow us to an exam room?" When Josie nodded, she added, "Thank you for being patient with us. We'd like to get this properly sorted out."

Once they were in the room, the man, evidently a pediatrician, extended his arms and cooed, "Hey, little guy. How about playing with *me* for a while so the ladies can talk?"

"Are you sure you're not the baby's mother?" Brittle inquired, as the doctor removed the child's pajamas.

"What? No. If I were his mother, then why would I bring him to the hospital, claiming I found him on the sidewalk in the middle of the night?"

"You'd be amazed at the stories we get from parents who want to surrender their children."

"He's *not* mine!" Josie insisted. "I've never married or had children."

"You're obviously good with kids," the doctor noted after he'd listened to the baby's heart and lungs with his stethoscope. "Most abandoned children come in here screaming their heads off."

"He's never made a sound," she admitted. "All he did was grin at me and then...just be okay with whatever I did. How old do you think he is?"

The pediatrician shrugged and said, "I'd guesstimate eight months. He's underweight and not the cleanest, but he seems developmentally appropriate for his age. There are no overt signs of abuse."

Turning his full attention back towards the child, he grinned and lightly tickled him under the chin. When the baby giggled, the man's smile widened. He proceeded to examine the baby's eyes, ears, nose, and mouth.

"So, where do you think his parents are?" Josie asked Ms. Brittle.

"They're probably drug addicts or mentally ill," the woman replied. "We'll take him into State custody and investigate. He may be reunited with his family someday, depending on the circumstances. Otherwise, he'll end up with new parents, whether it's as a foster child or through adoption."

"If his parents are drug addicts or mentally ill, then he'd *better* be given to someone else!" Josie snapped. "Poor baby."

"You saved his life," the pediatrician said as he passed the child a toy. "He could have been hurt by someone or run over by a car. It's also freezing outside, as you obviously know first-hand." Shaking his head, he said ruefully, "Forgive me. I completely forgot my manners. We're really short-staffed tonight, and I was only thinking about my patient. I should have introduced myself right away and then thanked you."

"It's okay. It doesn't matter."

"I disagree. My Mama and Daddy would be ashamed of me." Extending his right hand while keeping the left one on the baby's back, he said, "I'm Stone Romero, a second-year pediatric resident here at the hospital. Thank you for what you did, Miss...?"

"Hollingsworth," she said, shaking and then quickly releasing his hand.

3

"It's a pleasure to meet you. You did an amazing thing tonight. The police will have to take a statement from you before you go. It's protocol. I'll finish up here and get this little guy situated."

Josie stared at the baby, who smiled at her again. For some reason, she felt less inclined to kill herself. She looked to Dr. Romero and nodded; then she followed Ms. Brittle to a waiting room. There, she retold her story to the police. By the time they informed her she was free to go it was 7:00 a.m.

As she left the hospital, Josie wondered if she could remember how to get back to her hotel. Wandering in a daze through an unfamiliar city in the middle of the night, she hadn't paid attention to street names or directions. At the time, she hadn't cared. Now, all she wanted to do was eat, find her way back to the Driskill, and sleep. When she woke, then she could decide whether or not she thought it was worth living for another day.

"Miss Hollingsworth!"

Pausing, she turned back towards the hospital. Dr. Romero, now wearing jeans, athletic shoes, a black shirt, and a black leather jacket, was hurrying towards her. As he walked, he slipped off his jacket. Once he reached her, he draped it around her shoulders before she could protest.

"You saved that baby's life. It's cold out here, and the least I can do is give you my jacket."

"Are you always this involved when it comes to your patients and what happens at the hospital?"

"Working with abused, neglected, and abandoned children is my pediatric area of concentration. I do treat 'regular' kids, but the other ones are my specialty. I'm good with children and know that the ones who require special attention will grow up and can either become healthy, well-adjusted adults or end up in damaging lifestyles and relationships. When I work with those kids, I feel like I'm making a *real* difference, helping one kid at a time."

"That's very noble, Dr. Romero."

"Noble? I never thought of it like that, but thanks. Please, call me Stone."

"Only if you agree to call me Josie and not Miss Hollingsworth."

"I can do that." Stone narrowed his eyes and said, "You look like you're about to faint. When's the last time you ate?"

4

"Earlier yesterday before I arrived in Austin."

"You just rescued a helpless baby. Let me repay your kindness by at least making sure you eat some good food and get some rest. No strings attached."

Too tired to argue, she shrugged and said, "Lead the way."

Josie had expected him to take her to a local diner or coffee shop. Therefore, she was surprised when he led her to an apartment building several blocks away from the hospital. As they climbed the stairs to the third floor, he asked her whether or not she was afraid he might mean to do her any harm.

"No. You're not the type."

"How can you tell?"

"I learned early on how to tell. I'm good at reading people. It's part of what made me such a successful realtor."

"You're not from anywhere around here, are you?" Stone asked, as he unlocked the door to his apartment.

"No. I drove here from L.A." As they went inside, she observed, "You don't talk like a Texan either."

"I'm not. I'm from Louisiana."

"You don't sound Cajun."

"Not all Louisianans are Cajun. That's a common misconception the tourist brokers like to promote to draw in more visitors. I grew up in northern Louisiana. No Cajun accent there."

"What brought you to Austin?"

"A pediatric residency in a location I liked. You?"

"I was tired of life in L.A. I quit my job, sold my house, and just started driving. If I keep going, then Louisiana will probably be the next state I visit."

"Do yourself a favor and stop where you are, unless you prefer regressive instead of progressive."

She was about to ask him to elucidate then decided against it. Whatever his thoughts were regarding his home state, they didn't matter to her. At that moment, nothing really mattered to her except food and sleep.

"Why don't you sit at the breakfast bar while I cook?" Stone suggested. "Do you like veggie omelets? I make them with egg whites, but people tell me they taste just as good as the ones made with whole eggs."

"I like anything."

5

Anything that doesn't come out of a dumpster, she added silently.

While the man pulled out a skillet and the makings of their breakfast, Josie scanned her surroundings. The apartment was comfortable but upscale. The couch and chairs were neutral and over-sized, and they rested on a rug that was decorated with dark red, green, blue, and black geometric patterns. The coffee table and end tables were black, and the light fixtures were made of sleek brushed steel. The dining table and chairs were also black, as were the stools at the granite breakfast bar. The appliances were all stainless steel. The artwork was abstract and eye-catching. The place was trendy and attractive.

When Josie glanced back at Stone, she noted that *he* was also very attractive. He was muscular but lean and had chiseled cheekbones and a mouth that had enticingly full lips. She loved the way his dark brown hair was always in rakish disarray and the gleam in his brown eyes. He seemed at ease with himself and others and appeared to be a genuinely caring human being. After spending over a year working in real estate for the wealthy in California, Josie found him extremely refreshing and appealing. This made her inexplicably uncomfortable.

Once their omelets were ready, Stone sat beside her. The food smelled wonderful, and Josie's stomach growled loudly. Acknowledging that she was ravenous, she eagerly took her first bite. She then hastily took another and then another.

"This breakfast is chef quality," she said between mouthfuls.

"Thanks," Stone said with a small smile. "I've always loved to cook."

"Did you learn from your mother?"

"Both of my parents enjoy cooking although not food like this. Mama makes pretty standard stuff like pot roasts and potatoes. Daddy cleans and cooks whatever he kills when he hunts or fishes and taught me how to do those things. I learned to cook in other ways when I was in college and medical school. I find it relaxing."

"*You're* a hunter?"

"You don't grow up in a state labeled 'Sportsman's Paradise' without learning how to hunt and fish. Well, not where I came from. I'm certain inner city kids in Shreveport, New Orleans, and Baton Rouge aren't out hunting deer or going fishing on weekends."

6

"No, probably not."

"We always eat what we kill." After finishing his omelet, he added, "We were raised never to waste anything."

Josie stared morosely at her empty plate and said, "Us, too."

Stone cleared his throat and then asked if he could take her dish. Without waiting for her to answer, he picked it up and carried it to the sink. Once he'd rinsed their plates and forks and loaded them in the dishwasher, he asked Josie if she wanted more orange juice. Barely able to keep her eyes open, she shook her head.

"You don't look like you're going to make it to the hotel," Stone observed. "I have a guest bed if you want to crash there for a while once your food's gone down."

"I don't think I can stay awake that long."

"You have to sit up for at least thirty minutes," he insisted. "Rule of thumb."

"Thank you, Dr. Romero," she said with sarcasm. "How about if I use the bathroom and walk *really* slowly to the bed? Would that be good enough for you?"

He flashed her a heart-stopping grin and said, "Only if you walk *really, really* slowly."

"If you put a blanket on top of the bedspread, then I won't get it dirty. I'm sure my clothes aren't that clean after everything that's happened tonight."

"Bedspreads and sheets can be washed, but you probably won't be very comfortable in your jeans and shirt. You want some of my pajamas?" He gave her a once-over with his eyes and said, "I'm six feet one and pretty solid, and you look like you're about half a foot shorter and a lot thinner. The pajamas will swallow you but would be a lot more conducive to a restful sleep."

Josie accepted his offer. The pajama bottoms were several inches too long and too big at the waist. Luckily, they had a drawstring. Even when she pulled the string as tightly as she could, they hung low on her hips. Fortunately, the heavy knit top that accompanied them was way too long. She rolled up the cuffs on the sleeves and left the modern-style guest bathroom, feeling as if she might not make it to the bed.

Stone was suddenly by her side, guiding her towards the guest bedroom and the full-sized black iron bed topped with a multi-colored patterned quilt that awaited her there. Once she was lying

7

down, he covered her with the sheet, blanket, and quilt. Josie shut her eyes and imagined that she felt him gently stroking her hair.

"So, which was it for you?" the pediatrician asked softly.

"Which was what?" she mumbled.

"Were your parents drug addicts or mentally ill? I saw the way you reacted when Ms. Brittle made that comment in the exam room. It had an obvious and immediate emotional impact on you. And the fact that you came home with me afterwards, seemingly unconcerned about your safety, tells me that you need help. That leads me back to my original question about your parents. Were they addicts or were they mentally ill?"

No one in Josie's adult life had ever suspected how odd her home environment had been during her childhood. She should be affronted that this person she barely knew would ask her such an intimate question, yet she found she wasn't angry. Surprisingly, she felt relieved.

"Mentally ill," she murmured. "All but me now." Recalling her earlier desire to kill herself, she added, "Maybe me, too."

"I don't believe that you're mentally ill," he said reassuringly. "Perhaps a little mentally under the weather. Get some sleep. I'll be in the apartment if you need anything. I'm off work today and tomorrow. Sleep as long as you –"

Josie woke, disoriented and frightened. After a few anxious moments, she remembered where she was and took several deep, cleansing breaths. She tried not to think of how despondent she felt, of how her life had no purpose, and of how terrified she was that she might soon succumb to madness. She wanted more than anything to experience the release that came after prolonged weeping, but she shed no tears. Instead, she glanced at the digital clock on the bedside table and noted that it was 6:42 a.m. She'd slept for almost twenty-four hours.

Wondering if Stone would be awake or asleep, Josie carefully opened the door of the guest bedroom and peered out into the main living area. All was quiet. She used the bathroom before going out into the open-concept living, dining, and kitchen space. Her jeans, shirt, socks, bra, and panties appeared to have been freshly laundered and were stacked neatly on a chair by the couch. Her iPhone wallet was nowhere in sight, but her athletic shoes rested on the floor in front of the chair.

"I muted your phone so that the ringing wouldn't disturb you," a fully clothed Stone said from the kitchen, startling her and making her jump. "While you were asleep, you had twelve calls from one number, twenty-nine from another, and one from a third."

Livid, Josie asked, "You listened to my messages?"

"Of course not."

"Then how could you know?"

"Because most people don't get that many calls in one day unless they're using their phone for serious business purposes. You said you're a realtor, but you made it sound like you weren't currently doing that. When the thing kept vibrating, I got curious. I didn't listen to any messages, but I did scan the numbers. Unless you're a drug dealer whose runners are trying to contact her, I'm thinking your family's attempting to reach you."

Josie held out her hand and asked, "May I have my phone back?"

"Here you go," he said, passing her the wallet. "Sorry."

Opening it, Josie scanned the numbers listed on her phone's Voicemail screen. Twelve messages were from her father; twenty-nine were from her mother; and one was from her sister. When she bit her lip and began to cry quietly, Stone came directly over to her and placed his hands on the sides of her shoulders, urging her to tell him what was wrong.

"I don't want to unload on you. You've been so good to me since we left the hospital yesterday."

"Unload all you want. I think you need a friend right now. I can take it, Josie. Go ahead."

"You're sure?"

"I'm sure. Talk to me."

Gesturing to the phone with her free hand, she exclaimed, "I can't do *this* anymore! It has to end! I'm trapped by my family's insanity, and I'm beyond *done*!"

When Stone put his arms around her and pulled her against him, Josie gave in and wept. He sighed, but it wasn't a sigh of exasperation. No, it was a sigh rooted in deep sadness.

The pediatrician extricated the iPhone from Josie's hand, pocketed it, took her to the couch, and urged her to sit beside him. He then drew her into his arms once again, passing her some tissues from the box that rested on an end table. She wiped at her face and nose and then closed her eyes. She savored the comforting feeling that came with being held by someone, being able to share a burden that had weighed her down for twenty years.

"Why are you doing this? Why do you care?"

"My grandmother, Memaw, is mentally ill," he confided. "She's bipolar. It was terrible for me to see her suffer and act crazy when she'd go off her meds, but I didn't live with her when I was a boy. I can't imagine what it must be like to grow up with two mentally ill parents."

"And now my sister," Josie confided tearfully. "My sister isn't there."

"Shhh," he murmured. "*You're* going to be all right."

"I'm not. I can't handle anymore, and I might end up just like them. I'm twenty-five, and people usually develop schizophrenia in their teens or twenties."

"Is that what your parents and sister have?"

"My mother and sister. My father has Obsessive-Compulsive Disorder and severe anxiety issues."

"And your parents have been like that since you were born?"

Josie laughed bitterly and said, "My parents met in a mental institution. When they got out, they got married. Of course, both of them were on their meds and were functioning members of society at the time. Then my mom got pregnant and had to get off her meds so they wouldn't harm her baby. According to my father, she was totally whacked out during her pregnancy, thought my sister was an alien's baby, and wanted to kill her. Once my sister was born, my dad insisted my mom get back on her meds. Things were okay again until she got pregnant with me, and the same thing happened."

"Were you an alien's baby?"

"No, I was the next Christ child. I suppose when I turned out to be a girl that blew her theory right out of the water."

"Your mother got back on her meds after you were born?"

"Yes. My early years were happy and stable, but then my dad's meds stopped working for him when I was five and my sister was seven. He was never right after that. Nothing else the doctors tried worked or else they worked but then he'd feel better and quit taking them. My mom went on and off her meds all the time, starting when I was six. Zelda and I got used to it. We had to."

"I've never heard of anyone named Zelda."

"I've never heard of anyone named Stone."

He grinned and said, "My parents haven't ever told me why they chose Stone for my name, but I like it. What about your sister?"

"My father has a Ph.D. in English. One of his favorite authors is F. Scott Fitzgerald. He thought my sister would be a boy and wanted to name her Scott. When she was born, he decided to name her Zelda after Fitzgerald's wife. I guess it was fitting, since Zelda Fitzgerald was also super smart but crazy."

"Your sister's super smart?"

"She was a very successful stock broker on Wall Street until she manifested the schizophrenia."

"And your mother?"

"Has a Ph.D. in Psychology."

"Naturally," Stone said sardonically. "Did you have grandparents or aunts and uncles who helped you and your sister through all the chaos when you were growing up?"

"No."

"And no one tried to take the two of you away from them?"

"Neighbors or teachers would call Child Protective Services when things were glaringly unacceptable. They didn't know the half of it. We lived with foster parents here and there. When my parents would temporarily get it together, the courts would give us back. Zelda and I moved out as soon as we could once we were of age."

"When did your sister manifest schizophrenia?"

"About six months ago. She's lost her boyfriend, her career, and her home. She won't tell me where she lives, because she says people are trying to kill her."

"A paranoid schizophrenic." Sighing, he asked, "Where do your parents live?"

"Virginia."

"When's the last time you saw them?"

"Last March. Zelda and I always go to see them for a few days each spring. I talk to them on the phone once or twice a week."

"Do they always call you so much in-between your conversations?"

"My father phones twelve times a day to each of us girls. It's part of his OCD. He feels as if he has to call every hour on the hour from 7:00 a.m. to 7:00 p.m. All he says is 'hello' and that he loves

11

us and to be safe. Mom usually phones once or twice a day and rambles until the voicemail times out. Lately, she's been calling dozens of times."

"And Zelda?"

"We used to talk on the phone off and on all the time."

"And now?"

Josie shook her head slightly and admitted, "I get a call every day or two, but she's talking crazy like Mom. I haven't answered her calls since she told me she was being hunted by the President of the United States because she knew he'd been personally responsible for letting aliens experiment on human beings. I couldn't listen anymore. She's not Zelda anymore."

Stone pulled another tissue from the box and dabbed at Josie's damp cheeks. He asked her if she'd ever had counseling related to her family's mental illness issues.

"Off and on since I was a child. Some of the therapists were okay, and some weren't. I always get told how patient I am and that I'm doing everything right, but there is no solution. Things are what they are. My parents and sister can't help that they're sick, but I can't take dealing with them anymore. *I'm* going to go crazy soon. With two mentally ill parents and now my sister, I worry about going crazy as it is. I'm totally drained and alone."

"Is that the real reason you quit your job and set out on a road trip to nowhere?"

After a brief pause, she admitted, "Yes."

"And you have no idea what you're going to do with your life?"

"No."

Stone was silent. Josie was fine with silent. Just having another person hear her story and sympathize was tremendously comforting. She listened to the sound of the steady beating of his heart and drifted back to sleep.

Chapter Two

"What time is it?" Josie mumbled when she woke in Stone's comforting embrace.

"9:00. Are you ready for breakfast?"

"If *you're* cooking."

She heard the rumble of laughter in his chest and smiled. Reluctantly moving away from the man, Josie stood and stretched before thanking him for washing her clothing and informing him that she was going to get dressed.

"I hate to put on the clean clothes," she admitted. "I feel grungy."

"You can shower in the guest bathroom," he offered. "Take your time, and I'll get things ready in here."

Josie carried her clean clothing to the guest bathroom and placed it on the counter before removing Stone's pajamas and depositing them in a nearby hamper. She then proceeded to enjoy a long, hot shower, emerging refreshed. Once her skin was dry and her blonde hair only somewhat damp, she reached for her underwear. She experienced a feeling of embarrassment as she envisioned Stone handling her undergarments and hastened to put on her panties, bra, jeans, and shirt. Then she used a brush she found in a drawer to work out the tangles in her hair.

Josie studied her reflection in the mirror. She *was* too thin and seemed unusually pale. The mental strain was physically wearing her down. She wondered how long she'd looked so weary.

Did my friends and colleagues in L.A. notice, or were they so wrapped up in their own lives that they didn't see how much I needed help? Did they even care? Stone seems to care, and he barely knows me. Perhaps he's like this with everyone. Or is there something in particular about me that appeals to him? Shaking her head, Josie thought, *He works with abused, neglected, and abandoned children. Look at my background. He feels sorry for me; that's all there is to it.*

She padded barefoot back to the living area and saw that Stone had set out placemats, napkins, plates, glasses, and silverware on the dining room table. A covered round dish and a platter of muffins rested between the place settings.

"You didn't have to do all this," she protested. "We could've eaten at the breakfast bar again."

"We could have. This was no trouble. You deserved a little something special, and I had the time to do it this morning."

"Thank you. What's on the menu?"

"Blueberry muffins and a bacon and cheese quiche I made earlier."

"Not very heart healthy. Aren't doctors supposed to promote good eating habits?"

"Definitely. That doesn't mean we stick to them all the time. I know some doctors think they're God, but none of us are perfect."

"Do you think of yourself as God?"

He laughed and said, "Not even close. I'm just a man trying to do his best."

"You seem to be doing a great job." After eating a bite of the quiche, she added, "I wish I'd been taught to cook like this."

"Are your parents good cooks?"

"Adequate when they remember to buy food. They tend to eat fast food most of the time."

"So, you were raised on fast food?"

"Fast food or no food. When our parents were off their meds, Zelda and I became foragers. You'd be amazed at what gets thrown into dumpsters. People are so wasteful, but I shouldn't complain. We'd find food, clothes, shoes, and other useful things during our excavations."

Stone grimaced and asked, "What did you do with the useful things *you* couldn't use yourselves?"

"Brought them to local shelters so other people could use them." Breaking off a piece from a muffin, Josie asked, "Could we change the topic?"

"Sure. What led you to become a realtor?"

"We never had a house. Our parents rented apartments. It was one eviction after another. I wanted to have the satisfaction of helping people purchase their own living space. I bought my own house in L.A. last year."

"Do you still own it?"

14

"I put it on the market once I quit my job. After the closing last week, I just piled what I hadn't donated to charity into my car and started driving."

"Did you make enough money to live for a while until you decide what you want to do?"

"I was a realtor for high-end properties. I have a lot of money in savings and investments and a good profit from the sale of my house. Knowing how to live economically, I could probably exist indefinitely with the funds I have. The thing is that I don't want to exist. I honestly don't know what to do with myself."

"Do you want to continue being a realtor?"

"I'm not certain."

"What's your undergraduate degree in?"

"Business administration."

"There are administrative jobs open at the hospital. They don't all pay much, but it doesn't sound like money's a big concern for you at the moment. Maybe you could apply for one of those, work for a while, and see what you'd like to do after that."

"I just got to Austin and am staying at a hotel. I've been a realtor for the last three years. What makes you think they'd want to hire me for a job at the hospital?"

"Because they always need competent employees. You're in your twenties and were successfully selling high-end properties in L.A. I'm thinking you can more than handle an administrative job at a hospital. As for the living situation, you're a realtor. You could probably find an apartment this afternoon. There's actually a one-bedroom unit available on this floor. I could put in a good word for you, both here and at the hospital."

"In exchange for...?"

"I like you a lot. I'd like to keep seeing you on a regular basis. You're different from other women."

"*That's* putting it mildly."

"Don't be self-deprecating. I find you very attractive and intriguing."

"Everyone thinks I'm attractive."

"Is that a bad thing?"

"I'm pretty and blonde, so others assume I must be an airhead." Josie's face flushed as she said, "But you mentioned that I was intriguing. No one's ever said that about me before. What's so intriguing about me?"

"Your outlook on your life and the way you survived and made a success out of such an abnormal situation. I'm in awe of you."

"Awe? All I did was keep going."

"Not true. You managed to thrive despite your home environment. You helped others when you could barely take care of yourself. It seems like you're still doing it. Look at what you did for the baby you found yesterday. I could immediately tell that you were in a bad place emotionally, but you focused on saving him anyway." When Josie said nothing, Stone asked, "Are you interested in me? Even if you're not, I'll help you find a place to live and a job if I can. You need someone to be here for you right now."

"I find you extremely appealing and attractive. If I weren't so tired and confused I'd ask you to make love to me this minute, and I don't usually go to bed with men until after I've dated them for several months at least."

"Nice to know."

"Which part?"

"That you want me, like me, and don't sleep around. I'm drawn to you, Josie. Tell me more about yourself."

"I've done a lot of talking since we met. Tell me more about *you*. I know you're a pediatrician and a fantastic cook who knows how to hunt and has a mother, a father, and a bipolar grandmother. What else should I know?"

"My younger brother died a year ago. I have an older brother who owns a bar and strip club. My nephew is sixteen. Daddy's the sheriff of the town, and Mama's a housewife. They live in an ass-backwards town with a bunch of ass-backwards people. I couldn't wait to get out, although I do love my family. They'll never change, and neither will the people in that area. They have a whole different mindset than I do."

"How often do you see your family?"

"I haven't seen them since my brother's funeral. I talk briefly to my parents on the phone every few months. We spoke more often before my brother died. I do still call my grandmother once a month and have a long conversation with her. *That* hasn't changed."

"But you don't talk to your older brother?"

16

"*No*," he said emphatically.

"Is your brother married?"

"Divorced. His son is wonderful but is hanging out with the wrong crowd. I worry about him. He calls me once in a blue moon to talk, and I try to be supportive and give him good advice. I don't think he takes it, but he keeps calling. That gives me hope."

"You said you talk to your grandmother once a month. Are your other grandparents still alive?"

"No. There's only my Memaw. The others all died early of either cardiovascular disease or COPD. Everyone in the family smokes, except me."

"Ugh. My parents may be crazy, but they never smoked."

"You see? It's not all bad, is it?"

"I guess not," she smirked. "What's a lifetime of insanity versus cardiovascular disease and COPD?"

Her iPhone rang, and Josie tensed. She knew the only way to stop the calls was to ask that her number be disconnected. However, if she did that then she was completely cutting herself off from her parents and sister. If there was an actual emergency, they'd have no way to reach her.

"You aren't listening to their messages any longer as it is," Stone pointed out when she voiced her concern. "Something could've already happened, and you'd never know. Why don't you tell them the truth?"

"Because it wouldn't stop them. They're not rational. Also, they love me, and I love them. They're my family, even if I can't take dealing with them anymore. I don't want to hurt their feelings."

"Keep your old number so that they can call like they have been. You get a separate line that'll be the primary one you'll use, but don't give that number to your family members. That way, your parents and sister can do their usual thing, but maybe you won't feel so hounded all the time. You could listen to the messages whenever you want and delete them without being so…haunted by them."

"I could try that."

"Then put on your socks and shoes, and let's take care of it right now. Otherwise, you won't be able to think of anything else."

Before lunchtime, Josie had purchased an inexpensive, serviceable phone and had transferred her old line to it. Her iPhone now had a new number that would not be shared with her mother, father, or Zelda. She felt exuberant as she switched off the cell phone and slipped it into her purse. As they walked towards a local organic market that also served lunches, Josie gave Stone her new number, put his name and number in her Contacts list then called the Human Resource Department at the hospital to inquire about employment opportunities. Soon, she had an interview scheduled with a woman named Bridget Juarez for the following day at 10:00.

"Damn, you're good," Stone remarked once she'd finished the call. "I can see why you were such a successful realtor. You really know how to work people to get what you want."

"Survival instincts. People should always use their best attributes to get what they need. Well, within reason. I know that a lot of people find me attractive. It's that whole Barbie Doll image thing. I'd never dream of using it for my own gain though."

"Why not?"

"Because I watched Zelda do it, and it made me feel like she was prostituting herself to get her way. She used her body in combination with her brains in order to climb the Wall Street ladder at such a fast pace. She didn't see anything wrong with it. I love Zelda so much, but I thought less of her for doing that."

"As well you should. I've seen it happen a lot in my field. Men and women always seem to be trying to use sex to advance their careers or to 'snare' a doctor. You never know who's sincere and who's just out to get a promotion or become a trophy wife or husband."

"Who wants their lifetime job description to be 'ornament' when asked?"

Smiling, the pediatrician inquired playfully, "Are you being sincere or trying to snare a doctor for a husband?"

Grinning back at him, Josie said sweetly, "Well, I would make the most perfect trophy wife. After all, I look like Barbie, know how to get my way, and would probably make classically beautiful babies with a handsome doctor. Of course, they might all be schizophrenic, OCD-laden, anxiety-ridden children, but the Christmas card pictures would look fabulous!"

Stone stopped walking, which caused Josie to stop as well. When she turned towards him, he was rubbing his chin, looking contemplative. Bewildered, she waited for an explanation.

"You could never be a trophy wife for any man," he said quietly. "You're too honest for that." Hesitating, he asked, "Have you ever seriously considered marriage and children?"

"Marriage, maybe. But children? With my family's mental illness genes? After Zelda went crazy, I decided that having a family was not in my future."

He nodded thoughtfully, and Josie's heart sank. She truly felt an emotional longing for Stone Romero and a connection to him that she'd never felt with any other man she'd known. He was a pediatrician who was good with kids. It was only logical that he'd want to have a family of his own someday. Would he actually continue to move towards a relationship with her if he knew she had no intentions of procreating with any man?

He surprised her by asking, "Do you have pictures of your family?"

"Only one. It's back at the hotel."

"Let's go there after lunch. I'd love to see it."

"I'll show you mine if you show me yours," she said in an attempt to lighten the mood. "I want to see a picture of your family, too."

Relaxing, Stone nodded and said, "Okay. Let's do it."

After their lunch, they went to the historic Driskill Hotel and then took an elevator up to Josie's third-floor room. While Stone sat on the edge of the bed, she withdrew the framed photo of her family from one suitcase. She sat on the mattress beside him and handed him the picture, watching his face as he studied it. She tried to read his expression but felt as though she were failing miserably.

"You all look very happy," he eventually commented. "Your dad's a handsome guy, and your mom and sister are almost as beautiful as you."

"Thank you. That was a long time ago. My parents don't look like that anymore. Time and mental illness have taken their toll."

"All blonde-haired and blue-eyed. Interesting," Stone murmured. "What are your folks' names?"

"Clark and Rhonda."

"They look middle-aged in this photo, even though you and Zelda look very young."

"They married at thirty-seven, had Zelda when they were thirty nine, and had me when they were forty-one. They're sixty-six now."

Touching the glass with one fingertip, Josie said, "This was taken right before The Last Christmas."

"The Last Christmas?"

"That's the way I always think of it. For the first five years of my life, everything was really good. I had loving, highly intelligent, witty parents who were very involved with both of their children. My parents were respected college professors. Our family had lived in the same large, well-kept apartment since Zelda was a baby. This photo was taken right before the last normal Christmas we ever had, before our mother and father started to permanently fall apart. Then things were crazy, and we were moving all the time and never knew what to expect from them or from life."

"Did Santa Claus still come after The Last Christmas?"

Josie shook her head before saying, "When I was seven, there was a Santa at the mall near where our apartment happened to be at that time. It was free to sit on Santa's lap, and I told Zelda I wanted to ask Santa some questions. She took me, and I asked Santa why he hadn't come to our apartment the year before. I told him my sister and I were always good girls, but there hadn't been any presents when I was six. I wanted to know if we'd done something wrong so that we could make it right.

"The man assured me we hadn't done anything wrong and said that every once in a while there was a mistake on his list. The elf who was in charge of it was very old and was forgetful sometimes. He asked if we'd moved from where we used to live when he'd last come to our apartment. I told him that we'd moved twice and were about to move again. He explained that this may have been the reason he hadn't visited the previous year and apologized before suggesting we wait for him inside the pretend house behind his chair. He said he'd be there in a few minutes when he took his break. We complied, and soon he was kneeling next to a red sack that had a rope tying the top. He undid the rope and removed two wrapped boxes for each of us, one for the last year and one for the current year. He said we didn't have to wait until Christmas morning to open them. He also told us he may not be able to find our apartments in the future, but he wanted us to know that we were on the 'good girl' list and that he expected us to stay on it. We thanked him, and he smiled but it looked like he was sad, too. I asked him if he'd tell the elf who'd left us off the list not to feel bad. Zelda seconded the motion and said that everyone made mistakes. He assured us that he'd pass our message along and wished us a merry Christmas. Then we ran home and hurried to our room."

"What did he give you?"

"We each got a necklace that had a jingle bell on it and a little stuffed toy. Mine was a snow leopard, and Zelda's was a polar bear cub."

"Do you still have the toy and the necklace?"

"No. Both toys got lost during one of our hasty moves. As for the necklace, it wasn't an expensive thing. The chain broke somewhere a year or so later while I was out and about. I didn't know where it fell off. Zelda's had already broken. It was okay. We both knew by then that there was really no Santa Claus and were simply thankful for the man's generosity. We obviously weren't the first kids he'd helped at Christmas. I wish I'd been able to thank him once I realized the truth."

Josie was suddenly very tired again. Stone asked her if she wanted him to leave and come back another time.

"No. A deal's a deal. You still have to show me your family picture."

"We can do that tomorrow. Right now, you look sick. I'm worried about you."

Instantly panicked, she demanded, "Don't worry about me! I'm fine! I'm not sick! Nothing's wrong!"

Stone took her by the shoulders and said gently, but firmly, "It's natural for people to worry about each other sometimes."

"Not in our house it wasn't," she offered. "My father...the OCD and anxiety...everything's worry and danger and fear. I hate it! I've always hated it! We can't control everything or anyone –"

"And I understand."

She drew in a shaky breath and then asked, "Stone, will you just make love to me now and get it over with?"

He chuckled and said, "Well, when you make it sound romantic like that, it's awfully tempting."

"You know we're going to end up in bed together."

"I'd rather be lying in my bed with you than anywhere else, but that would be wrong. We hardly know each other, and we have no protection. We need to wait."

"You're probably right," she said wearily.

"I *know* I'm right."

"Could we go back to your place to look at the picture now? I don't really want to stay here at the hotel by myself."

"You could stay in my guest room. You'll need a local address for your interview tomorrow."

"And you don't believe the Human Resource people will think it's odd that you and I have the same address?"

"Our human resource manager will grill you even harder if the connection's made. She won't hire you unless she thinks you're supremely qualified." Rising from the bed, he said, "I'll help you gather your suitcases, and we can drive to my place. I have two parking slots allotted to me, but I only have one car. I usually leave the other slot open for guests. You're my guest."

Beginning to have misgivings, Josie said, "Maybe this is a mistake. I have so much emotional baggage, and it's not like it's going to go away."

"I have my own baggage. You've yet to learn about my family weirdness."

"It can't compare to mine."

"I try not to compare baggage. Come on."

Within the hour they were back at Stone's apartment, and Josie's belongings were in his guest room. Stone had her sit on the couch while he retrieved a framed photo from what she assumed was his bedroom. He sat next to her and said, "Here you go."

She studied the smiling Romero family. The picture looked fairly recent and featured Stone, a middle-aged couple who were obviously his parents, an elderly woman who must be his Memaw, two men who must be his brothers, and a boy who appeared to be in his early teens. She asked him to tell her each subject's name and relation to him.

Stone pointed to the elderly, slender woman with white hair and glasses and said, "Memaw, my father's mother. She's eighty and lives in a house behind my parents' place. She's amazing."

"And those are evidently your parents. Your father's hair is dark brown like yours, but your mother is almost blonde."

"Their names are Vin and Dumpling respectively."

"Dumpling?"

"I think her folks thought it was endearing. She's plump, as you can tell. Her parents were kind of large themselves, so I suppose the name fit as it turned out."

"Your father's not heavy."

"He stays pretty active when he is and isn't at work. Like I said, he enjoys hunting and fishing."

"And the boy is your nephew?"

"Tommy."

"He looks like you and the one brother. Which one of your brothers is his father?"

"The one he doesn't look like." Stone pointed to the heavyset man with sandy brown hair and said, "That's Cheek."

"Cheek?"

"No one can remember when or where he got the nickname. His real name is Larry."

"And your other brother? The two of you look exactly alike although you have different hairstyles."

"That's because we're identical twins. I was the first to be delivered. We were very close."

"What was his name?"

"Nelson."

"Was he a doctor, too?"

"He was an interior designer. He was really good at it and should have gone someplace like Chicago, New York, or L.A. The farthest he got was New Orleans."

"How come?"

"Because he always wanted our parents and brother to accept him for what he was and hoped someday they would. So, he didn't go too far. Our parents loved him, but they could never accept that he was gay."

"If he was your twin, then he was young when he died. How did it happen?"

Stone looked away but said, "He made a trip home for Thanksgiving last year. I didn't go, because I'd contracted a stomach bug. I should've gone anyway. I should've known."

"Known what?"

"I was always Nelson's protector. We were identical twins and had one of those bonds you read about or hear of on television. I knew he was gay from the time we were little, maybe even before he

23

was aware of it himself. As he got older and it became pretty apparent, people talked and kids bullied. Daddy and Cheek used to say that Nelson needed to 'man up' and act more masculine. Nelson couldn't be anything other than what he was, although he tried to appease them by hunting and fishing with us."

"What happened when he went home for Thanksgiving last year?"

Stone placed the picture on the coffee table, saying angrily, "Cheek decided he was going to 'convert' Nelson to heterosexuality. There's a brothel, a place on the outskirts of the parish. I guess Cheek thought if Nelson had sex with a woman that it would turn him into the man he was supposed to be. It didn't work out that way.

"I don't know the whole story. What I was told later was that Cheek brought Nelson to the brothel and had called ahead to let the Madam know the situation. She had one of her prettiest, sweetest girls on hand for Nelson. When Nelson realized what was going on, he protested and tried to leave. Cheek told him he should keep an open mind." Shaking his head, he snapped, "As if Cheek ever had an open mind about anything!"

"And Nelson wanted to please, so he went with the girl?"

"Yes. Nelson tried to…perform, but he couldn't. When he and Cheek left, he seemed shaken. Cheek said he dropped Nelson off at our parents' home around 5:00 in the morning. Nelson never went inside. Some people saw him jump off the bridge over the river when they were on their way to work at 6:00. His body washed up on the banks a mile or so downstream."

Josie's eyes stung with tears as she said, "It wasn't your fault."

"I would've stopped Cheek if I'd been there. I could've saved Nelson. I lost half of myself that day. Cheek and I haven't spoken since. He has no idea that Tommy calls me to talk and would forbid him to do so if he did.

"I hate my brother, and I hate that my parents didn't blame him for Nelson's death. They actually lauded Cheek's desire to 'save' Nelson from being gay. They're so fucking backwards! My Memaw's the only one who understood. She's civil to Cheek because he's her grandson, but she told me after Nelson's funeral that she would never feel the same about Cheek again. She said if God hadn't meant for there to be gay people on Earth, then there wouldn't be any. She told me she thought that small-mindedness was appalling and that it was that kind of thinking that led to cross-burnings, hangings, and other hate crimes." Smiling slightly, he said, "I do so love my Memaw."

"You didn't kill your brother."

"I might as well have. At least he's at peace now, but I'd rather have him be at peace and alive." Standing, he announced, "I have to go to work in a couple hours. After I put this picture away, I'll make us some dinner and head out."

"Or we could just have sex," Josie said earnestly.

"And get it over with? If we have sex, then we won't be doing it just to get it over with and keep going. If we have sex, we need to be ready for whatever happens afterwards. I have no idea what that'll be. Plus, we still don't have protection."

"You don't have condoms?"

"You told me you don't sleep around. Well, neither do I. The condoms I have are over a year old. I wouldn't trust them not to break."

I'll have to add condoms to my shopping list for tomorrow, Josie thought, as she waited for Stone to return to the room. *This whole thing is crazy, but then what should I expect with my background? Things between us are moving so fast, but Stone seems more than all right with it. Maybe he's just lonely. Maybe it's simply part of his nature to want to help people. But he hasn't had sex with anyone in over a year, and he's talking about doing that with me. He must really like and want me, whatever the reason. I certainly like him. If this doesn't work out, then I'll survive and move on. Or not. I'll have to wait and see.*

Chapter Three

When the alarm clock rang at 6:00 the following morning, Josie woke filled with energy and anticipation. According to Stone, there was a grocery store on the next block that opened at 7:00, and she intended to visit it for necessary supplies, return to the apartment, shower, get ready for her interview at the hospital, hopefully gain employment there, do some shopping for clothing, and then have lunch with Stone at a nearby restaurant. She was counting on the fact that he'd return home while she was at the store and that he wouldn't see her until they were scheduled to meet for lunch.

Josie rose from the iron bed, dressed in jeans and a sweatshirt, and ate a leftover blueberry muffin. After brushing her teeth, she headed for the other side of the apartment to rooms she'd never seen. It was time for her to forage.

She had a specific purpose for her reconnaissance mission. She wasn't snooping because she was nosy. What she needed to know was very important, and she figured it could only be found in Dr. Stone Romero's bathroom or bedroom.

She went to the bathroom first. It was modern, neat, and clean like the rest of the apartment. Feeling uncomfortable, she went through the cabinet drawers and the medicine closet. She didn't find what she was looking for, but she *did* find a prescription bottle that had Stone's name on it. Curious, she read the label but didn't recognize the name of the medication. Replacing the bottle exactly where she'd found it, she moved on to the bedroom.

The furniture in the bedroom had a very masculine feel to it. The dresser and chest of drawers were stained an ebony color, and the king-sized bed had a black leather headboard that had two rows of linear black stitching bisecting it. The comforter was a dark brown. Sixteen photographs of rural areas had been put in black frames and hung in a square pattern over the dresser. A painting of a cityscape also framed in black hung over the chest of drawers.

It was in the top drawer of the dresser that Josie found the box of old condoms Stone had mentioned. She wanted to buy some when she went to the store but didn't know what he preferred. She'd suspected that he'd kept the old ones and was glad to be proven right.

What if he hates these and this is what his last partner liked? she asked herself. *Stop it. Don't think about him with another woman. Imagine him with me. Imagine that sex is beautiful and phenomenal like it's supposed to be. We kissed last night before he went to work. He does kiss better than anyone I've ever dated. I wonder if he's better at sex, too.*

She glanced at her watch. It was 6:46. Deciding she would have to take a chance on the brand and style of the condoms, Josie carefully put the box back and closed the drawer. Hurriedly returning to the living area, she slipped on the jacket Stone had loaned her the morning they'd met. It was too large, but it was warm enough and made her feel happy when she had it on. He'd told her to keep it until she bought a jacket or coat of her own. He had a coat he could wear until then.

Taking the extra key he'd left for her, Josie attached it to her keychain, exited the apartment, and headed towards the store. She walked quickly, turning up the collar of the jacket against the cold wind. She was glad the store was only a block away and arrived just as the front doors were unlocked.

The grocery store was spacious but had low ceilings that made it feel less impersonal than the large warehouse chains. After retrieving a hand-held basket, Josie wandered up and down the aisles but didn't linger. She was on a tight schedule and could come back another time to explore the store more thoroughly.

Ending up in the pharmacy area, she headed straight for the condom section. Still undecided, she pondered her selection for a few minutes and worried she was wasting precious time. She picked up the box like the one at Stone's, put it back, and then picked it up again.

"May I help you?"

An older man wearing a pharmacist's lab coat stood beside her. He had a pleasant face and nice smile. Josie blushed slightly and asked about the box of condoms in her hand.

"Those are more expensive but worth the money," he said seriously. "They're durable but made to feel as natural as possible for both partners. They're also hypo-allergenic and have no spermicides."

"Oh. Okay. I'll take them then."

"I can check you out here in the pharmacy," he offered. "You don't have any fresh fruit or vegetables and have less than ten items."

Josie brought her basket to the counter. Once she'd placed it next to the register, she queried, "May I ask you another question?"

"Of course."

She told him the name of the medication she'd found in Stone's bathroom and inquired about its purpose.

"It's a prescription drug used to treat hypertension, congestive heart failure, and heart attack. It can also be used as a preventive for retinal issues and renal failure in diabetes sufferers. It's very effective for most patients requiring that type of drug."

"What's considered high blood pressure?"

"Normal blood pressure is 120 over 80. Normal pulse rate is 60 to 80 beats per minute. Well, that's optimal for blood pressure and pulse rate. Some people's run a little higher or lower, but you get the idea."

She thanked the man as she paid her bill, assured him she'd return to the store for her grocery and pharmacy needs, and left, mulling over the information she'd just learned about Stone's prescription. She doubted he was diabetic, although anything was possible. It was more probable that he had high blood pressure or a heart problem since he'd told her that cardiovascular disease was prevalent in his family.

If I remember right from watching all those television series about hospitals, Stone would have four years of college, four years of medical school, one year of internship and two years of residency. If he started right out of high school and he's in his second year of residency like he told me, then he'd be twenty-nine. That'd be awfully young to be on that sort of medication. But why else would he have it in his medicine closet and with his name on it? Has he already had a heart attack? If I have sex with him, then will it be bad for his heart?

Troubled and conflicted, Josie returned to the apartment and entered as quietly as possible. Stone's bedroom door was closed, and she tiptoed to the guest room and withdrew her purchases from the cloth bag she'd bought at the register. After putting them and the bag away, she gathered the one professional pantsuit she'd kept from her realtor days in L.A. and some clean undergarments. Then she showered, dressed, styled her hair in a sophisticated up-do, and applied makeup. She examined herself in the mirror then prepared to leave.

She wasn't about to wear Stone's large, leather jacket over her pantsuit. She would merely have to be cold until after the interview when she intended to buy a warm coat and a few other articles of clothing. It struck Josie then that she was actually excited about something for the first time in a long while.

More than one something, she reflected. *I hope the feeling lasts.*

Arriving at the hospital fifteen minutes later, Josie went to the front desk in order to get directions to the Human Resources Department. Once there, she was introduced to Bridget Juarez. Juarez, the Director of Human Resources, was fortyish, attractive, polite, and direct. Once they'd reviewed Josie's resumé together, the woman grilled Josie regarding her background, motives, and commitment towards her possible future employer.

Juarez finally declared, "I want to hire you and am trying to decide which available position would suit you best. I have a proposition for you. I'll lay it all out then leave it up to you to decide if you're interested."

Half an hour later, Josie left the hospital elated and followed the route on her phone's map app to the closest mall. There, she bought a black wool coat that had a soft lining, a demure lavender-colored cotton nightgown, some light pink knit pajamas and a fluffy pink robe. Her final purchase was a man's black-and-gray scarf.

Rushing to get back to the mall entrance where she'd parked, Josie took a wrong turn and ended up staring at a huge Christmas tree that had been beautifully-decorated with multi-colored lights and ornaments. Santa Claus sat in a chair in front of the tree, and his photographer, Mrs. Claus, stood waiting for customers. Since it was 12:20 on a school day, there weren't many children at the mall. Josie walked purposefully over towards the man, who brightened and said, "Ho! Ho! Ho! How are you today, young lady?"

She smiled and said, "Today, I'm very well."

"Would you like to take a picture with Santa?" Mrs. Clause asked expectantly.

"No, but thanks. However, I do want to give you some money."

"Money?" the woman echoed.

"Yes. Santa helped me and my sister a long time ago, and I want to do something to thank him."

"We can't accept money without providing you with our services," Santa protested. "That wouldn't be right."

"Then let me give you some money so that if a child comes along who wants a picture with you but can't afford it, you use what I gave you to give him or her a treat."

When she withdrew four twenty-dollar bills from her wallet and handed them to Mrs. Claus, Santa exclaimed, "You're a very good girl, young lady!"

"This will be enough for four children to have a small portrait package with Santa," Mrs. Claus said. "Bless you, my dear."

Josie smiled at both of them and said, "No, bless you. Have a nice holiday season."

"And to you," Santa offered. "You may find an extra-special gift under the tree this Christmas."

Still smiling, she shook her head and said, "I haven't had a tree since I was five. You gave me my last presents when I was seven. It's okay. You made it all right. Thanks again."

Josie knew that the man was not the same man who'd helped her and Zelda, but it didn't matter. He was aiding other children and would continue to do so as long as he donned the red suit each year and helped little ones to still believe there was something magical in the world. She wished she still believed.

She made her way back to downtown Austin and found the Vietnamese noodle restaurant where she and Stone were supposed to meet for lunch. It was almost 1:00 when Josie hurried in. The place was crowded, and Stone was nowhere in sight. When the hostess asked her if she wanted to get a table or wait, Josie opted for the table since she only saw one with two chairs left. As the woman seated her, she described Stone and asked the hostess to direct him to the table once he arrived. She didn't have to wait long.

"I didn't recognize you when I came in," Stone told her as he took his seat. "I'm impressed. I didn't think it was possible for you to look more beautiful, but I was wrong."

"Thank you. I think you looked more handsome every time I see you."

He laughed, ran his fingers through his perpetually unruly brown hair and asked when she'd last seen an ophthalmologist. Then it was her turn to laugh.

"You're in a really good mood," Stone commented once they'd ordered their food. "I take it you got a job."

"I did."

"And your job will be…?"

"Interim Director of Marketing. Marketing is what I specialized in while I was getting my degree, and I took those skills and used them to market real estate very successfully. I pointed out that I'd never worked in hospital marketing before, but Bridget Juarez didn't seem concerned. She says they'll have to conduct a formal search for a replacement Director but feels confident that I can do a great job in the position until it's filled. She gave me all sorts of materials to review and the promotional items of my predecessor. I asked her whether or not the other people in the department would resent me coming in and taking over, but she said the whole staff was being fired." Taking a sip of her water, Josie added, "You can't tell anyone that, by the way. I'm not supposed to tell anyone, but I kind of *have* to tell you in light of everything that's going on. Don't say a word."

"I won't, but why is the whole staff being fired?"

"Something about gross misconduct in that office. So, it'll be me and several other new employees."

"When is this mass firing taking place?"

"The beginning of January. I'll have a month to prepare and get started on my own marketing plan. The Director and I will meet once a week to go over my progress and make certain the higher-ups like my approach. I have to meet with them in two weeks."

"You sound enthusiastic."

"I am. It's something I like in a different context than what I've had."

"I'm glad to hear it."

"How was your shift?"

"Pretty slow and routine. There was one case of a bad virus that led to dehydration, another where a boy fell out of a bunk bed and needed stitches and a wrist cast, and three with bad cases of the flu." Once their waiter had deposited their bowls of noodles and autumn rolls in front of them, Stone asked, "Have you had a flu shot?"

31

"Yes. My father's such a germophobe that we got all of our vaccinations plus had to take the flu shot every year. He made me promise not to stop taking them once I left home, and I promised. So, I still get them."

"If you weren't going to be working in a hospital, then I'd say you didn't need to take the shot. I personally don't think it's necessary if you're a healthy younger person. It's not optional if you're employed in a healthcare facility though." Picking up some noodles with his chopsticks, he asked, "How did you like the grocery store I told you about?"

"It was really neat. I was in a hurry, so I'll have to go back and spend more time there soon."

"I see you bought a coat. Anything else?"

"A few things. I also had an unexpected encounter with Santa Claus and Mrs. Claus while I was in the mall. It was good. Santa said I might get a special present under the tree. I think he was disappointed when I told him I hadn't had a tree since I was five."

The pediatrician lowered his chopsticks across his bowl and asked, "You mean you and Zelda never put up Christmas trees after you left home?"

"For what purpose? They're pretty, but they're also in stores and all around towns during the holidays. Why should we put up trees in our homes each year? It would have been a sad reminder of all those trees we didn't have." After taking a bite of her noodles, chewing, and swallowing, she asked, "Do you put up a tree in your apartment?"

"Usually, but I don't have to this year if it will make you sad."

Giving him a half-shrug, she said, "It's not my house or apartment, so it's fine. I don't want you to change your tradition because you have a houseguest with Christmas baggage."

Heaving a sigh of relief, he declared, "That's good since I put my artificial one up before I came here this afternoon."

"You must not have slept much. If you got off at 7:00 a.m. and then came here at 1:00 and put up the tree in the middle –"

"I'm okay with it," he interrupted. "This is my last week of working nights for a while. Seniority. After all these years in med school and beyond, I'm used to having odd hours. I am looking forward to day shifts though."

"What do you want to do when you finish your residency?"

"I'd like to stay in Austin and work at the children's hospital, but I'm open to other opportunities if things don't pan out there."

Their waiter came by to refill their glasses of water, and both of them concentrated on eating. They each left with a take-out box and agreed to meet back at the apartment. Stone's Honda Civic was already parked in its slot by the time Josie pulled her Volvo into its designated space.

Gathering her purse, two shopping bags, and take-out box from the seat beside her, Josie shut and locked her car then hurried for the door of the building and jogged up the stairs in an effort to get warm. She wondered if it was always freezing in Austin in late November. She was going to ask Stone once she got into the apartment, but what she saw when she opened the door made her forget what she'd intended to say. After a moment, she exploded with laughter. Stone, who was standing in the kitchen, grinned at her and asked, "You're not impressed?"

Lowering her bags and purse to the floor, she closed the door and carried her take-out box to the breakfast bar. She put it down beside the two-foot high artificial Christmas tree. It had white lights and small red and gold ball ornaments hanging on the few branches available. There was no star. When asked about this, Stone told her that if he put a star on top the tiny tree would probably topple over. She giggled.

"I live in a two-bedroom apartment and don't have room to store a big artificial tree," he explained. "I don't want to lug a live one up two flights of stairs, deal with watering it and picking up pine needles, and then lug it back down after the holidays. Hence, my convenient little tree. I keep it in a bag up at the top of the laundry closet."

"There's a laundry closet? Where?"

He took her hand and led her to his bedroom. They walked around the bed to what turned out to be a large walk-in clothes closet. A folding door was at the far end. When it was pulled back, it revealed a washer, dryer, and shelving. Stone pointed to the high shelf that would've been impossible for Josie to reach without a stepstool.

"That's where the tree goes," he explained. "That and other odds and ends I don't need easy access to."

Josie eyed the few cardboard boxes that rested on the shelf and idly wondered what they contained. Then she asked matter-of-factly, "Do you mind if I use your washer and dryer tonight?"

"You're my houseguest. Knock yourself out."

"I'll wait until you go to work. I'm thinking you need sleep right now."

"Yes, I do."

"I'll read over some of those materials I was telling you about while you sleep. Then we could have our leftovers for dinner before you go to work."

He smiled down at her and said, "Sounds nice. See you in a couple hours."

She returned to the living room, realized she'd left the materials the Human Resource Director had given her lying on the backseat of her car, and braced herself for another trip out into the cold. It didn't take her long to go down the two flights of stairs, get the books and papers, and begin her ascent. She was halfway up the second flight of stairs when she almost collided with Stone, who was barreling down in pajama bottoms and a t-shirt. He was barefoot and looked rather panicked.

"Stone, what's wrong?"

"I didn't know where you were."

Looking down at the books and papers, she said, "I forgot to bring these up. I didn't think you'd notice I was gone."

"I noticed." Taking some of the things from her, he muttered, "You worry me, you know?"

"Please, don't."

He stopped and looked directly at her then asked, "What aren't you telling me?"

"More than you could ever imagine. What are *you* not telling *me*?"

"The things I haven't had time to share, yet. I'm a guy. What you see is what you get."

Back in the apartment, they deposited the articles they were carrying onto the dining room table. Stone kissed Josie, telling her he would see her later. Then, he retreated to his room and shut the door.

Josie removed her coat, withdrew the scarf she'd bought during her shopping trip, and took off the price tag. She folded the scarf and stuffed it in one pocket of Stone's coat. Then she sat in one of the dining room chairs and began to read. She was soon engrossed in a book on the hospital's history and its mission. When Stone emerged from his room and asked her if she was hungry, she blinked in surprise.

"It's been that long?"

He nodded and said, "Time for me to eat and run."

"Speaking of running, do you work out? I wondered if you knew of a gym nearby where I could get in some exercise."

"The one I go to for weight training and kickboxing is five blocks from here."

"How long have you been kick-boxing?"

"Since Nelson killed himself. I was just using the treadmill and weights before that. Afterwards, I needed to hit something on a consistent basis. You?"

"Resistance training and the elliptical machine mostly. If I really want to be a glutton for punishment, then I do Spin class."

"I'll take you tomorrow if you want."

"How do you have time to work out?"

"Exercise is important. I make time. It's typically an hour of exercise a day, although these last few days I haven't made it to the gym. Working out helps to keep me in shape and healthy."

They ate their leftovers at the dining room table. It was then that Josie realized there was no television in sight. When she asked Stone about this, he replied that he hadn't owned a TV since college. He used his computer or iPad for all of his media needs. If he wanted to watch a football game on a big screen, then he went with male friends to a sports bar or to one of their houses.

"Do you have lots of male friends?"

"I'm friends with most of the other doctors and nurses I work with at the hospital, both male and female. We get together and hang out off and on."

"Do you have a best friend?"

"Nelson was my best friend. Nobody could replace my brother."

"No one has to replace him in order to be close to you."

"Do you have a best friend?"

"Zelda was my best friend," she admitted.

"Guilty as charged, eh?"

"I guess so."

Stone glanced at his watch and said, "I have to go to work. I'll see you tomorrow morning."

They kissed before he left. This time Josie pressed her body close to his. He pulled her to him; then he stepped back and slid his hands to the front of her waist and up to the top button of her suit jacket. There, he paused before lifting his palms to cup her cheeks.

"I so want you," he murmured. "But it's not time, yet. We're moving *really* fast with everything here."

"I don't mind."

He kissed her lightly, slipped on his coat, and left. Josie immediately went to wash her dirty clothes plus the nightclothes she'd bought at the mall and the pajamas Stone had lent her on her first night at his apartment. In-between washing and drying the laundry, she kept reading and learning about the hospital and previous marketing strategies. None of them seemed particularly innovative. Feeling a stirring of her creative juices, Josie began to work.

Chapter Four

Later, Josie decided to check her new phone to see how many times her parents and sister had called since she'd last reviewed her voicemails. Not surprisingly, her father had phoned twelve times the day before and the requisite amount of times so far that day. Her mother had called seventeen times. There was one voicemail from Zelda.

As she prepared to listen to the voicemails, Josie took a deep breath and held it before slowly exhaling. It had been days since she'd listened to any of them, and she felt she was in a much better position emotionally to hear them than she'd been when she'd left L.A. She had to learn if things were still the same with her family, although she suspected she already knew the answer.

True to form, her father's voicemails were all the same.

"Josie, it's Dad. I love you. Stay safe."

Her mother's first message was, "I don't…I don't know why they think I'm part of a conspiracy to overthrow the…a conspiracy to…to overthrow the Canadian government. End-of-Days tells me that it's because I have radiation in me from Red Rain, but I think she's lying. She's lying. Don't you have times where you think she's lying? I think it's her yellow dress that makes her say things like that to me. I don't want to talk to her, but she won't…I don't tell her how to find them…and I have to use the radiation to make a difference. They think I'm mentally ill, but what is mentally ill? I think Jesus Christ told me yesterday that I should tell Pretty Kitty not to be so sad. I won't go back there. They told me they don't want me at the Institution. End-of-Days is angry with them for thinking it's my radiation that's making them think…making them…they might see me. If they see me, then they might find out where we live and kill us. The President of the United States might kill you and Zelda, too. You can't tell –"

The voicemail timed out. Josie deleted the other messages from her mother without listening to them. She was visualizing her mother's pacing, rocking, and gesturing the entire time she was on the phone. Pacing, rocking, and gesturing were things she did every

37

waking moment while she talked, which was pretty much every waking moment of her life.

Although she was dreading it, Josie forced herself to play Zelda's voicemail.

"The Ghost Men are hunting me," she heard her sister say. "I saw them at the facility where the President is letting the aliens…the aliens' testing facility. I know where it is. They don't want me to tell. The magical puppy is with my hovercraft. I'm going to use it to try and get away from the Ghost Men. I'm going to make it to Calendoria to the place where the planets align in the other dimension so that they can't get me. I'll call you again when I can. I have to go."

Why did I do that? Josie asked herself, as she put on her new pajamas. *I knew what it would be like. I'm better off not hearing their messages. Why am I keeping the phone number and letting Mom, Dad, and Zelda call like this? I have a chance to live a normal life here and maybe Stone will actually want to continue to be with me. Or I might just go crazy like the rest of the family and then Stone won't matter. If I become like Dad, I'll be dominated by fear of everything all the time. If I'm like Mom and Zelda, I'll be living in a world of hallucinations and only those will matter. Stone will move on, and I'll be oblivious.*

Shutting off the phone and placing it in the drawer of the nightstand beside her bed, Josie made up her mind to keep it charged and check the number of messages from each family member every night. She would try not to listen to the messages again unless her father called more or less than twelve times a day. If that happened she would know something was terribly wrong.

Terribly wrong in a different way, she thought wryly.

When she woke before 8:00 the following morning, she listened for sounds of movement in the apartment. Hearing none, Josie deduced that Stone must have come in exhausted from his long shift and gone directly to bed. Therefore, she was startled to see him sitting on the couch when she walked into the living area in her pajamas. She said his name and went to stand in front of him. When he lifted his head to look up at her, she could tell that he'd been crying.

"What is it?" she asked with concern. "Did something happen to someone in your family?"

Shaking his head, he said, "No. You'll get used to this if you stay here with me. It happens sometimes."

"What does *'this'* mean?"

"It's the result of what I do for a living and what I see with the kids."

"Something happened on your shift last night?"

He nodded.

"Tell me about it."

"Why? So you can be outraged and tormented by it, too?"

"You have to share it with someone."

"I shared it with everyone else in the ER who helped me with the patient. I talk with a counselor at the hospital on a regular basis about dealing with what I see and the stress of my job. All hospital employees have access to counseling anytime if they need it."

"That's great, but talking to therapists isn't like talking to someone who really cares about you on a more personal level. I know that all too well."

Stone dropped his head, and she sat beside him on the couch and tucked her bare feet beneath her.

"I like your pajamas," he remarked without turning towards her. "Light pink. Barbie would definitely approve. I figured you'd buy something sheer to try to seduce me."

"Sheer isn't my style," she told him. "And I've never set out to seduce any man. I had a certain image to maintain in California because of my clientele, but that ended every day when I walked through the front doors of my house. And if I slept with a man, then it was because I thought he had substance and cared about me. That's why I didn't sleep around." Folding her arms across her chest, she demanded, "Stop trying to change the subject by discussing my nightclothes. I *am* glad you like them, but they're not important right now. Talk to me, Stone."

Sighing, he began, "I'd only been at work for about forty minutes when I heard a girl screaming. I mean screaming as in screaming in agony, not just pitching a fit. I took off running towards the Waiting Room. Some other doctors and nurses obviously heard it, too. We all converged on the girl at the same time. She was curled on the floor near the sliding doors. It took us about two seconds to figure out what was going on, and I picked her up and ran for an operating room we have in that area."

"What was wrong with her?" Josie asked in a small voice.

"She was in labor. I got her on the table and told her she was safe and asked her name and age."

"Why the operating room?"

"Because she looked like she was about thirteen, and I doubted if her pelvis was the right size to deliver a baby. One of the other doctors called an OB/GYN to perform an emergency C-section." Stone clenched his jaw and then said, "There wasn't time. The baby was coming fast, and I delivered him moments after the call was made. The boy suffered a collapsed lung and damage to one shoulder. He has fluid on the brain. A shunt had to be inserted by a surgeon."

"Oh, my God. And the girl?"

"Her name's Brittany. She's twelve. She's got a cracked pelvis, internal and external damage that had to be surgically repaired, and the memory of being impregnated by her mother's boyfriend and then suffering through labor for an entire day at home before her mother drove her to the hospital and dumped her there. The mother didn't want the boyfriend to get in trouble for molesting and impregnating her daughter." Stone asked rhetorically, "What is *wrong* with people? How could the mother knowingly let her boyfriend have sex with her child and get her pregnant? And then to let the girl suffer for hours trying to give birth at home so the guy wouldn't get sent to jail? God! You can't imagine what it was like for us to witness this twelve-year-old screaming in pain and fear, her body literally breaking as the baby was born."

"How is she now?"

"Sedated. It's going to take her a long time to physically heal. God only knows about her mind. She wants nothing to do with the baby, which is understandable. The police have already gone to the mother's home and arrested her and the boyfriend. Brittany's younger brothers are in State custody. At least the two adults will go to jail. That won't ever make it right for Brittany."

"Have you ever had this happen before with a patient?"

"You mean deliver a baby when the mother was a minor? Once, but it was nothing like this. That girl was sixteen and had consensual sex with another teenager. The two of them came in together right before she gave birth. She was older and able to deliver the baby without problems. She and the boy kept the baby and seemed like they really loved each other and wanted to be good parents. Not what I'd encourage but a thousand times better than what happened last night." Rubbing tiredly at his eyes, he added, "I'll probably be called to testify at the trials of Brittany's mother and her boyfriend. I'll hate having to go over the details, but I'll do whatever it takes to get that child molester and his accomplice off the streets."

Josie felt sick to her stomach, and her skin tingled as if bugs were crawling all over her. Feeling wronged, violated, and betrayed, she was working hard not to remember a moment in time she'd never be able to forget. She wasn't being very successful.

"Josie? What is it?"

"I'm trying to not think about something disturbing."

"Brittany?"

"No."

"What then?"

"I can't tell you." Hugging herself tightly, she said, "You'll find it off-putting."

"How old were you when you were molested?" he asked bluntly.

"I wasn't molested," she answered defensively.

"Tell me," he ordered gently but firmly.

"No. I...I don't want to lose you. You're the first man I've ever really trusted, and I want there to be more between us."

"You're not going to lose me no matter what you say. Who molested you?"

"I wasn't molested!" she insisted vehemently.

"Then explain it to me."

"I'm afraid to."

"Then don't tell me now. Let me hold you. Tell me another time."

Before she could object, Stone put his arms around her and pulled her closer until her face was buried against his neck. His hold on her was solid, and she tucked her arms close to her chest and nuzzled him with her cheek and temple. He exhaled sharply, and she wondered if he would move to touch her breasts or other parts of her body.

"I know what you're thinking," he murmured. "Nothing sexual is going to happen between us this morning. We're both upset, and we still don't have protection."

"I bought some," she confided. "It's in my room."

He raised his hand to the back of her head and said, "You are the most complicated and confounding woman I've ever met. I rarely know what to expect from you. You can't imagine what you do to me."

Not certain how to respond to this admission, Josie relished the feel of Stone's body next to hers, one hand on her back and the other behind her head. She thought of the handful of other men with whom she'd been sexually involved. They'd been nice, intelligent, and stable. Yet, she'd never felt safe enough to tell them any of what she'd shared with Stone from the first day they'd met. It seemed as if he hadn't shared much with any of his previous partners, although she wasn't certain and wondered if it was wishful thinking on her part.

"Your brother decorated your apartment, didn't he?" she asked on the spur of the moment. "He was very talented."

"Yes. His life partner still works in New Orleans at the same firm where Nelson once worked. He's very talented, too."

"Did your family allow the partner to come to the funeral?"

"I insisted on it. Cheek took Nelson away from the man. I wasn't going to let them take away the man's right to grieve properly. They'd been together for six years."

"Do you still talk to him?"

"Once in a while he'll call me or I'll call him. All we do is catch up and reminisce about times we spent with Nelson. Neither of us has really moved on. It makes it hurt worse when we talk, but we agree that we usually feel better afterwards." Lowering his hand from the back of her head to her hip, he asked, "Do you ever talk to Zelda's ex-boyfriend?"

"No. He couldn't deal with her descent into schizophrenia, and he distanced himself pretty quickly. I don't blame him. I grew up with it, and it's a terrible mental illness. All of those years of watching my mother talk to people, animals, and creatures that weren't there gave me insight but didn't make it any easier."

"How many people, animals, and creatures did your mother talk to on a regular basis?"

"I kept track the year I was seventeen. I had a log of sorts. There were one hundred ninety-seven that I was aware of. Each one had its own personality, function, and frequency of appearance. Some were daily visitors, while others only showed up periodically. I think my favorite was Hedgehog, who was very playful and enjoyed games of all sorts. The most dangerous was End-of-Days. Sometimes Mom would talk about how End-of-Days was telling her to hurt people or one of her hallucinations like Hedgehog, but the other hallucinations would tell her not to listen to End-of-Days."

"How old was your mother when she manifested schizophrenia?"

"Twenty-seven. The same age as Zelda was when it happened to her."

"And your father?"

"His parents first took him to a psychiatrist when he was four. He did so well on one particular medication from the time he was about thirteen until he was in his mid-thirties. The drug suddenly stopped working for him. That's when he ended up in the mental institution where he met my mother. She'd been there for a year before he arrived. If only they could have stayed all right like they were when they got released."

"Most schizophrenics are socially withdrawn and tend to be either emotionless or act out. What's your mother like?"

"Mom used to be very loving and liked to hug and kiss when we were small and she was on her meds all the time. We got used to her not being physically affectionate with us after that year when she pretty much went off the deep end."

"And your father?"

"Dad was always loving, but he was such a germophobe that he'd hug or kiss us then make us wash our faces in case he gave us any germs. He'd wash his hands dozens of times before touching us in any way so that he wouldn't get us sick. Despite the germophobia, he's also a hoarder. So, it makes for a weird combination of things being scrubbed with Clorox or piled with dust." Sighing, she confided, "My parents have lived in special housing for people with disabilities for the last five years. The apartment's a disaster. You can barely walk in it. There are pathways to different things, but it's pretty tight."

"How in God's name did you know what 'normal' was when you were growing up?"

"We had 'normal' until I was five. Well, Zelda had Crazy Mom while Mom was pregnant with me and not on her meds, but Zelda was under two and didn't remember that."

"And after the permanent insanity took over at home?"

"I'd read books and watch television shows about wholesome families and how they acted. Nice families we came into contact with felt bad for us and let us hang out at their houses a lot. That helped. If only we hadn't moved so much when I was growing up. It would've been good for us to not be so transient. We were frequently changing schools, changing apartments, and changing friends. We could never just *be*."

"All we did was *be* when I was growing up. There wasn't much else to do in Clayville, Louisiana."

"How many people live in Clayville?"

"About twenty thousand now. There were about fifteen thousand when I was younger, but an underwear factory was built in a nearby area, so more people moved to Clayville because of the work. They finally opened a Walmart Supercenter on the outskirts of town last year."

"Wow. I can't imagine living in an area without malls, large grocery stores, or places like Target. Are you going back for Christmas?"

"I do have Christmas week off, but I don't know if I want to go home for the holidays. After what happened with Nelson last year, I'm still really angry and upset with Cheek and, by default, with our parents. On the other hand, I want to see my mother and father, Memaw, and my nephew."

"I think you should go. I could watch your place and explore Austin while you're gone. I still don't know much of anything about where I'm living now."

"You think I'd leave you here alone for the holidays?"

"They don't mean anything to me," Josie said truthfully. "Not since Santa gave me and Zelda our last Christmas presents."

"I don't understand. Your mother might have literally been out of it, but your father never, ever put up a tree or got his children presents?"

"He was worried that the lights would catch the tree on fire. As for presents, he decided that Christmas was too commercialized after The Last Christmas. He said it was supposed to be about Jesus, not Santa."

"Did he take you and Zelda to church?"

"He thought there were too many germs. It would've been dangerous to shake hands with people or hug them. So, we didn't go to church."

"Yet, you went to school."

"Because the State people said we had to or else they'd take us away from him and Mom. They did that after he kept us home for the first three weeks when I was in the second grade."

"What did he do when either of you actually got sick?"

"Gave us over-the-counter medications or rushed us to the doctor's office. He was always worried he wasn't doing the right thing and that we were going to die because he did or didn't take us in for treatment. After all, there are so many germs at the doctor's office."

"It's a wonder neither of you grew up to be hypochondriacs."

"It's kind of like the worry thing. We knew the way he was acting was extreme, so we became dismissive about it. I got really sick once in college with a chest cold and didn't go to the doctor because I didn't want to overreact like Dad always did. When I started having trouble breathing, Zelda and I decided I probably needed to see a doctor. I had double pneumonia. After that, I tried to be sensible about it and not let my father's mental illness issues color my views on healthcare."

"And sex? Who told you about sex?"

"Zelda. A friend explained it to her, and she told me." Looking up at him, she asked, "Who told you?"

"Daddy. I was eleven. You?"

"Eight." Burying her face against his neck again, she asked, "How old were you your first time?"

"Young. You?"

"I was twenty." Josie bit her lip then asked, "What do you like in bed?"

"Sex."

"Well, I figured that. I meant…do you like anything…different?"

"What do you mean?"

Relieved that Stone couldn't see her scarlet cheeks, she offered, "Games. Costumes. Role-playing. BDSM."

"No. You?"

"No."

"We haven't known each other for a week, yet you've already bought condoms and are asking me what I like in bed."

"I know. I'm usually *so* cautious. With you, everything's been different. I knew we were going to have sex pretty soon. Buying the condoms was sort of unnerving though."

"Why?"

"Because I've never bought any before. Each man provided his own."

"So, how did you make your selection this first time?" When she didn't answer, he said with a trace of humor in his voice, "Josie, I know you went through my things."

Immediately pulling away from him, she asked, "How? I put everything back exactly like you had it!"

"You told me you were a forager. I expected it."

"I wasn't spying," she insisted desperately. "I only wanted to find out what you liked so that I could please you."

"What about which product would please *you*?"

"That's irrelevant."

A look of astonishment spread across Stone's face. He sputtered, "Your...your pleasure's irrelevant compared to mine?" When she stared down at her hands, he asked, "Who told you that women didn't deserve to have equal gratification during sex?"

"Nobody."

"Who molested you, Josie?"

She got quickly to her feet and shouted, "Stop asking that! I was never raped!"

Stone was instantly off the couch, shouting back, "You don't have to be raped to be molested! Who was it? Your father? Someone in one of the foster homes?"

She hastened to retreat to the guest room, but Stone easily blocked her path before asking, "Who touched you when you were a little girl?"

"A neighbor!" she blurted out.

"What was his name?"

"I don't remember! I haven't been able to remember no matter how hard I try since it happened!"

"Since what happened?"

"Since he kissed me," she confessed. "He kissed me on the mouth and asked me to go inside his apartment with him. I wouldn't since he had a mean dog."

"How old were you?"

"Six."

"How old was he?"

"Sixty-something."

Stone fisted his hands and appeared to be vacillating between anger and anguish. He encouraged Josie to describe exactly what had taken place between her and the neighbor. For the first time in her life since that day, Josie did.

"I was standing next to his rocking chair, and he told me what a sweet little girl I was and how he wanted to give me a kiss. I thought he would kiss me on the cheek like other old people I'd known, but he kissed me on the lips. His moustache felt rough against my skin when he did it. He let his mouth linger on mine. I knew it was wrong, but I didn't understand. He asked me to go into his apartment with him. I looked at the mean dog sitting on the other side of his screen door and told him I had to go home. He tried to kiss me again, but I ran back to our place."

"Josie, that's molestation. It's okay to call it what it is." Without moving closer to her, he asked, "Did you ever tell anyone?"

"I told my parents right away."

"What did they do?"

"Nothing. They were both pretty clear-headed that day and wanted to call the police, but they were worried the police would take me and Zelda away from them because of their mental problems. Mom and Dad told me not to go near the neighbor when I was by myself. My Dad…my Dad would go talk to him and…and pet the dog. I felt so betrayed. I think my Dad thought if he pretended to be friends with him then the man would leave me alone." Beginning to cry, she said, "Dad even tried to get me to stand near the man and pet the mean dog. I didn't know what to do. I didn't want to go near the man, but I didn't want to not do what Dad said."

Stone put his arms around her, pulled her close to him, and asked quietly, "What do you feel when you have sex?"

"It hurt the first time, but I expected that," she managed to say. "The other times…it was okay. I did what I'd seen women do in movies or what I'd read about in books. I guess I was convincing. My partners seemed to enjoy it."

"But you didn't?"

"It wasn't bad, but no, not really. I don't think I've had an orgasm."

"You'd know," he told her. "You *will* know."

"What if I can't because of what the neighbor did?"

"You mean because you were molested?" When she didn't respond, Stone urged, "Say it. It'll make it easier to deal with."

Josie forced herself to ask, "What if I can't have an orgasm because I was molested?" Then, she declared more adamantly, "I was molested."

Relief instantly flooded through her, and her knees gave out. Stone caught her as she collapsed, slipped one of his arms under her knees, and then lifted and carried her to the guest bed. Lowering her onto the mattress, he covered her with the top sheet, blanket, and quilt then left the room in order to retrieve a box of tissues. Josie lay under the covers and wept, as he wiped her face and stroked her hair. She cried herself to sleep while Stone Romero told her no one was ever going to hurt her as long as he was around. Although she appreciated the words, Josie wanted to tell him not to make promises he couldn't keep.

Chapter Five

"How'd you sleep?" Stone asked from his position on the couch when Josie entered the living room that evening.

"Great." Glancing at the clock on the wall, she exclaimed, "It's 9:00 p.m.!"

"Yes."

"But you're supposed to be at work, not sitting on the couch reading a book."

"I called in sick. I haven't done that since I had that stomach bug last year. Another doctor's covering my shift."

"How is Brittany?"

"You're always thinking about others, no matter how bad things are for you," Stone mused. "Brittany's a little better today but not much. Her recovery time will be very long."

"And the baby?"

The pediatrician grimaced and said, "He suffered a cerebral hemorrhage this afternoon and died."

"Oh. Is it better that he died? I know that sounds terrible, but what do you think from a doctor's perspective?"

"It's not my place to make those kinds of calls. He could have been severely disabled because of the traumatic birth; he could've grown up healthy and become a criminal because of his circumstances and parentage; or he could've grown up to become the next President of the United States. We'll never know. For whatever reason, God took him now. It's a shame that Brittany had to go through what she did only to have the literal cause of her mental and physical pain die. It makes her entire experience seem senseless."

"Does she know?"

"Yes. She says she's glad. Later, she'll feel guilty. Hopefully, the social workers will help her deal with all of this mess."

"Good luck with that. They can only do so much. I suspect not enough staff, lack of resources, and too many children in need are problems all over the world. I know they were when I was growing up in Virginia and needed help."

Standing, Stone asked, "Are you hungry?"

"Yes. Did you sleep?"

"All day until my alarm went off at 6:00. I had a salad for dinner. You want one?"

"Sure. I can make it myself though."

"Allow me. It's nice to prepare food for someone else besides just me."

"Stone, may I ask you a question?"

"Only if I can ask you one."

"Okay. When I was looking for the condoms, I came across a prescription bottle you had in your bathroom. Why are you taking high blood pressure medication?"

"Because I have high blood pressure," he answered casually. "When I was seventeen I went for my yearly physical, and my pressure was perfect. The next year, it was pretty high. I was tested for a variety of causes, but the doctors couldn't find any reasonable explanation for my hypertension except heredity. I take my medication, exercise regularly, try to eat low-sodium foods most of the time, and live with the knowledge that I'm at greater risk for heart trouble or stroke than the average person."

"It doesn't scare you?"

"It is what it is. I deal with it. If I lived in fear, then I wouldn't be living."

"Does your family know?"

"Yes. Mama's only fifty-nine, but she's already had a mild heart attack. Cheek was diagnosed with hypertension two years ago."

"How old is he?"

"Thirty-nine."

"Your parents waited ten years after they had Cheek to have you and Nelson?"

"Supposedly, my mother got pregnant on her wedding night with Cheek. She and Daddy wanted more babies, but she never got pregnant again even though they never used preventive measures. When Cheek was nine, she turned up pregnant and had me and Nelson. Cheek wasn't too happy about that. He'd gotten used to being the center of attention."

Josie nodded absently and asked, "You aren't mad at me for asking about your high blood pressure?"

"I figured you'd seen the prescription bottle when you were foraging that first day. I have nothing to hide from you, so I'm not upset. I was wondering when you'd ask." Moving closer to her, he said, "My turn."

"To ask your question? Of course."

"How do you feel after sharing the circumstances of your molestation with me?"

"Still hurt, violated, and betrayed by the neighbor and my parents but also liberated in a way. These last few days have been more liberating than my last twenty years."

"I'm happy I could help," he said sincerely. "Now what would you like on your salad?"

Stone sat with Josie at the dining room table while she ate her salad and some bread. He spoke of life in Austin, the local attractions, and the culture. She absorbed every word but was also focusing on the way the man talked to her. He seemed to radiate gentleness and intensity at the same time. It was a magnificent combination.

"Josie?"

"Sorry. I let my attention drift for a minute there. I really was listening. I'd love to go to Zilker Park, McKinney Falls, and Ladybird Lake. I'd also like to see the famous second largest colony of bats in the United States when they return to the Congress Avenue Bridge in April. Austin sounds like a great place to live."

"Have you ever been truly emotionally attached to any of the places where you lived in the past?"

"Each city had its plusses and minuses. I liked some better than others. None of them were home."

"Speaking of home, I think I am going to Clayville to see my family for Christmas week. Why don't you come with me?"

"Don't you think it'd be awkward?"

"Maybe. But I don't think I can go back without you. I need you to be with me."

"Why?"

"Because you make me feel safe."

"*I* make *you* feel safe?" she asked in disbelief. "How?"

"I can't explain it. You just do. I feel happy and in control when I think of you."

"Probably because I'm such a freak that it gives you a sense of –"

"You're not a freak!" he interrupted. "You're so tenacious. It inspires me."

"How can I be an inspiration to you when I can hardly keep myself going? The night I found that baby on the street I was planning to kill myself."

"I know. I specialize in treating messed up children, remember? I told you kids who need help and don't get it have serious issues as adults. You think I wasn't trained to recognize the signs in adults who had destructive upbringings? I saw those signs in you while we talked as I examined the baby."

"I thought of that right away. I figured that was why you wanted to help me."

"I've helped other adults who've had rough childhoods. I've never wanted to have a relationship with any of them. The moment I met you I knew there was something special about you. I was afraid I wouldn't be able to find you before you left the campus of the hospital and that I'd never see you again."

"What do you expect from me?"

"That you give me an opportunity to be your partner. I want to love you and to make love to you. I want to have you love me and make love to me. I want to experience life with you."

"Stone, this sounds like a proposal."

"It is. I'm proposing that we see if we were meant for each other."

"How? Why? Do you want to have sex tonight?"

"And get it over with?" he asked darkly. "I understand that reference now."

"I didn't mean for it to come out that way."

"But it did, because that's the way you felt inside. The fact that you said it to me shows you trust me. Have you ever said it to any other man?"

"No."

"Have you ever trusted any other man?"

"I trusted my father until…."

"Until what?"

"Until I was molested and he didn't protect me."

Stone nodded and reached across the table so that he could touch her cheek with his fingertips. He drew them downwards then brushed them along her jawline.

"Did you ever tell Zelda what the neighbor did to you?"

"No, but I told her once that I was uncomfortable about having sex with any man."

"What did she say?"

"That all men cared about was their own needs and gratification, and women should use what they had to exploit that. I disagreed with her, but I secretly wondered if she was right."

"I don't think of sex the way she described it, and I'm a man. The molestation could have been a lot worse, and you shouldn't dwell on it. That doesn't mean you shouldn't acknowledge it or how it colored your views on sex."

"I understand that now."

"You told me about the neighbor, and I still want to touch you."

"That's what you say."

"Do you think all I'm interested in is my own needs and gratification?"

"I don't think so. I'm just afraid you have some hidden agenda."

"No hidden agendas here. I love the way you look and act. You're totally yourself. Comfy pink pajamas are much sexier to me than some flimsy nightgown." When she blushed and gave him a little smile, he noted, "I've never seen you wear any jewelry. I kind of like it. I've never met a woman who didn't wear jewelry of some sort. Why don't you wear any?"

"I never cared about jewelry. I do love to have a nice manicure and pedicure." Looking down at her bare fingernails, she added, "I haven't done either since the day I decided to leave L.A."

"How come?"

"I didn't even care about living. What difference did it make if my nails looked pretty?" Glancing up at him, she remarked, "You take good care of yourself. You're always clean-shaven and your hair is cut so perfectly. The way it's short but then a little longer and messy on top is exactly right for you. It's like a mixture of mature and playful."

He laughed and said, "Thank Nelson for that. One of his friends cut my hair like this right before I started my residency. I liked it because it was easy to care for this way. I just wash it and let it do what it wants. As for the clean-shaven part, Daddy told us to shave every day unless we were camping. He said respectable men knew how to use their razors."

Sitting back in her chair, Josie said, "I'm sure every unattached woman you work with wants you."

"They want a doctor."

"No, they want Dr. Romero."

"Do you want Dr. Romero?"

"I want Stone."

"You have him."

"For how long?"

"Forever if you want."

"Forever is a long time. I can't do that to you."

"You're not doing anything to me. What do I have to do to convince you that I'm only interested in being with you, Josie?"

After swallowing hard, she said, "My family's insane."

"I know."

"What if I go insane?"

"I'd get you help."

"And if nothing worked?"

"I'd remember who you really were inside. I'd love you no matter what. I'd never stop trying to reach you."

"It's not that easy."

"I like challenges. What about you?"

"What do you mean?"

"I have high blood pressure. I could have a heart attack or stroke out early. What would you do if that happened?"

"Whatever I had to in order to help you get better."

He nodded and smiled then leaned across to kiss her. She automatically parted her lips so that he could slip his tongue inside her mouth. He gently teased her with it and used his teeth to tug at her lower lip. When they broke apart, he asked, "What do you feel when I kiss you?"

"It's pleasant." Rising to bring her dirty dish to the sink, she added, "More pleasant than when I've kissed any other man. I like it."

"Nice to know, but I want you to think of my kisses as more than 'pleasant.' We'll work on that. Why don't you get dressed and let's go out?"

"Where?"

"I'll drive you around and show you some of the city."

"But it's late."

"So? I was prepared to work the night shift. We've both slept most of the day. Let's go out."

Josie showered, brushed her teeth, and dressed. As she slipped on her coat, Stone buttoned his and wrapped the black and gray scarf around his neck.

"Thanks for my present," he said, as he reached forward and slowly buttoned the front of her coat. "It was a cool surprise."

"I wanted to do something special for you. I wish I'd had time to do more."

"Your trust is the best present I've ever gotten in my life. I don't need anything else except your love." When Josie rolled her eyes, he said, "Okay, so I'm a sentimental man. Thank Nelson for that. Because we had that twin bond and he was gay, he made me more conscious of certain things a lot of heterosexual guys don't think about much."

"Then I'm very thankful for Nelson. I wish I could have known him."

Stone nodded, and it seemed as though he wanted to say more but couldn't. He took her hand and led her downstairs to his Honda. They were soon on a nighttime tour of Austin. At midnight, they pulled over at a truck stop. Sitting at a table under the fluorescent lights, they drank coffee and ate hash brown casserole made of potatoes, sour cream, cheese, sausage, peppers, and onions.

"Mm," Josie remarked. "This is delicious, but I'm sure it's horrible for my health."

"It is, but it's good comfort food."

"What's your favorite thing to eat?"

"One of the worst things in the world for someone with high blood pressure," Stone confided. "Pepperoni pizza with extra cheese."

"Yummy."

"And your favorite?"

"Nutella chocolate hazelnut spread. If I get a jar I'll take the top off and eat it all with a spoon. I have no self-control when it comes to that. I always say I'll only have a couple tablespoons, but I can't stop myself once I start. It's not just the taste; it's the texture."

"I've never tried it. I'll have to get some."

"If you do, then you'll have to hide it from me."

"I'll keep that in mind."

They returned to Stone's apartment at 2:00 a.m. Once they'd hung up their coats, they sat on the couch and talked about Austin, the hospital where Stone worked, and Josie's future employment at the same facility. They agreed it was time to go to sleep shortly after dawn. Before lying down, Josie turned on the cell phone dedicated to her family's calls and looked at the number of messages. There were twelve from her father, six from her mother, and one from Zelda. She switched off the phone without deleting the messages and left it on the nightstand. She would put it away when she woke and check it again the next night. For now, she needed to sleep.

However, once she was lying in the guest bed in her pink pajamas, Josie found she couldn't rest. She kept thinking about Stone, about herself, about her past, and about her future. The more she thought about life with Stone, the more anxious she became. He seemed to love her, despite their brief acquaintance and all that he knew regarding her. How could she possibly make him happy?

Light rapping on her door made her jump involuntarily. When Stone asked her if he could enter, she found herself unable to answer. He instantly opened the door and stepped inside. The moment he saw that she was in bed and awake, he muttered, "You're okay. Good. I was worried about you."

"Why?"

"I don't know. I had a feeling something wasn't right."

"That something is me." Sitting up, she announced, "I should go."

"Go? Go where?"

"Away from you. You should be with a nice girl from a nice family who can give you good sex and babies and –"

Stone was immediately sitting on the bed beside her with his mouth covering hers. She could sense the passion in him, even if she didn't understand what it was like to feel physical passion herself. She kissed back and enjoyed it. Slipping her arms around

56

his neck, Josie felt Stone's strong arms pull her closer to him. His right hand snaked around so that he could massage her left breast as he continued to kiss her. He startled her by slipping that hand downward, moving it underneath the waistband of her pajama bottoms. He slid his fingers between her legs then stopped and withdrew them.

"Why are you stopping? Do you want me to get the condoms?"

He was breathing hard but shook his head.

"Why not?"

"Because your body's telling me you don't want me in it. If you don't want me, then I don't belong inside you."

"But I *do* want you," she insisted.

"Josie, you don't understand what arousal is. Your body's not reacting the way it should if you desired me."

"I *do* desire you."

"Mentally and emotionally maybe, but not physically. If you wanted me in you, then you'd be wet for me. You're not."

I'm such a freak, Josie thought. *Who was I kidding? Did I really think there was a chance to have a normal relationship with this man?*

Moving around Stone, Josie climbed out of bed. When he asked her where she was going, she told him she needed to take a walk. When he objected, she asked him on what grounds and went to get dressed once more. She wondered if he'd follow her to the bathroom, but he stayed where he was while she put on some clothes, retrieved her coat and purse, and went out of the apartment.

She ended up at the grocery store where she'd purchased the condoms because she could think of nowhere else to go. Pushing a rolling cart, she wandered blindly around the store. She had no intention of buying anything. She simply didn't know what else to do with herself and couldn't clear her head. Eventually, she ended up on the aisle filled with peanut butter, jellies, and spreads. She put several jars of chocolate hazelnut spread in her basket and kept walking.

"Josie?"

She turned and saw Stone behind her. Vowing not to cry, she turned back and resumed walking. He came up beside her and matched her stride. When she paused to let someone else pass with their cart, Stone asked her to come home with him.

"It's not my home," she said dully. "I have no home."

Stone rested a hand on the handle of the shopping cart and stopped walking. Josie was forced to stop as well. She couldn't bring herself to look at the pediatrician. Although it was the last thing she wanted, she knew she should push him away, allowing him to move on with his life.

"Listen to me," he said urgently. "I need for you to come back to the apartment with me."

"I'll go back and get my things. Then you can get some rest and forget about the last few days. Forget you ever met me, finish your residency, and marry a woman who can give you what you want."

"I want *you*." When she said nothing, he continued, "After you left this morning, I listened to your phone messages."

"It doesn't matter anymore."

"It does. I'm a doctor. I've done my rotation in psychiatry plus extra because of specializing in dealing with children who've suffered more than most at the hands of their parents or others. I've interacted with the mentally ill as part of my training. I shouldn't have been shocked or rattled by listening to the voicemails, but I was."

"Why?"

"Because it's been your life since you were five, and it made it more affecting. You're not insane, although you probably should be. You're so strong, Josie. You've lived with the insanity for so many years and still love your family. You have to suffer 24/7 knowing how they are, knowing that they'll probably never get well. They love you, I'm sure. But they're incapable of helping you when you've needed it. I want to help you."

"Because you pity me."

"Because I love you!" he declared. "Because I need you as much as you need me! Because I think you're the bravest, most caring, and most attractive woman I've ever met! Will you give me a chance to be your partner in every sense of the word?"

"I don't know how."

"That's okay. I don't either."

She looked up at him and confessed, "I'm terrified to try."

"That's because every person you've truly cared about has betrayed your trust, albeit unintentionally. You told me you trust me, but I don't think you know what real trust is. Absolute trust

58

means being able to relinquish control. Your ability to control your life has been so limited that your self-control is all you have. I don't want to take anything away. That's why you can put your trust in me and not be so afraid."

Josie hesitated, wanting to truly trust Stone.

"Come home with me," Stone urged. "I swear I'll keep you safe."

"You can't."

"I swear I'll try."

"Okay," she said softly.

Stone breathed a sigh of relief and then insisted on paying for her jars of Nutella. They checked out quickly and were soon walking back to the apartment.

"You've got me curious about this stuff," he informed her as they walked to the apartment building. "It must be great."

"*I* think so. I hope you like it. If not, then I'll have to force myself to eat it all."

"Sounds like a big sacrifice."

"I'm used to sacrifices. At least that would be a nice one for a change."

Chapter Six

Stone placed the bag of Nutella jars on the breakfast bar next to the small, artificial Christmas tree. Then he turned back towards Josie, raked his fingers through his hair, and asked, "Can you remember the happiest day of your life?"

"That's easy."

"Ah, something easy. And here I thought everything about you was supposed to be challenging."

She grinned and said, "Not this. I was twenty-two. It was my last semester of college, and there was a Renaissance festival near the campus. Some friends and I decided to go and dressed in period costumes. I wore a blousy white top, a red corset, and a long, full black skirt. I left my hair loose. One of the actors was making cornets out of wildflowers and gave me a white one to put in my hair. My friends and I ate some great food, looked at beautiful, well-made art, clothing, dinnerware, and swords, and ended up where the musicians were playing on a stage. There were people teaching visitors how to dance like the country folk of those times, and my friends and I tried it. We danced for over an hour. I'd never felt so carefree in my life. We took a break then danced some more. My friends practically had to drag me out not long before the festival ended. I hated to go. I felt wonderful for days afterwards."

"Did you ever do it again?"

"No. I graduated and went to work and remembered it fondly every now and again. It makes me happy to think about it even now. I was full of joy and let everything else fall away."

"I wish I could have seen you like that. Maybe we should go to a Renaissance festival, and you could teach me how to dance like the country folk." Stone came to stand in front of her, rested his palms on either side of her neck, and said, "Dance with me, Josie."

"Here? In the living room?"

"No. In the bedroom."

She imagined he was joking, but he took her hand and led her towards the guest room. Trying to remain calm, Josie went with him, allowing him to lead her to the bed. He kissed her then slid his fingers into her hair and deepened the kiss. She began to feel something indefinable.

Stone brushed his full lips along the nape of her neck as he started to undress her. She automatically began to undress him. It was something she knew was expected of women who were about to have sex. She'd done it before, although her actions during those encounters had always been merely routine. This time, she felt anticipation.

When they were both naked, Josie skimmed her palms over Stone's bare chest. Again, the caressing was something she'd learned was expected, but she found she was deriving great pleasure from feeling Stone's muscles and skin under her hands. The fact that he wanted her to keep touching him was quite obvious, but she was beginning to realize that she was craving his touch as well. This reaction from her was foreign and slightly frightening, but she didn't want him to stop.

"You okay?" he murmured as he trailed his fingertips along the sides of her hips.

Unable to speak, Josie nodded. When he asked her where the condoms were, she looked at the drawer of the nightstand. He kissed her tenderly then removed the box, placing it beside the lamp. He then pulled Josie close to him and asked her if she trusted him and herself enough to make love. Her answer was affirmative but lacked conviction.

"Stop trying not to think about what happened with the neighbor," he directed. "Focus on how you felt when you were dancing at the festival. Hold onto that feeling while you and I are together."

They were soon lying on the mattress. Stone's hands and mouth were exploring Josie's body with a thoroughness none of her other partners had demonstrated. She felt as though her own movements were awkward and clumsy and realized exactly how little she really knew about the actual meaning of the word "intercourse."

"Dance, Josie," Stone said huskily, as he splayed one palm across her belly. "Just dance."

Her breasts became warm under his ministrations, and her nipples tingled as he swirled his tongue around the tips and sucked on them. An unfamiliar ache began at the apex of her thighs, and she gasped and stiffened as he slid his middle finger inside and rubbed his thumb just below the triangle of blonde curls.

"Remember the dance," he breathed then drew his tongue along one of her shoulders. "That's it, Josie. You're doing it."

"Doing what?"

"Reacting the way every woman is made to react during sex. You're wet. You're aroused. Do you want me in you now?"

"Yes," she whispered. "Please."

He withdrew a gold packet from the box and handed it to her. When she hesitated, he asked what was wrong.

"I've never…I didn't put…the men I was with usually put these on themselves. I've never done it."

He smiled encouragingly and said, "There's a first time for everything. Go ahead."

"What if I do it wrong?"

"We have a whole box at our disposal. I want to feel you put it on me."

She tentatively tore the foil and removed the condom. Placing the center of it on the crown of his erection, she slowly and carefully rolled it down. He groaned. When the thick shaft was fully encased, he took one of her hands in one of his and brought it lower, moaning as she caressed him there.

"Are you ready to dance a little faster?" Stone asked in a low voice. When she nodded, he murmured, "Then let's make love."

He parted her knees then rose and knelt between them. She tensed, but he immediately began to rub the insides of her thighs with his hands. She relaxed and realized with relief that she *wanted* to feel Stone Romero inside her.

Josie had been with three other men and had assumed that she knew what sex was like. Except for the first time, the encounters hadn't been painful, probably because the condoms used had lubricant on them. However, she'd never experienced pleasure during any joining. She'd merely pretended to enjoy it and had allowed the men to thrust until they came. She'd always been relieved when they were finished so that she could cease pretending.

Sex with Stone was wonderfully different. As he slowly sank into Josie, she pulsed around him. When he began to thrust, she heard herself whimper with pleasure. When he took one nipple in his mouth, she gave a little cry of delight and drove her fingers into

62

his hair. As he brought his mouth up to meet hers, she rested her hands on his biceps.

When his lips moved to below her ear, Josie gave herself permission to allow the rise of passion in her body. Stone plunged in and pulled out more rapidly, and she throbbed around him and deeper still. She was suddenly terrified, but it was too late to stop.

"Stone, I'm scared!" she cried, even as she thrust her hips upwards to meet his.

"Don't be," he said through ragged breaths. "My beautiful, brave Josephine."

In her entire life, Josie had rarely heard anyone call her by her given name. That, in combination with the way Stone gently slid one hand up her right thigh until her knee was bent and her passage tightened around him, proved to be Josie's undoing. She climaxed hard, gripping Stone's shoulders and repeatedly crying out, riding the waves of ecstasy. At the peak of her climax, Stone buried himself to the root and uttered a hoarse "Josephine!" before giving in to his own release.

Josie lay stunned underneath Stone for a few minutes after they'd finished. She felt physically and emotionally spent. Shocked by the force of her body's reaction to their lovemaking, she held on tightly to the man and thought, *I'm okay. I really am a normal woman, at least when it comes to sex. Thank you, God.*

When she began to cry with relief, Stone withdrew and took her in his arms. As he held her securely against him, he uttered reassuring words and told her he'd never had such an intense sexual experience with any woman. He murmured that he loved her and remarked on how thankful he was for her trust. Exhausted and relieved, Josie slept.

She woke alone after 8:00 that night. The apartment was empty, but Stone had left her a note, telling her he'd made steak, broccoli, and potatoes for dinner and that there was a plate waiting for her in the refrigerator. The note was addressed to "Josephine" and signed, "Looking forward to our future dances together. Love, Stone." She smiled to herself and went to heat up her food.

The meal was, of course, delicious. Once she'd eaten and loaded her utensils and plate into the dishwasher, Josie showered, put on a faded red thermal-weave shirt she'd always loved to wear while working from home, and jeans. Then she sat at the table and poured over the hospital materials the soon-to-be former Director of Marketing had prepared. By the time dawn broke, Josie had already outlined her prospective new marketing plan for the hospital. She was in the middle of typing a report on her laptop when she heard the key turn in the lock of the door. She smiled and twisted around in her chair, expecting to see the pediatrician smiling back. He wasn't. In fact, his expression was one of utter despair.

"Stone, what's wrong? Is it Brittany?"

"She's the same. I –"

He suddenly appeared dizzy, and Josie hurried across the room in order to steady him. His face was slightly red, and she instantly thought about his blood pressure. As she helped him towards the couch, she asked him if he was having a stroke.

"I doubt it, but it wouldn't surprise me if my pressure was through the roof. I have an electronic monitor in my bedside table. I should probably use it."

She darted to his room, found the monitor, and took it to him. He removed his coat and shirt then adjusted the cuff on the upper part of his left arm. He shut his eyes and breathed deeply once he'd pressed the START button on the machine. It whirred as the cuff tightened and then there were clicking noises. Finally, there was a beeping sound. Opening his eyes, Stone glanced at the screen and swore quietly.

"It's that bad?" Josie asked nervously.

"Yes. It's 197 over 95. My pulse is 94. The only other time everything's been this high was when I found out what happened to Nelson."

"What can I do? Should I take you to the hospital?"

"No. I just need to get calm."

"What made you so upset?"

"If I tell you, then my pressure will keep climbing. I need to think about something else for a while until I can get my emotions under control."

Snuggling beside him, Josie wrapped her arms around his waist and ordered, "Tell me *your* best memory. Maybe that will help you to relax."

"Okay. You're right." Sighing, he began, "Nelson and I were walking in the woods when we were seventeen. We were talking about what we wanted to do with our lives. We loved and hated

64

where we lived, and we knew we had to leave if we were ever going to be happy as adults. We eventually agreed we'd have to go to college in New Orleans because that's probably the most accepting city in the whole frigging state of Louisiana. We could go there, and Nelson could be accepted for who he was. So could I. No judgments about our views on life, religion, sexuality, or anything else. Well, no judgments from most people there. We knew Mama and Daddy would be upset; Cheek would be pleased that we were out of his hair; and Memaw would miss us but would understand. We were working out the details of how we were going to accomplish our goals when we heard something moving somewhere up ahead in the woods. We froze and stayed very quiet. That was when we saw them."

"Them?"

"Two wolves. They were gorgeous animals, but we knew how dangerous wolves could be under certain circumstances. So, we stood completely still and admired them from a respectful distance. They were sort of reddish-brown and had amazing eyes that were full of intelligence and feeling."

"How long did you stand there?"

"A few minutes. Then both of the wolves walked slowly towards us. They came right up to us. There was no fear on our part or theirs. Nelson and I looked at each other; then we both knelt on the ground. The slightly larger of the two wolves came over to me and circled around me once before nuzzling my hand. The other wolf went straight up to Nelson and nudged his knee. After a minute or so, both wolves moved away from us and walked off into the woods. They stopped once to look back at us then kept going. It was a surreal encounter. I've never spoken about it to anyone else – until tonight."

"It sounds almost mystical."

"It was." Kissing the top of her head, Stone asked, "Will you press the button on the monitor for me?"

Stone's blood pressure had dropped significantly but remained high. His pulse had slowed to below ninety. Josie suggested he lie back on the couch and be quiet for a while.

"Think about the wolves," she directed. "I'll lie beside you while you relax."

The bare flesh of his chest was cool under her cheek, and she asked if he was cold. He assured her the heat in the apartment was more than adequate and that he was not going to freeze by being shirtless for a while. When she told him he could go shirtless as often as he liked around her, he smiled drowsily and took his blood pressure again. It was continuing to drop steadily, which greatly relieved Josie.

"Josie?"

"Hm?"

"I think I'm going to have to change my career plans. Would that bother you?"

"Change them how?"

"I don't think I can continue to focus on the kids who are abused, abandoned, or neglected. I know I'll see some in a regular practice, but it won't be as prevalent as in a hospital setting. I think I'm going to work on mainstream pediatric medicine."

"Will you be content doing that?"

"Practicing pediatric medicine is rewarding for me no matter what. I just...I wanted to make a difference to kids with those special challenges. Now, I'm thinking that wouldn't be wise for me, not with my hypertension. If I keep pushing myself, I'll definitely die young or be permanently impaired. I don't want to do that, not now that I met you."

"You didn't care before?"

"Not really. I figured my goal was worth the risk, but I wasn't in love with anyone and had no plans for my personal future other than career plans."

"I don't care what you do as long as we're happy together."

"Good. Tell me how happy we'll be."

"We'll love each other, our jobs, and Chaucer, Frost, Shakespeare, and Aristophanes."

"I thought we weren't going to have kids."

"You think I'd saddle children with author and playwright names like those? No, those are some of my favorites, but I'd never do that to an innocent child. Those will be the names of our wolves. We'll have a nice house with a huge backyard and a pack of wolves. They can have lots of pups, and I can have fun naming them after every writer I adore. There are quite a few, so we might have to live out in the country."

He chuckled but admitted he'd never read any of the works written by the writers she'd mentioned, except Shakespeare.

"That's okay. Most people haven't. When you're the daughter of an English professor, you get exposed to a lot of works others don't often read."

"How many books or plays have you read?"

"Too many to count. Reading is an entrancing thing for me. It's a great escape. I love just about every genre. Dad's obsession with literature spilled over to me. Zelda never cared about it much, but she did appreciate Dad's stories. He could always tell the most fantastic tales. One story he told us lasted for an entire year."

"How'd he do that?"

"We got fifteen minutes of it a night before we went to bed. The story was very simple on the surface but became more and more complex as the days passed. I wish I'd written it down. I can't remember everything he told us. The ending was so perfect and tied up every loose end he'd left during the first three hundred and sixty-four days. He said it was the way people used to tell stories and keep legends going before the written word. I wish people still did things like that."

The next time Stone took his blood pressure and pulse, both were within the acceptable range. As he removed the cuff of the monitor, Josie asked him if he wanted something to eat.

"I'll try some of that chocolate hazelnut stuff you like."

"What do you want me to spread it on? Waffles? Pancakes? Toast?"

"I'll try it on a spoon and see if I even like it."

To her delight, Stone loved it. She heated two frozen waffles for each of them then drizzled some of the spread on top. They ate in silence, and she wondered how she was going to get Stone to talk about whatever incident had triggered his blood pressure episode. He looked completely drained. There was so much she didn't know about him, and she sensed it was imperative that she learn as much as she could as soon as she could. After all, they were going to raise a pack of wolves together, weren't they?

"What are you smiling about?" Stone asked with a gleam in his brown eyes.

"Our future."

"At least you're smiling."

"I am, aren't I?" Growing serious, she asked, "Are you sure you're okay with us not having any children?"

"I'm okay with us not having any biological children. I understand your concerns about the mental illness genes. With your family history and my grandmother's mental illness, the odds of our kids having emotional problems are greatly increased." Cocking his head, he asked, "Would you consider adopting?"

"Um…maybe. If I make it past twenty-seven without becoming schizophrenic, we'll talk."

"Deal." After yawning, he declared, "My head's killing me. It's because my pressure was so high for an extended period. I've got to get some sleep. Will you join me?"

"I'd love to. Which bedroom are we going to sleep in?"

"It doesn't make a difference to me as long as I'm sleeping next to you."

"Your bed is twice the size of the one in the guest room, so that one would probably be best. Let me go change."

While Stone showered, Josie went to her room and put on the lavender, cotton nightgown she'd bought at the mall. She put the box of condoms that had been in the guest room in the drawer of Stone's nightstand next to the blood pressure monitor. As she did so, she vowed to learn more about high blood pressure in general.

Josie moved to Stone's dresser and opened the top drawer. The old box of condoms was gone.

"I threw it away yesterday," Stone said from where he stood in the doorway of the bathroom. "I didn't want us to get the old and new mixed up." Walking across the room to where she stood, he asked seriously, "What would you do if a condom broke and you got pregnant?"

"Have an abortion then cry a lot."

"You seem pretty certain about how you'd react."

She nodded disconsolately and offered, "At least I'd cry. At least I'd feel horrible."

"How many abortions has Zelda had?"

"How –?" she began then shook her head and continued, "Never mind how you figured that one out."

"How many, Josie?"

"Two. She terminated the first pregnancy early, but she didn't find out that she was even pregnant the second time until she was fifteen weeks along. She was still having periods."

"How old was she?"

"The first time she was fourteen. She got pregnant by a boy in a foster home who used her sexually. He wanted me, but she convinced him to have sex with her instead."

"Who paid for the abortion?"

"I don't know. I don't know if Zelda knew. The woman who ran the foster home took her to the doctor, so I guess she paid the bill."

"And the other abortion Zelda had?"

"Was last year. She said she had unprotected sex with her boss. She asked the doctor who did the abortion to sterilize her at the same time. She knew she should never have kids. He refused. He told her what the doctors have told me, that I'm young and may change my mind and have no medical condition that would require sterilization."

Stone seemed lost in thought for a while then asked, "Have you ever had sex without using condoms?"

"No. I tried taking The Pill, but it made me sick. My doctor said I shouldn't be on it."

"So, you've never felt what it's really like."

"I did last night."

"Last night was phenomenal, but you have no idea how intoxicating it can be to feel skin upon skin during sex. You don't know what it's like to feel a man release directly inside you. If we're never having children together, then I'm going to look into having a vasectomy. I don't want to spend the next twenty to thirty years using condoms. I want to be in you naturally and for you to know what that's like. I also don't want us to have an unplanned pregnancy and abortion that will be devastating for both of us."

"But you can't have a vasectomy!" she insisted. "What if I die young and you fall in love with someone else and want to have children with her?"

"I can't imagine that happening. Even if it did, I'd suggest adoption like I have with you but because I'd had the vasectomy. If that woman loved me, she'd understand."

69

"But what doctor would do it? You're not even thirty. They'll tell you what they told me and Zelda."

"As sexist as it is, sterilization's done more readily for men than women. I'm also a doctor. I could have it done tomorrow if I wanted."

"Stone, we haven't known each other for a week! We've made love one time, and we're not married. We have no idea where we're headed with our careers. My family is crazy, and you seem to be estranged from yours. Yet, you're willing to have a vasectomy tomorrow?"

"If that's what I need to do in order to be totally with you."

"Are you sure *you're* not mentally ill?"

He laughed and said, "Sane as can be. I've just been desperately in love with you from the moment we met. I need you, Josie."

"Why? I can't understand it. It doesn't make sense!"

"Just because something doesn't make sense doesn't mean it's crazy. You complete me."

"Like Nelson completed you?"

"No. That was totally different. Nelson and I were parts of the same person. You and I are definitely two separate individuals."

"The concept's the same."

"Perhaps it is. That doesn't mean I need it any less. I've been the shell of a man ever since my twin died last year. You make me feel…filled."

"And you fill me," she admitted.

"I'd like to fill you," he said with a wicked grin.

"Well, that wasn't what I meant, but I'd like that, too. Not right now though. You need to rest. You weren't well earlier, and you have to work tonight."

"No, I don't. I've been placed on administrative leave, pending an internal investigation."

"Wait! What? Why are you on administrative leave?"

"Because I punched someone in the ER."

"Punched someone? Who? Why?"

"I really don't want to talk about it. My pressure will shoot up again if I have to review it with you."

"So, give me the short version."

Staring at the floor, he said quietly, "During my shift, I treated a fifteen-year-old boy who'd been put out on the street two years ago by his parents when he confessed to them that he was gay. He's been turning tricks to survive. The kid came in thinking he had the flu. He had pneumonia. I'm not sure how long he's had HIV. He was in bad shape. A staff member helpfully contacted his parents, thinking they might want to come to see their child. They came all right. They came and told him it was God's judgment on him that he caught AIDS because he was performing unnatural sexual acts. When the father told his son that he hoped he'd die and would burn in Hell, I punched the man. I think I shocked everyone in the ER." Stone covered his eyes with one hand and said, "That kid is their *child*. How could any parent wish for their child to die a horrible death because he's different? How could anyone be so heartless?"

Going over to him and slipping her arms around his waist, Josie said, "No wonder you were so upset. Come here."

Urging him towards the bed, she instructed him to lie down then climbed in beside him. Pulling his head across her chest, she stroked his hair and rubbed his back until he fell asleep. Josie lay awake, grateful she'd been able to help him. Stone had taken such good care of her. It gave her great satisfaction each time she reciprocated. She wished she could do more and suspected she'd get many chances in the future. They *did* seem to need one another. Josie wondered how they'd managed separately before fate had brought them together. She now understood what Stone must have felt towards her all along – love, attraction, and an overwhelming need to strengthen a connection he'd obviously felt with her from the beginning. If she hadn't been so worn down and emotionally cut off from the world when they'd first met, she might have realized the truth much sooner.

Chapter Seven

"We don't have to do this," Josie told Stone as he turned his Honda onto the long, winding, gravel driveway that led to his parents' home. "Things have changed so radically for you and me in the last few weeks. Your family doesn't know any of it. Maybe it's too soon. There's still time to turn around and go back to Texas."

"No. It's stressing me out not to talk to them or see them, regardless of how angry I am about Nelson. It's the day before Christmas, and I want to see my parents, Memaw, and my nephew."

"And Cheek?"

"No. I don't ever want to see Cheek again."

"But what if he comes?"

"Then I'll have to deal with him."

As the car wound its way through the woods towards the house, Josie asked, "How are you feeling?"

"You mean because of the vasectomy? That was a week ago. I feel fine. They've made a lot of improvements in techniques since the olden days. I've been cleared for intercourse. We could have sex tonight if you want."

"At your parents' house? But we're not married, and you said they were very traditional."

"They may not approve of premarital sex, but they're not fools. Once I introduce you and tell them we're living together, they'll know we're having sex in Austin."

"But they won't know about the vasectomy."

"And they never will. It's none of their business."

"When can we have sex without condoms?"

He flashed her a rakish grin and said, "Eager, are you?"

"Yes, thanks to you. When?"

"It takes a couple months after the procedure for a man to not have any more viable sperm left. I'll go back to the doctor and be certain before we have unprotected sex."

"What if your family hates me?" Josie blurted out.

"They'll love you. What if your family hates me?"

72

"They're disturbed. Besides, we're not going to visit my family anytime in the foreseeable future."

"At least you talked to each of them and told them you were safe and were in love."

"I wouldn't have been able to do it if you hadn't been sitting beside me holding my hand. I didn't tell them where I was living. I've made the obligatory calls and don't have to call again for quite a while."

"I know it was difficult, but you have to admit that it did remind you of how crazy they are and how certain you are that you should never try to have kids. I totally agree. That solidified my decision to have the vasectomy."

The Romero home came into view. It was a two-story house that looked like a log cabin. The wood was a light pine color, and the construction seemed solid. Nestled in the woods, it appeared very rustic and homey. Josie wondered if Stone had grown up in this house or if his parents had moved into it once their children had reached adulthood. It definitely wasn't palatial and would be downright small for a family of five. She asked Stone about the house.

"This was Daddy's family's camp. When he and Mama married at eighteen, his disapproving father told them they could move into the camp so they'd have a decent place to live. He looked down on Daddy for marrying Mama, who didn't come from a prominent family, and for wanting to be a policeman."

"What did your father's father do?"

"He was the town doctor. He was good at his job, but he could also be a mean son of a bitch. I often wondered why my Memaw married him. She's so sweet."

"You were raised here in this house then."

"I was literally born here. Mama had Cheek, me, and Nelson in the bedroom downstairs." Scanning the area, he said, "My folks love this place. They'll never leave it. That's why Memaw had her house built behind ours after my grandfather died when I was twelve. It's Daddy and Mama's home. They raised their kids here and love these woods. I love them, too. I just wish the whole place was located somewhere else, someplace more accepting. If only that were true, it'd be the idyllic location for any family."

As Stone parked the car, Josie unbuckled her seatbelt and said, "I'm sorry."

"For what?"

"Not being able to chance having children. Making you have a vasectomy."

"The vasectomy was my idea, remember? I seem to recall you saying something about raising wolves. I may hold you to that."

She smiled and said, "You can hold me to anything, Dr. Romero."

"Mm. Later."

Stone got out of the car before she could comment, coming around to open her door. Suddenly anxious, Josie was about to voice her concern when the front door of the house was flung open and Dumpling Romero hurried down the steps and came as quickly as she could towards them. She was surprisingly fast despite her ample figure. Her long, light brown hair practically flew behind her as she hurried towards the car.

"Stone! My baby! Why didn't you tell us you were coming?"

"That would've ruined the surprise. Merry Christmas Eve, Mama." He hugged her, kissed her on the cheek, and said, "There's someone I want you to meet."

Josie felt as if she were a deer caught in the headlights of a truck. Momentarily petrified, she wasn't certain what she should say or do. Dumpling took one look at her and beamed then hastened around to take her hand, practically pulling her out of the car. The woman took her other hand and said, "Now, aren't you the prettiest little thing I've ever seen? You look like a real-life Barbie Doll!" Turning to her son, she said, "Knowing you, she's got a lot of brains, too. She's just so cute!" Looking back to Josie, she asked, "What's your name, Baby?"

"Josie Hollingsworth."

After giving Josie a hug that almost suffocated her, Stone's mother introduced herself and exclaimed, "I'm so excited to meet you! Are you two married?"

"Mama, please," Stone said with a shake of his head. "Give Josie and me a break. We just drove a long way to get here and surprise you, Daddy, and Memaw."

"And we're real happy you came," said a man Josie knew must be Vin Romero.

They turned *en masse*, as Vin ambled down the steps and walked towards them. The brown-haired man went over to his son and gave him a bear hug then directed his attention to Josie.

"You're a fine-looking young woman," he said genially. "Not as fine as my Dumpling, but mighty fine in your own right."

Josie blushed and thanked him. She felt like an object that had been taken to school for Show-and-Tell. She reminded herself that this meeting of the family members over a year after Nelson's funeral was probably unimaginably awkward for Stone and his parents. She remembered Stone telling her that he wouldn't be able to go home to see his mother and father without her by his side and hoped that her presence somehow made things easier for them all.

"Are you two married?" Dumpling repeated.

"No, Mama."

Vin frowned and asked, "She's not pregnant, is she? If you're not married, then that just wouldn't be right."

"We're living together, but Josie's not pregnant."

Josie noted that Dumpling looked disappointed and felt a pang of disappointment in her own heart. Her feelings must have been evident on her face, because Dumpling asked her what was wrong. Reminding herself not to be too open about her own family situation with Stone's parents, she said diplomatically, "It wouldn't be advisable for me to have children. I wish it weren't so, but it is."

Dumpling immediately hugged her and said, "Now, don't you go thinking about that. If you shouldn't have children, then the Good Lord has a reason for it. We don't always understand His ways, but He knows best."

Vin nodded and said, "Dumpling's right, although we were both looking forward to having more grandchildren someday."

"Vin, the poor girl's only just arrived, and you're making her feel guilty for something she can't control," Dumpling said reprovingly. "I'm just so happy to see Stone and to meet Josie here. Oh, my sweet girl! Why don't you come inside and meet Memaw while Stone and Vin unload the car?"

Dumpling led Josie up the steps and in through the front door. The living room was full of comfortable furniture, framed prints of wildlife, and family photos. Deer antlers were mounted over the fireplace. Everything was well-kept but also well-worn. Vin obviously didn't make much money as a sheriff.

"Memaw!" Dumpling called out. "Guess who's here?"

"Who?" Josie heard an older woman call out from what she assumed was the kitchen.

"Stone! And he's brought his girlfriend!"

Stone's grandmother hurried into the room, wiping her hands on a towel. The thin, gray-haired woman wearing glasses apologized for not being able to hug Josie right away and explained, "I'm preparing the turkey for cooking tomorrow and should wash my hands before we hug.

"I understand," Josie assured her. "It's so nice to meet you."

"They're living together," Dumpling informed her mother-in-law in a conspiratorial whisper.

Memaw smiled at her son's wife and said, "You don't have to whisper. We're all adults here."

"But they're living in sin."

"We're all living in sin," Memaw pointed out. "And God can hear you whether you whisper or not."

Josie grinned. She was quickly beginning to understand why Stone got along so well with his grandmother.

"Daddy, no," Stone said, as he and his father entered the house with the suitcases. "That's ridiculous. I'm almost thirty; Josie's twenty-five; and we're living together."

"I'm sorry, Stone. If you're not married then you're not sleeping in the same bed in our house. Your Mama and I don't believe in sex before marriage. We won't tolerate it in our home."

"You won't tolerate premarital sex, but you'll tolerate Cheek owning a bar where women take off their clothes and give men lap dances?"

"None of us approve of Cheek's club," his mother said seriously. "But he doesn't do it in our house. We can't control what he does when he's not here anymore than we could control Nelson's choice to engage in unnatural sexual behavior or –"

Stone dropped the suitcase he was holding onto the floor and asked, "You think Nelson had a *choice* about his sexual orientation? Why would anyone choose to be ostracized by the people in their community and those in their own family?"

"He could have fought those urges," Vin suggested. "He could've abstained."

"And be alone for the rest of his life?"

76

"It's against God," Dumpling said sincerely. "It says so in the Bible."

Josie moved forward, feeling helpless and worried about what this exchange was doing to Stone's blood pressure. He'd been fine since the day after he'd punched the man at the hospital, but she could visualize his heart rate increasing and his arteries narrowing. She had to diffuse the situation somehow or else it was only going to get worse.

"How about if I sleep at Stone's grandmother's house while we're here?" she interrupted. "If she has an extra bed, then I could sleep there. If not, then I'll sleep on her couch. I don't want to be disrespectful if you feel uncomfortable about Stone and me sharing a bed during our visit."

The look Stone gave her was filled with a combination of gratitude, relief, and a hint of betrayal.

"Of course you can stay with me," Memaw declared. "I'd love the company and have a nice guest room."

"How long are you staying?" Dumpling asked her son. "We haven't seen you in so long."

"And we need to get to know Josie," Memaw pointed out. "Please tell me you'll stay for at least a week."

"If we don't talk about Nelson and if Cheek keeps away," Stone stated evenly.

"Cheek and Tommy are coming for Christmas dinner tomorrow," Vin informed them. "I'm not going to call your brother and my grandson and tell them they can't come because you're here."

Stone took a deep breath, exhaled, and then declared, "You tell Cheek in advance that if he so much as mentions Nelson's name, Josie and I will leave, and I'll never come back."

"Don't say that!" Dumpling pleaded. "We've already lost one son! We don't want to lose another!"

"No one's going to lose anyone," Memaw announced. "Everyone will play nice tomorrow and have a good dinner. Cheek won't stay once the food is gone, and we can spend the rest of the week with Stone and Josie. Maybe Tommy will be around more if his uncle's here."

"I'll call Cheek," Vin said reassuringly. "Please, stay."

77

Stone nodded and picked up the suitcase from the floor before saying, "This is Josie's. I'll bring it to Memaw's house and be right back."

Once he'd gone through the kitchen and they all heard the backdoor open and close, Vin urgently asked Josie, "How is my son's blood pressure?"

"Um...."

"Please, tell us. His mama and I are worried but don't want to make things worse by asking too much at once."

"He had a bad episode a couple weeks ago where it got really high. Other than that, I get the impression it's well-controlled."

"How high?" Memaw prompted.

Josie chewed on her lower lip for a moment before admitting, "The top number was close to 200, and the bottom number was almost 100. His pulse was in the mid-90s."

"Oh, Vin!" Dumpling exclaimed with a trace of fear in her voice. "That's way too high."

"He blames us for Nelson's death," Vin stated.

"He blames Cheek, but he's angry with you and your wife, too," Josie corrected.

"We understand that. Our views about Nelson's sexual behavior are different from Stone's and my mother's," Vin said. "We aren't going to change our position, and Stone and my Mama aren't going to change theirs. That doesn't mean we don't love them anymore. It doesn't mean we didn't love Nelson."

"Stone knows that," Josie told the man. "He loves you, but...but half of him is gone. I –"

The backdoor opened again, and she stopped talking. Memaw took this opportunity to suggest that Dumpling show Josie around the main house while Memaw recruited Stone to help Vin and her in the kitchen. Curious, Josie agreed and went with Stone's mother into the dining room. It was small and filled by a table and six chairs. There was a painting on one wall of a man, woman, and boy.

"That's Memaw, Pepaw, and Vin," Dumpling said helpfully. "Vin was six at the time."

Josie studied the oil portrait, which had been painted by someone with decent ability. The father came across as stern and in charge. The mother seemed to emanate kindness and love. The boy had an uncertain smile on his lips.

"What's your mother-in-law's name?"

"Gertrude."

"And your father-in-law?"

"Vincent. Vin was named after him."

"What was he like?"

"He was a good doctor, but he was a mean man. I honestly don't know why Memaw married him. She's always been so giving. He was cruel. I thank God that Vin never hit me like his father used to hit his mother. He cheated on her, too. When niggers used to come to his office for treatment, he'd make them sit in an unfinished room in the back, while the whites sat in a nice area out front. He thought niggers weren't human, but he'd treat them because he said someone had to help the poor creatures. He was awful!"

Josie wasn't sure what shocked her more, hearing Stone's mother call African-Americans "niggers" or what she'd shared with Josie about Dr. Vincent Romero's abusive behavior towards his wife and his attitude regarding blacks. She wanted to say something but could think of nothing appropriate. So, she mutely followed Dumpling to the master bedroom, which was small, neat, and clean. A handmade patchwork quilt covered the full-sized mattress, and frilly white curtains hung in the window. The house's only bathroom was across the hall.

The women climbed the stairs to what had once been the boys' bedrooms. The two rooms were large but felt smaller to Josie because of the pitch of the roof. She wondered whether or not the space was a converted attic. There was a full-sized bed and a dresser in Cheek's old room and matching twin beds and chests of drawers in the room that had been shared by Stone and Nelson. All of their childhood things had been removed, and there were no personal items remaining to suggest that the Romero children had ever occupied those spaces. Josie thought this odd but said nothing.

When she and Dumpling returned downstairs all seemed to be well in the kitchen. Stone was smiling and laughing with his father and grandmother. The air of tension that had surrounded all of them earlier seemed to have dissipated. Josie allowed herself to relax and accepted the bottle of root beer Stone offered her.

"So much for having sex tonight," he told her later as he kissed her goodnight on the front porch of his grandmother's large, one-story, white wooden home.

79

"Maybe we can have sex in the woods," she suggested playfully. "Keep some condoms in your pocket just in case. After all, exercise is good for your blood pressure."

"Too true." After he'd kissed her again, Stone murmured, "You're really enjoying making love as often as possible, aren't you?" Before she could answer, he kissed her once more and then added, "You don't know how happy it makes me."

Josie rolled her eyes and muttered sarcastically, "I can tell how happy it makes you every time we do it."

Stone pressed his lips to her forehead and then insisted, "That's not what I meant. I'm just so happy that I could make you –"

Placing two fingers over his mouth, she interrupted, "I understand, and I love you even more because of it."

Smiling, Stone knocked lightly on Memaw's front door. The woman quickly opened it and ushered Josie inside then hugged and kissed her grandson goodnight before saying, "We'll see you in the morning. You sleep well, Stone. I love you."

"And I love you, Memaw."

Once he was gone, Memaw took Josie on a tour of her house. The interior was well-appointed and filled with tasteful antiques. It was nothing like the former hunting camp that served as the Romero family home.

When Josie remarked on the difference in décor, Memaw laughed and said, "My son and daughter-in-law are country people with country tastes. My family had money and education, as did my husband's. We knew the value of fine things. Stone and Nelson took after us in that respect, but Cheek took after his parents. To each his own.

"Vin is a very bright, active man who earned his college degree, became a policeman, and has been the sheriff for years, but he and his wife are content in their limited world. If that's what they want, then let them have it. I'm glad Stone wants more. Nelson wanted more, too. I was so devastated when he killed himself last year." Taking a seat on the couch, she gestured for Josie to sit beside her then added, "My Daddy killed himself when I was thirteen."

"I beg your pardon?"

"Yes, it was pretty horrific. I found him, you see. That's when I started having mental illness problems. If I hadn't been so disturbed, then I would have had more sense than to marry Vincent

Romero." Offering a slight smile, she continued, "I did *not* mourn my husband when he died. I've been much happier in the two decades or so since he's been gone. I have a nice, violence-free life and enjoy volunteering at the library and belonging to several book clubs."

"You love books then."

"My major in college was English. I *adore* books."

"My father has a Ph.D. in English. I inherited his love of literature."

"Fabulous! Does your father teach?"

"He used to. He hasn't been able to work in a while."

"Poor health?"

Josie nodded and said, "Very poor. My mother, too. She's a psychology professor."

"Do you have siblings?"

"One sister."

"What does she do?"

"She worked on Wall Street up until this year."

"I see. So, they're all nutcases like me?"

Flustered, Josie answered, "Yes. No. I mean, you're not a nutcase. You're okay. They're not. And please, don't tell Stone's parents. I get the impression they wouldn't approve."

"Honey, I won't say a word to anyone, but remember to whom you're speaking. I'm mentally ill myself. Vin knows this. I raised him and wasn't always stable. He still loved me. He and Dumpling are actually very understanding about mental illness because of me." Patting Josie on one knee, Memaw asked, "Is that why you aren't supposed to have children?" When Josie nodded, she asked, "That bad?"

"Yes. I can't risk passing on the mental illness genes to any child I might have."

"Well, they wouldn't only be your genes. Look at our family. I've been diagnosed as bipolar although I am on my medications and have been for the past ten years without fail. But my husband was a sadist, and my daddy and Nelson both killed themselves. Our side's got its share of instability in the emotional area, too."

"Not like my family."

"I feel for you. I feel for Vin, having to live with me being emotionally up and down all the time when he was a boy. Maybe

81

someday you'll feel comfortable sharing your experiences with him. It'd probably do you both some good to talk about what it's like to be raised by parents with mental illness."

"I'm so glad you're on your meds," Josie told the older woman. "I wish things were different for my family."

Memaw nodded and proclaimed, "I believe you and Stone are going to be very good for one another. I'm certainly happy to know you."

"Thanks. I'm happy to know you, too."

"What did you get Stone for Christmas?"

"A watch I had engraved on the back and a seat at a private cooking demonstration given by Chef Kat Cora."

"That Iron Chef lady who was on the Food Network?"

"Yes. Working in L.A. for several years and selling high-end real estate, I made some unusual connections. One of those people is very involved in the culinary world. He's sponsoring this charity event in Austin in March, and Kat Cora will be the main attraction. I know how Stone loves to cook and thought it would be a different type of gift. I really didn't know what else to give him. I've never bought anyone a Christmas present before. I hope he likes it."

"I'm sure he'll love it. He *has* always loved to cook, and it's a charity event. He'll appreciate your thoughtfulness on more than one level." Frowning, she asked, "You've never bought a Christmas present for anyone in your life?"

"No."

"Are you Jewish?"

"No, but we didn't celebrate Christmas in our house after I was five, and I don't really remember what our celebrations were like before then."

Memaw's brow furrowed as she inquired, "Was that because of your parents' mental problems?"

"Yes, Ma'am."

"No tree or Christmas dinner?"

"No, Ma'am."

"No presents?" When she shook her head, Memaw asked, "Church?"

"No, Ma'am."

"So, Christmas means nothing to you."

Josie shrugged and said, "It's the date someone picked to celebrate the birth of Jesus Christ. Christians who have 'normal' families participate in religious and non-religious traditions related to the holiday."

"Did you ever try celebrating, just your sister and you?"

Josie stiffened and rapidly shook her head. She thought of the year when she'd been six and had suggested to their mother that the two girls attend a Christmas parade sponsored by a local community organization. Her mother had announced that End-of-Days had threatened to kill anyone participating in the festivities. Josie had never again attempted to engage in any organized holiday activity.

"Well, tomorrow we're going to have a nice Christmas dinner," Memaw told her. "I hope we are anyway. I'm worried about Stone and Cheek and how the holiday festivities will go. I think things will be tense, but we all have to try to repair this family a little at a time."

"Were Stone and Nelson as close as I think they were?"

"Always. It was like one knew what the other was thinking before the other one did sometimes. They'd often finish each other's sentences. They also experienced cryptophasia until they were about four."

"Cryptophasia?"

"It's a phenomenon in which twins develop a language only they understand. Of course, Stone and Nelson spoke regular English to the rest of us, but they had their own language, too."

Making a mental note to read up on twin behaviors, Josie asked, "Were their personalities alike?"

"Stone and Nelson were both smart, kind, and good-looking young men, but there was never any doubt that Stone was all man while Nelson was definitely not." Sighing, she asked, "What did you get Stone for his birthday?"

"His birthday? When is his birthday?"

"It's tomorrow. He was born on Christmas."

"I had no idea. He didn't say anything about it being his and Nelson's birthday."

"Well, it's Stone's birthday but not Nelson's."

Completely bewildered, Josie asked, "What? Did he come right before midnight and Nelson right after?"

"I wish it'd been that easy. Stone was born Christmas afternoon. Cheek was very put out. He was ten and felt that the birth ruined his holiday."

"But if Stone was born on Christmas afternoon, then when was Nelson born?"

"Four days later."

"How is that possible? They were identical twins. Aren't twins born one right after the other?"

"Not in this case. Vincent delivered Stone, just as he'd delivered Cheek. But then Dumpling's labor stopped, and Vin and I suggested that Dumpling go to the hospital. Vincent insisted that the baby would come when it was ready. Dumpling had sporadic contractions for the next three days. Vincent told her to do a lot of walking to get the labor going again." Narrowing her eyes, she declared, "I told Vin and Dumpling to go to the hospital anyway, but they trusted Vincent, the sadist. I think he was hoping the baby would die. He didn't think Vin and Dumpling should have any more children since he wasn't fond of Cheek to begin with."

"That's horrible! Was Nelson okay when he was finally born?"

"Yes, thank goodness. Stone didn't do so well those first few days of his life. The moment Nelson was delivered, Stone's coloring improved and he started to nurse better. It was like he was in limbo until his twin joined him in this world."

And he's been in limbo since his twin left it, Josie realized. *He's lost without his brother. Enter Josie Hollingsworth.*

She almost began to laugh but decided that would be impolite. She'd met Stone on the day she was about to kill herself, and he'd basically pulled her from the precipice. Perhaps he'd been on the edge of a precipice as well and was relieved to finally find someone he connected with, someone he intuitively recognized as a person he could love and trust. It was the only conceivable explanation she could imagine.

And speaking of conceivable, perhaps Stone's quick suggestion of his sterilization hadn't been so hasty after all. He had a sadistic grandfather, a great-grandfather who'd committed suicide sixty-seven years earlier, a bipolar grandmother, and an identical twin brother who'd killed himself by jumping off a bridge. It wasn't quite like living with Josie's family, but Memaw was correct in her assessment that mental illness was an issue for Stone's family, too.

Relieved, Josie let go of her guilt about refusing to procreate and relaxed.

Chapter Eight

"Are you hungry?" Memaw asked an hour later during a lull in their conversation.

"Stone and I ate at a small burger place off the highway. The food was terribly greasy but very tasty."

"Burger Barn," Memaw declared. "They have very good tater tots there."

"We had some with our cheeseburgers. They were to *die* for!"

Memaw laughed and asked, "How about some hot chocolate?"

"I'd love some. I guess I lived in Los Angeles too long and got used to that climate. I've been *so* cold ever since I came to Texas and Louisiana."

"It has been an unusually cold winter in the Austin area, but this is normal for northern Louisiana. Most people who don't live here think all of us southerners go around fanning ourselves and dripping with sweat no matter the season." Rising from the couch, she asked, "Why don't you come with me to the kitchen while I make the hot chocolate, and we can talk some more? As you can tell, we're pretty chatty here. Ask me anything.

As Memaw heated milk in the microwave so that she could add it to the hot chocolate mix, Josie asked, "How did you and your husband end up in Clayville?"

"There was a need for a doctor in this area, and Vincent decided to open his practice here. It was a wise business move. He had no competition. The town has grown, and there are more doctors nowadays. They're general practitioners, internists, or OB/GYNs. No pediatricians. Vin and Dumpling have tried to convince Stone to move back and open a practice here, but this isn't his kind of place. He loves it because it's where he was raised, but he hates it, too. I don't blame him. I'm used to it after fifty years and have likeminded friends here and in the surrounding towns. However, we are a select few. I would've moved a long time ago myself, but I love my son, daughter-in-law, and great-grandson very much and enjoy the beauty of the woods. I don't want to leave my family or what's become my home."

"What about Cheek?" Josie asked curiously.

"I love Cheek because he's my grandson, but I don't really *like* him. He's not a good example for Tommy at all."

"Where's Tommy's mother?"

"She divorced Cheek and died when Tommy was twelve."

"Stone worries about Tommy."

"So do his grandparents and me."

After the two women were seated at the kitchen table, Memaw asked, "Do you have questions for me about Stone?"

"Tons, but I'm too tired to ask them right at this moment." Sipping her hot chocolate, she prompted, "I'd like to know more about you. Did you have a happy childhood before your father died?"

"Happy enough. My parents didn't have a good marriage, but I knew they loved me. My bachelor uncle, Wade, was wonderful to me and my cousin, Sidney. Wade never married or had children, and he did very well as the owner of a local honkytonk. He had a bad heart and was told he shouldn't drive after he had a heart attack when he was thirty-one. So, he hired a friendly, older, black man named Auggie to be his driver. They became close friends, and it was quite scandalous since Wade sat up front with Auggie when they went places. Back then, it was unheard of for a white man to sit up front with his black driver.

"When Uncle Wade died at thirty-seven, Auggie was beside himself. We all thought it was because he was grief-stricken. About a month later, Auggie died of a stroke. My mother was talking to her black maid, Auggies' sister, about how sad it was that Uncle Wade had passed and then Auggie so soon afterwards. The maid said that Auggie had known he was going to die. When my mother asked how he could know, the maid told her Uncle Wade had said that he'd come back to take care of Auggie if he passed first. Auggie took that to mean that Uncle Wade would come take Auggie to Heaven with him. The poor man had lived in fear ever since Uncle Wade had passed, sleeping with the lights on and the covers pulled up over his head every night. Poor Auggie. I'm sure he worked himself up until he had that stroke and died. I guess Uncle Wade took care of him after all. Knowing Uncle Wade, he's probably driving Auggie around in Heaven. Both of them would've gotten a kick out of that!"

"What a great story. My parents never told me stories about their families when I was growing up."

"I'm full of stories and would love to tell them all to you. Everyone else has heard them many times over. Ever since I was a child, telling stories exhilarated me. Would you like to hear more?"

An hour later as Josie got ready for bed, she tried to recall a time in her childhood when she'd felt exhilarated. She remembered an afternoon spent at a park with her parents and Zelda before the adults had begun their descent into the living hell that would become their lives. Her mother had twirled each girl round and round in her arms until they were laughing and dizzy. Her father had tossed each of them high into the air then caught them as they squealed and fell back into his arms. They'd raced down the hill several times and then collapsed, giggling. It had been an exhilarating afternoon.

At least there was one, Josie thought. *The only other exhilarating thing I remember is my dancing at the Renaissance festival.*

She peered out of the window at the Romero home and thought about Stone. She wished she was lying in bed next to him or, better yet, had him inside her. Once she'd experienced true lovemaking, she couldn't get enough of it. Every time she and Stone were intimate, it grounded her as well as made her feel a sense of utter freedom. She reveled in the way her body and mind reacted during sex. Thinking about making love to Stone, she drifted to sleep with a smile on her face.

"Josie? Honey, please wake up."

The first thing she saw when she opened her eyes was Dumpling Romero's worried face. The first thing she asked was, "What's wrong with Stone?"

"We don't know! It sounded like he was throwing things a little while ago, and Vin and I went upstairs to see what was wrong. The door to his room is locked, and he won't come out. Vin threatened to break down the door, and Stone yelled and told him to go away. I came to tell you and Memaw, and she's at our house, seeing if Stone will unlock the door for her. We're scared it's his blood pressure, but what if it's not? If he's mad at us then breaking down the door won't make it better."

Trying to remain calm, Josie hurriedly dressed in jeans and a sweater. After slipping on socks and shoes, she followed Dumpling back to the main house and went up the stairs with her to where Vin and Memaw stood near the door that led to what had once been Stone and Nelson's room. Vin appeared to be extremely agitated, pacing back and forth across the narrow area between the two bedroom doors. Memaw was asking Stone to let her in. Josie heard his muffled refusal. Something about his voice sounded different, but the barrier provided by the door was making it difficult for her to hear clearly.

When Memaw saw Josie, she motioned for her to come closer and stepped back. Josie put her mouth near the doorframe and said Stone's name. For several seconds, there was no reply. Then he told her he wanted everyone else to go away before he unlocked the door. Vin looked stricken, as did Dumpling. Memaw simply nodded and suggested to her son and daughter-in-law that the three of them go downstairs. Stone's parents reluctantly complied, but Vin kept looking back up at Josie with what seemed like fear in his eyes. She was surprised. She'd figured that the sheriff wouldn't be afraid of anything.

Descending the stairs, Josie touched Vin on the arm and said, "I'll come and get you if he needs help. Otherwise, please leave us alone. I don't know what's wrong, but I'll do what I can to fix whatever it is."

"Thank you," he said quietly. "Take care of my boy."

"I will."

She ascended again and then knocked on Stone's door. After confirming that she was alone, Josie waited. Within a few moments, she heard the lock release, but Stone didn't open the door. So, she grasped the knob, turned it, and entered.

Looking haggard and sick, Stone sat on one of the twin beds. He wore pajama bottoms and a tee shirt. It was evident that he hadn't slept and that he'd been crying for a long time. He seemed exhausted and distressed, but Josie wasn't certain if this was the result of something physical or emotional. His face was red, which frightened her. At his request, Josie shut and locked the door behind her.

"I shouldn't have come," he proclaimed. "I missed my family and this place, but it was a mistake. I didn't realize how bad it would be."

"How bad *what* would be?"

"Being here without Nelson. I've never slept in this room without Nelson before. Ever."

"What about when you returned home for his funeral?"

"I stayed at a motel. I was so angry and upset over Nelson's death and what had led to it that I refused to come here before and after the service and burial."

"So, this is your first overnight visit since before his death."

"Yes. We were in the same room whenever we were here from the day Nelson was born. It…it hurts so much to be here without him. When I came up last night and unpacked my suitcase, I thought I could handle it. After all, Mama and Daddy had removed all of our personal articles, probably in an effort to make it easier for me if I ever came home again. But the longer I was here without Nelson, the more I realized just how permanent things are. I knew he was gone, but it didn't really hit me until I was alone in our room. Our things are gone; Nelson's gone; and nothing will *ever* be the same! How do I live with that?"

Josie went to stand in front of Stone, put her hands behind his head, and then drew him towards her. He buried his face against the area above her waist. His arms went around her hips, and he held on tightly as if he could never let her go. She stroked his hair and cradled his head between her breasts.

"Your parents thought they heard you throwing things," she said, scanning the room but seeing nothing out of place.

"I punched and kicked at the wood on the walls a few times, and the pain jolted me out of my rage. But it didn't stop the anger and hurt."

"What do you want to do right now?" Josie asked softly.

"I don't know. I *can't* see Cheek. I want to see Tommy but don't want *him* to see *me* like this. I'd like to be with Mama and Daddy the way we were before Nelson died, but I can't forget how they acted after he killed himself." Swallowing hard, Stone continued, "I wonder exactly what he thought about when he was standing on that bridge. Did it hurt when he hit the water? Did the impact kill him, or was he injured then drowned afterwards? Did he suffer long? What was the last thing he thought before he died? Was he at peace or in pain?

"During the night, I kept looking over at his bed, expecting to find him there. Every time I rolled over or turned around I thought he'd be looking back at me. It hurt each time, but I couldn't stop doing it. I kept hoping. God, I don't know what to *do*!"

"Well, you don't have to see Cheek *or* Tommy today," Josie said soothingly. "Tommy can come another time or else we can go somewhere to meet with him. You also don't have to try to make amends with your parents right this minute." As she felt Stone relax slightly, she went on, "Sleeping alone in your room was a bad idea, and I think you should sleep with me at your Memaw's place for the rest of the visit. Your parents will understand. If they don't, then we'll get a motel room or leave."

He nodded against her but said nothing.

"Did you take your blood pressure medicine last night?"

"No. I was thinking about Nelson and didn't remember it at all."

"Where's your electronic monitor?"

"In my old chest of drawers with the clothes I unpacked."

"We should take your blood pressure and pulse."

"It's been fine since that night I lost control in the ER and hit that sorry excuse for a human being."

"Yes, but you didn't take your medication like you usually do and have been under an inordinate amount of emotional stress since you came up to this room hours ago. Let me make sure you're okay."

Stone released Josie then wiped at his eyes. She knew he was capable of feeling deep sadness. That had been evident after he'd helped the girl who'd given birth in the ER and again after he'd had the encounter with the father of the teen who had HIV. However, she had a feeling that Stone hadn't truly allowed himself to grieve the loss of his twin, a man who'd literally been part of him at one time and would always be absent from his future. He needed to mourn without any hesitation, judgments, or time limits. After all, he'd lost the person he'd been closest to in the world since the moment of conception.

Retrieving the blood pressure monitor, Josie brought it back to the bed and asked Stone to extend his left arm. She was now well-versed in how to use the machine and was pleased that her own blood pressure tended to be around 120 over 70 and her pulse rate was typically in the mid-50s.

91

Between his daily dose of medication, exercise regimen, and generally healthy diet, Stone's pressure was normally 131 over 85, and his pulse rate was around 75. That morning, his pulse was 96, and his blood pressure was 210 over 97.

"I need a shot," Stone told her when she informed him of the readings. "Tell Daddy to call Flynn Carmody."

"But your readings aren't much higher than they were when you hit the guy at the hospital. You didn't have a shot then."

"Because I knew I could get control. I can't...I don't think I can right now. My...my head hurts, and I'm going to stroke out pretty quickly if my readings don't drop soon."

"We should get you to the hospital."

"Carmody's an internist whose practice is five miles down the road. It'll be quicker to call him, assuming he's home on Christmas Day. Help me to lie back then go tell Daddy to get Flynn here right away."

Josie wiped Stone's face with several tissues once he'd stretched out on the bed. After kissing him and telling him that she'd be back as soon as she could, she unlocked the door and jogged down the stairs. Vin, Dumpling, and Memaw were clustered at the bottom.

"He needs a shot," Josie said as evenly as she could manage. "He said to get somebody named Flynn Carmody to come give him a shot."

"A shot?" Dumpling repeated.

"His pressure's really high. Either you get the other doctor or we need to leave for a hospital now."

"I'll phone Flynn," Vin declared. "Dumpling, you come with me while I make the call."

"But I want to stay with Stone," she protested. "I'm his mother. People would expect me to stay. God would expect me to stay."

Frightened and frustrated, Josie hissed, "Go! Get out! This is *your* fault, all of you except Stone's Memaw and nephew! You and your stupid way of thinking pushed Nelson to his death and may well kill Stone! Stop worrying about what people will think and what you believe the Bible says and just love your remaining twin enough to save his life!"

Tears stinging her eyes, Josie turned without waiting for a response and dashed up the stairs. Stone lay with his eyes closed. His face was a darker shade of red, and he muttered that his head hurt worse than it had minutes earlier. Josie sat on the edge of the bed and began to massage his temples with her fingers. She prayed that the other doctor would arrive soon.

Chapter Nine

Dr. Flynn Carmody arrived within fifteen minutes. Blonde-haired and brown-eyed, he didn't look any older than Stone. Josie surmised by his height and bulk that he must have been a linebacker at some point in his life. This impression was given added credibility because of the faded high school football jersey he wore. He nodded to Josie as they exchanged introductions but wasted no time in asking her to move so that he could see to his patient. She sat on Nelson's empty bed.

"Jesus," the internist muttered after taking Stone's blood pressure. "212 over 99. Your pulse is 101." As he placed his stethoscope on Stone's chest, he listened for a while and then said, "Of course your heart's pounding like you've been climbing Mount Everest, but you don't have any irregular beats. Any chest pain?"

"No."

"Fatigue?"

"Hell, yes. I've been up all night and am wound pretty tightly."

"How's your head?"

"It hurts."

"Well, *duh*. Severe pain or tightness?"

"Tightness and throbbing."

"Are you having trouble breathing?"

"No."

"Stone, look at me. Are you experiencing any vision issues?"

"No. I can see you clearly."

"Good. When's the last time you urinated?"

"A few hours ago while my parents were still asleep."

"Any blood in the urine?"

"You know I would've called you right away if I'd had blood in my urine."

"I had to ask. Did you take your daily dose of meds yesterday?"

"I never skip, but I did last night. It's a long story."

"I'll hear it another time. Right now, we'll try the shot and then see how it goes."

"Dr. Carmody, what are you giving him?" Josie asked, both nervous and genuinely interested as she watched the internist give Stone the injection.

"A medication that dilates blood vessels, thus lowering blood pressure. It's going to make him feel dizzy, more tired, and possibly give him a different type of headache because of the resultant rapid drop in pressure. And call me 'Flynn,' please." Looking back to Stone, he asked, "Have you had any other episodes like this?"

"Only once in the last ten years and that was a couple weeks ago."

"Was its cause situational?"

"Yes."

"And this incident?"

"Yes."

"Is there a way to avoid said situations?"

"Not as long as there are bigots and ignorant people in the world." Lifting a hand to his head, he noted, "This feels weird. It's almost like I'm on a ride at the amusement park."

"That's encouraging," Flynn assured Josie. "Time to check his pressure again."

Stone's blood pressure gradually dropped to 137 over 83. His pulse rate went down to 41. The low pulse rate displeased Flynn, who explained that it was not a totally unexpected reaction when forcing pressure to drop radically in a short amount of time. He asked Josie if she'd mind getting him and Stone something to drink since the water bottles Stone had brought up to the bedroom the previous night were long gone.

Josie returned to the first floor with some trepidation. She knew that she'd been downright rude to Stone's parents. Part of her felt bad about this, and part of her didn't care. She stood by what she'd said, but she wished she'd had time to present it in a more tactful way and felt a pang of regret. As she headed for the kitchen, she thought of Stone, who could have easily died, and of Nelson, who *had* died. Josie's feelings of remorse lessened considerably.

"You made Mama cry."

She turned slowly and faced Cheek Romero. He had short, sandy brown hair and wore jeans and an Oxford shirt that stretched tightly across his belly. There was a meanness reflected in his eyes. Josie instantly detested him.

"You must be Cheek," she said with saccharine sweetness. "I can tell by the sadistic tone in your voice and the look in your eyes. I guess you take after your grandfather."

"Don't you be talking about my grandfather!" he growled. "You didn't know him at all!"

"I know what I've heard," she shot back in a low voice. "I know that he probably would've been happier if Stone and Nelson had died at birth."

"*I* would have been happier if Stone and Nelson had died at birth! They ruined my life!"

"You self-centered bastard!"

He raised his hand, and she instinctively put up her arm to block the impending blow.

If End-of-Days were real, she'd kill you for what you just said and what you're about to do.

The thought was so unexpected that Josie dropped her arm and soon found herself on the floor, the side of her face temporarily numb.

"Cheek, stop right there!" Vin ordered as he appeared in the living room, blocking Josie from further assault. "God, I never thought I'd have to arrest my own son!"

"You won't have to," Josie said quietly. "I'm not going to press charges, not today. Stone needs all of us. Just make Cheek go away."

"Josie, he hit you and –"

"Just get him out of here!" she cried.

Sighing, Vin turned back to his son and said, "I want you to leave this house! You just hit a woman, the woman Stone loves. And we all heard what you said about wishing Stone and Nelson had died at birth. You told your mother and me that you took Nelson to that place to try to save him. I'm thinking now you knew it would break him and did it on purpose. How could you do that to anyone, much less your own brother?"

"He was a faggot!" Cheek yelled. "If he'd died at birth it would've spared all of us from the shame of what he was."

"You should leave," Memaw said coolly to her eldest grandson. "I pray that Tommy becomes a better man than his father."

"But Memaw –"

"Just go, Cheek," Dumpling said from the kitchen doorway. "I love you because you're my boy, but I can't have you here, especially not today."

"Stone needs your Mama and me, and we need him," Vin said firmly. "For the time being, you're not welcome here, Son."

Cheek glared at Josie, who sat on the floor and rubbed the side of her face where he'd slapped her, and spat, "This is your fault! You're like every pretty girl who dances at my club. You've fucked my brother and got what you wanted. Are you happy?"

"You don't *ever* speak like that to a woman!" Vin commanded.

"I'll speak to a woman any way I like! I'm going, and I won't be back! Neither will Tommy!" He threw a final glance at Josie and shouted, "Bitch!"

Everyone stayed where they were once the door slammed behind Cheek. Vin then came over to Josie, crouched in front of her, and gently asked, "Are you all right?"

"When Cheek was about to hit me I thought..."

"You thought what?" he asked, concern evident in his expression.

She shook her head, unable to explain about her schizophrenic mother and End-of-Days. She wanted Stone, but he was in no shape to comfort her. On the contrary, he was the one who required comforting at that moment. She still needed to bring him and Flynn something to drink.

"How is Stone?" Dumpling asked anxiously.

"Better," Josie answered and heard a collective sigh of relief from the others. "He's exhausted, but at least his blood pressure's down."

"When you go back upstairs, Flynn'll need to look at your face," Vin told her. "Cheek's a big man, and you're a skinny little thing. He might have done you some real damage in your head."

"I'm fine," she assured him, although she was fighting a wave of nausea. "I need to get back to Stone."

"Please let us do something for you, Honey," Dumpling implored. "You look mighty shaky. I'm worried about you."

Anxiety washed over Josie, and she threw up onto the hardwood floor. Apologizing to the others, she promised she'd clean the mess after she'd brought Stone and the internist something to drink.

"No, indeed," Memaw said kindly but authoritatively. "You haven't eaten anything since last night, and there's hardly any mess at all. I'll take care of this. You take care of yourself and Stone."

After thanking Stone's grandmother, Josie walked unsteadily to the refrigerator and withdrew a bottle of water and two bottles of Gatorade. When Dumpling suggested that she and Vin help Josie take the bottles upstairs, she thanked her but refused.

"I'm sorry about the way I spoke to you earlier," she added.

"We're sorry you had to say it, but we're not upset that you did," Vin remarked soberly. "We've been thinking some of the same things ever since Nelson killed himself. We just haven't been able to bring ourselves to say them to anyone else. We feel guilty about a lot, although we still believe Nelson shouldn't have had sex with other men. That doesn't mean we don't miss our son every single day and wonder what we could've done to save him."

"It's so hard for everyone, especially with it being Christmas and Stone's birthday and then with Nelson's birthday coming up in a few days," Dumpling confided. "He was such a sweet boy."

A sweet boy whose older brother and father kept pushing him to "man up" and change, which he couldn't, Josie thought as she tried to ignore the throbbing of her injured cheek. *I see what Stone meant about his family having its own weirdness.*

"I should get these drinks upstairs," she said wearily. "We can talk more once Stone's okay."

"I hope he doesn't leave," Dumpling said anxiously. "Coming home seems to have made him worse." Looking to Josie, she asked, "Speaking of home, don't you want to call your family and wish them a merry Christmas? You could use our phone."

"Thanks, but no. My family doesn't celebrate the holiday."

"Aren't they Christian?" inquired Dumpling, who had a slightly horrified look on her face at the thought that the Hollingsworths might not be Christian.

"My father is but he doesn't...he wouldn't...."

"Yes?" Dumpling prompted.

"I can't talk about this right now. I need to go back to Stone."

She hurried past Vin and Dumpling, passed Memaw, and climbed the stairs, hoping she didn't fall. Her leg muscles felt as if they were made of Jell-O. When she made it to the top step, Josie heard Stone say, "Don't hit a man while he's down, Flynn."

"I'm not. We need you. Clayville has no pediatrician, and I'm the only white doctor who'll treat black patients in the area. The kids aren't getting the care they need."

"Look at what coming back's done for me today. Clayville's a know-nothing, wants-to-know-nothing place that has no willingness to change. Racism, bigotry, ignorance, or whatever you want to call it doesn't seem to have diminished much from when I was here as a kid."

"How can anyone make a change if no one leads them?"

"And I'm supposed to lead them while they're causing me to stroke out?"

"You weren't here in Clayville the last time this happened."

"Low blow."

"It's the truth. Look, I'd love to expand my practice and have you join me. Think about it."

"I'll think about it. Thanks for the offer. And thanks for coming over to help me on Christmas."

"What was I supposed to do? I was going to sit at home and let you die? I couldn't do that to a stranger, much less a friend. We grew up together. You, Nelson, and I were different. We were all on the same wavelength."

"Why'd you come back?"

"Because I want more people to think outside the box. I want more equality, more education, and more acceptance of diversity. I figure it starts with me and with others like your Memaw. She's made a real difference in this community during the past fifty years she's lived here. We need more men and women like her."

"And I'm thankful for that. I know change comes slowly to these parts. I just wish she could have made more of a difference when it came to Daddy, Mama, and Cheek."

"Your grandfather kind of brainwashed them, but I think your parents have started to come around since Nelson died. They're the same, but they're different, too."

"And Cheek?"

Josie slowly pushed open the door and said, "Cheek not so much."

Flynn was instantly on his feet, asking her what had happened. Stone looked up, saw the left side of her face, and tried to rise. She hastened to put down the bottles and placed her hands on his shoulders in order to gently push him back onto the mattress.

"Your father stopped Cheek from really hurting me," she told him once she'd explained about the exchange in the living room. "Your parents and grandmother told Cheek to leave. He says he's never coming back and won't let Tommy come either."

"Tommy's sixteen. He'll come over whenever he damn well pleases." Touching her injured face, Stone noted, "You're on the verge of tears." Turning his head towards Flynn, he asked, "Will you check her out?"

"You know I will. Josie, sit on the other bed so that I can make sure you're okay."

After Flynn gave her a brief, but thorough exam, Josie asked, "Did I pass?"

"Not yet." As he scrutinized her cheek once more, he said, "You know, it would help if you'd put a cold pack on that side of your face."

"I'll be fine," she insisted. "Will you please just finish with me and go back to helping Stone?"

"I can't force you to get an ice pack," he grumbled. "Did you vomit after Cheek hit you?"

"Yes, but it wasn't because he'd given me a concussion or anything."

"Why then?"

"I got nervous about Stone's mother being worried about me."

"What?"

"It's okay, Flynn," Stone said quickly. "I understand. Would you mind leaving us alone for a while?"

"I'll go, but you have to promise me you won't try to come down the stairs by yourself. Josie, come get me or Mister Vin once you're done talking. Stone needs to be on the first floor of this house or at his grandmother's. Got it?"

Once he'd gone down the stairs, Stone asked, "What made you want to cry?"

"Your mother asked me if I wanted to call my family because it was Christmas."

"That's not all. You're trembling. Something scared you, and it wasn't only Cheek's attack and Mama worrying about you."

"Will you hold me while I tell you?"

Stone scooted over to one side of the twin bed so that she could lie beside him. Josie rested her head on his chest. Breathing in the scent that was unmistakably *Stone*, she slipped one arm around his waist and tucked the other one between them. He rested a hand on the arm that was draped across his middle and stroked her blonde hair with the other. Then he urged her to talk. She began to cry, and he murmured that everything would be fine, that they could fix anything together.

"I thought about End-of-Days," she admitted. "When Cheek was about to hit me, I thought that if End-of-Days were real she'd kill him for what he'd said about you and Nelson and for what he was about to do to me. Why would I think about End-of-Days? What if I'm starting to lose it like Zelda?"

"Think about what you just told me. You thought that *if* End-of-Days was real that she'd kill Cheek. You didn't think that End-of-Days *is* real and *will* kill him or make you do it. That's a huge distinction." He paused then continued, "You grew up in two worlds. One was real, while the other was filled with your mother's hallucinations. I'm sure you had to pretend to interact with them or talk to your mom about them in order to have any semblance of functionality in your household."

"Of course, I had to pretend they were real. The hallucinations rule Mom's life." Remembering her parents playing with her and her sister at the park so many years earlier, Josie buried her face against Stone's chest and said, "I miss my mother and father. I've missed them for so long. I barely remember what they were like before." Hesitating, she added, "I'm sorry I'm dumping on you like this, especially when you've been through so much already today. Plus, it's your birthday, which I didn't even know until last night. Why didn't you tell me before?"

"Because I was worried it would make you sad. If your family never celebrated Christmas, then I assumed they didn't do birthdays."

"We never had parties like most kids, but Dad always got us a cake and a present from Mom and him. One year, Calla Lily even made me a bow for my hair out of a ribbon belt Mom had."

"Calla Lily?"

101

"One of Mom's hallucinations. She made Mom good; End-of-Days made Mom bad. At least that's what Mom always used to say. Some of the hallucinations were nice, and some were mean."

"How old were you when you got the bow?"

"Eight. I told Mom to thank Calla Lily for me. The bow wasn't well made, and it fell apart pretty quickly. I still appreciated it, especially after what had happened the previous day."

"I'm afraid to ask, but I will. What happened the day before?"

"End-of-Days made Mom stab me in the leg with a fork. She caught Zelda in the arm when Zelda tried to take the fork away from her. Luckily, it was a clean fork. Otherwise, Dad would've freaked out, thinking my leg or Zelda's arm might get infected and give us blood poisoning or something. Even so, we had to let him clean the puncture wounds a dozen times each and glob on a ton of Neosporin before he bandaged us up. Mom was oblivious about what she'd done and asked me why my leg and Zelda's arm were bandaged. She asked if we were zombies."

"Good God. Did the hallucinations make your mother violent often?"

"Sometimes she'd break things but not hurt anyone else. If she did get violent, then Dad would intercede if he was around. He stopped her from killing herself a bunch of times. Zelda and I always slept with the door to our room locked. It was the only way we could sleep without being afraid of what might happen. End-of-Days and the other bad ones never slept. I used to pray every night that Calla Lily would keep Mom calm all night so that she could rest. Zelda and I learned to sleep through all kinds of noise. If we hadn't, then Mom would've kept us awake almost every night while she wandered the apartment talking to her hallucinations."

Stone kept stroking her hair but was quiet for a long time. Josie began to drowse in his arms. She wondered idly what Vin, Dumpling, Memaw, and Flynn were doing downstairs. She hoped that they'd cooked the Christmas dinner and were eating it. After all, it shouldn't go to waste regardless of what had happened. She knew everyone must be hungry by now, whenever *now* was. She wasn't quite certain of the time.

Stone suddenly asked, "Would you think I was crazy if I told you that I wanted to go into practice with Flynn?"

"No, but I thought this was a backwards, racist community that was slow to change and not where you wanted to be."

"It is, and I don't. At least I don't on one level. My relationship with my family is strained, and I hate the mentality of the average person here. There's also not much in the way of diversity and cultural events."

"And alternately?"

"There's no pediatrician around and no other white doctor besides Flynn who'll treat the African-Americans in Clayville. The kids are underserved, and it's not their fault. No one else wants to help. A part of me feels obligated, but the other part wants to say that I can't change anything that's so deeply ingrained in the minds of those in the community." Pulling her closer to him, Stone muttered, "I can't believe I'm even considering it."

"You're considering it because you're a good man who wants to help those who need treatment but can't easily get it. Plus, I can tell that you want to be close to your family again."

"If I move back, I may drive myself to an early grave."

"I wouldn't let you do that. I need you."

"I need you, too. Will you stay with me if I go into practice with Flynn?"

"Yes."

"Yes? Just like that?"

"You and I *do* need one another. We can try life here. If it isn't what we want, then we'll move after a while."

"Have you ever lived in a small community?"

"No, so I might as well try it."

"From L.A. to L-A?"

She smiled and said, "Why not?"

"Life here will be difficult for someone who's always lived in larger towns or cities."

"Difficult? You're talking to someone who lived with a couple hundred of her mother's hallucinations while she was growing up. I think I can handle this."

"What would you do here?"

"Does Flynn have a receptionist?"

"Josie, you're going to go from brokering high-end real estate deals to being a receptionist?"

"Practice manager," she corrected. "I'll be your practice manager."

"You don't know anything about medical offices."

"I'm a fast learner."

"You want this," he said slowly. "Why?"

"Because you'd be with another doctor all the time. If you have trouble with your hypertension, then Flynn would be right there to help. I like him, and he seems to be a good doctor. He also seems to be a good friend of yours."

"He is, but I'd be with other doctors if I were in a practice anywhere. You seem intent on settling in Clayville. Why here?"

"I need a home and want to make one with you. I'd like to be part of a community, not just moving from one place to another. I want to make a change in people's lives, to have a family of some sort, and to have our pack of wolves."

"We might have to settle for dogs since it's illegal to keep wolves as pets."

"I'd be okay with that."

"And the lack of diverse culture?"

"We're not marooned on a desert island. There have to be *some* people in the area who are into more than hunting and fishing. We can drive or fly to bigger towns or places like Little Rock, Arkansas or Jackson, Mississippi or New Orleans or…I don't know…Shreveport?"

He laughed and said, "I don't know about Shreveport. We'd have to check that out. I've never actually been to Jackson. I think we'd find a lot in the way of cultural activities in New Orleans or Little Rock."

"Your grandmother volunteers at the library and belongs to book clubs. I wonder what else is around?"

"Nothing that I know of, but you'd have to ask Memaw." When his stomach growled loudly, he said, "We should both eat something. Maybe it's the lack of food that's making me delusional enough to think I could live in Clayville again."

"Speaking of living in Clayville, where would we live?"

"I have an idea about that. I'll show you tomorrow and see what you think. If we haven't changed our minds by then, that is." Turning towards her, he asked, "Would you get Flynn? I'm ready to go downstairs, shower, dress, and eat."

As the internist checked Stone's vital signs, Josie went down to the first floor and glanced at the clock in the living room. It was only 11:33 a.m. It felt much later to Josie, who stood for a moment and admired the live Christmas tree strung with lights and hung with ornaments. It hadn't been there the previous day when she and Stone had arrived. She figured Stone's parents had set it up after she, Stone, and Memaw had gone to bed.

"How's your face, honey?" Dumpling asked from the kitchen doorway. "Do you want to put a steak on it or something?"

Josie thought momentarily of what her father would do if a piece of raw meat was placed anywhere on her body. He would be worried about bacteria getting into her eyes, nose, mouth, or pores. The part of her that despised his mental illness wanted to declare, "Bring on the steak! It won't kill me. Maybe it will help my face, and it'll prove that nothing terrible will happen to me if I do it."

Her father wasn't there, and he wouldn't have believed her no matter what she said. She didn't really believe that putting steak on her sore cheek would help her heal any faster, so she thanked Dumpling but told her that she'd simply take some ibuprofen after they ate and would be fine. Dumpling didn't look convinced but didn't push the issue.

Josie knew that there would be a time when she'd have to tell Vin and Dumpling about her family. If she and Stone were going to stay together – and she certainly hoped that they would – then his parents would need to know. However, Christmas morning, especially *that* Christmas morning, was not the time to tell them.

Chapter Ten

"Dinner's ready," Memaw announced. "Josie, why don't you set the table with me while Vin carves the turkey in the kitchen?"

Intrigued, Josie asked, "Could I watch him carve the turkey instead? I've never seen a whole turkey being carved before."

"Of course you can!" Vin called out. "Come in here, and I'll show you how it's done."

She sat at the kitchen table and watched in fascination as he expertly cut the large turkey into pieces. As Vin worked, he explained why he was performing each task in that particular way and said that preparing any animal for cooking or eating was an art unto itself. When Josie asked if his father had been the one to teach him how to do those things, he scowled.

"My father was a cruel man who hated any sort of outdoor activity. Maybe that's why I started hunting and fishing at such a young age. That was a good way to get out of the house and away from him. All he liked to do was sit in the den and smoke while he read. That and yell at me or Memaw when we weren't doing things his way."

"Stone said you all smoke, but I haven't seen anyone light a cigarette since I got here."

"Shhh. Don't say anything. It's our big Christmas present to Stone. We all gave it up starting on Stone's birthday last year. He wasn't here, but we thought it would be a good present for him on his birthday that year and for this one. Cheek didn't agree to it, but Dumpling, Memaw, and I haven't had a cigarette for the past three hundred sixty-five days."

"That's wonderful. He'll love it."

"He obviously loves you." As Vin put down his carving tools, he said, "I hope he'll love our decision to quit smoking. I don't even know if he still loves us anymore."

"He does," she assured him. "He's angry, upset, and scared."

"Scared of what?"

Pushing some stray blonde strands of hair from her face, Josie said, "He's lost half of himself and can never get it back. I think he feels like someone's sliced him in two, and he doesn't know how to fill in the empty space. Sometimes, I think that's why he fell in love with me so quickly. He believes I can fill the void. I don't know if that's good or bad."

"It's good," Vin told her. "He's never loved a woman in his life, not that he's gay like Nelson. Stone dated various women, but I could tell he never loved any of them. He *liked* them and found them attractive, but there wasn't a spark in him like there is now that he's with you."

"All I am is trouble."

Vin sat in the chair beside her and asked, "What is that supposed to mean? You seem real sweet, smart, and pretty."

"Thanks, but I also have two severely mentally ill parents and a mentally ill sibling," she admitted, deciding she couldn't withhold the information any longer. "Any children I might have will be at greater risk of being mentally ill, so I can't take a chance and have any."

"You and Stone can adopt. Hell, you could adopt a nigger baby if you want, and we wouldn't care." When Josie stiffened and told him she couldn't stand hearing anyone use such a derogatory word, he said, "It's a bad habit I picked up from my father. Dumpling got it from her folks, too. We don't think less of blacks than whites. 'Nigger' is just a word to me, but my father used it in a bad way. He thought of blacks as animals. He was so smart, yet so stupid. We don't ever use that word in public."

"I wish you wouldn't say it at all. It's so degrading, whether that's how you mean it or not."

"My father certainly meant it that way. Lots of folks around here still do. I wouldn't have been sheriff for as long as I have if the blacks didn't support me as much as the whites. They know I'm fair, unlike a lot of other white people raised around Clayville." He hesitated then said, "As for you not being able to have kids, I'm sure you know between what Stone's told you and your stay with my mama last night that mental illness is nothing new to our family. It's nothing to be ashamed of."

"I'm not ashamed. Most other people simply don't understand."

"Damn straight. You think it was fun for me to be the son of 'Mean Doc Romero' and 'Whacky Miss Gertrude' when I was growing up?"

"For me, it was 'Crazy Clark' and 'Looney Rhonda' when other people talked about my parents."

"It's a hard way to grow up."

"Yes. Yes, it is."

Vin rose and announced, "Let's get this bird plated and set everything out on the table. Stone should be ready soon, and we can eat. I think we're all pretty hungry, and I've asked Flynn to join us."

"Doesn't he have family in the area? I thought this was where he grew up."

"His cousins and aunt all live in Texas now. His folks divorced when he was eighteen. His father moved to Oklahoma City with his pretty, young secretary, and his mother moved to Fort Worth to live with her sister. The poor woman never recovered from the shock of Flynn's father having an affair and leaving her, and she died of a broken heart about a year later."

"People don't die of broken hearts," Josie objected. "That only happens in books and movies."

"I disagree."

They both turned to see Flynn Carmody standing at the edge of the kitchen. Josie's face flushed. She wanted to apologize for talking to Stone's father about Flynn's parents, but she felt as if that would make the situation worse.

"The mind has a lot to do with the body," the young internist informed her. "It may not list 'broken heart' as the cause of death on my mother's death certificate, but that's definitely what killed her. The depression and stress caused all sorts of health issues that contributed to her passing away so soon after the divorce. She never gave up loving my father, even after what he did to her and to me. It was really sad to watch her slip away."

"Enough of this sadness talk," Memaw declared as she entered the room. "It's Christmas; it's Stone's birthday; Josie is here; and Flynn is here. It's a beautiful day. I think we should put all of this aside for a while and enjoy our dinner. The table is set, and everything's already set out except the turkey. The food's going to get cold, even with the covers on the dishes!"

Josie had thought that the covers on the dishes were glass lids. When she entered the dining room, she saw that she'd been mistaken. There were actual red-and-green quilted covers on top of the containers that rested on trivets along the middle of the table.

Vin placed the platter holding the turkey in the center of the table as Stone came in, wearing jeans and a heavy black sweater. Vin sat at one end of the table with Dumpling to his right and Memaw to his left. Stone pulled out the chair beside his grandmother so that Josie could take that seat then sat at the other end of the table across from his father. Flynn took the seat between Stone and Dumpling.

"Time for us to offer up a blessing, then we can eat," Dumpling proclaimed as she reached out one hand to Vin and one to Flynn.

Stone extended one hand to Josie and the other to his friend. Memaw stretched out one hand to her son and the other to Josie. Josie hesitated then forced herself to hold hands with the others. It wasn't that *she* feared this simple act, but years of conditioning by her father about holiday gatherings, germs, and coming into contact with others without knowing if they'd washed their hands had long-lasting effects. The fact that she also had never been involved in a traditional holiday dinner was intimidating to her.

"Josie, would you like to say the blessing?" Dumpling asked with a smile. When Josie thanked her but declined, Dumpling looked confused but didn't stop smiling and said, "Why don't you do it, Stone? It would be nice to hear you say it since you…weren't able to be here last year."

Stone's fingers tightened around Josie's. She knew he wanted to say something to his mother and remind her of why he hadn't come home for Christmas. He refrained and instead offered, "Lord, bless this food we're about to eat. Thank you for taking care of those of us who're here to enjoy it and those who aren't. Amen."

As the quilted covers were removed, Dumpling described what was in each container. There was a marinated vegetable salad, oyster dressing, cranberry sauce, sweet potato casserole, macaroni and cheese, and gravy. Buttered rolls were snuggled within a towel in a tan wicker basket. Josie stared at the food and wondered what she should do. Was there some etiquette about who went first at such dinners? There was so much food, and it was all so…normal.

She glanced at Stone, who was watching his parents talk and laugh as they discussed a Christmas dinner years earlier when their dog had gotten to the cooked turkey before they had. He was smiling but looked very tired. This gave Josie an idea.

"Why don't I fix your plate?" she asked in hopes that he'd agree and spare her from committing some social gaffe. "You look worn out."

"That would be nice. I am tired. The shot was necessary, but I'm definitely dragging now."

"You're also dragging because you almost had a stroke," Flynn muttered quietly. "After the meal, you need to chill on the couch for the rest of the day."

Stone nodded as Josie rose and put some of everything on his plate. She felt as though she should be wearing a nice dress, an apron that tied around her waist, and a short strand of pearls like women in 1950s TV sitcoms. Oddly enough, it made her feel happy to picture herself in such garb. The corners of her mouth turned up slightly as she placed Stone's plate in front of him.

The meal was relaxing, and the food was delicious. Everyone except Josie told stories, talked about local people and places and Christmas gatherings of the past, and discussed their work. Josie enjoyed merely sitting and eating as she listened and experienced her first Christmas dinner. She was pleased that everyone seemed to be getting along well and mending fences within the Romero family. She liked Flynn Carmody a great deal and thought that a medical practice involving him and Stone would be good for the two men.

After the table had been cleared, everyone moved to the living room to watch football. Josie cared nothing about the game but was happy to sit beside Stone, rest her head against his chest, and feel his arm around her. The others seemed very involved in the game and were rooting for one particular team.

As one player caught a ball in the last few seconds of the game even Josie got excited. If the man made it all the way across the field for a touchdown, his team would win.

"Run, Nigger!" Vin yelled. "Run!"

"Daddy, would you *please* not use that word?" Stone asked with more than a hint of exasperation.

"Sorry! Run, African-American! Run!"

Josie laughed, and Stone smiled and shook his head. Vin grinned broadly then cheered along with the rest of them as the man made the touchdown.

Flynn departed after they'd enjoyed leftovers together. Once he was gone, the Romero family exchanged Christmas gifts and gave

Stone his birthday presents while Josie watched. Vin, Dumpling, and Memaw were upset that they had no gifts for Josie, but she reminded them that her appearance had been a surprise. She'd brought each of them gifts that Stone had suggested would be to their liking. They seemed to love them all, as well as the ones from each other and Stone. Stone declared that he was happy with his presents and thanked his family. No one mentioned the absence of Cheek and Tommy, but Josie knew the two absent Romeros were never far from the minds of the others.

"You haven't opened my presents, yet," Josie told Stone. "They're in the boxes wrapped in gold and silver paper under the tree."

He sobered and gave her a soulful look that conveyed, *The first Christmas present you ever got someone on your own.*

He unwrapped the first box. It held the invitation to the charity event that would feature Chef Kat Cora, and Stone was ecstatic. Once he'd kissed Josie and thanked her multiple times, he reached for the second box and opened it. Inside was an expensive, black watch that had brushed silver hands and tiny lines in lieu of numerals. The watch had reminded Josie of Stone himself – totally masculine, totally classic, and totally humble. She suggested that he turn the watch over and see the surprise on the back, an inscription that read, *For Ever. Love, Josie.*

"It sounds so much better when it's two words instead of one," he murmured. "I love it. Thank you." As he leaned over to kiss her, he said, "I love you."

"I love you, too."

"Are you ready for your present?"

"You already gave me a present."

She was referring to his vasectomy, and they both knew it. However, this would never be said in front of the family, and she understood that. After her talks with Vin and Memaw, she didn't think they'd mind but wouldn't say a word about Stone's surgery unless he agreed to it.

"That present was for both of us," Stone said. "This one is just for you."

He handed Josie a square box that measured approximately one foot wide, one foot long, and one foot high and was wrapped in an

111

iridescent silver paper that had a rainbow-colored ribbon bunched on top. The ribbon had been fashioned into a rather odd-looking bow.

"I tried to do it myself," Stone admitted. "I guess bow-making isn't one of my talents. Nelson would've done a fabulous job with that."

"I appreciate the effort."

And no one had to stab me in the leg with a fork the day before this time, she thought with a mixture of happiness and sadness. *It's nice to be able to thank him and not have to tell Mom to thank Calla Lily for me.*

She carefully removed the bow from the top and placed it beside her before unwrapping the box. Slowly lifting the lid, she viewed colorful tissue paper. Raising it up, she saw something metal glint in the light of the lamp beside her. Reaching inside, she touched the object and freed it from the tissue.

It was a silver bell meant to be displayed for decorative purposes and was as big as the size of a large man's fist. She held the end of the bell and shook it. She was not disappointed. It jingled as what sounded like dozens of tiny silver bells shook around inside.

"I don't think this one will get lost," Stone told her. "Although it might be a bit big for you to wear around your neck."

"It's perfect," she said softly then shook the bell again. "I'll put it someplace where I can see it and shake it every day."

"I'm glad you like it. I hope you like the other present that's in there, too."

"I don't need another present."

"I say you do."

She rummaged around in the box but felt nothing else inside. When she remarked on this, Stone offered, "Let me. It *has* to be in there."

He placed the box in his lap and proceeded to perform a thorough search of the tissue. His brow creased as his efforts seemed to prove fruitless. Then he smiled and said, "Here it is."

"What?" Josie asked curiously as she attempted to see into the box where his hand was. "What is it?"

"Well, I don't really know if you'll like it. Maybe I should wait to give it to you."

"If you think you should, then that's fine."

112

Stone put his free hand behind Josie's head, pulled her towards him, and kissed her hard. When he drew back, he declared, "It's *not* fine! You know you want to see."

"Of course I do, but I can wait. I have an endless amount of patience. It's a learned trait."

"Patience isn't always a virtue," commented Memaw. "Sometimes it can be downright detrimental to a person's soul."

Josie opened her mouth to say that she wanted to see what was in the box, found herself unable to speak, and hurriedly rose from the couch and went out through the front door into the frigid night air. She stood on the porch and hugged herself tightly, allowing tears to stream uninterrupted down her cheeks.

The door opened and closed behind her, but she didn't turn. A blanket was draped atop her shoulders then Stone crisscrossed the front pieces by bringing first one arm around her then the other. He kissed her hair and asked her to tell him why she was crying. Without moving, she said, "Just because."

"Just because why?"

"Dinner. Watching the football game with your family and Flynn. Having the leftovers for supper. Seeing everyone opening their presents. Getting a Christmas present. It was all so…stereotypical and nice. I could never dream of having those sorts of experiences with my parents and now Zelda. Even if we did those things, Dad would be worrying about everything and doing everything a dozen times, and we'd have to include Mom's hallucinations. One of us might even get stabbed with a fork or…."

"Or what?" Pulling her closer to him, Stone asked, "What happened that made you so patient?"

Closing her eyes, she quietly said, "One day, Mom got a box in the mail. Zelda and I thought maybe there were books in it but weren't sure. Being former college professors, our parents bought lots of books from Goodwill or the used book shop. Sometimes, people would donate them to us since they knew we didn't have much money. Our only income came from Mom's and Dad's Social Security Disability checks."

"You and Zelda wanted to see inside the box," Stone deduced. "And something bad happened."

"It hadn't been that long since our parents had stopped taking their medications. Zelda and I were still getting used to the craziness. When we tried to look inside the box in Mom's lap, Six-Six-Six tried to strangle Zelda. I started screaming, and Dad came in and pried Mom's hands off Zelda's neck then held Mom pinned to the ground for a long time until she went limp. She apologized to Zelda later, saying Six-Six-Six had made her do it. Zelda and I agreed we'd never be impatient with Mom again. We didn't know which hallucination might do what; it might be good or bad. We couldn't take the chance."

"I wish to God that *someone* would have gotten you out of there."

"I wish we could've lived a normal life with our parents. If someone had just taken us away, who knows if our parents would've survived?"

"They've survived since you and Zelda moved out."

"That was a dozen years or so later. They'd learned how to make it on their own by then."

He didn't argue, but she knew he wanted to. Instead, he asked, "So, what was in the box?"

"Books Mom had gotten somewhere for me and Zelda. The box actually *was* filled with something for us, but that didn't stop Six-Six-Six from lashing out. We learned our lesson."

"No one will do that to you outside your parents' apartment."

"I know. I just got scared. Old habits die hard."

"That's totally understandable. Do you want to come back inside and see what's in the box?"

"Yes," she said in a whisper.

"Good. It's freezing out here." Pulling her around to face him, Stone kissed her then held her tightly to him before informing her, "Memaw's going to sleep here in Cheek's old room so that you and I can stay at her house."

"But what about your parents? I don't want to do anything that would make them disapprove."

"They can disapprove of our choice to sleep together before marriage all they like. I don't give a damn about that anymore, and you shouldn't worry about it. They really like you. After my incident this morning, I don't think they'd say 'no' to anything I asked for right now. I scared the crap out of them."

"And me. I really like your parents and grandmother, even though I see what you mean about your parents. They're good people who were raised to believe that certain things were acceptable that I strongly disagree with. I know they're doing their best. They love you so much, and they definitely loved Nelson. They love Cheek, even after what happened this morning."

"Exactly, like you love your family despite their situation. True love is unconditional."

"Love me."

"I have since the day we met at the hospital. Do you love me?"

"You know I do."

"Then prove it by coming inside and accepting your other present."

They returned to the living room where Vin, Dumpling, and Memaw waited. Josie wiped at her face with one edge of the blanket that remained draped over her shoulders, while Stone headed for the box he'd left on the couch. As he bent to retrieve it, Vin asked him to stop.

"We want to give you our last present before you give Josie whatever else you have for her. We also have presents for Josie."

"But you didn't know I was coming," she protested.

"Well, we discussed it and think we've remedied our lack of gifts," Memaw announced. "I'm going to stitch a special quilt for you. Stone has one of my best pieces in his guest room. You tell me the colors you want, and I'll start working on it right away."

After Josie had thanked her, Vin said, "And Dumpling and I are going to give you something we hope you'll like, even though you can't see it."

"We're not going to say the 'N' word ever again," Dumpling proclaimed. "We should stop, and if we give you that as a gift then I know we will. Saying it would be like taking back a present."

"I couldn't have asked for a more thoughtful gift," Josie said sincerely. "Thank you so much!"

"You're very welcome," Vin said graciously. Looking to his son, he said, "As for your big present from the three of us, it's that we stopped smoking last year on your birthday. None of us have had a cigarette in a year."

Stone's face almost split with his grin. He beamed and said, "Thank you so much. I know that had to be really difficult for y'all. You've been smoking your whole adult lives."

"It was real hard," Dumpling confided. "It's like a drug. I know you always told us it *was* a drug. We had some rough moments, but we did it because we knew you'd always wanted us to."

Stone hugged his mother, father, and grandmother. Once things had settled down, he said, "And now for the final present of the evening. Josie, do you want to see?"

Although her stomach muscles twisted with anxiety, she forced herself to say, "Yes, I want to see."

Smiling, he said, "That was a great gift you just gave yourself. Now for mine."

He withdrew a plain gold band and got down on one knee. Josie wanted to tell Stone that no one did that sort of thing anymore, but she was deeply touched by the chivalrous gesture.

"Would you do me the honor of marrying me?"

"Are you *kidding*?!?" she squeaked, her heart pounding with excitement and surprise.

"I would never kid you about something as important as this." Glancing at the ring in his hand, he continued, "I know you don't like to wear jewelry, but would you make an exception for a simple wedding band?"

"Only if you agree to wear one, too. I'd like to be traditional when it comes to that."

"I wouldn't have it any other way."

"You know this is crazy."

"Love makes people do crazy things."

Smiling, she said, "Yes, it does. Yes, I will. I love you for *ever*."

Chapter Eleven

"What do you think?" Stone asked as they stood at the end of a long driveway that led to an enormous home on the outskirts of Clayville. "The house is surrounded by woods on all sides except this one that faces the road."

Josie slowly scanned the home with its white paint, two stories, thick columns, and the pair of wide, winding steps that curved up towards each other and the landing that led to the porch. The home was constructed in the Plantation style, but it didn't appear to have been built during the appropriate era. To Josie's practiced realtor's eye, it seemed to have been constructed within the last decade. Around ten thousand square feet, the house was perhaps a fifth the size of a grand plantation home of centuries past. It was like a scaled-down version of its opulent inspiration.

"What *is* this place?" she asked, as Stone extended his hand and inclined his head towards the house.

"It's my house," he answered nonchalantly, as she put her hand in his.

Following him along the driveway and away from his car, which he'd parked just past the iron front gate, she asked, "Yours?"

"Mine now," he answered. "It was Nelson's until he died."

"I don't understand."

"I know. I'll explain in a while. Will you walk with me now and take it all in? Once I've shown you everything, then we'll talk."

As they wandered around the perimeter of the home, Josie admired the attention to detail its designer and builder had shown. The woodland setting made the house paradoxically more impressive and more intimate. There was no pool or garden in the back of the home. There were only more woods.

Josie wondered how Nelson had done this and why. He was a gay man with a long-time partner and a thriving career who'd resided in a much more accepting city. Why would he go through all of the time, trouble, and expense to build a huge, plantation-style home in the middle of nowhere on the outskirts of Clayville?

Stone and Josie climbed the wide steps that led up to the back porch. Josie waited while he removed a set of keys from his coat pocket and undid the locks. The whine of an alarm sounded as Stone pushed open the door, and they hurried inside so that he could punch in a code, disarming the security system. The whining stopped, and Stone rearmed the system.

"People know the house is deserted," he told her. "The place would be trashed if there was no alarm or the high iron fence surrounding the area near the home. That's why the electricity can never be shut off out here. Getting electrical, water, and sewer lines run for all this practically took an Act of Congress, but Nelson got it done. I never asked him how or how much he paid for it." As he switched on the lights, he asked, "Are you ready for the tour?"

"Very, although I wish the heat were on. I understand why it's not, but it's so cold inside. I can only imagine what the heating and cooling bills are like."

"The house is well-insulated to keep in heat in the winter and keep things cool in the summer. There are fireplaces in many of the rooms, so that would help with heating bills. In the summer, all of these tall windows on both floors can be opened to provide a cross-breeze to help cool things down, plus the house is raised so that helps as well. There are ceiling fans in almost every room. There is central air and heat if someone needed it. The house is fitted with tankless water heaters to save electricity. All of the appliances are energy-saving. It may be huge, but it's not as wasteful as many might think. If it had been built in other areas of the state or country, then even more would've been done to make it eco-friendly. Because it was built in this location, it was simply too cost-prohibitive – or so Nelson said. Daddy comes out here periodically and runs the heat or air and all the faucets so that things keep working."

"Stone –"

He placed a finger over her lips and said, "No questions, yet. We're not done with the tour. Once we're finished, then you can grill me for hours if you like."

During the tour, Josie was shocked to find that the enormous house was completely furnished and was beautifully decorated, no doubt by Nelson. It reminded her of Stone's apartment, but the house was more balanced between masculine and feminine. The furnishings were not quite as modern but were not antiquated, and the finishes were a combination of contemporary and antique. The place needed to be photographed for an architectural or design magazine. Nelson's talent rivaled any of the top designers Josie had known in Los Angeles.

The last two rooms Stone showed Josie comprised the master suite of the house. The entire bathroom was white and included a soaker tub, a separate tiled shower, a long counter with double sinks, cabinets, a hatbox toilet, and filmy curtains. The master bedroom was awash with deep, vibrant colors and rich fabrics, accentuating dark wood furniture that looked as old as the house was supposed to be.

After directing Josie to sit on the end of a dark brown chaise-lounge, Stone started a fire in the hearth of the fireplace across from the foot of the bed. Within a short time, the chill of the room began to dissipate, and Stone removed his coat and hung it on the hook of the closed bedroom door. Josie removed her coat and handed it to him when he asked her for it. She watched, as he hung it next to his and then announced, "The tour's over. Ask whatever you want."

"Why did Nelson build this house?"

Stone rested his hands on his hips and turned his brown eyes towards the hearth before beginning, "Nelson started designing this place when we were five. Pepaw took us all to Nottoway Plantation in White Castle, Louisiana. Our family members were fascinated, except Cheek. Memaw had been there before as a girl, but she said she loved seeing the place again. We spent the night in White Castle and drove back to Clayville the next day. Nelson and I couldn't stop talking about the plantation house the whole way back, and Pepaw was intrigued. As much as the man hadn't cared whether or not we'd live or die at birth, he'd actually come to appreciate us once we'd arrived. He treated us nicer than anyone else, which pissed Cheek off to no end. Pepaw said he saw great intelligence and the drive to use it when he looked at Nelson and me. He wasn't close to us, but he was proud of us in his own way." Walking over to sit in front of her, Stone draped one arm across Josie's knees before continuing, "The moment we arrived home, Nelson got pencils and paper and began to sketch 'our' plantation home. Even at that age, he was a wonderful artist who had fantastic vision for good design. The rough sketch of what he drew was actually very similar to what you see here today. Pepaw was impressed. He asked Nelson a lot of questions about the house, what materials he'd use, and other things like that. Nelson had a quick answer for everything, including where he'd build the place. It's where the house sits now. Pepaw asked him why he'd select this piece of land, and Nelson said because part of the land was wide-open and wouldn't have to be cleared while the other part was completely wooded and would give the home a dignified feel." When Josie looked skeptical, he hastened to say, "Nelson did actually use those words. He and I were...advanced for our ages."

"So, Nelson wanted to build this house when he was five because of your visit to Nottoway Plantation and his love of art and design. Why did he build it when he reached adulthood? Wasn't this a regressive area he wanted to escape? Did he ever intend to live here? Where did he get the money? How long did it take?"

"Pepaw's family had a lot of money. A lot. He made a good living as the area's only internist. Memaw's family had money, too. When Pepaw died, Nelson and I were twelve. Pepaw left Daddy and Mama the camp and the land around it, which is considerable. He left Cheek fifty thousand dollars, which incensed Cheek, who thought he should've gotten more. Cheek used the money to buy the bar and strip club he still runs today."

"I'm sure your grandfather would've been thrilled," Josie said sarcastically.

"He would've hated it, which is why I think Cheek did it."

"And you?"

"Pepaw knew I wanted to be a doctor, and he definitely wanted to ensure that I was able to follow through so there'd be another Dr. Romero in the family. He left me enough money to pay for college and medical school. I couldn't stand the man, but I'm thankful for that. I have no enormous loans to pay back as most doctors do when they finish school."

"And Nelson?"

"Pepaw left Nelson the money to build his plantation home on this particular piece of land, which Pepaw had already purchased several years earlier. The money was only to be given to Nelson if he used it for that purpose. The rest of the estate was left to Memaw."

"Did your grandfather know Nelson was gay?"

120

"If he did, he never admitted it to anybody. As I said, he respected me and Nelson for our abilities and would never have said a negative thing about us to anyone. His admiration may have blinded him to what he would've surely seen as a failing of Nelson's. I'm glad he didn't see it for whatever reason. It allowed Nelson to do this."

"But why build it if he knew he'd never live in it? And why don't your parents and Memaw live here?"

"I'll answer the second question first. My parents love their comfortable, small house. They've lived there since they were eighteen and first got married over four decades ago. We boys were born and raised there. They have no desire to move." Sighing, he said, "When Pepaw died...well, Memaw needed taking care of at that point in her life because of her mental illness. She sold her house and had the other one built behind Mama and Daddy's so that she could be closer to them and us. She's been there for almost twenty years now and says she's happy where she is."

"I can understand that. But what I don't understand is why Nelson built a house he'd never live in."

"Whether he lived in it or not, it had always been a dream of his to build his plantation home. If he didn't build it, then the money would have been given to various organizations that were not very accepting of diversity, if you get my meaning. Nelson's attitude was that he might as well make his dream come true, even if he couldn't live in his house. He said it'd make a great home for someone someday. That gave him a huge amount of satisfaction."

"How wonderful and sad."

"Yes. It took years and all of the money Pepaw left him, but he did it. It was completed the month before Nelson died. I drove here the week it was finished to tour the place with him and Chas. Nelson was so happy with the finished product, regardless of the fact he'd never planned on spending even one night here."

"Chas?"

"His partner. He'd worked on the project with Nelson the entire time. He told me after Nelson killed himself that the project had given my brother so much joy, but Chas felt like it was a bittersweet victory of sorts. I had to admit I saw both sides. Nelson left me this house and property and left everything else he had to Chas. I never intended to live here either, but I knew I could never sell this place. *This* was Nelson."

Josie took Stone's face in her hands and said, "Nelson built this house for you as much as he did for himself. I didn't know him, but I've worked with plenty of interior designers and have some insight into their approaches. When you gave me the tour, I could tell that the place was furnished in a combination of styles representing what you would like and what Nelson would have liked. It's a nice blend." Bending to kiss him, she added, "It's also ridiculously large for only two people." After a long, deep kiss, she asked, "When do you want to move in?"

"Josie, you just said the house was too large for only two people."

"We're going to have lots of dogs, remember?"

"But –"

"But nothing. You want to live here, and I love this house and property. I've had a house once before, but I've never had a home. This is a *real* home. It's a little girl's dream come true, especially for a little girl who was raised by crazy parents who kept getting evicted from every apartment they ever inhabited. The house is paid for, so we'll just have to maintain it and keep paying the insurance and property taxes. You have no loans to pay back, and I have money from my lucrative realtor days and the sale of my house in L.A. Considering you'll be a pediatrician in a small, backwards town and I'll be your practice manager, we probably won't make tons of money. I've never cared about money. What I care about is having love and security."

"You'll have both with me," he assured her. "But I'm still worried about what you'll think of life in Clayville. You haven't even been into town, yet. This is a whole other world. What if you hate it?"

"You have a love/hate relationship going with it. Maybe I'll have the same feelings towards Clayville. I told you if we don't like it we can always move." Scanning the room, she asked, "Does this house have a name?"

"What?"

"Plantation homes always have names. Did Nelson name his?"

Stone rested his head on one of Josie's knees and said quietly, "Wolfwood."

She ran her fingers through his perpetually unkempt brown hair and murmured, "How perfect."

"*I* thought so."

They stayed as they were for a long while. Josie continued to weave her fingers through Stone's hair, and he closed his eyes, his head remaining on her knee. The room became pleasantly warm, and Josie felt a tension she hadn't realized was being held within Stone's shoulders and neck ease.

"Will you make love to me?" she asked suddenly.

Without moving or opening his eyes, Stone asked, "Right here? Right now?"

"Yes."

"I scared you yesterday morning, didn't I?"

"Yes. I was really worried about how much you were suffering emotionally and physically. I thought you might die. We've only just found each other, and I know things have been moving forward at an accelerated rate for us. I wondered if I'd find you, fall in love, and lose you. What happened yesterday really frightened me."

"It frightened me, too. I don't want to leave you."

"Good."

"When do you want to get married?"

"Why don't we do it during our trip? Everything has been happening at breakneck speed, so why not add our marriage to the list? We could exchange vows here at Wolfwood."

"I think it takes longer than that to process all the paperwork. We'd need birth certificates and maybe even blood work. I vaguely remember when Cheek got married to Tommy's mother that it took about a month after they applied before the marriage license was approved."

"What happened to Tommy's mother?"

"She was a stripper at Cheek's club. He married her because she was pregnant. He didn't love her, and she didn't love him. I think she thought he had more money than he did. I have to give her credit, though. She was a good mother and stuck it out for a long time before leaving Cheek."

"But if she was such a good mother, then why didn't she take Tommy with her?"

"She was diagnosed with cancer not long after filing for divorce. Her chance for survival was nil. She knew it and so didn't fight for custody. She died two days after the divorce was final. A lot of people wondered why she went ahead with the divorce when she knew she wasn't going to make it. She said it was better to die a free woman than to die as Mrs. Cheek Romero."

"Ouch."

"I know. You'd think Cheek would get the hint. I guess he's like Pepaw in that he'll never understand that *he's* the problem in his life and not everyone else."

"Poor Tommy. I want to meet him."

"You will. Cheek can't stop me from seeing him. I plan on taking you to meet him today. I'll take you all around Clayville if you want. You should know what you're getting into before you commit."

"Speaking of commitment, let's go back to the marriage thing. If we can't get married at Wolfwood while we're here, then why don't we just fly to Vegas and get married there?"

"You don't want a 'normal' wedding?"

"I've led an abnormal life, and we've had an abnormal courtship. Why not have an abnormal wedding ceremony?"

"Lots of people get married in Vegas."

"I know, but we could do something different."

"You want Elvis to marry us?"

"Too traditional. How would you feel about Mark Twain?"

"Mark Twain?"

"I read an article last year about a man who *is* Mark Twain. That's his job, to *be* the author. He's also licensed to marry people. I bet if we went on the Internet we could find his contact information and set it up. The English professor's daughter in me would love it if Mark Twain married us."

"Let me get out my iPad, and we'll see if we can make it work this week."

"Later. Right now, make love to me."

He lifted his head and confided, "I wish getting started each time wasn't so difficult for you."

"At least once I do get aroused I *really* get aroused. No more pretending like I did with the three other men I slept with before you."

"What do you think it would take to have you get aroused spontaneously?"

Shrugging, she volunteered, "Go back in time and tell the neighbor not to molest me?"

"Try it."

"What?"

"That's actually a valid technique used by therapists. No one's ever tried it with you?"

"I talked to the therapists about my crazy family, not the molestation. I couldn't talk to anyone about that until I met you. I couldn't even think of it as molestation."

Stone rose from the floor and sat beside her on the chaise-lounge before taking her hands in his and commanding, "Close your eyes."

"But –"

"If you trust me, then close your eyes." Once she'd followed his directive, he continued, "Go back to when you were a little girl and replay what happened with the neighbor. When he says he wants to kiss you, tell him what you would say to him if you knew then what you know now. Talk it out."

Josie squeezed Stone's hands and forced herself to relive the incident. When the neighbor when to kiss her on the mouth, she said, "No! Don't touch me, you pervert! I'm going away and never coming near you again! I'm running away *now*!"

As she opened her eyes, Stone asked, "Well?"

"Oh, my God. I feel…freed, like what I envision really happened. How could that have worked?" Josie asked hoarsely. "I know the actual event was different, but it's like I changed it for real…inside. I *feel* different when I think about it. It doesn't scare me like it did before. How is that possible?"

"I'm a pediatrician, not a therapist. I can't remember the name of the technique and don't know why it works, but it obviously does for some. I'm elated that it worked for you."

"What if it's temporary?"

"Then do it again. If it keeps working, do it every day if you have to. Or get some more therapy for *your* problems, not only those relating to your parents and Zelda. You need that anyway."

She nodded and announced, "I want to see if it actually changed anything when it comes to me, my body, and sex."

"So, touch me," he said in a voice roughened with arousal. "Kiss me and see what happens."

125

She leaned forward and lifted her head to kiss him. Even before their lips met, she felt the ache between her legs that had previously only come after Stone's caressing and verbal encouragement. Josie found herself instantly wanting him inside her. She slid her arms around his neck and deepened their kiss.

The sex was quick and explosive, and Josie experienced multiple orgasms for the first time in her life. Unable to find her voice afterwards, she collapsed into Stone's arms, trembling. Their skin was damp with perspiration, and she inhaled the fragrance that was the unmistakable scent of her, Stone, and sex. She felt his lips on her head and snuggled against his chest.

"That was amazing," she murmured. "I wanted you in me before I even kissed you. I can't wait until we don't have to use condoms and I can feel you come inside me."

"That was definitely amazing, and I can't wait either. Too bad we have to. We need to be sure the vasectomy worked." When she sighed dramatically, he chuckled and said, "One thing at a time. We can't take chances. We won't go *au naturel* until we're sure the procedure was a success. We have a lot of other firsts ahead of us. We'll get married, and I'll finish my residency. Then we'll move here and see how things go. We might hate it and end up in a condo somewhere with no pets and no kids."

"Promise me no condos unless there aren't any other alternatives. I've spent most of my life in apartments. I want a house with a yard."

"You certainly have a yard here at Wolfwood."

"A nice big one," she agreed. "Just how big *is* the property?"

"Ten acres although the iron bars only extend two acres around the house. The rest is outside the fence and gates."

"Wow. And everything's woods, except this main area?"

"Yes. The back of the property actually sits on the edge of a river."

"Will you teach me to hunt and fish? I didn't get to do those things in the places where I lived growing up."

"You really want to learn to hunt?"

"Why not? I doubt if I'd want to do it more than once, but I'd like to learn how it's done. If I'm going to be living in redneck country, I should learn how to shoot something, right?"

126

"Definitely," he replied with mock seriousness. "We might actually want to trade in one of our cars for a truck, especially living on this big piece of land and with this big house to keep up. Four-wheelers might not be a bad idea."

"I thought those were dangerous."

"If you're thrill-riding. If you want to get from Point A to Point B on a ten-acre property, they're not so bad and help to save time and effort."

"This is getting more and more interesting by the minute. What else do we need in order to be true country estate owners?"

"We could have chickens and a henhouse so that we'd always have fresh eggs."

"No. No roosters crowing and dirty chicken coops. Yuck. Maybe horses?"

"Horses are expensive to care for. Plus, are you going to muck the stalls? I'd rather spend my time with you, at work, with the family, or doing something else."

"Just dogs will be fine."

Stone kissed her, and Josie felt the heat spark instantly within her body. He quickly drew back and asked, "Why are you crying?"

As she wiped at her cheeks, she admitted, "I hadn't realized that I was. Don't worry. They're happy tears. You don't have to coax me into arousal before sex anymore."

Pushing some hair away from her face, he said, "Once I'm fully healed, we'll have to test our stamina."

Josie carefully climbed off his lap and stood beside the chaise-lounge. He studied her admiringly as she stretched. When she bent over to retrieve her clothing from the floor, he asked, "Are you doing that to torture me?"

She gave him a mischievous grin then retreated to the bathroom. When she returned to the bedroom, Stone sauntered into the bathroom to clean up and get dressed. While she waited, Josie sat in front of the dying fire and watched the glow of the embers. She ached constantly for Stone.

I'm the one who's being tortured now, she thought. *God, it's a wonderful feeling.*

Chapter Twelve

Once they arrived in Clayville, Stone took Josie on an informal tour of the town. They drove through run-down neighborhoods and middle-class neighborhoods. Stone pointed out schools, the business district, fast food restaurants, hometown restaurants, a quaint shopping area, a dilapidated shopping area, the "bad" part of Clayville, and, finally, the Walmart Supercenter. There was a sign next to it proclaiming the upcoming construction of a Lowe's.

"What are we going to do about a gym?" Josie asked. "You have to keep working out in order to help maintain good blood pressure levels, and I want to stay in shape, too."

"I'll keep you in shape," he teased. "But don't worry. There is a gym we can join that's not far from Wolfwood. It isn't huge, but it's well-kept and more than adequate."

"Does it have a pool? I like to swim."

"No pool. We could put one in at Wolfwood."

"With all those trees around? The amount of leaves that would end up in the pool would be ridiculous!"

"Unless we had a cover on it for when it's not in use."

"Maybe," she said noncommittally. "We can decide on that later."

"Later it is. Ready to meet Tommy?"

"Sure, but where?"

"Where I know he'll be."

Recalling what Stone had told her early on about Tommy's questionable friends and recent choices, Josie wondered if they were heading for a run-down trailer filled with a bunch of stoned teenagers. Therefore, she was surprised when they pulled into the Walmart parking lot. Stone got out, came around to open Josie's door, and urged her to take his hand.

Everyone they passed seemed to know Stone, despite his many years spent living away from Clayville. Of course, most of them had known him from the time he'd been an infant. Josie was introduced as his *fiancée* and was startled by the warm greetings of the locals

128

and the many welcoming hugs she received. Each person seemed genuinely pleased when Stone told them he planned to move back in a few months and take up residence with his new bride at Wolfwood. As he repeated this to various locals, Josie wondered if she was about to have a panic attack. She'd never been so overwhelmed by well-meaning people in her life. It was refreshing and slightly scary.

"You okay?" Stone asked once they'd made it inside the store.

"This is all so different than the places I've lived in the past. I'm feeling a bit off-balance."

"Welcome to life in Clayville. Remember that there's good and bad here."

"That's true of any town in various ways. You may have backwards and racist here, but when's the last time you had gang warfare, a roaming homeless population, massive substance abuse, and hoards of mentally ill men and women wandering the streets?"

"Point taken."

Glancing around, Josie remarked, "Speaking of points, I'd like to point out that there are black people and white people shopping here. I thought the racial lines in Clayville were pretty well drawn."

"They are, but Walmart's got no racial lines inside it. Neither do the McDonalds and Subway. The Lowe's should be the same. It's not like the local places. The expanding presence of the national chains will help to blur some of the racial barriers outside the stores, too. At least that's what I hope."

"Stone Romero!"

They both turned to face a short, silver-haired, well-built man of perhaps fifty. He was smiling, but Stone's grip on Josie's hand tightened even as he smiled back and introduced his *fiancée* to the stranger, whose name was David Skinner. She was informed that Mr. Skinner was in fact the pastor of a local church. A petite, perky, forty-something-year-old woman with dyed-blonde hair stepped up beside Pastor Skinner in an overtly possessive fashion.

"It's wonderful to meet you," Skinner replied once Josie had offered him a friendly greeting. "This is my wife, Mary Ann. Mary Ann, you remember Stone." Once she'd confirmed this with a nod and an insincere smile, her husband said, "This is Stone's *fiancée*, Josie Hollingsworth."

"It's a pleasure to meet both of you," Josie said graciously. "I'm looking forward to getting to know the town of Clayville and its inhabitants once Stone and I move to Wolfwood."

"Oh, that is such a lovely place, at least from what we can see on the outside," commented Mary Ann. "Although I can only imagine what sort of sinning went on in that house." Looking at Stone, she said, "Your brother was quite a designer as many homosexuals are."

"Yes, he was a fabulous designer," Stone said tightly. "And you know full well that no one has ever resided at the house."

"I do hope you're not planning on living in sin at Wolfwood," Pastor Skinner said seriously.

"Of course not," Josie assured him with a sweet smile. "We're living in sin now. We plan to get married before we move into Wolfwood."

The pastor looked stunned by her candor. She supposed no one had ever spoken freely to the man for fear of repercussions within the community or because they didn't want to engage him in a controversial debate. She had no qualms about speaking freely to the Skinners and would relish a debate with the pastor or his wife.

While Skinner attempted to think of something to say that would put Josie and Stone in their places, his wife exclaimed, "What happened to your face! I see a bruise under your make-up!"

Automatically lifting her hand to her cheek, Josie echoed, "My face? Oh, that. It's nothing. Stone's brother slapped me yesterday when he was being a jerk and I called him on it. It won't happen again."

"That's for damn sure," Stone muttered. Nodding to David and Mary Ann Skinner, he said, "We have to go. We'll be seeing you around town when we move here. Have a good day."

Once they were out of earshot of the Skinners, Josie opened her mouth to speak. Stone looked angry and shook his head then practically dragged her towards the back of the store. Her heart pounded hard, and she wondered if she'd been too frank. Would it hurt Stone's pediatrics practice in the area? Would his parents and grandmother be harassed because of her forthrightness?

Stone said nothing to her until they'd passed through the swinging doors that led to the warehouse area. He then stopped, turned towards her, and declared, "I love you, Josephine. You are the most fantastic, beautiful woman I've ever met."

"You're not mad at me?"

"I doubt if I could ever be mad at you, although who knows? You seem to do the unexpected with alarming frequency. No, I'm mad at that prick, David Skinner, and his small-minded wife, Mary Ann."

"He's just a sheep. A lot of pastors are sheep instead of shepherds. No one should talk about others the way the Skinners do. That's not very charitable."

"Doesn't anything phase you?"

"My family and my fear of becoming like them," she reminded him. "Other than that, I think I'm only afraid of losing you. People like the Skinners are weak fools. They aren't intimidating to me. They can't compare with End-of-Days or any of the other hallucinations that inhabited our apartments."

"I think Clayville is in for a major adjustment when we move here. Flynn, Nelson, and I were always pretty vocal about how things needed to change, but no one listened to us then. Maybe people will be more receptive now."

"Adjustment is good. It sounds like it's about time."

There was movement to their right, and a young man cried, "Uncle Stone!"

Tommy Romero had matured since he'd appeared in the family photo Josie had seen. He was a sixteen-year-old boy who looked almost exactly like Stone and Nelson. Josie was certain that it must have driven Cheek insane. A portion of her was glad, but another wondered if Tommy suffered because of it.

Uncle and nephew hugged, and Josie was introduced to Tommy, who didn't hesitate to reach out and firmly shake her hand.

"What do you do here at Walmart?" she asked.

"I help in the warehouse. I've been working here since I turned fifteen." Turning towards his uncle, he proudly declared, "I'm back on the Honor Roll. *And* I'm the President of the Book Club. You were right about my friends dragging me down. I wasn't going to be happy hanging out with them, getting high. The friends I have now are motivated at school, and we hang out and have fun without using pot or anything."

"That's awesome," Stone said, clapping him on the back. "I'm so proud of you, Tommy."

"Thanks. I'm sorry I couldn't come to the house yesterday. Dad was pissed and said I could never see you again. I told him he was a royal asshole and that I'd see you whenever I wanted."

"So, why didn't you come?" Stone asked in a non-accusatory tone. "Once your dad was gone from the house, everything went well. We had dinner, watched football, and opened presents. Flynn Carmody joined us for everything, except the present part."

"Dad got all teary and started saying how if I left he'd be alone on Christmas and that nobody loved him. I felt sorry for him, so I stayed. I have your Christmas and birthday presents as well as ones for Memaw Gertrude, Pepaw Vin, and Memaw Dumpling. I figured I'd come over tonight when I get off work. Things have been crazy today with it being the day after Christmas." Looking hopeful and much younger than his sixteen years, Tommy asked Stone, "How long are you here for? I want to spend time with you before you leave again."

"Several more days. Once my residency's finished, Josie and I are going to move here and into Wolfwood."

The boy's face reflected shock and excitement, as he exclaimed, "No fucking way!"

"Yes, way," Stone countered. "And you should leave the 'F' word out of your vocabulary." Leveling his gaze at his nephew, he asked, "And speaking of that word, are you still using protection when you have sex?"

"Not with *her* here," Tommy said with obvious embarrassment, as he avoided looking at Josie.

"Later then. We'd better let you get back to work. We'll see you tonight."

"I'll be there for supper. Dad'll be at the club as usual now that one of his two holidays off is over."

"What's the other one?" asked Josie.

"Easter. He's a real religious man, my dad," Tommy snorted. "See you tonight. It was great to meet you, Josie. Or should I call you Aunt Josie?"

"I kind of like that," she confided. "You'll be my only opportunity to have a nephew."

"You don't have any brothers or sisters?"

"One sister, but I doubt if she'll ever marry or have kids."

"Oh. Well, then I'd definitely better call you that. Bye, Uncle Stone. Bye, Aunt Josie."

They made their way back through the Walmart and to Stone's car. Once they got in, Stone drove directly back to Wolfwood, punched in the security code at the main gate, drove through, and parked by the house. When Josie asked him why there was no garage, he replied, "Have you ever seen a plantation home with a garage? That would've ruined the aesthetics for Nelson."

"Can we light another fire when we go in?"

"I'm planning on it. Actually, I'm planning on lighting more than one fire."

Once they were inside, Josie understood. Stone had barely reset the alarm when he pinned her to the wall with his body and slanted his mouth across hers. The ache she'd been feeling since their earlier encounter was instantaneously almost crippling, and she wished she'd worn a skirt despite the cold so that she could unzip his jeans and take him inside right away. She moaned his name as he stroked her neck with his tongue.

They were soon once again in the master bedroom with the fire blazing in the hearth. Josie was seated, naked, in Stone's lap again, but this time they were on the bed and her back was against his chest. He groaned when she leaned forward with him still inside her and slid her inner thighs to the outsides of his legs. Stretching out her arms in front of her, Josie felt the coolness of the sheets under her breasts and the heat inside her. When she began to move back and forth, his breathing quickened. So did hers. She picked up the pace and gave a little cry of pleasure when he shifted his position and began to meet her thrust for thrust. They continued like that for what felt like a deliciously long time before surrendering to climax.

Afterwards, they lay under the sheets and duvet and slept. When Josie woke, Stone was sitting on the *chaise-lounge*, watching her. He'd showered as was evidenced by his damp, brown hair. He was fully dressed.

"It's 1:00. Are you hungry?"

"A little. You?"

"Yes. Why don't we grab some lunch and then I'll take you to Flynn's office. You can see where it is and if you really want to work as our practice manager."

"Okay. I want to shower first."

"Go ahead. I'll call Mama and Daddy and let them know that Tommy's coming to dinner."

They ate a sandwich at a local restaurant owned by another man and woman who'd known Stone from birth. Once they'd visited with the couple and shared some pie, they went to Flynn Carmody's medical practice, which was located in a lovely, old, two-story house that looked like a mini-castle with a stone facade. Stone explained that it had been Carmody's childhood home. His father had given it to him when he'd divorced Flynn's mother, and Carmody eventually converted the first floor into his offices and turned the second floor into his main personal living space.

"So, he's always on call?" Josie asked. "If people know the doctor lives here, then don't they show up at all hours?"

"Only if it's an emergency. They respect his right to have a normal schedule. It *is* convenient for him to live right above his practice though, especially in a small community. All of his supplies are literally within his reach. Since he lives at the practice and has a security system, no one's ever tried to break in and steal drugs or equipment. Pretty sweet."

Josie glanced at the sign that read Carmody Internal Medicine Clinic.

"I guess we'll have to add one for Romero Pediatrics," Stone told her, as they passed the sign.

"Definitely. Did you come to this house a lot when you were growing up?"

"Yes, but Flynn was at our house more often. His parents fought all the time. Even so, I think his dad's affair caught him and his mom off-guard. They never suspected. Flynn's still furious with his dad, especially after the way his mom died not long after the divorce." As they climbed the porch steps, he confided, "I worry about Flynn. He avoids commitment at all costs."

The sign that hung in the window was turned to OPEN, and they entered to find Flynn standing behind a counter, accepting payment from a smiling, heavy, older black woman whose gray hair was pulled into a bun behind her head. She sweetly greeted Stone and Josie on her way out. Once she'd left the office, Josie remarked, "She reminds me of the Pretzel Lady."

"Who?" Flynn asked blankly.

"The Pretzel Lady."

"The pretzel lady?" echoed Stone.

Josie nodded distractedly and said, "She caught me and Zelda dumpster diving behind her little shop. It was when we were pretty new at it and weren't so stealthy. We were worried she was going to call the cops, but she simply asked us to come inside the store, which was closed. When we did, she asked why we were digging through garbage disposed of by the neighborhood restaurants. Zelda and I were tired, hot, and hungry, so we did. The woman told us she was called 'The Pretzel Lady' and would save four large pretzels for us every day. We could pass by on our way home from school to pick them up." Smiling to herself, Josie continued, "When she'd give us the pretzels, she'd ask how our schoolwork was going, what kinds of games we were playing with friends, and how our parents were. She instructed us to always keep ourselves clean, do our homework, and eat and sleep as much as possible. She also told us how smart and pretty we were.

"Five months later when our family got evicted from our apartment, Zelda and I went to The Pretzel Lady's shop to thank her and say goodbye. She gave us all the pretzels she had left that evening. We ate pretzels for a week. It was nice. *She* was nice." Shaking her head, Josie murmured, "I wish I could talk to Zelda. I miss her."

"Zelda is your sister?" Flynn asked.

Nodding, Josie faced the man and said, "My parents are crazy, and now my sister is, too."

"Enough said."

"Thank you. Could I have a tour of the clinic now?"

"It'd be my pleasure."

The waiting room was large and filled with old-fashioned furniture. A rectangular, wooden counter and a desk had been positioned so that the two formed an L-shaped administrative area at one end of the room.

"This used to be two rooms," Flynn explained. "I had a wall knocked down. Thank God it wasn't a load-bearing wall."

To the right was a hallway that led to three examination rooms and a bathroom. The entire section of the house reminded Josie of any other modern doctor's office. Each exam room held an examination table, a bottom row of cabinets with a sink, and cabinets above, as well as one rolling stool and two stationary chairs. Flynn told her that what lay on the other side of the waiting room looked identical but had never been used. The back half of the first floor had been converted into a file room, a small lab that Josie guessed was used for basic blood and urine tests, a locked room that held medications, a private bathroom and kitchenette for Flynn, a room that held general medical supplies, and one that held an array of cleaning products. The internist volunteered that he cleaned his own equipment, the waiting room, and the exam rooms at the end of each workday so that the correct standards needed for a medical office could be maintained. Stone said he'd be doing the same on his side of the first floor.

"I could help," Josie suggested. "You could teach me how to clean the right way for a medical practice."

"Not a bad idea," Stone mused. "If one or both of us is unavailable, it would help if someone knew proper cleaning protocol."

"True enough," Flynn agreed. Looking directly at Josie, he asked, "Are you sure you really want to do this? I mean, you were some big-time realtor from what Stone says. Now, you want to be the practice manager for a small-town doctors' office that just got off the ground and is barely paying a living wage?"

"I'm sure."

"You're probably going to hate me after you look at my…ah, system," Flynn said awkwardly. "I've never had a receptionist or bookkeeper or anything. I was a darn good linebacker in high school and college and an excellent med student, but I never actually had anyone teach me how to run the administrative side for a medical practice."

"I'll fix it," Josie said with a smile. "I'm really good with business and people."

"I'd be thrilled if you could straighten it all out and streamline things. It's exhausting to work all day, clean up, and try to manage the business for the practice."

"I'd love to help."

"Great." Glancing at Stone, he asked, "How've you been doing today? How's your blood pressure?"

"Fine. Thanks again for yesterday."

The front door of the clinic opened and a young, white girl with short, black hair entered the waiting room where the three of them stood. She looked about thirteen, and Josie thought instantly of Brittany, the child who'd given birth to the baby who'd later died. Stone had updated Josie on Brittany's condition before they'd left Austin for their trip, telling her that Brittany was in a foster home and was recovering as well as one would expect.

This girl looked nervous and uncertain. She fidgeted as she asked to see the doctor. Josie immediately looked to Stone, who shook his head and reminded her that he was not yet licensed to practice medicine in Louisiana. Flynn explained to the girl that he had no nurse and didn't examine under-aged patients unless their parents or guardians were present.

"But I'm bleeding!" she cried as tears filled her eyes.

"Are you hurt?" Flynn asked worriedly. "I don't see any blood."

When the girl shook her head, Josie went forward and asked, "What's your name?"

"Rhonda."

"My mother's name is Rhonda," Josie said with what she hoped was a reassuring smile. "Rhonda, why don't you come with me so that we can talk?"

She took the girl's hand and led her down the hall to one of the exam rooms Flynn had shown them earlier. She gestured for Rhonda to have a seat in one of the stationary chairs and sat in the other. It took her only a few minutes to learn that Rhonda was, indeed, thirteen and that she knew absolutely nothing about her developing body and the onset of menstruation. She came from a very religious family who attended Pastor Skinner's church and had been given no sex education whatsoever. She tearfully confessed to Josie that she'd been curious about her own body and had touched herself the day before to see what she felt like "down there." Now, she was bleeding and wondered if God was punishing her for being sinful and doing something bad. Josie assured her that she'd done nothing wrong, explained the facts of life, and asked her to wait in the room while she got her a Kotex pad.

"She's started her period," Josie said in a quiet voice to the two men when she returned to the waiting room. "Flynn, do you have any pads here?"

"Of course. But –"

Josie cut him off by saying, "I'll talk to you when she's gone."

Once she'd returned to the exam room with the pads, she explained how to use them then sent Rhonda to the bathroom. The girl emerged looking less frightened, although she confided that she wasn't very excited about bleeding for several days each month for the next thirty-five or forty years. Josie commiserated with her but said it was natural and a part of every woman's life.

Rhonda stood a little straighter and said, "That's right. I'm a woman now, aren't I?"

"A part of you is, but you're still a young girl. Don't be in such a rush to grow up. And remember what I told you. Go to your mom when you get home and tell her that you started bleeding. Let her explain it in whatever way she chooses. Some moms are embarrassed to talk about things like this, so don't contradict her. Just listen and do what you know you should."

"Was your mom embarrassed to talk to you?"

"She never did. Take care, Rhonda."

After the girl had left, Stone asked, "How could you know that quickly what was wrong with her?"

"Because I started my period when I was ten. Zelda didn't start hers until she was fourteen. When I started bleeding, she and I both freaked out. Knowing Dad, we figured he'd think I was dying if I told him I was bleeding like that. *We* weren't sure if I *was* dying, but we certainly weren't going to get him involved in case I wasn't. Zelda brought me to the local health clinic, and I got a lecture and a bag of pads." Sighing, she said, "That girl's family goes to Pastor Skinner's church. No sex ed and everything's a sin. It's disgraceful."

"Did you tell her about sex?" asked Flynn.

"Of course I did. She's gotten her period. She knew absolutely nothing about how men and women procreate. Don't worry. She won't tell her parents about my explanation of the facts of life."

"How can you be so sure?"

"Because she knows if she does they'll be mad at her for not coming to them first and won't understand that she's afraid of their narrow-minded approach to life. I suspect they have that 'spare-the-rod-spoil-the-child' mentality. What a waste. I hope she can break away from it."

Flynn looked to Stone and said, "You're right. Having the two of you move here is going to be one heck of a shock to Clayville. I hope we all survive."

Stone grinned and said, "We'll definitely keep the ass-backwards people on the edge of their seats, won't we?" Slipping his arms around Josie's waist, he asked, "Are you ready to find Mark Twain?"

"Ready, willing, and able. Las Vegas, here we come."

"I must be missing something," Flynn muttered.

"You have *no* idea," Stone and Josie said simultaneously before looking at one another and then exploding with laughter.

Part Two

Chapter One

"Happy Valentine's Day, Mrs. Romero," Stone murmured as he feathered Josie's neck with kisses. "I take it by your reaction that you enjoyed making love without us having to use condoms."

"It was fantastic," she answered with a grin. "Although it would seem to limit our ability to have sex anywhere we want at any time. It's definitely messier than when we used protection."

"But?"

"Being able to feel you like that made the experience even more beautiful and intense. I'm so happy the vasectomy was a success. Let's never use condoms again."

"Fine by me."

Glancing at the clock, Josie yawned and then said, "We should get some sleep. You have to get up in a few hours to go to work."

"I know. How are you handling not working?"

"I *am* working. I'm spending most of each day while you're at the hospital learning everything I can about medical practices and how to be a practice manager."

"I meant not working at the hospital. You were only there for a month before they hired a new Director of Marketing. They kept all of your ideas and want to implement them. Aren't you upset?"

"No. I'm quite pleased actually. I knew the position was only temporary, and they happened to connect with the right person for the job early on in their search. He and I were on the same page, so to speak. I got paid for my time and effort and have documented credit for my work at the hospital. Now, I have a few months to focus on Carmody Internal Medicine and Romero Pediatrics. I've already learned quite a lot in my two weeks of research. I'm looking forward to our move this summer."

"You know it's going to be hard for us in Clayville."

"I'll miss Austin and everything we've done here. Living in Clayville will certainly be different, but I think I'm ready. How do *you* feel about the move and your switch to mainstream pediatrics now that it's a certainty?"

Stone didn't answer, and Josie realized he'd fallen asleep. She smiled and nestled closer to her husband of six weeks. As she lay in his arms, it was difficult for her to remember how despairing she'd felt that first night in Austin over two and a half months earlier. She'd been ready to kill herself, unable to imagine having any sort of positive future. Stone Romero had rapidly and radically changed her outlook. In a few months, her life would be dramatically altered again when they made the move to Louisiana and began the next interesting – and potentially difficult – transition in their lives.

When Josie woke the following morning, it was to Stone's gentle kiss. He told her he was going to work and would see her at 7:30 that night. She nodded then went back to sleep for another hour before rising, showering, and putting on jeans and one of Stone's flannel shirts. Then she set to work on her research. At some point she ate lunch then returned to her studies. She didn't look up again until Stone entered the apartment.

"How was school today?" he teased.

"Great. None of the other kids bullied me for being a bookworm."

As he moved to the kitchen area and pulled out a wok and a bamboo utensil, Stone asked, "Did you get bullied a lot when you were in school?"

"Sometimes. People expected me to be an airhead because I was blonde and pretty. Since I was serious about my schoolwork, I'd get teased by other kids who were mean or jealous. I ignored them. I'd had practice with a lot worse bullying from Mom's hallucinations. The school bullies couldn't compare." Checking the time, she said, "I might as well go through the messages on my cellphone. Maybe I'll call my parents and sister this evening. It's been two weeks since I last talked to them."

"Eat first. Then you can delete the twelve messages from your dad and all the other ones from your mom and Zelda before calling them back. When you call them before dinner, you tend not to want to eat."

"Really? I hadn't noticed. I'm so used to checking the number of messages, but I've only actually spoken to them three times in the last two months. And you noticed that I didn't eat afterwards?"

"Of course, I noticed. You're always very tense for about twenty-four hours after you talk to them."

"*You* were tense after *you* talked to them."

"It was my first time. You'd just told them about me and that we were married, and your dad was in a panic because I'm a pediatrician and am around so many germs every workday. Your mom and sister only seemed concerned that I might be a plant from the government who was sent to kill you. Our exchanges weren't your typical 'meet-the-family' conversations."

Josie looked down at her lap and mumbled, "I wish they *had* been."

"You shouldn't feel bad about the way it went. They're sick."

"I know. I still feel sad about it." Before he could continue to reassure her that everything was all right, she said, "I'll at least delete the voicemails while you cook; then I'll call Dad, Mom, and Zelda after dinner. I'll even wait for thirty minutes so that my food will have gone down if you like."

"Rule of thumb," Stone said with a forced smile. Sighing, he came over to kiss her then said, "Don't be long. I'm making stir-fry vegetables, and the brown rice is already cooked from yesterday, waiting in the fridge."

"You spoil me with all this healthy cooking. My parents are so used to fast food that they'd probably get sick if they ate the types of meals you prepare."

"I'd hate to see their arteries. At least you and Zelda got away from it once you moved out."

"Who knows what she's eating now? She's probably dumpster-diving like we did when we were kids."

"Josie –"

"Don't, Stone. I'll try not to dwell on it. I'm just tired from being in one position for most of the day."

"Maybe we can get you into some different positions tonight," Stone said with a lopsided grin. "I'll think of a few while I cook."

Josie went to the guest bedroom where she still kept the cell phone used only for her family's calls. She turned it on and pulled up the message screen. She was about to automatically hit her father's first voicemail so that she could begin to delete the twelve messages when she noted the number of voicemails from him. There were twenty-one.

She checked the times of the calls. Starting at 7:00 a.m. there had been one every hour until 11:00 a.m. All of the rest had come at odd times including the last one, which had been left at 7:17 p.m. Josie hit the *Play* button with a trembling finger. The first five messages were all routine calls. She waited anxiously for the sixth to play.

"Josie, it's Dad!" Sounding frantic, he cried, "Mom's collapsed! I've called 911! Call me! I love you!"

The next fifteen messages were updates: The paramedics had come. Rhonda had been taken to a hospital. The doctors said she'd suffered a heart attack and a stroke. She was on a ventilator and was unconscious. Then she was conscious but unable to communicate. Then she was unconscious. The doctors said she was in bad shape. There were so many germs at the hospital that Clark wondered if he should insist they take his wife home so that she wouldn't catch anything. Her room wasn't clean enough. Josie's mother's condition was critical. No one would listen to her father. Her mother was stable. Her mother was worse. Her father couldn't reach Zelda. They needed Josie and her husband to come right away.

Shaking, Josie hit the button to listen to her mother's three voicemails. The first two were the typical ramblings of a paranoid schizophrenic. The last one was similar, but Josie could hear the slurring of certain words as her mother spoke. The time for that call had been 10:48 a.m.

Zelda's call had been all about government agents with special laser guns tracking her and her alien baby. She didn't mention their parents, so Josie assumed she either didn't know about their mother or that she was incapable of understanding at the time she'd called, which had been shortly after 6:00 that evening.

Josie phoned her father. The call went directly to voicemail. She left him a message, stating that she'd gotten his voicemails and would be there as soon as she could. Before she hung up, she told him she loved him and her mother.

"Dinner's ready!" Stone sang out from the other room. "What do you want to drink?"

Feeling sick, Josie lowered the phone into her lap and didn't answer. She knew what she had to do, but she dreaded it. It was something she'd lived in fear of for many years. It hadn't been a question of *whether* or not one of her parents would die; it had been a question of *when* and what she was going to do with the remaining one. They couldn't exist independently of one another, and she'd always known that there was no way either of them could live with her. Her own descent into insanity would be a given if that were to happen.

"Josie?"

Stone stood in the doorway, looking worried. Josie blurted out, "Mom's going to die!"

He came over and sat beside her. Taking the phone from her hands, Stone pulled her to him as he listened to the voicemails one by one. When he was done, he put his free arm around Josie and told her they were going to take care of everything together.

"Your mom might not die," he said encouragingly.

"I hope she does. She'd finally be at peace. I can only imagine what it's like for her, if she's still aware but has a tube down her throat and can't move. She's trapped inside her own body with the hallucinations! It's already like hell on earth for her when she can talk to them and feels like she can try to fight off the bad ones. But if she's totally incapacitated? She must be terrified! Hedgehog, Calla Lily, and the other good hallucinations are no match for End-of-Days, Six-Six-Six, and the other bad ones if Mom has no control! She's been existing in misery for twenty years." Burying her face against his chest, she prayed, "Please, God. Let her die."

Stone said firmly, "Everything will work out, Josephine. I'm here with you. I'll book our flights to Virginia, pack, call to let the family in Louisiana know what's happening, and then phone work to let them know."

"What am I going to do with my father? He can't live by himself, but he can't live with us. He can't live *near* us."

"One thing at a time. We have to learn your mother's current status. Depending on her condition and the outcome, then that'll affect what happens with both of your parents."

"And Zelda? I should tell her."

"Wait until we get to Virginia and find out what the facts are. You lie here and rest while I arrange things. I'll be back, all right?"

She nodded against him and confided, "I've wished for my parents to either get better or pass away for years, but now that it's finally happening, I'm scared. I always hoped for the 'getting better'

146

part, even though I knew the chances were slim. I want my mom to die, but I *don't* want my mom to die. Does that make sense? Or am I just a horrible person?"

"You want her suffering to end. That makes you a wonderful person."

Josie allowed Stone to lay her back on the guest bed before he went to make the necessary calls and to pack. She listened absently as Stone booked their flight reservations, made arrangements for them to stay at a hotel near the hospital where her mother was currently a patient, phoned his work to explain the situation, and called his family. He then moved out of the main living area. She supposed he'd gone into the master bedroom in order to pack their things.

When he returned to the guest bedroom, Stone urged Josie to come with him to the table to eat. He'd reheated their dinner, insisting that they needed food in their stomachs before leaving the apartment in order to take a taxi to the airport.

"I don't think I can eat," she told him. "I'm too nauseated."

"I'm not giving you a choice. You have to eat something, even if it's only enough to placate me."

Josie walked with him to the table and took a seat; then she stared down at the plate of stir-fried vegetables and rice. Normally, the sight would have made her mouth water. That night, it made her want to throw up. She forced herself to eat until there was nothing left, and Stone seemed relieved.

"I called the hospital in Virginia," Stone told Josie an hour later, as they climbed into the taxi that would take them to the airport.

Normally, they don't give out information regarding a patient over the phone, but once I explained that I was a physician and a relative they checked it out with your dad and cut me some slack."

"What did they say?"

He frowned and admitted, "If what they're telling me is accurate, then it's unlikely your mom will improve. Her kidneys and liver are failing. They can't perform surgery on her heart because she's too critically ill. Her heart's already stopped once, but they were able to bring her back."

"*What?!?* They *resuscitated* her? If there's no hope, then why?"

147

"Because your dad refused to sign a Do Not Resuscitate form. He's her husband. They have to follow his directives."

"So, they'll just keep bringing her back each time until her body finally gives out?"

"Yes."

"Does it hurt the person who's resuscitated?"

"It can if they use the paddles and electricity. If they're able to bring the patient back with medications only, then there's no residual pain."

Josie wiped at the corners of her eyes with a gloved finger. Her poor mother was being tortured because her father couldn't let her go. They were so codependent that they'd formed a symbiotic relationship during their married life.

She and Stone caught a flight out of the Austin-Bergstrom International Airport that took them to Atlanta. There, they changed planes, continuing on to Reagan International Airport in Washington, D.C. After landing and deplaning, Stone rented a car, and they drove for thirty minutes through darkened streets to their hotel in Alexandria. Upon arrival, they checked in, leaving their suitcases in the room, then drove to the hospital where Josie's mother was a patient in the Critical Care Unit. They entered the building before dawn.

Stone pulled Josie to one corner of the lobby before she could approach the elevators. She asked him what he was doing, citing the need to go up to see her parents as soon as possible.

"I want you to be as prepared as you can be. Have you ever seen anyone on a ventilator?"

"On television."

"It's different when it's an actor on TV and when you're in the same room with the real patient, especially when that person is someone you know."

"I'm sure it is. That doesn't mean I can avoid it. I have to go to her."

"I want to talk to the doctor on duty before we go in."

"But –"

"Trust me. I'm trying to do right by you. I'm your husband and better informed than the vast majority of people who have family members in CCU. Give me a few minutes with her doctor before we go in so that I'll know what to expect and can prepare you for what you might see or experience."

Josie agreed to this, her heart pounding with anxiety. She allowed him to lead her up to the CCU floor and deposit her in a waiting room where other patients' family members were sleeping in chairs or staring vacantly at a cooking show that was playing on the television. Some looked as though they'd been camped out there for weeks or months, while others appeared to be new arrivals like her.

Stone was gone for quite a while, and Josie began to fidget. Twice, she stood then returned to her seat. She watched the cooking show with the few others who were awake. Eventually, Stone came back to the waiting room and then sat beside her.

"Well?" she asked in a small voice.

"Her kidneys and liver are definitely failing. Her body can't purify itself the way it should. Her heart rhythm is almost nonexistent. Frankly, I don't know how she's still alive. I suspect she's waiting for you and Zelda to come before she lets go."

"We don't even know where Zelda is! How long do you think Mom will hold on?"

"I can't say. No doctor can."

"Is she conscious?"

"Off and on."

"And Dad?"

"Hasn't left her room since they brought her here." Sighing, he said, "Josie, there's something else."

"Bad?"

"Very bad. She has *C. diff.*"

"What's that?"

"*Clostridium difficile.* It's a Gram-positive bacteria. Basically, she's had so many antibiotics that it's wiped out all the good bacteria in her gut and has made her susceptible to invasion by bad bacteria. She's suffering from intestinal bleeding. This is a highly contagious bacteria. We'll have to wear gowns and gloves when we're in the room and strip them off when we leave. Even a healthy younger person who catches *C. diff* might battle it for months. But if a newborn, young child, or someone with a compromised immune system is exposed, it could easily kill him or her."

"But Mom hasn't even been here one full day! How could she have had that many antibiotics already?"

"She wasn't given them here."

Josie blinked in surprise and asked, "If not here, then where?"

Running his fingers through his disheveled, brown hair, Stone answered, "Your dad has been giving them to her. I don't know where he got them. He won't tell the doctors. All he'll say is that he's been giving her antibiotics for a long time to keep her healthy. He didn't realize that an overabundance of antibiotics can kill good bacteria as well as bad."

"What if Mom keeps bleeding a lot?"

"She could bleed out."

"Can't they give her medicine to clot her blood?"

"They could if she hadn't had a stroke followed by a massive heart attack. Coagulants could lead to more life-threatening blood clots. It's a Catch-22."

"So, Dad gave her all these antibiotics for who knows how long to keep her healthy and it's killing her."

He nodded solemnly.

"And yet he's in there with her and all these germs."

"The doctor I spoke with said your dad is terrified but won't leave your mom's side. The staff seems to be dealing with your folks' mental illness issues pretty well. They feel sorry for them and are trying to be patient and understanding."

"Did you see my father, yet?"

"No. I figured we could go in together. We'll have to put on the protective garb and leave all of our belongings outside the room. I want to stop by a drugstore to buy antibacterial soap, Hibiclens, and garbage bags before we go back to the hotel. We need to be very careful for our sakes and for the sakes of others. I don't dare catch *C. diff* and pass it on to my patients. Their little systems would be especially vulnerable."

"What's Hibiclens?"

"An antibacterial antiseptic skin cleanser. We'll use it in conjunction with the soap."

"This bacteria is that powerful?"

"Yes," he answered grimly before rising. "Are you ready?"

Her head spinning from all of this new information, Josie stood and followed Stone down the hall and to a room that was cordoned off from the others by sliding glass doors. There were warnings posted on each of the doors about the *C. diff* threat and the need for protective garb. Stone and Josie removed their coats and left them, their hats, scarves, and gloves on a desk outside the room along with Josie's purse and Stone's wallet, phone, and keys. Then they put on special gowns and gloves before entering the room.

Josie halted just inside the doorway. It *was* a shock to see her mother, lying in the bed with the tube down her throat. She had physically deteriorated dramatically since the previous spring when Josie and Zelda had last visited. Josie estimated that her mother had gained thirty pounds in the past year, and she'd already been about forty pounds overweight. Her short, blonde hair stuck out in various directions all over her head. Her blue eyes were closed; her skin was too white; her hands lay at her sides; and the machine was breathing for her. It was almost as if Rhonda Hollingsworth was already gone, and the husk of the woman lay in the hospital bed, mocking them all.

Clark Hollingsworth had also suffered great physical deterioration since his daughters had last seen him. Formerly too thin, he was perhaps now fifty pounds overweight and had deep lines etched across his features. His thick, blonde hair fell to his shoulders and was unkempt. His skin, like that of his wife, reflected an unhealthy pallor.

"Dad?"

His blue eyes darted towards his daughter, and he immediately hurried over to her, extending his arms as if he was going to hug her. When he was a foot away, he stopped, shook his head, and said, "There are too many germs. I can't hug you until we're all scrubbed clean."

Josie intended to tell him that she didn't care how many germs there were, that she wanted a hug and wanted to give him one. Stone touched her hand and remarked that her father was right in this instance. He also directed her not to touch her eyes, nose, or mouth with her gloved hands.

"You're a good doctor," her father said distractedly. "You need to talk to these doctors here. They don't know anything. They say Rhonda's terminal, but she's not terminal. She's getting better. I wish I could take her out of here, but what if that *C. diff* stuff spreads and kills someone on the way home? People could die."

"Yes, they could," Stone told him. "That's one reason why your wife needs to stay here."

"How long will it be before she's better?"

"I don't know how long she'll be in CCU," Stone replied diplomatically. "Once Josie's said 'hello' to her mother and I've been properly introduced, then I'll check out the readings on some of these machines and see what I can learn from that."

"You can explain it to me," Clark said. "I may be a crazy man, but I'm not a stupid one. I have a Ph.D. in English."

"I know. Josie's very proud of you and your wife. I wish we'd met under better circumstances."

The man nodded and glanced at the bed before saying, "She mouths things around the tube. Sometimes, I can't understand what she's trying to say; other times, I get it."

"What does she say?" asked Josie as she gripped the metal railing on the bed.

Clark looked distressed as he answered, "That she wants to get up and go home and that she wants someone to help her."

Josie's eyes filled with tears, and she lifted one hand to wipe them away. Stone stopped her and reminded her not to touch her eyes, nose, or mouth with her hands. She willed the tears away. At that moment, her mother jerked in the bed and opened her eyes.

"Mom? It's Josie. Can you hear me? Can you nod?"

Her mother looked up at her, nodded, and smiled around the tube. Josie smiled back and took her mother's hand in hers. It felt odd to have the glove separating their skin. Even so, she could feel the unnatural coolness of her mother's flesh. Forcing herself not to break down, she said, "Mom, this is my husband, Stone Romero. Stone, this is my mom, Rhonda."

Rhonda's eyes focused on Stone, and she smiled again. Josie released the woman's hand, and Stone took it. He lightly squeezed it and told her it was wonderful to meet the mother of his kind, beautiful, and intelligent wife. Rhonda nodded. Then her gaze flew to the area directly above her. She shook her head then nodded. She shook her head again.

Josie knew what was happening. The hallucinations were there, and her mother was communicating with them as best she could. Josie murmured this to Stone and asked him to use this time to check out the machines with her while Clark took his wife's other hand. Stone moved to study the monitors.

He pointed out various readings and quietly explained them to Josie. She understood that her mother's blood pressure and pulse were way too low. After all, she'd come to understand those things more completely than most people because of Stone's hypertension issue. He reviewed the oxygenation levels and what they should have been. He told her that her mother's creatinine levels were rising, meaning dialysis was required in order to keep her kidneys functional. However, because of her overall condition, Rhonda would not be a candidate for dialysis. Her albumin levels were dropping, indicating liver failure. Organ system shut-down wouldn't be long in coming.

Josie heard every word, but she couldn't tear her gaze away from the heart rhythm line on the monitor. She'd watched enough medical dramas on television to know what was normal. There should be a short, straight line followed by jagged lines and varying peaks as the heart contracted and released. Her mother's reading was a continuous snaking line with no peaks at all. She wondered how the damaged heart was pumping enough blood through the body to keep anything going. Without saying a word, Josie lifted a finger and pointed to the almost-flat line.

"That was the first thing I noticed," Stone said. "She has less than twenty percent of her heart functioning right now. I think you should try to reach Zelda. Why don't you go into the private room we saw at the end of the hall and call her while I stay with your dad?"

Josie nodded and explained to her father where she was going before carefully stripping off the gown and gloves and tossing them into a biohazard canister that sat near the sliding doors. Then she washed her hands twelve times with soap and water at her father's request before retrieving the cell phone from her purse and going to the private room. She stood with her back resting against one wall and dialed her sister's number.

"Zelda, it's me."

"I can't talk long," her sister said in a hushed voice. "I have to catch the bus to D.C. soon and bring my alien baby. No one would suspect I'd go to where the President is and leave it for the media so the world can know the truth. If they experiment on the baby, then maybe it will stop other aliens from having sex with humans. I was tricked into it by an alien in disguise."

"Zelda, please," Josie said pleadingly although she knew it was pointless. "Mom is dying. You need to come to the hospital in Alexandria right away."

There was a long pause.

"Zelda, did you hear me?"

"I heard you," her sister said slowly. "What's wrong with Mom?"

"She had a stroke and a heart attack. Plus, she has a bacterial infection caused unknowingly by Dad."

"Mom said they'd kill her this way. She said they'd try to make it look like a natural death but that it wouldn't be. She said they'd do it to Dad, too. We'd be next. I can't come. If I come, then I won't be able to leave the alien baby for the scientists. They'll kill me first, and other aliens will mate with more humans."

God, help her, Josie prayed. *If You're there, please make it stop for all of them and for me.*

"Will you do me a favor?" her sister asked quietly.

"If I can."

"Give Mom a hug for me and tell her that I love her."

Zelda disconnected the call, and Josie gave in and wept. She wasn't certain how long she stayed in the little room and cried. Eventually, she returned to the area just outside her mother's room, put on the gown and gloves, went in, and walked over to her mother's bed.

Stone stared at her. He looked tremendously sad, and she could tell he knew that she'd been crying and that Zelda wasn't coming. Her father asked her if her sister was on the way. She relayed the conversation to the men then stepped closer to the bed.

Bending low, she said, "Mom, Zelda can't come to see you because she's so sick. I talked to her on the phone, and she asked me to tell you that she loved you and to give you a hug."

Before Stone or her father could stop her, Josie had her arms around her mother's shoulders. Her mother weakly lifted her arms and put them around Josie, who couldn't recall the last time the paranoid schizophrenic had held her in an embrace of any sort. Their cheeks touched. She whispered to her mother that she and Zelda loved her very much and to tell Calla Lily, Hedgehog, and the others who were good that she loved them, too. She felt her mother begin to shake.

At first, Josie thought the woman was crying, but it didn't take her long to figure out that tears had nothing to do with Rhonda Hollingsworth's movements. Hastily disengaging herself from their embrace, Josie said frantically, "Something's wrong!"

"She's convulsing," Stone said and reached for the button on the wall that would summon help. "You both need to go."

"No!" her father cried. "Rhonda, you can't go! I love you! Don't leave me! I can't be without you! We've been together forever!"

"You two have to leave now!" Stone ordered. When Josie insisted that they should stay, he repeated, "*Now!*"

Josie prepared to argue. Then she saw the blood dripping from the side of the bed closest to her, and her heart dropped into her stomach. Doctors and nurses rushed in, slipping into gowns and gloves as hurriedly as they could. She turned to her father, who gaped in disbelief at the sight of his wife and the blood.

"Josephine!" Stone growled. "Take your dad and get out of here *now*! I'll stay with her until the end."

Chapter Two

Josie pulled her father to the doorway, assisted him in removing his protective clothing, took off her own, hastily washed her hands, insisted that her father only wash his once, and then led him into the hallway. She was dizzy, and her skin felt clammy. Her father was talking, telling her they had to go back. She pulled him forward into the small, private waiting room and shut the door behind them before stumbling towards a chair. She couldn't get the image of the blood dripping from the edge of her mother's hospital bed out of her head. Everything began to go black. She heard her father call her name before she passed out.

"Josie, wake up!"

She opened her eyes and looked into her father's anxious face. Her right shoulder, hip, and arm hurt. So did the right side of her head. When Josie tried to rise, pain shot through all of the places that had merely been sore while she'd been lying still.

"You have to get off the floor!" Clark cried with obvious panic in his voice. "Think of all the germs! We're in a hospital! People track things in here all the time!"

"What happened?"

"You fainted and fell. I couldn't get to you in time to catch you. I'm sorry."

"It's okay, Dad. Would you help me up? How long was I out?"

"From the time you fainted? Not long. Sixty seconds?"

Clark struggled to aid her to first sit, then stand. She noted with concern that he was out of breath from these simple activities. Her head, shoulder, arm, and hip throbbed painfully, but she would live. Her mother would not. She felt a surge of grief and then one of relief. There would be no more suffering for Rhonda. The hallucinations would die with her.

When Josie tried to hug her father, he stepped back. Looking guilty and miserable, he said, "You touched Mom's cheek and head without protection. We can't hug until you've taken twelve showers. I have to take twelve, too. So does your husband. That's the only way we can be sure we're clean. As it is, I have to wash my hands twelve times after helping you up."

Frustrated by her father's mental illness and exhausted, she stood slightly hunched because of the pain in her body and simply nodded before saying, "Okay, Dad. Later, we'll hug."

Josie forced herself to straighten when Stone pushed open the door to the private room thirty minutes later.

He doesn't need to be worrying about me any more than he already does, she thought.

"Will Rhonda recover?" Clark asked hopefully. "May I take her home now?"

"She passed away a few minutes after you left the room. They tried to resuscitate her as you'd requested, but they couldn't. She was bleeding too much, and her heart wasn't strong enough to restart again like it did the first time. I'm sorry."

"Dad, she's not in pain anymore in her body or her mind," Josie said quietly. "She's free."

He didn't look at either of them. Instead, he stared at the floor for a few moments before saying, "I want to be free, too."

"Dad, if you'd try some new medications it might help."

"Or it might not help at all and cause terrible side effects as a lot of them did. No more meds. Your mother and I agreed on that when you and Zelda were younger and our regular meds stopped working for us. The medications were sucking our souls right out of our bodies." Rubbing at his temples, Clark muttered, "I was microwaving a frozen dinner when Mom collapsed. What if it caught fire and I didn't notice? What if the building burned down while we were gone and people died? I don't care if I die, but I don't want other people to die."

"No one is going to die in your building because of you."

"But what if they do?" he asked worriedly. "What if they already have? I have to be *sure* nothing I did will cause other people to die."

Knowing that continuing along this line of conversation would prove fruitless, Josie said, "Stone and I are staying at a hotel. Why don't you stay there with us tonight?"

"Hotels are full of germs. I need to go home. I have to make *sure* the building didn't burn down if our microwave caught on fire."

"But Dad –"

"Go to the hotel with your husband, Josie. You've done so much already. Your life for the last twenty years has been about taking care of us and trying to take care of yourself. Don't think I didn't know it. Don't think I didn't feel awful about it. Your mother and I couldn't help what we were or what we did. We couldn't stop ourselves. We never should have had children. It was wrong, and we knew it but wanted children so badly. It was selfish." After a brief pause, Clark asked, "What if my frozen dinner caught fire and everyone in the building died because of me? Maybe I should have checked before we left in the ambulance."

"Dad, you have to stop! You have twelve smoke detectors, and I know you change the batteries in them every month. They're fine. You check each one every day."

"But what if nobody heard them going off while we were gone? What if my frozen dinner caught on fire and our building burned down? Maybe I should have gone back to the microwave to check before we left. I'm not *sure* I didn't smell smoke."

"Dad, you know how OCD works," Josie said patiently, attempting to ignore her own exhaustion, grief, anxiety, and the pain that had resulted from her fall. "You get caught in a mental loop. You'll never be sure. You'll always doubt yourself. If you resolve one worry, then you'll focus on another. The cycle goes on and on because you can't take control of it without help."

"It's a terrible thing to have to live like this." His blue eyes filling with tears, Clark asked, "How will I live without Mom? And what about the smoke detectors? What if there was a fire?"

Josie said calmly but firmly, "We're not going to talk about smoke detectors or fire any more today. You're going to come back to the hotel with us for now."

"No. I have to go home. I want to be home with your mother's things. I need to be near them. You can't stay with me; there's no room. You stay at the hotel and get clean. I'll go home and get clean. Then we can talk." Looking at Josie, he continued, "Mom and I already have funeral plots. Our families bought them for us as a wedding gift. We thought that was pretty cold, but I guess I'm glad they did it now so that Mom doesn't have to be buried in a pauper's grave."

"Your families bought you burial plots as a wedding present?" Josie asked, stunned. "You never told me that."

"Mom and I never told you anything about who we really were," Clark admitted. "You and Zelda were better off not knowing how truly sick we were."

"Dad, Zelda and I knew from the time we were little."

"No, you didn't. God willing, you never will. I know you don't understand, and I'm glad of it." Shaking his head, he said, "I wish I could hug you. I'm going to walk home. I need to clear my head. Come to the apartment tonight at 7:00, and we'll talk. I'll get out the cemetery paperwork and put it on the table so that I don't forget. I always kept that and our wills in the refrigerator in case there was a fire and the smoke detectors didn't work. That way, the important papers wouldn't burn." Looking anxious, he asked, "What if there's a fire today after I take out the papers and they get burned up? Maybe I should leave them in the refrigerator."

"Yes, Dad. Leave them there. We'll take it all out tonight when we come over."

"I love you, Josie. You and Zelda are beautiful creatures with beautiful minds." Looking to Stone, he said, "You seem to be a good man and a good doctor. Protect my little girl and put her well-being before your own. Do what her mother and I couldn't."

"I intend to take care of Josie for the rest of my life and am thankful she feels the same way about me," Stone declared.

Clark turned to his daughter and said, "F. Scott Fitzgerald wrote, 'Reserving judgements is a matter of infinite hope.' You always had hope and never judged me or your mother, regardless of how terrible things were. Never let go of that hope. Promise me."

"I promise, Dad," Josie whispered, her vision clouded by tears. "I love you."

"And *I* love *you*, my brave girl," her father said before leaving the room.

Josie mutely walked with Stone to retrieve her purse and their coats, hats, scarves, gloves, and phones. As they left the Critical Care Unit, he instructed her not to put on any of her winter outerwear. They left the hospital and moved hurriedly through the freezing Virginia morning air to their waiting rental car.

When they stopped at a drugstore, Josie stayed in the car while Stone went in to purchase the necessary items. She fell asleep for a few minutes and woke feeling worse than before. The pain in her body was now being compounded by stiffness, and her head felt as if it might explode at any moment.

When they reached their hotel room, it was almost 10:00 a.m. Stone instructed Josie to remove her clothing, place it in a garbage bag, shower with the Hibiclens, rinse, wash with the antibacterial soap and the shampoo he'd purchased, and then dress in clean nightclothes he would put on the counter. Once she was finished in the bathroom, then he'd take his turn. He'd dispose of the garbage bag holding their clothing so that no one else would be exposed to the *C. diff* and possibly contract the bacteria.

Eventually, Josie stood alone in the hotel bathroom, staring at her reflection in the mirror. Her blonde hair hung in tangled waves around her face, which was ashen and puffy because of her exhaustion and tears. Her blue eyes seemed dull in the bright light emanating from the bathroom fixture. Clean underwear and a long, pink nightgown lay folded on the counter beside the sink.

I wonder what Zelda looks like right now, she thought. *Are her clothes as filthy as I imagine? Does she even have a nightgown, or is she sleeping in her regular clothing on the streets? Maybe she's living with someone or somehow has a place of her own.*

Josie knew there was no place. Zelda was on the run from her imagined government persecutors and from the extraterrestrials, one of whom had tricked her into having sex and conceiving an alien baby. She was now willing to sacrifice said baby for experimentation. If the delusions hadn't originated in her sister's mind, Josie would have thought them a good plot for a movie.

She unzipped her jeans and leaned forward to push them off her hips. Pain and vertigo were the results. She involuntarily cried out and reached forward to steady herself by placing a hand against one wall. She felt hot and cold simultaneously and heard the door to the bathroom quickly open.

"What the –?"

"I'm fine," Josie managed to say as she fought the rising bile in her throat. "Don't worry about me."

Stone came over to her and said, "I *am* worried. You look sick. Actually, you look sick and hurt. What's the matter?"

"It's nothing."

"If it was nothing, then you wouldn't be yelling and trying not to lose consciousness. You can't fool me. I'm a doctor and your husband, for God's sake! What's wrong?"

"I – I fell at the hospital."

"You did *what*?"

"I fainted in the little private room. Dad didn't have time to catch me."

"You mean he didn't catch you because he was afraid of the germs you might pass on to him after you hugged your mother," Stone said matter-of-factly. "How'd you land?"

"On my right side."

"If I put my arms around you will it hurt you?"

"Yes. I hit my shoulder, arm, hip, and head."

"Head? You hit your head?"

"Yes."

Sighing, Stone rested his hands on his hips and asked, "Did you lose consciousness?"

"I told you I fainted, remember?"

"Oh, for crying out loud! You could have a concussion!"

"I didn't throw up or feel like I wanted to pass out again once I came to," she countered. "Dad let it go."

"You're going to take medical advice from your father, the mentally ill English professor, over that of your husband, the doctor?"

"I'd just lost my Mom in a terrible way!" she cried, her anger and anguish directed squarely at him. "I'd just talked to my formerly normal sister who said she's giving up her alien baby for experimentation! I'd just hit my head! My Dad wouldn't even hug me or stop me from falling because he's so sick! Forgive me for not thinking straight!"

"You don't need my forgiveness," Stone said softly, but firmly. "None of this is your fault. Forgive yourself for not being able to fix things, Josie."

"I don't know if I can!"

"I'll help you with that. Will you let me give you a quick physical exam first?"

"Can't we just go straight to bed?"

"Unfortunately, no. Because of the *C. diff*, we have to be really careful and get completely clean. I'll help you to undress, and we'll shower and go to bed after we've eaten and you've taken some Advil."

"Stone, please."

"This is nonnegotiable. I'm worried about you, and don't tell me not to worry. This kind of worry is natural. If I even *suspect* after I examine you that there's a problem, then we're returning to the hospital. I'm not going to take any chances on losing you, Josephine."

"Why do you love me?" she asked suddenly. "*How* can you love me?"

"'Beautiful creature with a beautiful mind.' Your dad was spot on about that. The one thing he left out was 'beautiful heart.' The moment I met you I knew I'd found the woman I was meant to love. You're so pure of heart and soul. You…restored me simply by being you."

Deeply touched by his words, Josie stood complacent as Stone unbuttoned her shirt, which happened to be *his* flannel shirt that she'd put on the previous morning.

When the front of the shirt had been unbuttoned, Stone eased it over her shoulders and slid it down her arms. Once he'd placed it into the garbage bag, he went behind her and unfastened her bra before moving to her right side and gently probing her shoulder and arm. She gritted her teeth against the discomfort, as he rotated, extended, and prodded the injured appendage in varying ways.

"Nothing appears to be broken, but you'll be sore and stiff for a while and will have some nasty bruises." Moving to examine her head, Stone lightly ran his fingers over the knot that Josie hadn't realized was there, muttering, "Let me get my pen light."

After seating her on the toilet lid, he left the bathroom in order to retrieve a small penlight from his suitcase. When he returned, he knelt in front of her and made her stare straight ahead as he checked her pupils. She was asked to follow the light and then to tell him how many fingers he was holding up as she closed one eye at a time. He seemed satisfied but announced that he reserved the right to change his mind about taking her back to the hospital for an MRI.

After slipping off her shoes and socks, Stone helped Josie to stand and pulled down her jeans and underwear. He frowned as he examined her hip. She winced at the pain resulting from his touch.

"It's a good thing you're twenty-five and like milk," he muttered. "If you were old or calcium-deficient, then you might have broken your hip. You have a huge bruise on your hipbone."

"I'm feeling really shaky and nauseated," she confided. "Can we wash and go to bed now?"

Stone quickly stripped off his clothing, put it in the bag, and then turned on the shower. Josie watched his muscles ripple under his skin as he twisted the levers and adjusted the water temperature. She reflected that his powerful but lean body was like a piece of art. Even in her present state, Josie was aroused. Stone looked quizzically at her and asked why she was smiling.

"Because even in the most abnormal of circumstances, I'm feeling something normal. That makes me happy."

"What are you feeling?"

"Desire for you."

He smiled tiredly and guided her into the shower then gathered the Hibiclens, antibacterial soap, and shampoo. Deftly utilizing all three until they were both as clean as they could be, he then lathered his hands one more time and slowly slid them over Josie's wet, naked skin, being mindful of her sore head, shoulder, arm, and hip. Although she continued to feel weak and drained, Josie began to relax and said she was ready to rinse off.

Stone toweled both of them dry before helping Josie to don her nightgown. He left her underwear on the counter and went to put on pajama bottoms and a t-shirt. Coming back to the bathroom, he picked up the clean underwear, took Josie's hand, and drew her towards the king-sized bed. Once she was seated, he returned the underwear to her suitcase then handed her a Room Service menu.

"I can't eat."

"You have to eat and then take some Advil. What do you want?"

She finally agreed to eat a waffle. Stone ordered a breakfast meal and ate the remaining waffle, yogurt, and fruit that Josie refused. After she'd swallowed the ibuprofen, he insisted that she sit up for thirty minutes before lying back on the bed. *She* insisted that he hold her while they waited for the appointed time.

"Is there anyone you want to call?" he asked while they waited.

"Your parents and grandmother."

"I called Daddy while I was picking up the supplies we needed at Walgreens. He wanted to get on a plane and come up here today, but I told him I didn't know what was going to happen and what you'd want."

"I don't know either. That was sweet of him though."

"I'm sure Mama and Memaw will have the same reaction once he tells them. All you have to do is say the word."

"What about Flynn?"

"I left a voicemail on his cell. He was probably with patients. He'll call when he can. I doubt if he'll be able to leave the practice, even for a day or two."

"I don't want him to feel obligated. Your family either. I just figured they should know."

"It's not a matter of obligation. It's a matter of love. You're part of the Romero family. That group includes Flynn by default. Everyone will be sad for you, including Tommy, of course. The two of you really bonded while we were there for the Christmas holiday. The only person who won't give a damn is Cheek, because he doesn't care about anyone except himself."

"Do you think he loves his son?"

"I really can't say what he feels about Tommy. At least the rest of us love him."

"Can I lie back now?"

"I guess it's been long enough."

"Stone?"

"Hm?"

"What am I going to do with Dad?"

"We'll figure that out later. Rest now."

She slept soundly and woke at 6:00 p.m. Stone slept beside her. She knew they would have to rise and get ready soon if they were going to go to her parents' apartment to meet with her father in an hour. Still, Josie hated to wake Stone, who looked so peaceful as he slept. She decided to use the bathroom first. That proved to be impossible, as her right side was so stiff that she couldn't turn and sit up. She tried several times before admitting defeat and taking Stone's right hand in her left, squeezing lightly.

He woke and yawned before asking her what time it was. She told him then explained her predicament. He was instantly wide awake and helped her to the bathroom then gathered their clothing so that they could dress and go to her parents' place. They reasoned they could take her father out for dinner then discuss the funeral plans for her mother along with her father's plans for his future.

They arrived at the shabby apartment complex at 6:55. The curtains of the Hollingsworths' unit were drawn, which was not unusual. Josie knew that her mother always kept them closed because of her paranoia. However, there didn't seem to be any lights on inside. Perhaps her father was still asleep. She knocked several times, but no one came to the door.

"I have a copy of their key," she told Stone. "Maybe he decided to be safe and take one more shower."

When the door was unlocked, Stone turned the knob and prepared to walk in. Josie stopped him and informed him that it wasn't safe. When he asked her what she meant, she remarked that he would soon see for himself and flicked on the wall switch. The living room was instantly illuminated.

"Holy crap!" he exclaimed when he viewed the mountains of papers, books, and junk. "Is it all like this?" When she nodded, he shook his head in disbelief and asked, "How do they exist in this environment?"

"I don't know. I couldn't. It's only gotten this bad in the last few years because Zelda and I started paying their rent each month and they weren't evicted all the time like before. Unfortunately, that meant that all of their stuff didn't get left behind with each move. It kept growing. They collected all sorts of items, from books to newspapers to broken chairs or other usable junk they'd find or that people gave them."

"And your dad's worried about things being clean? There's no way anyone could clean this place. It's a hoarder's paradise! If there was a fire, this apartment would be a death trap."

"Don't let him hear you say that. He's already fixated on the smoke detectors and fire enough, thank you very much. He used to call constantly when Zelda and I first moved out, because he was so afraid and wasn't sure about anything he did being exactly right. We'd talk to him for a while, and he'd tell us he was sorry for calling and bothering us and that he knew his worries were irrational. He'd swear he wouldn't call again anytime soon. Sixty seconds after we'd hang up, he'd call back with the same anxiety issues. Sometimes that would go on for hours. I guess that was when I really started dreading the calls. Eventually, he placated himself by calling each hour from 7:00 a.m. to 7:00 p.m. At least he stopped phoning us every few minutes. I was greatly relieved, and so was Zelda."

Josie walked into the living room via the narrow pathway her parents had left so that they could navigate the space. Since both of them had gotten heavier in the past year, she wondered how they'd moved around in such close confines. The mounds of stuff were taller than she was in various areas of the living room.

She followed the path to the two recliners and television, but her father wasn't sitting in his usual chair. Weaving her way to the kitchen, Josie turned on the light and stared at the junk along the floors and counters. There were no dirty dishes, but then she hadn't expected to find any. Everything was "clean" yet coated in dust. Because of her father's fear of germs, she knew that her parents only used paper plates, bowls, and napkins as well as plastic forks and spoons. They drank from Styrofoam cups. Everything was used only once then thrown away. It was wasteful, but it was also the only way Clark Hollingsworth could cope with that particular aspect of his mental illness.

"How many bedrooms are in this apartment?" Stone asked from behind her.

"One bedroom and one bathroom."

"You stay here, and I'll check those rooms out."

Josie could hear the strain in his voice and turned painfully to look at him. The Advil she'd taken after eating the waffle had long since worn off, and she was waiting until after dinner to take more. The discomfort in her right side was suddenly compounded by an icy sensation spreading out from the pit of her stomach.

"Don't touch anything," Stone directed. "Your mom had the *C. diff* before she was brought to the hospital. Right now, you've only touched light switches, and we've both touched the doorknob at the front. That's plenty. We'll wash our hands with soap and water when we leave." Glancing around, he muttered, "A controlled burn wouldn't be a bad idea for this place."

"Don't joke about that."

"I'm not."

"So, should I stand in the kitchen and wait for you or should I go to the living room and stand there?" she asked hotly.

"Here's fine," he said without a trace of sarcasm in his voice. "I'm sure I won't be long."

Fighting the urge to begin straightening and throwing things away, Josie stood in the center of the kitchen, closed her eyes, and began to count the seconds. It was a self-soothing mechanism she only used when she was at her parents' place. She'd taught herself how to do this when she'd been a child and her parents had slipped into complete mental instability. When she'd felt as though she couldn't take their behavior any longer, Josie would begin to quietly count until things got better. The highest number she'd ever reached during one of these episodes was one thousand. She was good at adapting to her circumstances.

"One thousand one, Mississippi. One thousand two, Mississippi…."

Stone interrupted by saying her name. Without opening her eyes, Josie asked him if he'd found her father in the bedroom or the bathroom. She already knew that he was dead. She could tell by the way Stone had spoken her name.

"Your dad's in the bedroom."

"How long has he been dead?"

"Josie –"

"How long?!?" she demanded angrily as her eyes flew open. "And did he die of a broken heart like Flynn's mother or was this some freaky coincidence?"

"I don't know why he died. It looks like he's been gone for several hours. I've already called 911. A medical examiner will have to determine the cause of death. I don't see any overt signs of foul play or suicide, but I can't tell from a cursory exam."

"I want to see my father before the paramedics get here."

Stone's expression hardened, as he said, "Absolutely not."

"You can't stop me!"

"The hell I can't! You've already watched your mom dying today, and now you want to see your dad's body?"

"Yes!"

"No."

Josie intended to hustle around Stone before he could block her. However, her injured hip proved to be an unanticipated hindrance, and she wasn't fast enough to hastily pass by. He hooked one arm around her waist, pulling her close to him. She yelled and fought despite her injuries. He tightened his hold on her, and she fought harder.

"Let me go! I want to see my father! I have to see him!"

"No, you don't."

"I do!" she insisted. "I *have* to!"

"Why? What purpose will it serve?"

Josie was wearing herself out, which she deduced had been Stone's intended goal. Regardless, she kept fighting until she heard the sirens. As they drew nearer, she slumped against Stone. He suggested they wait outside for the authorities, and she agreed. As they walked towards the front door, she pivoted and darted for the bedroom, careening through the maze of books, bric-a-brac, and clothing that littered the short hallway.

Before Stone could stop her, Josie was inside the room and had closed and locked the door behind her. She could hear Stone calling out to her from the other side. She ignored his pleas for her to let him in and turned to look at her father.

Chapter Three

Josie had expected to find Clark in bed. Therefore, she was surprised to see him seated at his desk. He was slumped forward in his chair, an open book positioned under a small reading lamp. She edged closer, using one of the pathways in the cluttered room. Lifting the cover of the book so that she could read the title, she saw that it was F. Scott Fitzgerald's *The Beautiful and Damned.*

Scanning her surroundings, Josie saw only books, books, and more books. Her parents' brilliant minds had been trapped in such distorted realities. All of that intellect had been lost in a sea of mental confusion. Their goodness had been constrained by their inner demons. Her mother had forgotten how to *feel*, and her father had been afraid to. He hadn't even been able to give his daughter one last hug because of his all-consuming fears.

"At least you're at peace now, too," Josie said to her father's body. "And you and Mom are together again." Cocking her head, she told him, "I'm glad your suffering is finally over and wish Zelda's could end, too."

Someone was pounding on the door, and it wasn't Stone. Assuming that the police had arrived, Josie took one last look at her father, Dr. Clark Hollingsworth. For an instant, she saw him as he'd been during the early years of her life – brimming with wit and love. He'd been a wonderful man, just like her mother had been a wonderful woman. That couple had left her life two decades earlier. She wished more than anything they'd elected to fight in an attempt to stay.

Stone's strong arms were suddenly around Josie, although he was careful not to put pressure on her sore shoulder and arm. Josie hadn't even heard the sound of the door being opened and wondered if the lock had been picked or if the police had forced their way inside the bedroom. Someone was asking her if she was all right. She didn't answer.

An older policeman escorted Stone and her through the apartment and out of the front door. Neighbors were loitering, drawn in by the police cars, ambulance, and a van Josie decided must belong to the Medical Examiner. A young woman was waiting, holding something in each hand, beside the van. When they approached, she instructed them to stretch out their arms and turn their palms up. Then she poured something clear into their hands. Josie stood mutely, as Stone cleaned her hands thoroughly and washed his own.

"Did you touch your hands to your face or neck?" Stone asked. "If so, then we'd need to clean those areas, too."

"No. All I touched was the book Dad was reading when he died."

The woman who'd offered them the soap held out a bottle of water, and Josie stared at it. Stone thanked the stranger, took the bottle, and unscrewed the top before holding it out to his wife. She didn't take it. He drank a few swallows and then placed the bottle in her left hand. She automatically gripped it then brought the opening to her lips. She supposed she sipped some water, because Stone allowed her to pass the bottle back to him.

Two policemen came over to take statements, but Josie had nothing to say. The woman who'd offered them the soap and the bottle of water led Josie to a police car and opened the door before helping her sit sideways in the backseat. The door remained open, and Josie leaned her left side against the seat, resting her cheek against the leather. Her feet touched the pavement. She gazed at the wheel of another police car and wondered if she should call her sister to let her know that their father was now dead, too.

Zelda will really think it's a conspiracy against our family if I do that, she thought. *She'll remind me that Stone could be an alien in disguise who's tricked me into having sex with him so that he could impregnate me. Thank God I won't be having any babies. No more of this. The family insanity ends with me and Zelda.*

She spotted Stone out of the corner of her eye and turned her attention towards him. He appeared in control, focused, and very serious as he spoke to the police and the medical personnel. Josie felt guilty since she was currently incapable of talking to them and answering their questions. It was *her* family tragedy, not his.

A man and a woman joined the others to whom Stone spoke. They both wore jackets and hats that identified them as members of the Federal Bureau of Investigation. Stone shook hands with each of them, and a brief discussion followed. At one point, Stone jerked his head back as if he'd been punched. He darted a glance at Josie, and she saw the shock reflected in his brown eyes. He said something to the two agents. They paused then nodded.

Stone walked slowly over to the police car where Josie waited. He crouched in front of her, resting his hands on her knees before saying, "We can't do any more here. We need to get something to eat."

"I'm not hungry. Why is the FBI here?"

"We'll talk about it after we eat. They have some questions for you."

"For me? Why? Was my mother right? Was the government conspiring against our family? Two looney parents and their looney kids are big threats to national security."

"In the first place, *you* are not looney. In the second place, the government is not out to get your family."

"So, why are they here?"

"After you eat and take some more Advil."

"No."

"Fine. You don't have to eat or take the anti-inflammatory pills. *I*, on the other hand, *do* need to eat and take my blood pressure meds. Today's been a little stressful for me, too."

Josie immediately felt guilt and reached out to cup his cheek with her left palm before saying, "I'm so sorry for this. You deserve better."

"*You* deserve better. *I* am blessed to have you as my wife. Will you please start thinking about yourself for a change? What do you need? What do you want?"

"There is no me." Gesturing towards the chaotic scene around them, she added, "There's only this."

"You're wrong, and I'll be damned if I let you go on believing that without challenging it."

"I'm too worn down to fight you."

"Excellent. So, keep trusting me and loving me. Do *not* go anywhere."

Refusing to comment on his last statement, she asked pointedly, "Did my mother or sister do anything that would draw the attention of the FBI? Is that why they're here?

He licked his lips and said, "They're here because both your mother and Zelda wrote threatening letters to the President."

"And they decide on the night of Mom's death to investigate?"

He shook his head, speared his brown hair with one hand, and then admitted, "There was an incident at the White House this morning. We didn't hear about it because we were at the hospital, at the hotel, and here. We haven't watched the news."

"An incident," she repeated, her mouth suddenly dry and her voice barely audible.

Stone hesitated then said, "A woman walked along the street towards the White House, placed a cardboard box on the ground, and began yelling that the President was allowing aliens to mate with humans so that a hybrid race could evolve. She said she had proof. When Security approached, she pulled out a gun, fired at one of the team, and hit a passerby in the arm with the bullet. Innocent people were all around where she was standing. She aimed again and was shot and killed by Secret Service agents."

"It was *not* Zelda," Josie said adamantly. "She didn't even know how to shoot a gun!"

"She obviously learned. She had a letter in her coat outlining what she planned to do. She said she knew it would get her killed but that it would be worth it. She signed her name, documented where she'd been living on the streets, and asked that you and your parents be notified so that you'd know about her noble sacrifice and the good that would come of it. She listed this address." Dropping his eyes to her knees, he added, "Since you seem to want to hear it all right now, I'll tell you the rest. There was a newborn in the cardboard box. When Zelda's body was examined it was determined that she'd recently given birth. Part of the umbilical cord was still attached to the baby boy. Several of the homeless people in the area where Zelda lived said she was always on the streets and often had sex with homeless men. They had no idea which one could be the father. The baby's in State custody at the moment. The FBI team wants to talk with you about what Zelda did so they can see if you're a threat, and the social workers want to know if you intend to take custody of the baby."

Josie's eyes widened, and she began to shake. Her mother, father, and Zelda were all dead, wiped out in one day's time in three very different ways. Her sister *had* given birth to a baby, although he was not half-alien as she'd believed. In Josie's mind it was just as bad since the odds were that her nephew's father was also mentally ill. A newborn baby with two mentally ill parents and at least one set of mentally ill grandparents would most likely be genetically doomed to be mentally ill himself, or so Josie supposed. She wondered why God had allowed the baby to be conceived and to survive what had probably been an unassisted birth in some dirty back alley in the freezing cold. She visualized the boy as a blonde-haired, blue-eyed young man talking to his hallucinations and telling anyone who would listen how the government had conspired to kill his mother and grandparents.

"Josephine!"

She blinked rapidly and looked into Stone's eyes. He seemed frantic, and she idly wondered why. It was only then that she realized how hard she was shaking. As he stood then bent awkwardly to embrace her, she choked out, "I can't take the baby! I know it's terrible of me, but I can't! He'll be like my parents and sister, and I can't do it anymore! I'll kill myself first!"

"You'll do no such thing," Stone said patiently but firmly. "You're hurt, exhausted, grief-stricken, and overwhelmed. You need food, medication, and a respite from all the trauma of the last twenty years and the last twenty-four hours. I'm going to make sure you get all that and more. You're everything to me."

"I can't take the baby, but I know I should. He's my sister's child!"

"If you take him in because he's your nephew and kill yourself because he turns out to be mentally unstable, then you definitely won't be helping him. Plus, if you kill yourself, then it will kill me. We are *not* going to take the baby. I feel terrible about it, but it would be irrevocably damaging to you and, therefore, to me. Call it self-preservation or being selfish. We just can't do it." As she continued to shake, he went on, "I'm going to get the medical people to give you a sedative before I bring you back to the hotel. You're going to sleep while I talk to the FBI. I'll examine the baby soon just to check him out and see what his condition is."

"I – I should go with you!" she stammered. "He's Zelda's baby!"

"That's precisely why you shouldn't go with me. If you see him, then you'll want to try to keep him. We can't, Josie. We'll tell the child welfare people about his background and then you can sign away your rights to him."

"You don't care about what will happen to him! He's not your flesh and blood!"

"I care. I care about you more. If you truly don't want to end up crazy, then you can't take your sister's baby. Every time he does something – *anything* – you'll be looking for signs of mental illness. He might be perfectly normal, but the uncertainty will drive you to a nervous collapse. I'll do whatever it takes to prevent that. Got it?"

"Help me," she pleaded with what little energy she had left.

"God knows I'm trying. Let me."

Josie let him. She was given a sedative and some other medication. Only once the sedative had started to take effect did Stone allow her to be introduced to the two FBI agents, who were kind and appeared sympathetic. They agreed to wait to interview Josie until she was feeling better but informed her that they wouldn't leave her unsupervised until then due to her mother and sister's threats against the President. The agents escorted Josie and Stone to the rental car, and she lost consciousness on their way back to the hotel.

Josie woke in her nightgown under the covers of the king-size bed. Her head didn't hurt anymore, but her injured shoulder was so stiff that she couldn't move it at all. She was grateful that her arm didn't pain her as badly and that she was able to shift on the mattress without adding to the ache in her right hip.

"Can I get you something?"

Josie turned her head towards the chair next to the bed. The female FBI agent occupied it, her feet resting on the ottoman. She'd been reading something on an iPad, but Josie couldn't see what it was from her position. What she *could* see was that the woman appeared to be in her mid-thirties, had brown hair and brown eyes, and was in excellent physical shape.

"I need the bathroom and some Advil," Josie answered. "Where's my husband?"

"With Agent Saghir at the hospital. He's examining your sister's baby. He's given us a pretty thorough explanation of your background and of recent events so that you wouldn't have to do it once you woke up."

"What time is it?"

"A little after 8:30 a.m."

"Has Stone had any sleep?"

"No."

"Has he eaten?"

"Yes. He told me to reassure you that he'd taken his medication. He said you worry about him, but you don't want him to worry about you. That's not exactly fair."

Josie wondered if she should be offended by the woman's candor, but she wasn't. The agent was right and had offered her opinion in a genial tone that bore no trace of reprimand. She was simply stating a fact.

"You know everything about me, I'm sure. What about you? What's your name? If you told me earlier, then I don't remember. I was kind of out of it."

"Agent Myra Katavich. And no, we don't know everything about you, although we do know an awful lot. We'll know the rest soon."

"What does that mean?"

"Two members of your family threatened national security. Our people will be pretty thorough when it comes to making certain you're not a threat as well. By tonight, your entire family history will be in a report. Your husband was extremely helpful in speeding up our legwork. He said you had nothing to hide and neither did he."

"You're investigating him, too?"

"Naturally. He's married to you. If he were a subversive, we'd need to be aware of it. Subversives aren't usually so cooperative. It's a big plus in our book."

"Will your agency go through my parents' things?"

"Yes."

"Will you dispose of what you don't need once you're done?"

"There's nothing you want to keep?"

"The important papers my father stored in the refrigerator. Any other important legal documents you find. Everything else can go. It means nothing to me. All I need is the picture I already have that was taken of my family right before my parents lost their minds when my sister and I were small. That's the way I want to think of my family."

"Your husband told us you brought the photo with you. He gave it to us so that we could make a copy for the file. We'll have it back to you by this evening."

"Can I ask for a favor?"

"You can ask. I don't know if I'll be able to deliver."

"Would I be able to read the report?"

"Doubtful. Why would you want to?" When Josie turned her head away, the woman said, "We might be able to give you a verbal summary of our findings. Would that suffice?"

"I suppose. I'd appreciate it."

The agent waited outside the door for the sixty seconds Josie was inside the bathroom then helped her back to bed before insisting that she order something from Room Service, eat, and take some ibuprofen.

"Did Stone tell you to say that?"

Katavich grinned and said, "Well, he is a doctor and was extremely insistent."

And extremely handsome, Josie thought. *If I don't pay attention, some other woman will take him from me. I can't let that happen.*

As if she'd been reading Josie's thoughts, Katavich said, "It's obvious that Dr. Romero is devoted to you. If you left him or died, then he'd probably die of a broken heart. It happens."

"So I've heard," Josie remarked, thinking of Flynn Carmody's mother. "I wonder if my father died of a broken heart yesterday or if he killed himself."

"We'll have to wait on the M.E.'s report for an answer to that. It'll be rushed because of the situation involving your mother and sister. We'll tell you the truth if you want to hear it."

"I have nothing else when it comes to my parents and sister, so I might as well have the truth."

"Even if it hurts?"

"I always hurt when I think of them. At least if I know the truth some of the hurt will make sense."

Josie ate, took the Advil, and was soon sleeping once more. Then she was dreaming of the Renaissance festival she'd attended in college. She was dancing, happy, and totally free. She never wanted to stop dancing. It felt so good. There was no fear, no sadness, and no dread. There was only pure joy.

When Josie began to wake, she fought hard against it. She didn't want to return to her present where death, madness, and despair surrounded her. If it hadn't been for Stone, she knew she would've killed herself the previous night. He was the only reason she had to live. He'd said he would die without her, and she believed him. She still didn't understand why he loved her, but he kept insisting that he did. Perhaps he was only saying this to keep her going and would divorce her after she'd had time to regain her emotional footing.

"How can you even think that?"

Josie opened her eyes and stared up at her husband, who was seated next to her on the bed. He looked worn out, worried, and baffled. She must have been mumbling to herself as she'd waked and felt heaviness settle in her chest. Josie had obviously wounded him with her words although she didn't know why.

"I'm not taking what you said as an attack on me," Stone explained when she asked him. "I'm taking it as an attack on you. That hurts worse. You're an innocent."

Tears pricked her eyes as she side-stepped the topic by asking, "How is Zelda's baby?"

"We're not done talking about you."

"We are for now," she said resolutely. "How is the baby?"

Running his fingers through his hair, he replied, "Not good. Something is severely wrong with him although it's too soon for an exact diagnosis. It could be some trauma caused during birth since we have no idea what occurred during labor and delivery. Your sister could have used illegal drugs throughout her pregnancy. The baby could be –"

"Mentally ill?"

"He's a newborn. A diagnosis of mental illness would be quite a ways away."

"What's wrong with him that makes you say that his condition is bad?"

"He didn't respond appropriately to the tests we perform in order to see if a newborn is normal and healthy. He cried the entire time I was there, which was over an hour. The neonatologist said he'd been crying continually, only taking a few naps in the twenty hours he'd been in the hospital's care. It didn't look like he was going to stop crying anytime soon. It was hard to watch him in such great distress."

"Why didn't they give him something to help him rest?"

"By the time I saw him, they'd already tried two different medications. They'll keep trying until they find one that works effectively and safely, but it's tricky because of his age and his mother's condition."

"Was he a preemie?"

"What? No. He was full-term. Why?"

"Because Zelda became schizophrenic last summer. It's February. I last saw her in June."

"She would've been early into the pregnancy. She might not have known."

"Could getting pregnant have triggered her schizophrenia?"

"No one knows what triggers schizophrenia, but the body does go through a lot of changes during pregnancy. I personally don't think the trigger in this case is as important as the result. Zelda became schizophrenic and was pregnant. Her baby is…well, he's a mess. I hope something can be done to help him."

"I should take him," Josie said weakly. "I should at least try."

"No, you shouldn't. We can't be the ones to try to help him."

"He's suffering. I'm his aunt. Why can't we try?"

"Because I have a feeling that he's beyond help, and I pity him and those who'll have to care for him. Stop trying to save everyone and save yourself."

"What if I don't want to be saved?"

"You want it as much as I do or else you'd already have committed suicide."

Her curiosity piqued, she asked, "Did *you* ever consider suicide after Nelson died?"

"No. I knew how much it devastated me, our parents, Memaw, Chas, and Tommy when Nelson jumped off that bridge. I could never do that to someone who loved me. So, I just turned off my ability to feel deeply after his funeral. I didn't really feel again until the morning I met you."

There was a knock on the door of the hotel room. Stone went to answer it. Josie noted he was in his pajama bottoms and a t-shirt and glanced at the clock. It was 6:14 a.m.

"Hey, Daddy," Stone said, as he opened the door. "It's good that you came. We need you."

Chapter Four

"Vin? Why are you here?" Josie asked nervously. "I'm so relieved to see you, but won't you get in trouble?"

He smiled at her and said, "Dumpling and Memaw know where I am."

"That's not what I mean. You're a sheriff. My sister...my mother...the FBI...."

"What happened with your mother and sister isn't going to reflect on me," he assured her. "Even if it did, I wouldn't care. Stone's my son, and you're his wife. That makes you my daughter-in-law, and I take my responsibility to you just as seriously as if you were my own daughter. People are always more important than money, titles, or what others think. The ones we love are more important than what *we* think. It took Nelson's death to make me realize that, although I still don't approve of the lifestyle he led." He shot his son a warning look and ordered, "No arguing about it today. I'm an ass-backwards fool who's slow to change. That doesn't mean your Mama and I didn't love Nelson as much as we love you." Looking back to Josie, he said, "I'm real sorry about all this. Memaw and Dumpling wanted to come, but Memaw tripped and fell yesterday and hurt her hip. Flynn says she'll be fine, but she needs to stay put. Dumpling's taking care of her." Clasping her left hand gently between both of his, he asked, "How's *your* hip? Stone said you fainted at the hospital and fell on your right side."

"My hip hurts but not as much as my shoulder. I guess I hit that first when I fell. My head and arm are better."

Directing his attention back towards his son, Vin asked, "What time are you two meeting with the FBI agents?"

"8:00."

"We are?" Josie asked, perplexed.

"You slept all day yesterday and last night. I slept from about 10:00 p.m. until you woke me a few minutes ago when you were talking in your sleep. When Agents Saghir and Katavich left last night, they said they'd be back here at 8:00 this morning. I was

179

going to wake you at 6:30 so that we could shower and eat before they returned."

"So they don't consider me a threat to national security?"

"No, but they do want to talk to you. Katavich said something about giving you a verbal report and wrapping things up for now."

"I want your father to stay if they'll let him."

"I've worked with the FBI a few times," Vin informed them. "Even small-town sheriff's join forces with the Bureau now and again. I'm sure they already know I'm your father-in-law. They should be fine with me staying if that's what you want."

Josie nodded then asked the two men to help her sit up so that she could go shower. Vin left in order to check into the hotel but promised to return before 8:00.

As Stone helped Josie to wash her body and hair, he said, "I talked to Flynn last night. He sends you his best and said he wishes he could do more for you."

"Flynn's very sweet. Does he have a girlfriend?"

"He dates, but he's never been serious about anyone in Clayville. There was a girl in medical school I think he loved, but she had no desire to move to a hick town. Flynn wanted to change the face of Clayville and make a difference. She wanted to make a difference in a big city like New York. They broke up before graduation."

"That's too bad."

"Yes, it is." As Stone toweled them both dry, he asked, "What do you want for breakfast?"

"A piece of toast."

"You have to eat more than that. It's not healthy for you to eat so little."

"A piece of toast and some jelly?"

At Stone's insistence, Josie ate toast with jelly, plus a strip of bacon and two eggs. He ate a veggie omelet and a bagel. Once they'd finished their orange juice, Stone handed her some Advil and a glass of water. She hoped that the ibuprofen would take effect quickly since her shoulder was throbbing and stiff.

Stone's father returned to their room at 7:50. He'd barely had time to sit in the chair closest to the bed before someone rapped on the door. Josie was not surprised when Stone ushered Agents Saghir and Katavich into the room. What *did* surprise her was how shaken they looked. Myra Katavich appeared to be wound so tightly that she might explode at any moment. Agent Andrew Saghir, whom Josie had only met briefly after she'd been given the sedative, had the dark skin of a Middle Easterner but somehow seemed pale.

"We have a couple of agents outside," the man remarked tightly. "It's not because we consider any of you to be threats. It's for your own protection if need be."

"Protection from what?" Josie asked in confusion.

The two agents looked at one another then to Vin Romero, who stood. He reached out his hand and introduced himself, and they didn't hesitate to return the greeting. They acknowledged they already knew who he was and that nothing that had happened with Josie's mother and sister would reflect poorly on anyone present.

"Perhaps it would be better if we spoke to you alone," Agent Katavich suggested to Josie. "Your husband and father-in-law could wait in your father-in-law's room."

"Why would it be better?"

Both the man and woman seemed to be extremely uncomfortable, and Saghir remarked, "There may be unsettling details about your family's past and their recent activities that you might not want your husband or father-in-law to hear."

"If the details are that unsettling, then I'll need both of them here to offer me their support."

Katavich conceded that this was true. She asked Josie, Stone, and Vin to sit at the foot of the bed, while she and Saghir each got a chair from the little table at the end of the room. They brought them over and set them in front of where the others waited.

Josie's anxiety level was rising with every passing second. She had a very bad feeling about the conversation that was about to take place. Stone held her left hand, while Vin held her right.

"How much do you know about your parents' lives before you were born?" asked Katavich.

"My parents were both from Virginia. They were the same age. He got his Ph.D. in English, and she got her Ph.D. in Psychology. My father manifested signs of mental illness early on, and his family got him help. He did well until he was in his mid-thirties when he had to be institutionalized. Mom was schizophrenic and had already ended up in the same mental health facility. They got treatment, got better, got out, got married, and had Zelda and me. Mom got off her meds both times she was pregnant, but Dad made her get back on after we were born. They were loving, brilliant, and normal until I was five. After that, our lives were hell."

"We understand that no other relatives were involved in your lives. Do you know why?"

"Zelda and I figured they couldn't take dealing with our parents' mental illness issues and stayed away. We hated that we never knew our grandparents or anyone else on either side of the family, but Zelda and I accepted it."

"You didn't think that was odd?" inquired Katavich. "One would imagine other relatives would remove you from the home."

"Everything about our lives was odd. Living with those who are severely mentally ill is indescribable. We dealt with it as best we could. We were children."

"You were in several foster homes over the years,"Katavich continued. "Were you or your sister ever molested?"

"What does that have to do with anything?" Stone asked tersely.

"Zelda Hollingsworth was killed yesterday because of what she did near the White House and because of what led her there. This is one thing of which we have no knowledge. Our profilers want to know, so Agent Saghir and I agreed to ask. Mrs. Romero, were you or your sister molested?"

"You want me to leave, Josie?" Vin asked solemnly. "I will if you want. No hard feelings."

"N-no," she stammered. "Please, don't leave."

"I won't. I just wanted to make sure it was what you wanted."

Josie squeezed Stone's hand as hard as she could and admitted, "A neighbor molested me when I was six. He was an old man, and he kissed me on the mouth and then asked me to go into his apartment with him. But I didn't. Zelda and I were living with our parents then, though, not in a foster home."

"Did your parents press charges?"

"No. They were afraid the authorities would take us away from them. They…they didn't protect me."

"And your sister?"

"Started having sex when she was fourteen with one of the boys in a foster home who wanted to have sex with me. I was twelve. She slept with him so he'd leave me alone. She got pregnant, and

182

the woman in charge of the home brought her to have an abortion. She had another one when she was in her twenties."

"Did your sister blame the government for what happened to the two of you?" asked Saghir.

"The government, our parents, and everyone else but me."

"And she only became schizophrenic this past summer?"

"Yes. She started talking crazy like our mother but never tried to hurt anyone like Mom did."

"We were informed that your mother periodically tried to kill herself or you, your sister, or your father," commented Katavich. "Is that true?"

"Yes. Her hallucinations often told her to do bad things."

"Did you know that your mother and sister were writing letters to the President that contained threatening sentiments?"

"No, but I'm not shocked by that. They were paranoid schizophrenics."

"Did you know that your father was writing a book about how much better off our country would be if the Presidency was eliminated from the United States government?"

Stunned, Josie said, "No. Do you have the manuscript?"

Saghir confirmed that they did and that they'd retrieved it from her parents' apartment.

"I don't share any of my family's beliefs regarding the government, if that's what you're after. I'm proud to be an American and vote in every major election. As a matter of fact, I voted for the current President."

"Yes, we know," Katavich said with a slight smile. "We also know that you and your sister both graduated with honors from college and that your sister did the same when she got her master's degree. Why didn't you go on to graduate school? You were certainly bright enough."

"Just because one is bright enough doesn't mean one has to get an advanced degree. I loved being a realtor, and I was extremely good at it. I didn't need an advanced degree to do that."

"Why'd you quit?"

"My family. I couldn't take it anymore. My past caught up to me, and I realized I hadn't truly been happy since I was five. I really had no plans for the future. I just knew I couldn't go on the way things were."

Pulling the photo of the Hollingsworths from her jacket pocket, Katavich said tensely, "We wanted to return this to you. We…need to talk about it."

"The picture?"

"No. The subjects in the picture. You, your sister, and your parents."

"What about us?"

Saghir cleared his throat and asked, "Do you know anything about your parents' families?"

"They never talked about their relatives. They said we didn't need to hear about people who cared nothing for us."

"Your parents were the same age."

"Yes."

Pointing to the picture, Saghir added, "And they looked remarkably similar."

Josie nodded, and Agent Katavich said, "The FBI uncovered some details about your parents' early lives when we started keeping a file on your mother years ago. We discovered some important information. Everything you told us about your parents, their backgrounds and education, and their institutionalization was correct. However, there is more to it than that."

"More to it?"

The agents looked at one another before looking back to Josie. Katavich said, "Your mother and father were fraternal twins who were put up for adoption and separated at birth. They were raised by families in two different towns. Each knew they were adopted, but they never knew they had a twin. They met at the institution and were instantly drawn to one another. They fell in love, got out, and got married. They had you and Zelda. Our people at the Agency didn't know if they were ever aware that they were actually brother and sister. However, upon reading your father's manuscript after it was confiscated, we found the answer. Your father noted their realization and confirmation of their biological relationship when you were five and your sister was seven. He didn't say how they'd figured it out, but he did write that neither of them could handle the truth. They knew that they shouldn't be married, but they also felt they couldn't be apart. They'd already had two children. Unable to deal with the truth, they eventually opted to go off their medications."

Josie closed her eyes and tried not to hyperventilate. She'd always wondered about the uncanny resemblance between her parents and their children. The odds of both of her parents looking so alike and having blonde hair and blue eyes were unusually low, and she'd always feared that Rhonda and Clark were related. However, not only had her parents been related, they'd been fraternal twins. At least they'd married unaware of the truth. It would have been worse had they wed and procreated knowing that they were involved in an incestuous relationship.

"We're sorry to have to tell you this," Agent Saghir said. "You wanted a verbal report, and this was one major point we figured we couldn't and shouldn't keep from you."

"I suspected my parents were related but prayed I was wrong," Josie admitted quietly. "At least they didn't know when they got married and had us."

"What will be released to the media?" Stone asked. "Because of what Zelda did at the White House, they'll want as many details as possible."

"The Agency has to divulge certain information about Zelda, Rhonda, and Clark Hollingsworth, but our people will do their best to minimize the release of details regarding Mrs. Romero," Saghir assured them. "We don't like to see guilt by association when relatives are victims and not accomplices."

"What will happen to my family's FBI files?" Josie asked.

"They'll be closed once we write our final reports after the investigations are complete. It will take a while. We may have further questions for you."

"I'm sure you know where to find me."

Josie may have appeared calm, but she was struggling not to faint. Disengaging herself from Stone and Vin, she reached out with a trembling hand to accept the photo from Agent Katavich. She looked at the image of the smiling people in the picture, blissful in their ignorance of what lay ahead. They had been so happy and appeared so normal. Josie wished it could have lasted a lifetime.

Stone escorted the two FBI agents out of the room and pulled the door closed behind him. Vin went to the bathroom, filled one of the hotel glasses with water from the tap, and brought it back to Josie. He held out his hand in order to take the family photo from her as he passed her the glass. He examined the picture as she took a drink, her hand still trembling.

"You had a nice-looking family," he remarked tensely. "How soon after this did things go wrong?"

"Not long."

"I'm real sorry that you had to live like you did."

"Me, too. I'm really sorry I was ever born."

"Don't say that. You were born for a reason."

"What possible reason? I'm an abomination. I'm –"

"A beautiful, smart woman who came from a horribly disturbed family. I understand part of it, because my mama is bipolar and my daddy was a mean jackass. Things at home were pretty bad, but not quite as bad as they were for you."

"Probably not. You're not the product of unwitting incest. I bet you never had to go dumpster diving for food or clothing, move all the time at the drop of a hat, live in foster homes, or get molested."

Vin took the glass from her hand and sipped some water before saying quietly, "You were right about the first four."

Josie gaped at him for a moment before asking, "You were molested?" When he nodded, she asked, "Was it a neighbor like it was with me?"

He shook his head and admitted, "A family friend who's long dead. No one knows except Dumpling and now you. I'd appreciate it if it stayed that way."

She nodded gravely and said, "No one knows about any of my experiences except Stone, you, and…well, the FBI."

"I don't think any of us will be sharing the information with anybody else. You don't have to worry."

"I'm still in shock about the confirmation of my parents' biological link. How will Stone feel about it? How do *I* feel about it?"

"You should talk to a professional. What you've had to deal with and what you'll have to deal with is too much for any person to handle."

"Stone…helped me to deal with what happened regarding the neighbor. Did *you* ever get help?"

"From Dumpling." Vin's face flushed, and he lowered his head before confiding, "She was real patient with me when we were first married. I had a rough time, figuring out how to separate what had happened to me from what I was supposed to be doing with her as her husband."

"Do you think about it a lot?"

"Not so much consciously, but it's always there. The memory of what was done to me comes at odd times. Of course, when I'm dealing with a child molester in my role as sheriff, I think about it every second I'm with the pervert and have to fight the sick feeling in the pit of my stomach. I feel the same way about rapists. They're all part of a perverse breed to me."

"We have a lot in common," Josie mused. "Both of us had mentally ill parents and were molested."

Passing the water glass back to her, he said wryly, "Great things to have in common."

"We have one really great thing in common," she offered.

He nodded his understanding and said, "Dumpling and I got it right with Stone. I wish we'd gotten it right with Cheek and Nelson. God knows I love all my boys, but Cheek's a lot like my daddy and Nelson was too much like my mama." Chuckling, he said, "I never put two and two together about that until this moment. Kind of explains a ton of things, doesn't it?"

"Stone seems to be a lot like you."

"I guess I should take that as a compliment, being as you married the man. He has a good heart, but it's a heart I worry about. I know what his high blood pressure can do to his kidneys, heart, and eyes. I don't want to outlive him. Does he really take care of himself like he should?"

"Most of the time."

"Good. Most of the time is all anyone can ask of any man. If we were perfect then we wouldn't be human."

"You know, for being an 'ass-backwards fool who's slow to change' you're pretty smart and kind."

"I think that's the nicest thing anyone's ever said to me," he declared with a twinkle in his eye. "I might just have to have them put that on my headstone when I go someday."

Josie grinned and rose to put the photo and glass on the chest of drawers. As she did so, she glanced again at the picture. Her smile faded as she realized that her mother, father, and sister would all need headstones in the near future. She momentarily wished that her newborn nephew would be allowed a merciful, early death rather than a lifetime of physical and emotional suffering. She imagined him lying in an incubator crying piteously and began to cry herself.

She was suddenly in Vin's strong arms. He offered her reassuring words and encouraged her to rest. Josie allowed him to guide her to the bed and to help her lie on her left side. She fell instantly to sleep and dreamed of the day fourteen-year-old Zelda had been taken to have an abortion.

Josie had been terrified of what they were doing to her older sister and worried that the boy who'd gotten her pregnant might come after Josie while the foster mother and Zelda were gone. He hadn't, and she'd been relieved about that. However, when Zelda had been brought back, she'd been shaking and bleeding. She'd kept repeating that she'd screamed during the painful procedure but that no one had helped her. She'd cried and declared vehemently that no one was *ever* going to use her again in any way. *She* was going to use *them* and get what she wanted from life.

"Promise me you'll do the same!" Zelda demanded through her tears. "Don't you ever let anyone fuck with you! If they do, then you get revenge on them! You make them pay!"

"No!" Josie countered, turning away. "That would make me like them! I won't do it! I won't"

Chapter Five

Pain shot through Josie's right shoulder, as her eyes flew open. Disoriented, she struggled to regain her bearings but remained confused. She suddenly realized she was lying fully clothed in the bed in the hotel room in Virginia. Stone slept beside her. Vin was nowhere in sight.

I must have tried to turn over, she decided. *In my dream, I was turning away from Zelda. I did turn away from her then and when she became schizophrenic. Maybe if I'd taken her in, I could have gotten her help.*

Josie diverted her attention from the "what ifs" and carefully rose from the bed. It was after 7:00 p.m., and she had places to be. She glanced at Stone's wallet and the items lying beside it on the dresser before writing him a note, stating that she had to go out but would be back by midnight. Leaving the paper near his wallet, Josie lifted her purse and coat from the chair then tiptoed out of the room.

Josie hurriedly left the hotel, hailing a cab and then telling its Indian driver the address for her parents' apartment. When they arrived there, she asked the man to park and wait; then she got out and stared up at the deserted apartment. She imagined her father, reading in his chair, while her mother paced through the narrow pathways and had conversations with her hallucinations. It was an oddly comforting image, and Josie climbed back into the cab, feeling slightly better.

"Where would you like to go next?" asked the driver, his Indian accent clearly present but not so thick that Josie had trouble understanding him.

"I'd like to see the White House. I've never seen it at night."

"You will have to get out and walk when we get close, and I cannot go with you. I must stay with my car."

"I understand. I want you to wait for me. I have a couple more stops after that."

Shaking his head, the man muttered, "You will have a very large cab fare."

"You only live once, right?"

"It is not so safe in Washington, D.C. at night, and you are a very pretty woman. You may not live much longer. Curiosity killed the cat, you know."

"Cats have nine lives," Josie asserted.

"You may be using one of them up this evening, but it is not my choice to make," the man grumbled. "Do not say I didn't warn you."

The taxi driver parked his cab as close as possible, but Josie still had to walk two blocks through the cold February night air in order to reach the White House. Once she stood across the street from 1600 Pennsylvania Avenue, Josie thought about Zelda's last actions and her death. She wondered if the President and his family were inside and felt sorry for them. She prayed that they would always be safe from crazy people like her sister and evil extremists who might wish to do them harm. She then walked back to the waiting cab and climbed in.

The next address Josie gave the driver was for the hospital where her nephew languished. She'd spied the identification badge Stone must have worn there when she'd scanned the area around his wallet. Once she'd entered and located the Neo-natal Intensive Care Unit, she produced her driver's license. A young, male nurse verified that Josie was listed as the unnamed baby's aunt and offered to take her to see her nephew.

"I feel so sorry for the little guy," confided the nurse. "He cries almost all the time. We have to keep him in a separate room so that the other babies in the NICU can rest."

Josie heard the warbling cries before the nurse opened the door to her nephew's small room. While the man stood off to one side, Josie stared down at the newborn, who was scrawny, wailing, and bright red from the uninterrupted crying. The nurse asked her if she wanted to hold the baby, but Josie shook her head. She knew that if she so much as touched the child with one finger, she'd never be able to let him go. And she had to let him go or lose her fragile hold on her own sanity. Praying that he would have some peace in his lifetime, Josie left the tormented infant and returned to the waiting cab. She needed to stop at an ATM and withdraw enough money to add to what cash she had in her wallet in order to pay the high fare. She also wanted to generously tip the driver, who had been polite and patient.

Josie had expected Vin and Stone to be waiting for her in the hotel lobby. They weren't. They also weren't in the hotel room she and Stone currently shared. Beginning to get nervous, she went down to the front desk and asked for Vin's room number. The clerk explained that the older Mr. Romero had gone out about 8:00 with the younger Mr. Romero and that both men had looked very worried. They'd asked the clerk to tell Josie to call her husband if she returned in their absence.

I left the iPhone in our room, she recalled. *The cellphone, too. Of course, I'll never need the cellphone again. Dad, Mom, and Zelda are all dead, and I'll never hear their voices again. I'll never see them again.*

Josie turned and walked back out of the hotel, suddenly numbed by recent events. Of course, she'd known that Rhonda, Clark, and Zelda Hollingsworth were dead. In one way, Josie had felt relief that they were no longer suffering and would no longer be able to inadvertently torture her. However, the finality of their passing obviously hadn't touched that part of her brain that could fully comprehend the loss. The impact of their deaths hit her hard, and she began to shake slightly as she moved forward.

Josie chose an indiscriminate path and paid little attention to her surroundings. She recalled her mother's horrible death, envisioned her father succumbing to a heart attack, and imagined her sister's fatal shooting. She thought of the baby, who was crying incessantly in the hospital incubator. She shook harder and wanted to throw up, but it had been well over twelve hours since Josie had eaten, and there was precious little food available in her stomach.

At some point, dawn broke. Josie kept walking. She was exhausted, lightheaded, and literally and figuratively lost. She eventually stopped and sat on some steps in front of a run-down sex toy store that was currently closed. Feeling as if she was going to pass out, she wondered what she should do next. Both of her phones were back in the hotel room.

Josie heard the woman before she saw her. The bedraggled person, wearing mismatched, dirty, and ragged clothing, emerged from around a nearby corner. Combat boots were on her feet. Her hair was limp and oily, and she looked and smelled as if she hadn't had a bath in several weeks. She was talking animatedly, gesturing in various directions as she did so.

191

"You shouldn't sit there," the woman said absently as she passed Josie. "It's almost the end of the world, and that's not a good place to sit. We have to find a place to hide from the monsters."

"There is no place," Josie responded dejectedly. "The monsters are all around and inside us."

The woman stopped walking and rapidly nodded at Josie with approval before announcing with delight, "*You* understand!"

"I do."

"You're one of us, the Chosen Ones."

"No, but I understand. Are you hungry?"

"Yes! Yes! Always hungry. Someday, I'll eat and then have the most peaceful sleep…."

Josie gave the woman ten dollars from her purse, saying, "Get some breakfast so that you can have more energy to fight the monsters."

"You must be the Virgin Mary, the Mother of God!" the woman exclaimed. "Thank you, Mary!"

Josie didn't correct her and watched as she pocketed the money while hobbling away. She couldn't have been much older than Josie.

"Mrs. Romero?"

Josie turned and stared at Agent Katavich. For an instant, she questioned whether or not she was hallucinating. Perhaps the events of the last two days had pushed her into the world of schizophrenia after all.

"Mrs. Romero, are you all right? We've been looking for you since last night."

"We?"

Katavich jerked her head towards her partner, who was standing several yards behind her.

"Why were you looking for me?"

"Because we were concerned. Your husband contacted us shortly after 7:30 last night when he woke and found you gone. He, his father, Agent Saghir, and I have been canvassing the city. It seems that we went to the same places you did but at different times than you. Your husband is pretty upset."

"But I left Stone a note and said I'd be back by midnight," Josie insisted. "I was, but he was gone."

Katavich frowned and said, "He didn't mention a note." Sighing, she admitted, "I suppose that was a mistake on our part, not leaving someone at the hotel in case you returned. We were a little short on manpower. Still, you set out again without retrieving a phone."

Josie nodded tiredly and asked, "Where am I?"

"In a really bad part of town. You're lucky we found you unharmed. Why'd you come here?"

"I wasn't even conscious of where I was going."

Saghir was talking on his phone, and Josie assumed he must be telling Stone that they'd found her and would be bringing her back to the hotel. She wondered in a detached fashion whether her husband would be angry with her. She also wondered what had happened to her note.

Stone and Vin were waiting in the hotel lobby when Katavich and Saghir escorted Josie inside. Both men looked drained and tense, and Josie immediately apologized for causing them to worry and swore that she'd left a note for her husband.

Perplexed, Stone declared, "There was no note. I searched the whole room before I called Daddy and Agents Katavich and Saghir." Stepping forward, he gently took his wife into his arms and kissed her before asking, "Are you all right?"

"I will be once I show you the note I wrote before leaving our room."

They went upstairs *en masse*. Josie stared at the top of the dresser. There was no note. Feeling short-winded, she battled a swell of anxiety until Vin suggested that perhaps the note had fallen or been accidentally moved. He went over to the dresser and looked around before checking behind the piece of furniture.

"Here it is," he proclaimed, his voice muffled as he strained to reach along the wall behind the dresser in order to retrieve the paper. "No wonder you didn't see it, Stone."

He scanned it then passed the paper to his son, who read it and handed it to Katavich and Saghir.

"I'm sorry I called and kept you out all night," Stone said. If I'd seen the note –"

"It wouldn't have mattered," Saghir assured him. "We were happy to help."

193

Once the two FBI agents had left, Vin hugged Josie and kissed her on the forehead before excusing himself to get some food and sleep. When they were alone, Stone came over to where Josie stood and took her purse from her.

"Have you eaten anything since breakfast yesterday?"

When she shook her head, Stone went to the phone and ordered food from Room Service then ushered Josie into the bathroom. For the third day in a row, he washed both of them and shampooed their hair before rinsing and drying them off. He didn't say a word as he assisted her with her nightgown once he'd slipped into his pajama bottoms and t-shirt. He then took his blood pressure but didn't tell her his readings.

When their food arrived, Stone accepted it from the server, took it to the little table, tipped the woman, and then closed the door behind her. Still, he said nothing to Josie. Taking her arm, he led her to the table then sat in one of the two chairs. Without looking at his wife, he began to eat. Josie simply stood and waited, not quite certain how to react.

"Will you sit and eat something?" Stone asked, as he prepared to spear a piece of French toast with the tines of his fork. Without looking up at her, he added, "Please."

"I'm not hungry. I feel sick right now."

Stone quickly got to his feet, fork in hand. Josie automatically extended her arms, palms facing him in a defensive gesture. She watched as his expression went from worried to puzzled to shocked. Without taking his eyes from her face, he lowered the fork to the table and murmured, "Josephine Romero, did you honestly think I was going to stab you with that fork?"

"Old habits die hard, remember? I thought you might be mad at me and reacted instinctively."

"*Mad* at you? I'm not mad at you! Frustrated as hell and worried out of my mind is more like it!"

"Don't say that!" she cried. "I know Dad's gone, but I'm so conditioned to react to his anxiety issues about my well-being! Mom is gone, and I don't have to be afraid of End-of-Days, Six-Six-Six, and the other hallucinations anymore, but the fear's so ingrained in me. And Zelda...Zelda was *wrong*!"

"Wrong about what?"

194

"About how the world works and what she had to do in order to survive in it! She was big on taking what she needed in order to get payback for everyone letting us down, but she allowed herself to have this poor baby who's going to go to some institution or an unsuspecting family! She should have had another abortion! It would've been better for him if he'd never been born, just like it would've been better for me and her to never have been born! They should've sterilized our parents at the mental health facility! They should do that for all of the lunatics who are locked up! They should never allow them to have children and place them in a world of insanity and insecurity! It's wrong! It's so wrong, but it's too late for any of us."

"I'm thankful your parents weren't sterilized. I know all this is...terrible for you, but you wouldn't be here if they'd never given you life. You're amazing, Josie. I so need you and love you. I wish someone had gotten you and Zelda out of their crazy world." Stone stepped forward and took her in his arms before saying softly, "It's not too late for you."

Burying her face against his chest, she asked, "How can you even stand to touch me knowing what I am?"

"You're my loving, smart, beautiful wife. The rest of your life is ahead of you, and there's no more insanity in sight, just little old ass-backwards Clayville."

"I want to go home to Wolfwood," she told him. "I want to go tomorrow. I'm not going to have a funeral for Mom, Dad, or Zelda. I just want them to be buried with their names and birth and death dates on their headstones. I don't want to be there when they put them in the ground. Can't we just leave and let someone here take care of it? No one else cares but me anyway."

"We can set it up so someone else can handle the burials of your parents and sister, but you have to sign the papers regarding your nephew before we leave. Also, we can't go home to Wolfwood until I finish my residency. Unless you want to live there alone for the next few months until I'm done and can join you, that is."

"Definitely not. I only...I need...couldn't we go back for at least a couple days before returning to Austin?"

"I think we could work that out. Now, will you please eat something and take some more Advil? Then we can sleep for a while before taking care of business."

Josie forced herself to eat her French toast and fruit. She took the Advil then sat in Stone's lap while waiting for the required thirty minutes to elapse. She fell asleep waiting for him to tell her that it was all right for her to lie down and woke to the ringing of Stone's iPhone later that afternoon. She lay with her eyes closed and listened to him answer, offer a greeting to another doctor, let out an exclamation of surprise and what sounded like relief, listen to whatever the other person had to tell him, and thank the caller for all his help.

"Who was that?" Josie asked, as she stretched her arms, pleased to note that her shoulder was no longer paining her badly.

"A neonatologist at the hospital."

"Did the baby finally stop crying?"

"He stopped."

The way he said it made Josie open her eyes and look over at him with suspicion.

"What did they give him?"

"They tried quite a few different medications, but none of them worked."

"So, what made him stop?"

Stone stared at the phone in his hand and said, "He died."

"Thank God," she breathed after a few moments of silence. "Thank you, Lord."

"Sad to say but I have to agree with you there. The baby seemed doomed from the start."

"Another grave and headstone," Josie remarked sadly. "Zelda's baby didn't even have a name."

"He needs one. What do you want to name him?"

"I think I'll name him Scott Hollingsworth. I told you about my father's love of F. Scott Fitzgerald's works. This will be a final tribute to the long and crazy saga of the Hollingsworth family." As Stone brushed some hair away from her tear-filled, blue eyes, she added, "I hope this is the end. I could still go crazy, you know."

"You won't."

"How can you be so sure?"

"I just am. You're a Romero now. There are no more Hollingsworths. You're *not* going to go crazy, partly because you're going to get some professional help with what's happened in the last few days and with the past. I know you said you'd been in therapy off and on since you were young, but I suspect you didn't have the greatest therapist and weren't totally honest with them."

"You're right about that. What if I don't want to go to therapy?"

"You have to."

"Why?"

"Because I'm not enough, and I can only take so much without it hiking my blood pressure. I need for you to do this for me as much as for yourself."

Feeling guilty, Josie asked, "What was your pressure last night when you didn't know where I was?"

"It was a bit on the high side," he answered vaguely. "It was fine this morning though."

"I'll go to therapy. I know I'm a lot to deal with."

"*You're* not a lot to deal with. Your past is a lot to deal with. I don't know how you've done it all these years. You're so strong."

"Me? Strong? I don't think so."

"I don't think so either; I know so. That's why we make such a good team. I'm strong, too. The only difference is that I recognize it in myself, and you don't see your inner strength at all."

Josie considered his words as she dressed and prepared to go with Stone to meet his father for dinner in the hotel restaurant. She supposed she'd always viewed strength as belonging to those who demonstrated their force of will to others on a daily basis. She'd thought of outspoken people like Zelda as being strong. Yet, Zelda had been miserable for the twenty years before she'd become schizophrenic and was now dead. Josie was the one who remained alive and in love. *She* had a chance to make a positive difference in the world. She *was* strong and had a future, unlike her sister, parents, and nephew. She had hope.

Chapter Six

Josie squirmed in her seat, as she watched Stone walk across the courtroom. She was nervous, not simply because he was there to testify regarding his experience with twelve-year-old Brittany in the E.R. She was also nervous because once the trial was over, her life in Austin would also end. Stone's residency had been completed, and they would be moving to Clayville and facing both the known and unknown in northern Louisiana.

Stone's parents, grandmother, and nephew had come to support him during the trial and would then help the couple move their personal belongings to Wolfwood. Vin and Dumpling sat to Josie's right, while Tommy and Memaw sat to her left.

The courtroom was full. Josie had expected Brittany's family to be poor white trash. She chastised herself for making assumptions. Brittany's mother had worked as a lawyer for a local firm, and her child molester boyfriend had been a bank executive. Josie reminded herself that child abuse came with no class restrictions. She thought briefly of her father-in-law's admission of his own molestation and of his parents' wealth. Dr. and Mrs. Romero's money and status in the local community hadn't stopped Vin's assailant.

Brittany's mother, no longer licensed to practice law, had entered into a plea bargain, surrendering her rights to all of her children and agreeing to serve a year in jail and then several years of probation. The boyfriend, who appeared smug and unapologetic, had refused to cooperate with authorities. He'd maintained his innocence up until the Medical Examiner had provided irrefutable DNA evidence that the dead baby had been fathered by the accused man. Even after that testimony, the defendant refused to change his plea.

After being sworn in, Stone took a seat on the witness stand. At the Prosecutor's request, he detailed the events that had occurred on the December night six months earlier when Brittany had been taken to the hospital and abandoned there by her mother. Josie flinched as he described the birth that had caused her excruciating pain and long-lasting physical and emotional trauma. Next, he reviewed the injury done to the baby and how that injury had contributed to the newborn's death.

Stone came across as a competent witness who was in control, but he didn't attempt to hide his anger and disgust regarding both Brittany's attacker and her mother. Josie found him to be a compelling witness, but she was afraid of what the day's events were doing to his blood pressure and pulse rate. Both had been elevated in the days preceding the trial.

Once the Prosecutor finished questioning Stone, the defendant's lawyer began her cross-examination. It had become evident during the trial that she didn't stand a chance of winning her case, and she knew it. Therefore, she'd been doing what she could to discredit or slander the witnesses in an obvious ploy to divert as much negative attention away from the accused man as possible. Stone had been warned about this early on and had declared he was prepared for anything.

"Isn't it true that you feel as though you have a mission to persecute those you perceive to be child molesters?" the woman asked coolly. "You have some personal experience with the subject from what I understand."

Stone blanched, and Josie held her breath. Had the defendant's attorneys somehow found out about Josie's molestation? Had they uncovered the secret molestation of Vin? If so, then how would Stone react to the news and what would Vin do if his secret was publicly revealed?

The Prosecutor objected, and the Defense was rebuked but allowed to continue.

The lawyer asked Stone, "How can you give impartial testimony when you were molested at age thirteen and fathered a child with the woman who molested you? Why didn't you say anything when the woman declared that her baby was actually your older brother's son and then married him?"

Stone's face grew red, but he didn't react with an outburst. He also didn't look in the direction of his family members, who were sitting in stunned silence. Instead, he set his jaw and said, "*I'm* not the one on trial here. We know who is and what he's done to his victim and their baby, who is now dead."

"Are you denying that you were molested and fathered the boy known as your nephew, Thomas Romero?"

"I'm not denying anything. I don't have to since I'm a witness and not a defendant. If you have more questions about what happened the night I delivered Brittany's baby and the agony I saw her experience, then go ahead. Otherwise, I'm done."

"Dr. Romero –"

"I said I'm done! I have hypertension, and I need to wrap things up here unless you want to call 911. Do you want me to stroke out on the witness stand so that people will forget that your client repeatedly raped a little girl and destroyed her life?"

The judge hastily interceded and excused Stone from the stand. He stood slowly, looking unsteady on his feet. One of the court officers present came over to him. After a brief exchange that none of them could hear, Stone allowed the man to escort him out of the courtroom. Josie could hear people talking animatedly all around them, but she paid no attention to what any of them were saying. The only thing she cared about was getting to Stone.

Josie and the rest of the family scrambled to their feet, hurrying out of the courtroom. She was terrified that Stone's life was in danger and that there would be a terrible backlash from what the lawyer had just proclaimed in public. It didn't matter that Austin and Clayville were not geographically close. People in Clayville would know about today's happenings as soon as the next edition of the local newspaper was released since one of the two reporters employed there had travelled to Austin. He'd expected to write about the return of Stone Romero, his new medical practice, and his testimony at the trial of a prominent man who'd molested and impregnated a little girl. The reporter had gotten much more than he'd bargained for during his trip.

If this is true, how is Tommy going to react? Josie wondered. *And Cheek? Cheek will be furious. What about Stone's parents and grandmother? Did anyone have a clue? Does Flynn know? Surely Nelson knew.*

None of the Romero family spoke, as they hurried down the hallway with a courthouse employee to the room where Stone had been led. Once they arrived, they found Stone lying on a bench with his eyes closed and his hands laced together across his waist. His face wasn't quite as red, and Josie was relieved but didn't relax. It was definitely too early to relax. She quickly knelt beside him, ran her fingers through his unruly hair, and kissed him before asking how he felt.

"Very tired," he admitted. "I have a wicked headache."

"Should we call 911?" Dumpling asked anxiously.

"No, Mama. I think I'll be fine once I calm down."

"Is it true?" Tommy asked impatiently. "Did my mother have sex with you when you were thirteen? Are you my real father?"

Without opening his eyes, Stone said, "Your mother did have sex with me when I was about to turn fourteen and she was eighteen. She did get pregnant with you about the same time, but she swore she was having sex with Cheek, too. She told him he was the father of her baby, and he obviously believed her and married her. I don't know if you're actually my son. I was fourteen when you were born and didn't really feel like I had any power to stake claim to you. What your mother did was wrong, but she was a good mother to you and I was still a kid myself. I didn't know what to do except be as involved in your life as I could."

"You could've come to me," Vin offered quietly.

"Not then I couldn't. We weren't that close when I was a teenager, remember? I was embarrassed and confused."

"But you let me stay by myself with that mean asshole the last couple years!" Tommy said angrily. "How could you do that?"

"Your mother was dead. I didn't want to tell you the truth and mar your image of her. She'd been molested herself and was pretty mixed up when she had sex with me, but she really turned her life around once you were born. Am I wrong? Was she a bad mother?"

Tommy hung his head and answered, "No. She was a great mom. She said her life had been a mess until she had me and that I made all the difference in the world to her."

"What she did was inexcusable," Vin declared sharply. "But she was a walking disaster until Tommy came along. Then she devoted her life to doing right by him."

"That still doesn't excuse what she did to you," Memaw told Stone. "You were a boy, and she took advantage of you."

"I'm not disagreeing with that," Stone responded.

"I want to find out if you're my father," Tommy declared. "I hope to God you are. That way, I never have to go back to that asshole's house or club ever again."

201

"You've been to the club?" Dumpling asked with horror. "During business hours?"

"Not when my mother was alive. She wouldn't let me near the place. Afterwards, I could go whenever I wanted as long as I didn't tell."

"You saw the strippers?" Vin asked angrily.

"Yes, Pepaw. I know all of them."

"Did you drink alcohol?"

"Sometimes."

"I'm going to arrest Cheek's ass for letting minors in his club and providing them with alcohol!" Vin snapped. "Did he let other kids in?"

"Nah, just me." Turning back to Stone, he asked, "Do you want to know if I'm your son?"

"Now that the truth about your mother and me is out, of course I want to know," Stone assured him. "I'm sorry I hadn't felt like I could tell you." Looking at Josie, he added, "Or anyone else."

Josie's mind was racing. She was hurt by the fact that she'd shared her molestation experience with her husband, but he hadn't done the same with her. She wondered if Tommy would live with them if he was, indeed, Stone's son.

On the one hand, Josie would welcome having Tommy as her stepson since she and Stone would have no children of their own. But Josie was only twenty-five. How would she feel about having a sixteen-year-old stepson? Reminding herself that Stone was only a few years older than she and might be the sixteen-year-old boy's biological father, she considered how he must feel. What a secret he'd kept for so long. She thought of Vin and the terrible secret he'd carried for much longer.

The Prosecutor for the case entered the room and asked to speak with Stone alone. The rest of the group stepped outside, standing awkwardly in the hallway while they waited. Fifteen minutes later, Stone and the lawyer emerged. He thanked her for her good work, and she thanked him for everything he'd done for the case and said she knew what it had cost him.

"It might have cost me *some* things, but it may have caused me to gain even more," he told her.

The reporter from the Clayville paper approached and asked Stone for a statement about the trial and the shocking revelations

202

regarding Stone's involvement with Tommy's mother. Stone said he had no comment at that moment but promised the man he would give him a statement once he had something definitive to say. The reporter, a white-haired, heavyset man in his sixties, nodded, thanked Stone, and then turned to Vin and said, "And people think small towns are dull. Damn, there's more going on in a small town than in most big-city suburbs! You got anything to say, Sheriff Vin? How about you, Miss Dumpling? Miss Gertrude? Tommy?" Turning to Josie, he added, "Miss Josie?"

"I think we'll all hold our tongues for the moment," Vin said casually, but firmly. "This is a family matter."

"You know where to find me once you're ready," the man said. "I've got to run this story, but you also know I'm not out to hurt anyone. I'll try to state what happened but do some damage control. See y'all back in Clayville."

"Are we going to stay for the rest of the trial and the verdict?" Tommy asked once the reporter had returned to the courtroom.

"The pervert will be found guilty," Vin declared. "I suspect he'll be sentenced to the maximum penalties."

"As well he should," Memaw said with conviction. "That poor girl and her poor baby. You know she'll never really recover from any of this."

They left the courthouse and stepped into the mid-June heat. Stone announced that he was tired and wanted to rest before they all went out for dinner that night. The following morning, they would load up the small U-Haul truck with the boxes that were packed and ready to go.

Stone had donated all of his furniture to a local thrift store whose proceeds went to help children battling cancer. He'd decided that Wolfwood was already fully furnished, so the furniture in his Austin apartment should go to a worthy cause. The thrift store moving men had taken everything the previous day, except the king-sized bed. They would come back for it the following morning.

Stone and Josie hugged the others before agreeing to meet them at 6:00 at a popular Mexican restaurant. As Vin, Dumpling, Memaw, and Tommy headed for Vin's extended cab Ford truck, Stone and Josie went to the Honda. Neither of them spoke during the ride home or the walk to the apartment.

Josie waited until they were inside and Stone had removed his tie before asking, "Why didn't you tell me?"

Sitting on the floor amidst the boxes and slipping off his shoes, Stone said, "Because I never intended to tell anyone. Tommy had enough to deal with when he lost his mother. He didn't need to learn about what she'd done or reflect on all those years that we'd lost. *If* he's my son, that is. I really don't know." Pausing, he asked, "If he is, then all hell will break loose with Cheek. He'll want to take out his indignation on me and Tommy."

"If Tommy's your son, then he should come live with us at Wolfwood. You two have a lot of time to make up for and a lot of time ahead to develop a good relationship as father and son."

Stone stared up at her for a while then asked, "You know what you're saying? You're only nine years older than he is! Are you really willing to take on the role of fulltime stepmother?"

"Are you really willing to take on the role of fulltime father?" she shot back. "I wouldn't be offering if I wasn't serious! What kind of a woman do you think I am?"

Josie stepped out of her shoes, leaving them where they were in the living room, then stalked off towards the master bedroom closet in order to remove her dress. She tossed it onto the floor along with her pantyhose and reached for a hanger that held the shirt she intended to wear to dinner. Stone came up behind her and wrapped his arms around her waist. Clad only in her bra and panties, Josie was instantly aware that Stone was naked and was amazed by how quickly he'd disrobed. His state of arousal was unmistakable, as evidenced by the hard length of his erection pressing against her back.

"What kind of a woman do I think you are?" he murmured before kissing her behind her left ear. "I think you're an amazing, intelligent, kind, beautiful, loving, and desirable woman. As for me, I think I might be like my Daddy, an ass-backwards fool who's slow to change when it comes to some things." After pressing his lips to her neck, he whispered, "I'm sorry I didn't tell you about what happened between Tommy's mother and me and the possibility that he was my son."

Josie closed her eyes and moaned, as Stone slid the fingers of his right hand inside the front of her bikini underwear. His breathing quickened as he eased a finger inside her channel, and she pushed her back against his front.

"You're not an ass-backwards fool who's slow to change," she said in a breathy tone. "And I...oh, God...Stone...I admire your father very much."

"He and Mama have come a long way since Nelson died," Stone admitted before drawing his tongue up one side of her neck. "I'm proud of them. They've adopted a more accepting attitude although not quite as accepting as I'd like. Still, it's a start. And no smoking for a year and a half and no 'N' word since Christmas. That's progress."

"How can you talk and touch me like this?" she panted.

Easing in a second finger, he asked mischievously, "Like what?"

"I want you in me now," Josie declared urgently. "I *need* you in me."

"There's no place I'd rather be," Stone said hoarsely before scooping her up in his arms and carrying her to the bed.

Later, they met Vin, Dumpling, Memaw, and Tommy at the Mexican restaurant for dinner. Josie observed Tommy's staring at Stone for most of the meal and prayed that he was actually her husband's child. He would be devastated if it were proven that Cheek was his biological father. Tommy and Stone had always been close, and he and Cheek had obviously never been close. This could be a huge turning point in the young man's life, but it could cause him to turn either in the right direction or the wrong one. From what she knew, he'd been headed down the wrong path after his mother's death but had gotten back on track. Would this new development derail him?

Before they left the restaurant, Tommy excused himself to use the restroom. While he was away from the table, Vin explained, "I called Cheek and told him what happened in the courtroom. I didn't want him to read about the shocking news in *The Clayville Daily Gazette* tomorrow morning. Cheek was livid and threatened to kill Stone for sleeping with his wife. When I pointed out that Stone had been thirteen at the time, Cheek asked me what difference that made and called Tommy's mother a whore. That was when I told him that Tommy would be staying with Dumpling and me until DNA tests could be performed. Cheek said he never wanted to see Tommy or any of us again, no matter the results. I told him that was an awful thing to say. I also asked him whether or not he wanted to be arrested for allowing Tommy to be in the strip club during business hours. I reminded Cheek that if he tried to hurt or slander anyone in the family, then I'd see to it that he lost his liquor license and, therefore, his business. Cheek slammed down the phone, and that was that."

"Does Tommy know any of this?" asked Stone. "What about his personal things at Cheek's house?"

"He and I talked about it. I'll go with him to the house while Cheek's at work and help him clear out whatever's his."

"If tests prove he's my son, then Josie and I want him to move out to Wolfwood with us."

"Are you sure about that?" Dumpling asked worriedly. "He's a teenager, and the two of you haven't even been married for half a year. You've had so much to deal with. It might put a strain on your marriage to add having Tommy living with you fulltime."

"If we can make it through everything else, then I think we can handle a sixteen-year-old," Josie said resolutely. "After all, it wasn't so long ago that Stone and I were sixteen."

Vin grimaced and said, "I still wish you'd come to me about what happened with Tommy's mother, Stone. I understand, but I wish things had been different. Did Nelson know?"

"Of course, he knew," Stone said, looking away. "He was…we were…the same but different."

Vin looked uncomfortable but asked, "How old was Nelson when he first…?"

Stone fiddled with a clean spoon on the table for several moments before answering, "Nelson didn't have sex until he met Chas in New Orleans. He said he was waiting for the person he'd spend the rest of his life with, and he found him."

"Do you still talk to Chas?" Memaw inquired. "How is he?"

"Still missing Nelson. He finally met someone last month he was interested in, but he said the whole time they were at dinner all he could think about was how the man couldn't compare with Nelson. I told him nobody else would but that someone else who was special might be right for him. He agreed, but he didn't sound convinced."

"Maybe he should come to Wolfwood for a visit once you and Josie are settled in," Dumpling suggested, startling them all. "Maybe if he saw that you two were living there and making Nelson's dream come true, it would help him to let go. I know we don't know him well, but it seems like he's a nice man. He deserves to be happy."

"That's a great idea, Mama," Stone said, as Tommy returned to the table. "Once we get a little more situated, then I'll talk to him about it."

The moment Stone and Josie began the short walk back to the apartment, he crowed, "That was unbelievable!"

"What was?"

"What Mama said about Chas. You have no idea how long I've wished that my parents would be accepting of...well, Nelson being gay. They never got there while he was alive, but the fact that Mama suggested that Chas come to Wolfwood...." He shook his head as if he still couldn't believe it then continued, "I don't think they'll ever accept homosexuality, but at least they can accept a person who's gay. I never thought they'd get there. It was part of why Nelson battled depression and insecurity most of his life. He knew how they viewed him, even though he knew they loved him. He couldn't change and didn't want to, except when it came to Mama and Daddy's perception of him. I miss him so much."

Josie understood that Stone would never truly get over the death of his identical twin, and she considered that to be natural. She hoped that being back in Clayville and at Wolfwood might somehow salve his wounded psyche and heart. If Tommy lived with them, then that would provide another distraction. Stone's medical practice would keep him focused on his work, and Josie would keep him focused on their life together, both at work and at home.

"What do you want for your birthday?" Stone asked, as they resumed their walk. "I have less than a week, and I have no idea what you'd like."

"I'd like to know why my mother named me what she did, but I doubt that will happen since she's dead and never told me when she was alive. I mean, I know why Dad gave Zelda her name, but what was the reason behind Mom's choice?" Taking his hand, she asked, "Where did she get Josephine Mamie?"

207

"That may be a tough one. I'll give it a try though. Any other ideas in case I don't succeed?"

"Nope."

"You're making it difficult for me. Let me try something more straightforward. What kind of cake do you want?"

"Strawberry with cream cheese frosting."

"I can do that."

"I know you can. You're a fabulous cook, much better than I'll ever be."

"You could learn."

"Why should I? Most men expect their wives to do the cooking. I think I'll be liberated and expect it from my husband."

"Only if you promise to do all the household maintenance," he shot back with a grin.

"I'm good at household maintenance. Zelda and I figured out a lot of that stuff, starting when we were young. I can fix various appliances, put in a box with electrical outlets, and even work on plumbing."

"Sounds like I have the better part of the deal."

"That's a matter of opinion."

They were lying in bed later that night when Stone's phone rang. He groaned and reached for it, muttering that it was too late for anyone to be calling unless it was an emergency. When he sat bolt upright in bed, Josie became instantly alert and sat close beside him. She strained to hear what the caller was saying but could only discern that whoever had phoned was female.

"So, he saved the good people of Texas some money," Stone said gruffly. "Good for him. I hope God has mercy on his soul, because I sure as hell never will. Yes, I know. Thank you. Tell her she's very welcome and I wish her well."

When he clicked off the phone, he looked at Josie and said, "The pervert banker hung himself in his cell. They told Brittany, and she asked the Prosecutor to thank me for helping her at the hospital and with the trial. She says she'll be all right now."

"She won't," Josie said quietly.

"No, she won't. At least she never has to be afraid of the bastard again, and her mother is locked away."

Josie rubbed tiredly at her eyes and admitted, "Sometimes, I wish there was a way people like me and Brittany could forget all of the horrible things that happen to us."

"There is. However, I like you the way you are, not all catatonic and stuff."

She smiled wanly at him and repeated, "And stuff? Is that a medical term, Dr. Romero?"

"No. It's a human one, and I like to remind myself I'm not God as often as possible, remember?"

"Oh, yes. That. I am very thankful you try to stay humble."

"Try?"

She grinned and declared, "I'm just messing with you. You are wonderfully humble. Promise me you'll stay that way."

"I'll do my best."

"Your best is more than good enough."

Chapter Seven

By the next afternoon, the Romeros were on their way to Clayville. Josie drove her Volvo with Memaw sitting beside her. Dumpling drove Stone's Honda, and Vin was behind the wheel of his truck. Stone drove the small U-Haul with Tommy in the passenger seat. The boy had insisted on riding with the man, and Josie prayed again that Stone was actually Tommy's father.

She found Memaw to be an excellent travelling companion. The older woman was highly intelligent, kind, and as well-read as Josie's father had been. Since Josie herself had inherited his love of reading and learning, the two women maintained an on-going discussion of novels ranging from Homer's *The Iliad* to Jeaniene Frost's *This Side of the Grave*. Josie reflected that it was a pleasure to be able to connect with someone regarding her passion for all things literary. Stone loved to read fiction but had explained to Josie early on that he'd rarely had time to do so since beginning medical school. He'd bemoaned this fact and declared he was eager to catch up to Josie, who had informed him playfully that she wanted to see him try.

The travelers stopped outside of Dallas so that they could eat and stretch their legs. Anticipating that they'd arrive in Clayville around midnight, they all agreed to go directly to Vin and Dumpling's property. Josie and Stone would sleep in Memaw's second bedroom, while Tommy would sleep in the bedroom that had once been shared by Nelson and Stone. He'd refused to sleep in Cheek's old room.

"I do hope Stone is Tommy's father," Memaw announced once she and Josie were back in the car. "Tommy is so thrilled by the possibility, and I'm afraid of how he'll react if his hopes are dashed. It's a shame that he loathes Cheek so much, considering he thought the man was his father his whole life." Sighing, she added, "Of course, none of us have ever really *liked* Cheek, but he is our flesh and blood. We don't get to pick our blood relations."

"No, we don't."

"How are you *really* doing, Honey? It's been four months since your family died. I know we discussed it right afterward when you and Stone went to Wolfwood for those few days, and we've spoken about it some on the phone. But it's not the same as talking in person."

Josie was surprised by how quickly her eyes clouded over with tears, but she rapidly blinked them away and said, "I do miss Mom, Dad, and Zelda, but it's also sort of liberating not to live being overshadowed by their mental illness issues. I think about Zelda's baby and how fortunate he was to be spared by passing away, kind of like Brittany's baby. What sort of a future would either of them have had?"

"We'll never know, but I agree that in those cases the babies' futures seemed bleak. Conversely, sometimes things are good for a child when he's born, then he turns out badly."

"Is that what happened to Cheek?"

"I'd say so. Vin and Dumpling loved that boy and spoiled him by not disciplining him at all. For Vin, I think it was because my husband was so strict, and Vin didn't want to be like that with his son. So, he went in the opposite direction, which was a bad move. As for Dumpling, she was simply so thrilled to have a baby that she felt he could do no wrong. When he went to school, he was always in trouble and people talked about how poorly he behaved. Vin and Dumpling tried to change their approach, but it was too late. He was an extremely dislikable boy by the time he reached third grade and was often the instigator of problems inside and outside of the classroom." Chuckling, she said, "I remember one of his high school teachers telling me about what took place one beautiful, sunny school day. It was hot, and the school had no air-conditioning. So, all the windows were open for ventilation. Cheek was being particularly belligerent. His teacher gave him detention, which was nothing new, and he made a very rude comment about where she could put the detention slip. She marched herself over to him and proclaimed that God was watching him and that if he didn't change his ways he would end up in jail or worse. He laughed defiantly. A lightning bolt came out of the clear, blue sky and in through the open windows. It struck a light bulb right above Cheek's desk, and the bulb shattered and landed all over him and the furniture. Talk about a sign from Above, but Cheek simply shrugged it off and said it was a coincidence. The other students didn't seem to think so, and the few friends he had stopped hanging around with him. It was sad, actually. I feel very sorry for Cheek, although I have no inclination to be around him."

"What was Tommy's mother really like? Did Cheek love her?"

Memaw looked dolefully out the window and said, "I can't speak for how Cheek felt regarding his wife. I felt sorry for Malinda from the time she was small. I didn't personally know the family, but everyone in town knew that things were bad for them. Her father was a drug dealer, and her mother liked to entertain other men when he was out peddling dope. Stone mentioned Malinda had been molested. I wonder if it was by one or more of those men or if it was by her own father. He was a terrible man."

"How'd she come to work for Cheek?"

"Malinda got into drugs early. After all, they were readily available and in use at the trailer where she grew up. She did finish high school somehow and became a stripper in Cheek's club on her eighteenth birthday. She was a beautiful girl with a very shapely figure. She'd been stripping in the club for almost a year when she approached Cheek to tell him she was pregnant with his baby. I suppose he must have loved her and thought Tommy was his. Otherwise, he would have probably told her to leave and never come back."

"Did she use drugs while she was pregnant?"

"No. That was the most wonderful thing that came out of Tommy's conception. Well, other than Tommy himself. When Malinda found out she was pregnant, she immediately stopped doing drugs, stopped stripping, and began to dress more conservatively. Overnight, she devoted herself to doing everything she could for her baby. She ate right, kept a clean house, and was a model mother to her child. Cheek continued to be Cheek, and it was more like they were sharing a house rather than living as husband and wife. Malinda made the best of it and raised Tommy right, shielding him from Cheek's temperament and world as much as possible."

"But she ended up filing for divorce."

"I think as Tommy got older she realized there was the potential for him to become like Cheek if she stayed. Unfortunately, she got the cancer and died although she was granted the divorce before her passing."

"It sounds as if you really liked her."

"We all did."

"Why didn't any of you petition to take Tommy after she died?"

"Biological parents always have the upper hand in custody disputes unless there's proven abuse. We simply all agreed to remain as involved as we could in Tommy's life. He began to go out with the wrong sorts of kids after his mother died, and we were very worried. He started cleaning up his act not long before you and Stone came to Clayville for the Christmas holidays. What a relief!" Looking to Josie, she admitted, "Of course, none of us had any idea that Malinda had sex with Stone when he was thirteen and that he might be Tommy's father."

"Does it change how you feel about Malinda?"

"No. She was a lost child herself but became a beautiful woman and mother. What she did by sleeping with Stone was very wrong, and I've been deeply affected by it. However, she was so confused herself, and Stone was filled with the raging hormones of a teenager. I'm not saying he was complicit. I have no idea. It's unfortunate for him that it happened, but I am thankful for Tommy's existence. It changed Malinda in the best of ways. Plus, if Tommy is Stone's, then at least Stone will have a biological child." Shaking her head, she said, "I'm sorry. I shouldn't have said that."

"It was one of the first things I thought," Josie admitted with a smile. "Don't feel bad."

"I only pray that Cheek doesn't do anything stupid because of this. Any man would be upset by the news, but Cheek's the type to seek retaliation."

"If he does, then we'll deal with it. It sounds like he has a major lesson to learn. Maybe this is what it'll take to make him learn it."

"I surely do hope so, but it does worry me. I think Cheek is a lot like my husband was, and that doesn't portend well for him or anyone around him. At least my husband had great intelligence. Cheek wasn't blessed with superior intellect, but he is good at being a business owner. From what people tell me, his club does very well as those places go." Looking disconcerted, she asked, "Has Stone talked to you about what happened with Malinda?"

"No."

"He will in time. Don't tell anyone else whatever he says. Keep it between the two of you. Some things were meant to be kept private."

Josie thought of Vin Romero and his admission that he'd been molested and had only shared that knowledge with his wife until Josie revealed her own molestation experience. She suspected if he hadn't been trying to help her and hadn't been confident she'd never tell another person what he'd said, then he and Dumpling would have gone to their graves harboring that secret.

There was an accident on the highway when they were about an hour from Clayville. Luckily, there were no fatalities, but the accident did slow what traffic there was on the road at that late hour to a crawl. By the time the Romeros arrived at Vin and Dumpling's property, it was almost 1:00 a.m. Everyone got stiffly out of their vehicles and declared they were going straight to bed. Tommy went with his grandparents to the main house, while Stone and Josie went with Memaw to her home. She wished them a good night before retiring to her bedroom. Once Josie and Stone had brushed their teeth and slipped into their nightclothes, they went straight to bed and to sleep.

They slept until 10:00 the following morning and snuggled together upon waking in the bed. When Josie asked Stone how his nine hours with Tommy in the U-Haul had gone, he replied that it had been great. He and Tommy had always gotten along famously, and the new development regarding Stone's possible paternity of the boy had only seemed to bring them closer together.

"We need to find out as soon as possible if I'm Tommy's father so that we can handle the fallout either way," Stone told her.

"He looks so much like you and Nelson," Josie remarked. "What did his mother look like?"

"She was tall with dark brown hair and really dark brown eyes. She didn't have the Barbie doll figure you do. She was bustier and had a rounder backside. It was the perfect body for a small-town stripper." He paused then said, "I know you're wondering what happened that time we were together, so ask."

"If you want to tell me, then that's fine. If not, then I'll accept that. I have no idea if it was consensual or not."

"It was, but it was still wrong. I was only thirteen and couldn't really make an informed decision. I was a kid, one about to jump out of his skin with all those hormones building inside me." Pulling Josie closer to him, he said, "I ran into her at the lake. It was a really hot day, and I'd gone out there to get away from my folks. Memaw wasn't on her meds at the time; Cheek still hated me and Nelson for being born; Nelson was struggling with a lot of bullying at school; and our parents were being…our parents. I was really pissed at them and wanted time to think, to get away from everyone. I figured that if I went to the lake I could just chill for a while. I found Malinda sitting on a dock, crying her eyes out. I sat beside her and asked her what was wrong. She blurted out her entire life story – her drug dealer dad, the crack whore mom, the parade of strange men her mother invited over when her father was out or too stoned to notice, and the fact that several of the men had used Malinda sexually from the time she'd been a young girl. She talked of how her father got her hooked on drugs when she was twelve and of how she'd wanted to go to college but had ended up a stripper at my brother's club. She'd started sleeping with him even though she really didn't love him because she felt like it would give her more job security. She needed all the money she could get to feed her drug habit. In short, she was miserable and felt like she had no hope of ever getting out of her abysmal circumstances."

"What did you do?"

"I told her she was only eighteen and that she could make her life whatever she wanted it to be. I poured out my heart to her about all my family's problems and insisted that Nelson and I were going to get out of Clayville and make something of ourselves. I was vehement that we weren't going to get stuck like everyone else. She quit crying and said she believed me and that she believed *in* me. Then she leaned over and kissed me. I reacted instinctively, and she didn't pull away when I slipped my hand under her shirt. She should have, but she didn't. I think she was so desperate and alone that she didn't care that I wasn't quite fourteen, yet. I'm sure I was clumsy because of my inexperience, but that didn't seem to matter to her. Of course, I enjoyed the sex, but she really seemed to enjoy it as well. When we finished, she told me that we probably shouldn't have done that, but she was glad we had. She said that I was a good lover, which I'm sure was an exaggeration. But it actually gave me a lot of confidence when I started having sex with girls my own age a year or so later.

"Malinda and I agreed never to tell anyone what we'd done, but she knew that promise excluded Nelson. It didn't worry her. She knew he'd keep my secrets, just as I kept his."

"What did you think when she turned up pregnant and said it was your older brother's baby?"

"That it might be, but it might also be mine. What was I going to do? I was perpetually mad at my parents and Cheek and would've loved to rub it in their faces that I'd had sex and was oh-so-grown-up, but I didn't want Malinda to be arrested for statutory rape and didn't want them to take her baby away from her. Once she announced she was pregnant, it was like a switch got flipped in her brain, and she straightened out her life. Nelson and I talked about it and decided it was best for everyone if I said nothing and assumed Cheek was the baby's father. I always wondered, though." As he ran his fingers through Josie's blonde hair, he said, "What I'm wondering is how the attorney in Austin found out about any of it. To my knowledge, no one knew besides Malinda, Nelson, and me. I know they were digging up dirt on all the witnesses, but that's some serious dirt and some seriously *old* dirt."

"Maybe someone saw you and Malinda have sex by the lake, and you never knew. Maybe the attorney came across this person, and he has something against you and your family. It would be a very public way to humiliate you and everyone else. That person just didn't count on the way Tommy, your parents, Memaw, and I reacted. I guess his plan backfired."

"That remains to be seen. This is a small town, and I'm starting a medical practice. If people are put off by what happened, then they may not take their kids to see me for treatment. You know how some people don't want to associate with those who've been raped or molested, even though it wasn't their fault. I can't worry about it unless it happens. We'll see how the good people of Clayville respond once I hang out my shingle."

"Did I detect some major sarcasm in that last sentence?"

"Yes, although I guess starting out with sarcasm isn't going to get me anywhere in Clayville. There *are* good people here. They just need to broaden their horizons and change their mindsets to something a little more accepting."

"Maybe the situation regarding you and Tommy will be a good catalyst for that change."

"One can only hope and pray."

Chapter Eight

In the days that followed, Stone and Josie moved into Wolfwood and prepared for the opening of Romero Pediatrics. Josie loved the colorful chairs, artwork, and toys that now filled the exam rooms. She and Stone hoped the patients and their parents would love it all, too.

"Wake up, Josephine Mamie Hollingsworth Romero. It's Saturday, the twenty-third of June, and you are now officially twenty-six years old."

Josie smiled but refused to open her eyes as she told Stone she wanted to sleep late in honor of her birthday.

"No sleeping late. I'm giving you your two birthday presents from me here; then we're going to my parents' house for lunch. After lunch, we'll eat the birthday cake I made for you, plus you can open your gifts from Tommy, Memaw, Flynn, Mama, and Daddy."

Josie frowned and asked drowsily, "You have two presents for me?"

"I do, but you won't get either of them if you don't open your eyes."

She did so, insisting, "Two is too many. One would be fine."

"Two will be just right this year," he argued. "Happy birthday, Josephine."

Stone lay in his silky, blue boxers beside her in their bed at Wolfwood. Josie wore a short pale green cotton nightgown that had spaghetti straps made of ribbon. All of the windows in their room were open, and she loved it. She'd never lived anywhere where it was safe enough for people to sleep with their windows open even on the second floor.

Since it was early in the day, the temperature in the room was perhaps seventy degrees Fahrenheit. Josie knew from the last several days of experience that the summer morning temperatures were quite pleasant, but the afternoons could be stifling in Wolfwood if all of the windows weren't open and all of the ceiling fans weren't running. However, she also knew that the cost of using central air would be prohibitive for their large home unless it was absolutely necessary. She would adapt and adjust to her environment, just as she always had.

"My eyes are open," she pointed out. "When do I get those first two presents?"

"Hm. Maybe I should make you work for them."

"I've worked hard to stay alive and sane for twenty-six years. I think that's enough."

Stone looked contrite, and she wasn't sure what to say to him. So, she kissed him and repeated her question regarding her birthday presents. He relaxed, and so did she.

"The first one is about your name. I can't be completely sure, of course. Only your mother knows exactly why she named you what she did. However, I did research on the Internet and think I found some plausible explanations."

"Enlighten me."

"I think you got your first name in honor of Joséphine de Beauharnais."

"Napoleon Bonaparte's wife?"

"Yes."

"Any particular reason?"

"You have the same birthday. Other than that, I don't know."

"And Mamie?"

"Well, I thought of Mamie Eisenhower but somehow figured that wouldn't be your mother's style since she was all about government conspiracies and things like that. I decided to search for famous women named Mamie who worked in psychology since your mother had a Ph.D. in the subject. Don't you know I found one? Her name was Mamie Phipps Clark. She and her husband Kenneth were African-American and did ground-breaking work during a time when simply being black and having opportunity in that field and most others was unusual. The couple's work and research were extremely crucial in influencing the 1954 decision made by the Supreme Court in *Brown v. Board of Education*."

"Separate is not equal," Josie murmured. "Having separate public schools for blacks and whites was declared unconstitutional. That Mamie *does* sound like someone Mom would've admired. We'll go with that Mamie." Putting an arm around his waist, she said, "Thank you. I've always wondered but was actually kind of

219

afraid to investigate. With Mom's schizophrenia, I wasn't certain what I'd find out."

"I don't want you to be afraid of anything anymore."

"That's very noble of you."

"You and that noble thing again. You told me not long after we met that I was a noble man. I'm just me."

"Okay, so I spell Stone N-O-B-L-E. What's my second present?"

"Put on your robe, and I'll show you."

Josie rose, slipped into her silky, white, long robe, and tied it at the waist. Stone padded around the bed and took her hand before leading her out of their bedroom. When she began to ask questions, he reminded her she trusted him but refused to say more. Completely confused, she allowed him to guide her down the stairs, through the rooms of the first floor, and out the backdoor. There, she hesitated.

Stone looked questioningly at her, and she said quietly, "My parents never allowed us to go barefoot outside. Dad was afraid that we might get bitten by ants, step on something that might cut us, or contract a rash. If we're going out onto the property, I should at least put on my slippers."

"You've never walked barefoot on grass or dirt in your life?" Stone asked, astonished.

"Not that I can recall."

"Then I guess you're getting three presents today."

He moved down the steps, but Josie stayed put. When he looked back at her, the smile on his face faded. She knew she probably looked petrified. She *was* petrified.

"Do *you* think you'll get bitten by ants, step on something that will cut you, or develop a rash? All of those things could happen, but they're all treatable. You need to feel the earth under your feet."

"I want to. I just…it's like when people say they worry about me and I instinctively feel panic. You're talking about fighting years of programming by my father. I'm scared."

"Will you try to do it?"

"For you."

"No, you need to try it for *you*."

"I'm really scared, and that's so silly."

"It's not silly. It's unfortunate. Come on. I'll walk right beside you and hold your hand all the way."

"How far are we going?"

"A ways. I'll keep you safe."

"But all you're wearing is your boxers, and all I'm wearing is my nightgown and robe. It makes me feel vulnerable."

"We'll be fine." He lifted his arms and flexed his biceps before saying in a deep voice, "Me big, strong man. Me protect my woman."

She grinned then slowly took his hand before descending the steps with him. When she reached the last step, she stopped and stared at the grass. Very tentatively, she lowered one foot.

"It feels so…different." As she lowered her other foot, she added, "I've felt it under my fingers, but it's different under my feet. Nice."

"I am glad it takes so little to make you happy," Stone said with an exaggerated Southern drawl. Lowering his voice, he told her, "Time to be quiet until I say otherwise."

As they left the area behind the house, passed through the gate, and entered the woods, Stone guided her along a dirt path. Inwardly, she marveled at the cool, clay-like earth as she walked on it. The woods were lovely, and sunlight filtered through the branches of the trees. Birds twittered, and she saw a butterfly further up ahead. It was enchanting.

They reached an area that didn't look much different from any other they'd passed on their walk, but Stone stopped. Josie peered around, expecting to find something outstanding that would catch her attention. There was nothing. She glanced questioningly up at Stone, but he wasn't looking at her. He was staring straight ahead and had a remote expression on his face. Josie stared in the same direction but saw nothing.

She was about to break her vow of silence and ask Stone why he'd brought her there when it came to her.

This is where he and Nelson had their encounter with the wolves, she thought. *I'm the only other person in the world who knows what happened here.*

Josie turned, lifted her free hand, slid it along one side of Stone's neck, and pushed it up into his disheveled brown hair. When he looked down at her, she nodded knowingly. He released her hand, wrapped both arms around her, pulled her to him, and slanted his mouth over hers before kissing her with ferocity. She responded with equal intensity and pressed her body against his, eliciting a groan from him.

Josie's breathing quickened as Stone undid the front of her robe and pushed it away from her shoulders. As it fell to the ground, he slid his hands under the hem of her short cotton gown and pushed up the material, bunching it at her waist. One of the spaghetti straps fell across her upper arm, exposing one breast. Stone quickly latched onto that nipple. Josie trembled and reveled in the feel of the tug on her breast, Stone's hands encircling her waist, and the gentle breeze that caressed her exposed flesh, deliciously whispering between her thighs.

"Free me, Josephine," Stone demanded in a graveled voice.

Does he mean free him from his boxers because he wants to pleasure us both? She wondered. *Or does he need for me to make him climax here and free him from being haunted by memories of Nelson? Either way, he wants to be inside me, and I want that more than anything, too.*

Stone's boxers joined Josie's robe on the ground. He growled with desire and pulled her closer, his erection pressing against her belly and making her wet with longing. She whimpered with need.

In one fluid movement Stone knelt and pulled Josie down on top of him. She cried out with surprise and pleasure as he filled her. The other strap of her nightgown slid down, and she crossed her arms over her front and grabbed at the cotton before pulling the gown over her head and tossing it into the pile. She had to lean back to do this, and Stone directed her to stay as she was.

He supported her back with his right hand and forearm, allowing his left hand to explore the flesh of her face, neck, breasts, belly, and inner thighs. When she began to undulate her hips, his breath hitched and hers quickened. Within a matter of seconds, they had found what felt like the perfect rhythm and kept it going for as long as they could. Josie wished it would never end; it felt so *right*.

When Stone stroked her folds where they surrounded his erection, Josie gasped and tightened inside. He grunted and reached his thumb up to rub at her clitoris, and her world exploded. Stone continued to support her as she climaxed, her back arched, her gaze fixed on the branches of the trees above her. Her screams echoed in the woods. She felt him come while she was finishing. Then, Stone lifted Josie up and cradled her against his chest. She sighed with lingering satisfaction.

"Josephine," he murmured.

"Hm?"

"Don't move," Stone said quietly.

"Why not? Did I hurt you?"

"No. Shhh."

"Stone –"

"We're not alone."

"What do you mean we're not alone? This is our property, and there are acres of it."

"Shhh. Be quiet and still."

She obeyed, waiting. At first, she wondered if someone had come onto their land to hunt without permission. Then she saw the pack.

For some reason, Josie experienced no fear as she watched the wolves circle them. She counted five during the next few minutes as she remained absolutely still in Stone's arms. The wolves seemed regal, calm, and curious. Josie, who had never seen a wolf outside of pictures or on television, was fascinated. She watched without moving as the largest one went over to the pile of their clothing and sniffed it. As he moved away, the others did the same before slipping out of Josie's line of sight.

She continued to remain motionless as Stone held her. He was obviously watching the wolves, whatever they were doing. She could hear the beating of his heart under her left ear. It was steady and strong. He wasn't afraid either. He seemed tranquil and relaxed. Well, most of him did. The part that remained inside of her was hardening again, and she felt herself quivering around him and fought the urge to move.

There was movement behind her as the wolves walked away from them through the woods. Before she could ask Stone why he'd just done what he had, he lowered her onto the ground and began to thrust in and out, surrendering to a punishing rhythm that soon brought them both to climax. Stone collapsed on top of her afterwards and lay with his head buried against her neck for a long time.

"Why?" was all she could manage to ask.

"The wolves accepted me and Nelson a long time ago. These wolves must be their descendants. They seem to have an understanding with me, and I wanted them to have that same understanding with you. They got a good whiff of our scents from the air and from our clothing, but I wanted them to know you were mine."

Josie laughed and asked, "You *marked* me like when a dog pees on a tree?"

"More like when a male wolf mates with a female. I wanted them to know that you and I were connected in the most primal of ways. Amateur wolf psychology. They seemed to accept it. I'd still be careful if you come across them while you're walking on the property. Wolves are wild animals and can be very dangerous."

"I'm losing track of how many birthday presents I'm getting from you today," Josie said with a contented sigh. "First, I got your explanation of my name. Then I walked barefoot on grass and dirt. You brought me here, a place that's so significant to you. We had some fabulous sex and then met the wolf pack. We had more fabulous sex. And I still have food, cake, and presents waiting at your parents' house? You are *so* spoiling me."

When they rose, Josie refused to wear the nightgown and robe she'd thrown on the ground. Stone intended to put his boxers back on but stopped when Josie argued that they were dirty and probably had wolf snot on them. Grinning broadly, he picked up all the clothing and took her hand before leading her back to the house. He laughed out loud when she darted from the edge of the woods across the grassy area behind the house to the backdoor. Josie hurried inside and stood in the doorway, admiring Stone's muscular body and lean hips as he casually strolled towards her.

"What if someone sees you?" she called out when he neared the house.

"My parents are the only other people besides us who have access through the gate and keys to the house."

"That would almost be more embarrassing than a stranger!" she exclaimed. "What if they saw us naked?"

"I'm sure they'd be as embarrassed as we'd be. They won't just come out here anymore. Wolfwood's not deserted like it used to be. They'll respect our privacy and call first." Coming inside and shutting the door behind him, he said, "That does make me think about Tommy though. If he is my son and comes to live with us, then we won't be able to do things like that unless we're sure he won't be home."

"How soon will the paternity report come in?"

"It'll go to Flynn's office since that's where we did the swabs. It all depends on the lab. It might be a few days or a couple weeks. Flynn will let us know as soon as he gets the results."

Josie took the clothing from his hands and immediately put it in the washing machine, poured in some detergent, and hit the Delicates button. She planned on laundering the nightgown, robe, and boxers several times before declaring them "clean." She'd been impressed by their encounter with the wolves, but she wanted to make certain any physical traces of the wild animals were removed from the articles before they wore them again.

After they'd showered, eaten breakfast, and dressed, they drove to Flynn's in order to pick the man up. His truck was at a mechanic's shop for repairs, and Stone had offered him a ride to the Romero home. As they pulled into the gravel parking lot, Josie watched an attractive black woman exit through the front door, go to a Buick, and climb in. As the woman drove out of the lot, Josie thought it odd that Flynn was seeing patients on a Saturday morning. She remarked on this to Stone, who smiled slightly and said he doubted the woman had been a patient.

"Flynn doesn't discriminate when it comes to the color of a person's skin, and that includes the women he sleeps with."

"I thought you said he didn't date much."

"I did. That doesn't mean he's celibate."

"Oh. Wouldn't a white man sleeping with black women be frowned upon in Clayville?"

"It could get him hurt or killed. He's told me that's why they don't go out. They have a meal, watch a movie, or do other things at his home so that no one can question what's going on. Most people would assume exactly what you did – that he was seeing a patient for some urgent care issue. I've warned him to be careful. He doesn't listen."

Flynn, whose blonde hair appeared mussed from sleep, answered the door wearing jeans and an LSU t-shirt. Josie wondered if he'd been a linebacker for Louisiana State University or if he'd gone somewhere else for college and had attended the LSU Medical

225

School. He invited them in and apologized, saying he was running a few minutes late as he yawned and rubbed sleep from his brown eyes.

"Yes, we saw the reason leaving on our way in," Stone remarked. "We're not in a rush. It's fine."

"How come you never told me you had sex with Malinda?" Flynn blurted out. "I thought you and I were tight, Man."

"I was a scared thirteen-year-old. And don't tell me I shouldn't have been afraid to tell you. You've never outright told me you were sleeping with black women, and you're thirty-one, not thirteen."

"Aren't there any biracial couples in town?" asked Josie.

"Only in the run-down trailer parks," Flynn answered. "And even those families are looked down upon. Their kids are treated pretty badly. If I were to go public with my choices of partners, then it could easily wipe out our careers and our lives. I'd rather not have the KKK burning down my house and clinic and hurting anyone."

"The Ku Klux Klan is still active?" Josie asked in disbelief.

"Not like it used to be, but radicals remain and keep the hate alive. It's not only the whites who are racist. Believe me, there are some blacks who'd castrate me if they knew I was sleeping with black women."

"We can change that," Josie insisted.

"Spoken like a true city girl," Stone muttered. "You both need to be careful or it could get all of us in trouble."

"I'll be good," she said without conviction. Flynn remained silent.

Stone smiled and kissed his wife before suggesting, "We should get going. It's almost lunchtime."

"Before we leave I have something for you," Flynn said to Stone. Holding out a sealed envelope, he stated, "Here are the DNA results. They came in yesterday afternoon's mail."

Stone accepted the envelope and stared down at it before admitting, "I don't know what to do. Should I open it here or wait until we're at my parents'? If I'm Tommy's father, then he'll be elated. If I'm not, who knows how he'll react. I don't want this to overshadow Josie's birthday party."

"I think you should open it," Flynn advised. "If you're Tommy's father, then you can tell him and everything will be good with everyone in the family except Cheek, who won't be there anyway. If you're not, then you can wait until later to break the news to Tommy."

"I agree with Flynn," Josie put in. "If you don't open it now that's all you'll be thinking about for the rest of the day. I want you to enjoy my birthday with me."

Stone opened the envelope and withdrew the folded paper from inside. He straightened it and scanned the contents without any visible change in his expression. Josie's heart sank. She wondered how Stone would break the news to his nephew.

"He's mine," he said quietly. "Tommy's my son!"

Josie threw her arms around Stone's neck and kissed him. Flynn congratulated him as they all expressed their immense relief. Josie suppressed the pang of remorse she felt for denying Stone more children and pushed away an image of Stone holding a baby in his arms, looking down at it with an expression of love and tenderness.

"How are you going to tell Tommy?" Flynn asked as they rode to the Romero home for Josie's party.

"I have no idea. Do either of you have any suggestions?"

"Just tell him the moment you see him," Josie urged. When Stone seemed uncertain, she added, "Trust me."

Stone laughed and said, "I thought that was *my* line."

"Well, I'm borrowing it for this afternoon. Actually, I might start using it a lot more often."

He grinned impishly and then laughed. Josie wished she could've seen him as a boy, being carefree with Nelson, Flynn, and other friends. Although he was often relaxed, happy, and calm, he was rarely carefree. Of course, Josie was *never* carefree, except when she and Stone were having sex. It was regrettable, but true. She was thankful for those moments and treasured each one.

Chapter Nine

As the next two months passed, Tommy, overjoyed by the results of the paternity test, alternated between residing at Wolfwood and his grandparents' home. He decided to call Stone "Dad" but addressed Josie by her given name, which suited her fine. She was thrilled that Tommy was Stone's son and was also relieved that Cheek had kept away from all of the other Romeros. For the first time in as long as Josie could remember, she had a true family.

Unfortunately, adjusting to life in Clayville had proven more challenging than Josie had anticipated. Residents in the community displayed outright bigotry on a regular basis. People tended to be complacent, showing little desire to change their prejudicial attitudes or to improve their circumstances. There was a lack of diversity regarding shops, restaurants, and cultural activities. Despite Stone's warnings before their move, Josie had thought she could easily handle these issues, but she had to admit that life in Clayville was often frustrating. Still, she remained committed to adapting to her new town and to generating change there.

One day during the last week of August, Josie stopped and glanced around the packed waiting room at Carmody & Romero. Flynn had told them that his practice always had a steady stream of clientele, but the number of patients had quadrupled the first week that Stone had joined the practice. Not only were children being brought in for treatment, but more of their adult relatives were now coming to Flynn for their ailments as well. It had been a win-win situation for both doctors, but their two months in business together had been more than frenetic.

Stone, Flynn, and Josie had ironed out a routine at the practice. Josie loved running the clinic, although she'd worked for hours every evening during that first month in order to straighten out Flynn's haphazard record-keeping system and financial accounts. He had plenty of money but had paid little attention to where any of it was until she'd created computer files, folders, and spreadsheets and explained everything to him and to Stone.

"So, are you going to stick around?" Flynn asked Stone once Josie had reviewed the details of the clinic's financial accounts.

"Looks like it. Why?"

"Because I own my practice, and you joined it and are paying me rent. I want you to own half if you plan on staying."

"I don't have that kind of money," Stone said frankly. "I have the house Nelson left me, but I wouldn't risk losing that for anything in the world."

"We have the money," Josie piped in. "I still have a lot of money I earned as a realtor and from the sale of my house in Los Angeles, remember?"

"That's *your* money," Stone pointed out.

"When we had the lawyer draw up our wills last month, I seem to recall your leaving me the house and a quarter of any assets you had. Tommy would inherit the rest. If I die before you, then you get whatever assets I have. What's mine is yours, and what's yours is mine. It's not *my* money; it's *our* money. If we put it into the practice, then you and Flynn can be equal partners, and there won't ever be any disputes regarding the actual business. Well, there may be disputes, but at least you'd be equal when it came to making decisions."

"You really do want to spend the rest of your life in Clayville," Flynn said with a smile. "After the last few weeks, are you sure?"

"Of course, I am. I love it here. I love my husband, my stepson, my in-laws, some friend named Flynn, the work I'm doing, and the area. It's nice to live in a town where everyone knows you and most people are genuine, whether they're genuinely sweet or nasty. At least you know where you stand with people. That's something I never had before."

"And the racist, undereducated, backwards mentality that seems to be prevalent?" Stone prompted.

"Can be changed. It *is* changing because of what we're doing here at the clinic. I want to help it change more."

"Well, you're certainly doing that. You interact the same with whites and blacks alike whether it's here, in stores, at restaurants, or at the gym," Flynn remarked. "And your car's only been egged that one time." Looking back to Stone, he asked, "So, are you in? Fifty-fifty?"

229

"You don't want a controlling interest? It was originally your practice."

"Fifty-fifty."

"No." When Flynn looked crestfallen, Stone continued, "You can own fifty percent. I want the other half to be divided equally between Josie and me."

Before she could voice any objections, Flynn said, "Done."

"But you're the doctors!" Josie exclaimed. "It should be between the two of you."

"It *is* between the two of us, and that might be a problem someday," Flynn pointed out. "We've been friends since we were babies. There might be a time when we disagree and get deadlocked. You're the tie-breaker, the negotiator, the voice of reason. You'll keep us both in line, and we'll do the same for you if you get carried away with something we know won't fly around here. Good move, Stone. You always were better at chess than I was."

As the memory of their exchange faded, Josie smiled. She pictured Stone and Flynn as teenagers, playing chess.

"Hello there, young lady!"

Josie glanced towards the front door of the clinic. She recognized Miss Iris, a sweet, elderly, well-spoken, terminally ill black patient. Once she and Josie had chatted for a few minutes, Miss Iris declared that she'd been feeling worse and had gotten a friend to drop her off at the clinic so that Flynn could examine her.

"I'm sure he'll see you after his last scheduled appointment. Would you sign in and take a seat?"

"It's not like I have anything better to do," Miss Iris chuckled. "Thank you, Miss Josie."

"Please, just call me 'Josie.' "

"That's not the way I was raised," the woman informed her. "But thank you for the offer."

The remainder of the afternoon passed quickly. Flynn appeared grim when he emerged with Miss Iris from the exam room at 5:30. The woman patted him on the arm and smiled tiredly at Josie and Stone, who stood together in the waiting room.

"Miss Iris, do you have a ride home?" Flynn asked quietly. "I can take you."

"I'd like for Miss Josie to drive me home. I want to visit with her over some coffee and cake."

"Of course," Josie said automatically. "Let me get my purse. Stone, I'll meet you back at Wolfwood."

Nodding, he said, "Call me if you're going to be too late so that I won't worry."

Ignoring the momentary flip-flop she felt in her belly at the mention of worry, Josie assured him, "I will. I have my iPhone with me. I'll be fine."

Stone didn't look convinced, but she ignored this and helped Miss Iris to her Volvo. Josie followed her verbal directions, as she drove them to the woman's house. It was a small, red brick home with an attached carport that held no car. The interior was pristine and was decorated in a style reminiscent of the 1950s. Josie smiled, thinking of how many people in present times were paying a lot of money to buy retro furniture and accessories that Miss Iris had kept in her home for decades.

"Home sweet home," Miss Iris told her, as they sat with their plates of pound cake and cups of coffee at the square Formica kitchen table. "It really has been a wonderful house, this little place of mine. My husband and I bought it a long time ago and took a lot of pride in decorating it just so. A year after we'd finished, he was killed. I was a week away from giving birth to our son. The nursery is the only room in the house that's changed over the years. Doing anything with the rest seemed disrespectful to my husband's memory. Plus, with everything the way it was I felt as if he was still here with me and our baby. I wish my son could've known his daddy."

Josie wondered what had happened to Iris's husband but was too polite to ask. As it turned out, she didn't have to.

"My husband, Isaiah, was a deliveryman who was killed because he helped a married white woman change a flat tire. What he didn't know was that she was driving home from having sex with a married white man. Her husband figured out when she got back that she'd been with someone other than him, and she accused Isaiah of rape to cover up her affair. He'd been spotted by several people changing her tire. He was arrested, tried, and found not guilty. We were so relieved."

"But if he was found not guilty, then how did he die?"

231

"A lot of white folks didn't believe he hadn't raped the woman. The day after his release, the Ku Klux Klan came, took Isaiah, and hung him in some woods. The woman, who was filled with guilt, stood up in her church and confessed about her lying to everyone. Then she went home and shot herself. She left a little baby boy of her own." Sighing, she went on, "Poor David Skinner. I think that's why he's so intolerant of sinners. His daddy was real bitter, and everyone knew his mama had been breaking her wedding vows, let an innocent man be falsely accused then murdered, and then went and killed herself."

"David Skinner? You mean the pastor?"

"The very same. I think David wanted to prove to everyone that he wasn't tainted by his mama's sins. He went too far the other way and is one of the most judgmental men I know. What a terrible burden he's had on his shoulders all his life."

"What about his wife?"

"Which one?"

Josie almost choked on the bite of cake she was in the process of swallowing. She took a gulp of coffee, scalding the back of her throat in the process, and then asked, "Mary Ann's not his first wife? Was he a widower?"

"Divorced."

"But David Skinner is obviously a Bible thumper. Why in the world would he ever get a divorce?"

"His first wife left him after ten years of marriage. He almost lost his congregation over that."

"Wait a minute. *She* left *him*, but *he* almost lost his job over it?"

"The people in his church are very narrow-minded, as you can well imagine. He was devastated when his wife left him – then doubly so when his followers threatened to oust him as their leader. They said they weren't certain they could trust him to lead them spiritually when he couldn't lead his own household. You reap what you sow."

"But he didn't. He's still the pastor."

"Because of Mary Ann. She saw an opportunity to further her own ambition. By stepping in and marrying David, she saved both him and his career. It's plain to see that Mary Ann has her own agenda, and she uses her position as the pastor's wife to do what *she* wants and to promote her interests and ideas. David is indebted to her for the rest of his life. At least they were already in their forties when they got married and never had children. Praise Jesus for that!"

Josie grinned and nodded, as she took another bite of pound cake.

"I've gotten myself a bit sidetracked," Iris declared. "I know almost everybody and everything that's gone on in this town since I was a little girl, and I sense that you need some guidance. I'm sorry I don't have more time left to live."

"You might be fine," Josie said earnestly. "You told me in the car that you got better the last time you had cancer."

Iris gave her a sad smile and said, "I can tell this time I'm fading fast. There are some things I think you should know that you don't because you weren't born and raised here and didn't have the same upbringing as the locals. I'll make it brief. You can sort it all out later. These are only my observations, but I'm a smart and observant woman, if I do say so myself.

"I've raised a lot of white folks' babies and have lived in this town all my life. You're not like most people around here. You need some background on those closest to you and on Clayville itself if you're going to make your life in this community."

"I'd love any advice or information you could give me."

"As you know, the people in this area are giving and helpful like typical Southerners are. Some blacks are better educated than most in Clayville, but they're either self-taught like I was or were able to go away to school. The majority of blacks get a piss-poor education in the public school system. The majority of whites aren't much better educated, but they do have more opportunity. The racial lines are starting to fade, which is good. But there are still a lot of very racist people in Clayville. You have to push for change but be careful, too."

"I understand."

"I don't think you do. It's going to take you years of trial and error to figure it out. Louisiana, Mississippi, and Alabama...this part of the United States is like a whole other country. That's why I worry so much about Dr. Flynn and his sleeping with black women."

"You know about that?"

"I've known for quite a while. I think most people in town know, but as long as he and his women don't do anything out in the

233

open, folks pretend like nothing's going on. I worry it won't stay that way forever."

"Maybe people will become more accepting."

"Or it will get him and the women killed."

"Do people still do things like that around here?"

"The last time was about twenty years ago, but the KKK remains. There aren't as many of them as there were when my husband was killed, and I'm grateful for that. It doesn't have to be the KKK though. As long as hateful people exist, they'll feel threatened by any unwelcome change and may act on their fear. I don't want to see you, Dr. Stone, Dr. Flynn, or anyone else in danger. That's why I wanted to talk straight with you. You're so innocent."

"Innocent?"

"Yes. You seem very street-smart and independent, but I also get the feeling that you know next to nothing about normal everyday life and tend to be a bit anxious. The combination isn't something I usually see in people, and I know people. You must have had a very unusual childhood."

"That's putting it mildly," Josie muttered.

She knew that the woman must have heard her comment, but Miss Iris simply proceeded to say, "Hold your own but don't do anything rash if you come into conflict with idiots, be they black or white. Pick your battles. Be charitable to those who are less worldly than you. Use whatever happened to you as a child to strengthen you as an adult. Don't let your fears rule your life."

Josie thought about Miss Iris's words. Her advice involved common sense, and the things she'd suggested were the things Josie always strove to do, not that she was successful in every instance. She was grateful for the woman's help.

"Miss Josie, I have this feeling you're going to be at the center of whatever change is coming, so I'd better prepare you as best I can. Ask about anyone, and I'll give you my thoughts for what they're worth."

"I guess I'll start with Flynn. He's part of my new family, even though we're not related in any way."

"Dr. Flynn has a big brain and a big heart. He'll never forgive his daddy for leaving him and his mama and for causing his mama's death. He's book smart but can't balance a checkbook. Lord knows

I tried to teach him when I was the family housekeeper years ago, but his mind just doesn't work that way. He's a loyal man and will stand by anyone he loves. He got thrown in jail once when he was fifteen for beating a fellow student who called Nelson a very ugly name. Flynn did a hundred community service hours for that and said he'd have gladly done thousands if it'd stop people from bullying those who were different. I was so proud."

"I didn't know that last part," admitted Josie. "How about Dr. Vincent Romero?"

"Dr. Romero was a brilliant, twisted man who liked to beat his wife and son and thought of us black folks as animals."

"Do you think he loved Memaw and Vin?"

"No. He married Miss Gertrude because of her family's money, and he didn't take care of Vin. He didn't protect him."

The tiny hairs on the back of Josie's neck stood up as she asked, "Protect him from what?"

"Evil, but I can't really say what kind." Looking shrewdly at Josie, she asked, "Your daddy didn't protect you from evil either, did he?"

Unable to speak, Josie rapidly shook her head, working hard to suppress the fear that was threatening to overtake her. Miss Iris seemed to sense this and went on to volunteer that Gertrude Romero was very smart, sweet, and productive as long as she was on her medications. Unfortunately for her son, she'd been mentally unstable for all of his childhood years.

"And Vin?" Josie asked when she regained her voice.

"He's a smart man, smarter than he lets on. He's always wanted to be accepted as 'one of the guys' but is more advanced than they are and knows how to deal with people in difficult situations. He also has an unwavering sense of right and wrong. That's why he makes such a good lawman. I personally think that whatever evil was done to him made him work harder to be a successful policemen, husband, and father."

"What do you think of Dumpling?"

"She's so nice but not anywhere near as bright as her husband. She's what he needed. All that boy wanted was love and normalcy, and Miss Dumpling's got plenty of that. She's not very imaginative, but I think that's what Mister Vin craved. He wanted predictable after all those years with his volatile father and unstable mother. As for Miss Dumpling, she's always been heavy and self-conscious about it. The fact that Mister Vin never seemed to care must have been a huge relief to her. I think she still wonders what she did to deserve him, which is sad."

"What about Cheek?"

"He's like Dr. Vincent but without the brains and genteel background."

"And Tommy?"

"He's like Dr. Stone. He went through some rough times, but I think he'll turn out well. I saw him at Walmart yesterday. Being with his father and you has done wonders for his self-esteem. Just knowing he wasn't really Cheek Romero's son would be a boost to *any* boy's self-esteem!"

"What about Nelson?"

Miss Iris smiled wistfully and said, "Curious, sensitive to others' feelings, artistic, smart, and talkative. He also tended to alternate between being excitable and depressed, kind of like Miss Gertrude used to be before she was on her medications. Not that he was that extreme, mind you. It was more subtle, but there. He so wanted to have his father's approval without changing who he really was, but that proved to be his undoing. Poor Nelson. I do miss him."

"What about Stone?"

"All man but not in that fool way some men have where they're full of themselves. He's brilliant about medicine like his grandfather but nothing like him in his personality, thank God. He's an excellent hunter and fisherman."

"What was he like as a kid?"

"Quiet, rebellious, angry, defiant, and driven." After taking a sip of her coffee, she went on, "Stone was very protective of Nelson as they got older and his homosexuality was impossible to miss. Nelson was bullied a lot and couldn't take care of himself in a fight. So, Stone did a lot of fighting for a while. That didn't go over well with Mister Vin, who'd already had trouble with Cheek. Stone and Mister Vin clashed a lot when Stone was a teenager." Looking chagrined, Miss Iris said, "Stone didn't feel like he could talk to his parents about important things, but he'd talk to me about what was troubling him. He'd known me all his life and felt comfortable around me. He once confided to me when I was the Carmody's housekeeper and he was about Tommy's age that he wondered if he'd ever find a girl who would love him for who he really was. He wanted someone to take care of him and who'd let him take care of her. When I assured him there had to be some girl out there who fit that description, he added that she had to be more interesting than any other girl he'd ever met. He said he wanted a woman who never failed to surprise him, even if it meant it made him frustrated. I laughed and said anything was possible." Cocking her head, she murmured, "I was right. You fit his description perfectly."

"I do? How can you tell? You barely know me."

"That doesn't matter. I told you that I'd raised a lot of babies. I lived in the world of white folks and black folks and had access to both cultures and viewpoints. I learned a lot. I could probably tell you everything about your life, even though I haven't spent much time with you and no one's really told me much about you other than that you're a city girl who's strong-willed but very likeable." Grinning broadly, she asked, "You know what my granddaughter likes to call me?" When Josie shook her head, Miss Iris said, "Sherlockeisha Holmes." When Josie laughed, the woman added, "She says they should make a TV show about me and my deductions. Lord, I think it's a bit late for that! I'm just an old woman who has a good head on her shoulders and has always liked learning and keeping my brain cells active!"

Josie laughed, but it was a nervous laugh. Unable to resist, she asked Miss Iris to tell her about herself. The elderly woman studied her for a long time before she spoke.

"You're actually scared most of the time, but you don't let that stop you when you have a goal in mind. You always have to have a goal or else you want to give up. Your parents were extremely well-educated, but there was something seriously wrong with them. You had an older brother or sister. You loved your family, but things were very bad for you. They're all gone, and you feel relieved and guilty about that at the same time." After eating her last bite of cake, she continued, "Evil was done to you when you were small, and your parents didn't protect you, just like Dr. Vincent didn't protect Mister Vin. You and Mister Vin are actually a lot alike and have some kind of bond, but you can't bring yourself to completely trust anyone except Stone. You don't even trust yourself." Rising slowly from the table, Miss Iris said, "You're unique and beautiful, and God loves you. Dr. Stone loves you. Never lose hope."

Josie sat subdued and somewhat shaken. The woman had done an excellent job of describing her. Her powers of perception were uncanny, and her advice was sound. Josie wished that Miss Iris had been around to help raise her. Perhaps she would have turned out differently. Perhaps every day wouldn't be such a struggle.

Chapter Ten

Josie left Miss Iris's house at 8:00 p.m. and then headed home to Wolfwood. She was relieved that it was Tommy's week to stay with his grandparents and great-grandmother. She wanted to be alone with Stone that night. She needed to talk with him, hold him, and have him hold her.

Josie thought about Miss Iris's comments regarding Clayville and those closest to her. The woman did seem to have a gift for being accurate in her observations and deductions, and Josie mulled over what they'd discussed. Most of it was not news to her. The only thing that did come as a complete surprise had been Stone's concerns about not finding love. He was Stone. What eligible woman *didn't* want him?

Remember what she said, Josie reminded herself. *It wasn't that he wouldn't find a woman; it was that he wouldn't find a woman who wanted him for who he was, who needed him, and who could comfort him and keep him…wondering. That's why he was so attracted to me. Remember when he said I was the most complicated woman he'd ever met? Who knew that my being screwed up and depressed would be a draw to a man someday? Maybe that's why I was born to two mentally ill people. If they hadn't messed up Zelda and me so badly, then would Stone have fallen in love with me? I would've been just another girl.*

She thought of the adjectives Miss Iris had used to describe Stone: brilliant, quiet, angry, rebellious, defiant, and driven. She'd also mentioned his penchant for fighting when Nelson was threatened. Josie recalled what had happened the previous December when Stone had hit the father of the gay boy in the Emergency Room and of how high Stone's blood pressure had risen. He was a quiet man who seemed to always be in control, but was that actually the case? Perhaps he was perpetually angry and kept that emotion in check almost all the time. That, combined with his family's genetic predisposition to cardiovascular disease, might have been the trigger for the onset of hypertension at such a young age.

Thank goodness he's a doctor who works with a doctor in case there are future problems. Well, I know there will be future problems. Am I really ready for them? What would I do if Stone really did have a heart attack or a stroke? How would I respond?

Thoughts of Clark Hollingsworth suddenly filled Josie's head. At least his death had been quick. Had he been alive, he would have lived in constant panic at the mention of his daughter's job, working face-to-face with patients in a doctors' office. Feeling guilty, Josie was relieved her father wasn't alive to worry about her.

She pulled up to the front gates of Wolfwood, typed in the security code, and then drove through when the gates swung open. She parked the car, took a deep, cleansing breath, and went to the house. Josie found Stone sitting with his eyes closed on the couch in the living room.

Without looking towards her, he said, "I don't want Miss Iris to die."

"I know."

"But she will. Soon."

"We all will at some point."

"Death doesn't scare you."

"No. It's life that scares me."

He looked across the room at her and asked, "How old *were* you the first time you considered killing yourself?"

Chewing on her lower lip, Josie thought about this before saying, "Ten, I think."

"How many times have you considered it since?"

She shrugged. She truly didn't know. It was a battle she'd waged off and on ever since that first time.

"Did you ever try it?"

"Stone –"

"Answer me," he ordered calmly. "Did you ever try to kill yourself?"

"Seriously try? I came close once when I was fourteen."

"What happened?"

"I don't want to talk about it."

"I don't care. I have to know."

"Why?"

"Because I can't live without you and want to know what I'm up against. Tell me what happened when you came close to committing suicide. What pushed you harder than usual? What were you going to do?"

"I, um, was going to jump to my death."

"Like Nelson," he said darkly.

"Not quite. There was no bridge involved."

"Tell me what happened, Josie. I have to know."

"End-of-Days told Mom to destroy everything I had when Zelda and I were at school one day. Dad was at the store. Mom left Zelda's things alone. Everything I had that was in the apartment was trashed. That included books, papers, trinkets, clothes, shoes, my bedspread and sheets, the mattress…." Shaking her head, she continued, "We couldn't afford to replace everything all at once, so Zelda and I slept together in her bed for about six months until I could get another mattress." Staring at the rug beneath her feet, she said, "But all of my things – what few things I had – were gone! Mom had cut them up or torn them or set them on fire in a big bowl. That set off all Dad's smoke detectors." Laughing bitterly, she said, "At least he knew they worked. When Zelda and I got home, I screamed at Mom and told her to tell End-of-Days to fuck off and never come back! I told Mom I hated her and End-of-Days, Six-Six-Six, and the others and wished they were all dead! Then I ran to the top of the apartment building, which was eight stories high. I got up on the edge of the roof and looked down and wondered why I was living when life was so horrible for me."

His voice graveled with emotion, Stone asked, "Why didn't you jump?"

"Because I spotted a little kid across the street and didn't want him to see me smash into the pavement. I was also afraid he'd run into the street and I'd accidentally fall on him and kill him. I backed away from the ledge and sat on the ground, and that's where Dad found me and apologized for Mom. He said she was sick and all the usual stuff. I told him I understood. He had no idea about what I'd almost done. It was just another day in our world of insanity for him."

Stone stood and came over to take Josie in his arms. She hugged him tightly and said, "Never let me go. Remind me why life is worth living."

"I try to do that every day. Remember your promise. You're never going to leave me. Remember, Josephine."

"I remember," she said softly. "I'm sorry about Miss Iris. You've known her a long time and are upset about her being sick and dying. She's a really nice, intelligent, wonderful woman."

"Yes. She was sort of my grown-up confidant when I was a kid. She was Flynn's parents' housekeeper for quite a few years, so I was around her off and on all the time while she worked for them. If I had problems with my family, I'd talk to her and felt better afterwards. She was like that with Flynn, Nelson, and me. Flynn's going to be devastated when Miss Iris goes. She was like his second mother."

Josie nodded against his chest and asked, "Could we not talk anymore about bad things tonight? I think I've reached my limit."

"Sure. Why don't we go upstairs, take off our work clothes, shower, and go to bed. I don't know about you, but I'm exhausted."

"Did you eat?"

"I picked up a pepperoni pizza with extra cheese on the way home."

"But that's one of the worst things you could eat because of your blood pressure problems!"

"It is. I needed it tonight. I haven't had one for so long, and thinking about Miss Iris made me sad. I wanted to indulge. It tasted amazing. There's some in the fridge if you're hungry."

"I'll have a piece for breakfast. I had pound cake at Miss Iris's. It was delicious. Too bad I'll get cancer now."

Stone stopped walking and asked, "What are you talking about?"

Josie smiled tiredly and said, "My father thought you could catch cancer. That was one of his fears. He'd read an article in some journal that stated there was speculation about cancer being contagious. He never forgot it and told us not to eat anything with a cancer patient. The cancer germs might be in the food or on anything they touched. We also shouldn't use bathrooms where cancer patients had been. And you couldn't even begin to talk to him about people with HIV or AIDS. He was so dominated by his anxieties. He had no idea that one of my closest friends in college was gay and that I went to her church with her a few times. It was a predominately gay congregation, and I shook hands with others, hugged people, and took Communion. Going to any church with all those germs would've scared him, but if he'd known I'd gone to *that*

242

church? There were a lot of people with compromised immune systems present."

Stone appeared as if he wanted to say something but kept silent as they climbed the stairs. They were soon clean, snuggling under the sheets in their bed. Josie fell instantly to sleep and had jumbled dreams of mean Dr. Romero beating Memaw and Vin, of Cheek drinking at what was surely his strip club, of young Tommy sleeping in his mother's arms, of Flynn and a black woman having dinner at a fancy restaurant, of Nelson drawing the plans for Wolfwood, and of Dumpling cooking and cleaning in her little house. In every scene, Stone stood with his hands balled into fists, his face red with suppressed rage. Josie wanted to tell him to stop, that his repressed anger would kill him. Instead, she found herself gagged and tied to a tree by something amorphous that she intuited was End-of-Days.

Josie woke, breathing hard. Her pulse was racing. Stone lay sleeping soundly beside her. Josie pressed her body against his and rested her head on his shoulder. She stayed that way until dawn broke and then rose and went downstairs to eat a slice of the pepperoni pizza.

"Why did you lie to me?" Stone asked seriously when he entered the kitchen clad only in his boxers.

"What are you talking about?"

"You said you didn't go to church because of your father and the germs. Last night, you said you went with your gay friend to her church several times."

"I never said I didn't go to church *ever*. Did I? I don't remember. I thought I said I never went with my family. The few times I went with my friend it was to support her in her decision to join that congregation. Her family didn't know she was gay. They wouldn't have gone to the church with her, so I did."

"But you took Communion."

"They're pieces of bread, Stone. I was curious to see what they tasted like. I didn't burst into flames the moment they touched my tongue."

"Do you want to go to church?"

"What?"

"Do you want to go to church?" he repeated more emphatically.

"No. Do you?"

"No, but Mama and Daddy are disappointed that we don't go."

"And Memaw?"

"Memaw doesn't go to church anymore either. That disappoints them as well. I wish I wanted to go, but I have issues with authority and have never felt anything but anger during church services."

Josie frowned and asked, "Are you angry all the time?"

"Not all the time. Just most of it."

"You hide it very well."

"I've had a lifetime of practice. Sometimes, I slip."

"Have you ever been carefree? I thought I saw a flash of that once and wondered if you were like that as a boy."

"Sure. When I was a kid hanging with Nelson and Flynn I was very carefree. We had some great times and adventures. When I'm with kids at any time, I'm a lot more relaxed. That's one reason I went into pediatrics. It can be stressful working with really sick children or those who are in bad situations, but kids are great and make me happy. They're typically so innocent. It makes me forget my anger when I interact with them."

"And when you're not Dr. Romero on the job?"

"It's not like I dwell on my anger, but I guess it's always there under the surface. I learned how to handle it over the years."

"Yes, you internalized it," she observed. "That's probably why you have hypertension."

"Are you telling me *you're* not angry all the time?"

"I'm not. I'm anxious and depressed a lot, but that's to be expected. My parents were crazy. What's your excuse?" Before he could answer, she continued, "Your parents love you so much and have their own baggage. Clayville may be a hick town, but there are good people of all kinds here, not only bad. Just because they don't know any better doesn't make them stupid!"

"Don't lecture me on what my childhood was like!" Stone snapped. "You have no right!"

"I have every right!" Josie shouted back. "I *dare* you to tell me your childhood was so terrible when I was raised in a living hell with hundreds of hallucinations and truly disturbed parents who didn't protect us, make sure we were always fed, and often scared us either with their actions or delusions. I wish I'd had parents like yours! They're great. They've spent their lives trying to do everything they could to take care of their family in the way they thought was best, whether it was the way *you* thought was best or not. They would die

244

for you and Cheek, even though they don't even really like Cheek and probably didn't like you very much either before you moved back! They would've died for Nelson, even though they didn't understand or approve of his homosexuality! I wish I could've said the same about my mother and father!" Stone was staring open-mouthed at her as she went on, "As I said last night, we're all going to die someday. You might die sooner than you should because of your hypertension, which is exacerbated by your suppressed anger. So, things were backwards here, and you resented all of it. That part of your life is over! I'm trying to let go of my family's ghosts, but you still have your family here and now! You can work on making things better every day that you have with them. You're wasting it! You're wasting time and your life and their lives and…and...and you should stop taking everything for granted!"

Josie darted out of the back door and across the lawn to the back gate. After punching in the security code, she ran down the path to the spot where Stone had taken her on her birthday, the spot where he and Nelson had first met the wolves. Once she reached it, Josie dropped to her knees, bursting into tears. She cried for a while.

When she eventually stopped, she realized that she was only wearing her lavender cotton nightgown and was sweaty and dirty from sitting on the ground in the woods. She was surprised that Stone hadn't followed her. Perhaps he was now *really* angry. Perhaps she'd crossed some indefinable line. She hadn't been able to help herself. She was afraid of losing Stone. He knew himself so well, but he couldn't seem to relinquish control in order to release his deep-seeded anger. If he didn't, then Josie figured it would lead to his premature death.

He talks about how people in Clayville won't change, but he's guilty of the very same thing, Josie thought. *He won't bend, even if it breaks him. I can't let that happen. How can I make him understand?*

She thought of the kickboxing Stone did at the gym while she walked on the treadmill or used the machines for resistance training. Flynn typically lifted weights but liked to jog around town to get his aerobic exercise. Perhaps if Stone started to jog with Flynn it would help. After all, any form of exercise was good for releasing endorphins in the brain and relieving depression and stress. It was also good for lowering blood pressure.

245

"Josie?"

Without turning around, she answered, "Yes, Stone?"

"Are you okay?"

"No. Are you?"

"No. Are *we* okay?"

"I don't know. Are we?"

"I don't know either. I'm really scared of losing you."

"Don't worry. I'm not going to jump off the roof of the house."

"That's not funny."

"It wasn't meant to be."

"Are you going to leave me?"

She looked back at him and echoed, "Leave? Stone, I'm terrified of losing you because of your health issues and because of my weirdness."

He sat beside her in the dirt and said, "I do have some serious anger issues, but that has nothing to do with you. You were right about me holding onto my anger and how it affects me physiologically. As for your 'weirdness,' I happen to consider you refreshingly unique and beautiful. I'd never leave you, not voluntarily anyway."

"So, what are you going to do about your anger problem?"

"After you left the house, I did some thinking. I went online and researched anger management retreats. There's one tailored to physicians that will be held in Little Rock over the Labor Day weekend. I registered for it. It sounds pretty intense with the requirements and program, and there are no clocks, watches, phones, tablets, or computers allowed. After the three-day retreat, there's one follow-up session per month that last an entire Saturday. That goes on for six months. A lot of doctors with anger issues recommended it, so I figure I'll give it a shot and see if it helps."

"And if it doesn't?"

"Then I'll figure out what does. I want to be around to spend the rest of your life with you. I want to be able to say to Mama and Daddy that I love them without having it be tinged with anger at the same time. I want to be a good example for my son." Kissing her temple, he said, "Speaking of sons, when are we going to talk more about adopting some children or at least getting some pets?"

"My goal was to reach twenty-seven and not become schizophrenic, remember? We have ten months to go. For now, we'll have to be satisfied with our pack of wolves here."

"And what about being satisfied in other ways?" he asked as he surprised Josie by slipping a hand between her legs.

"Being satisfied is good," she gasped. "So is stress relief."

Josie sensed the wolves nearby as she and Stone made love in the woods. Again, she felt no fear. It was almost as if they had their own private sentinels guarding them against everything beyond the trees in the world of men, a world the wolves had no desire to know. Josie wished that she and Stone could stay in the woods with the wolves for *ever*….

As Labor Day approached, Stone informed his family that he had a conference to attend over the holiday weekend and suggested that they stay at Wolfwood with Josie while he was gone. They were disappointed that he wouldn't be home with all of them but eagerly agreed to the weekend visit. Flynn was asked to join them but declined, citing previous commitments.

"I wish Stone were here," lamented Dumpling as she stirred the pot of beans she'd started cooking on the stove the Saturday morning she, Vin, and Memaw had arrived. "I know he had that doctor conference thing in Little Rock, but it's the holiday weekend and our first time staying at Wolfwood."

"You know it doesn't have to be a holiday for you to stay here with us," Josie pointed out. "The house is plenty big."

"We know that, but we don't want to intrude on your lives all the time," Memaw confided. "You're newly married in a new town with a new job and new in-laws. Plus, you have a teenager to raise."

"How's that going?" asked Vin, as he added some herbs to the venison stew he'd been cooking for hours. "Tommy seems happier than he's been since before his mama died, and he says his school year is going well. I know he likes his job at Walmart, but I'd like to see him doing more than stocking a warehouse when he graduates from high school."

Josie stopped stirring the iced tea and asked, "He hasn't told you?"

"Told me what?"

She shook her head and suggested, "Ask him at dinner."

Vin's brow furrowed, but he nodded before he asked, "How's the clinic?"

"Great. We have lots of patients, both black and white." Placing the iced tea in the refrigerator, she inquired, "How's your work?"

"I've always loved my job, whether I was patrolling, working at the jail, investigating, or being Sheriff. It gives me real satisfaction to know that I'm making my area of the state a safer place. I did have to fire a deputy yesterday, and that's never a fun thing to have to do."

"Why'd he get fired?"

"He beat a prisoner who was arrested for rape. Nobody beats any prisoners in our jail. It's an automatic dismissal if you do."

"That's a good policy, but I can see how it would be hard for policemen not to beat up some of the really bad people who get arrested."

"If a man can't control his anger, then he's not worth squat. I learned that lesson from my daddy, who took out his anger on my mama and me. I always told my sons it was better to deal with their anger inside than to plaster it all over their faces for the world to see or to use their fists to take it out on others. Cheek never listened, and Stone didn't listen much either until he was about seventeen or eighteen. Nelson was the only one who didn't have outbursts or get into physical fights, but I guess that's because he was gay. Hell, I don't know. I tried my best with all three boys, and look where it got me."

"I can't say anything about Cheek," Josie remarked. "My one encounter with him obviously wasn't a good one. I only know Nelson from what I've heard, but he seems to have been a very nice, intelligent person. As for Stone, I'm a little biased there."

"The twins were our pride and joy," Dumpling confided. "We just didn't quite know what to do with either of them. Memaw could reach them better than we could. They were in their own world, and we didn't know how to be part of it."

"It's my fault that Stone's sick, isn't it?" Vin asked rhetorically. "He's always been so angry, and I told him to bottle it up instead of teaching him how to deal with it. He's going to die younger than he should because of me."

Josie wanted to tell her father-in-law that this wasn't true in order to make him feel better. However, she believed it was an extremely astute observation and busied herself with taking the hash brown casserole out of the oven. She wished she could tell him Stone was trying to deal with his anger issues by attending the anger management retreat, but Stone didn't want anyone except Josie to know the truth about why he'd gone to Little Rock.

Tommy arrived home, quickly showered, changed into shorts and a t-shirt, and then came downstairs for dinner. As they ate, the family members chatted about mundane topics then listened in rapt attention as Memaw told them of the day long ago when a supposedly dead man had been found under her family's home. It turned out that he'd been a drunk who'd tried to crawl under the house for shelter and had passed out halfway there. He'd regained consciousness, scaring everyone gathered by "coming back to life" in front of their eyes.

Once the family had finished eating and moved to the living room, Vin awkwardly asked his grandson, "Tommy, what are your post-graduation plans?"

"What? I'm only a junior, Pepaw."

"I know, but it's good to have goals. That doesn't mean anyone's going to hold you to them. You can always change your mind. So, what do you want to be?"

"I want to be a sheriff like you."

Vin's eyebrows shot up in surprise. After a moment, he said, "I'm honored. What does your father have to say about that?"

"That he'd be proud of me if I followed in your footsteps."

"Stone told you that?"

"Of course, he did," Tommy said nonchalantly. "He's always looked up to you, Pepaw."

"I doubt that."

"That's the problem, Vin," his mother remarked. "Nelson and Stone thought the world of you, even though you were very different from them. You wanted them to be like you and conform, but they weren't the type to do that. That's caused many problems over the years. Cheek's another story."

Vin seemed lost in thought for a long time then declared, "I'd like to call Stone and talk with him tonight."

"The conference rules are very strict," Josie said casually. "No phones, clocks, computers, tablets, or television. It's all supposed to be focused on the attendees and what they can get out of the intensive weekend."

"Sounds more like a Marriage Encounter retreat than a doctor conference," Dumpling observed. "I guess when you're a doctor you have to get a lot done in a short amount of time."

"He'll be home Monday night around 9:00," Josie told Vin. "Maybe the two of you could have dinner on Tuesday and talk then."

"I'd like that. Things have been better since you came into Stone's life, but he and I have a lot of unresolved issues."

"You can say that again," Memaw muttered. "You're both such good men, but you can't seem to completely accept one another for who you are. You *have* been trying a lot harder since Nelson died, and I'm so proud of you for that. It took Josie's presence to make Stone attempt a reconciliation with the family, and thank Heaven for her."

"You've always accepted each of us in the family for who we were, Mama," observed Vin. "How do you do it?"

"God made us all different for a reason. It's not my place to try to change anyone. Each person has his or her own purpose, and I'm not God so I have no idea what that is. Therefore, I accept people as they are and try to be a good person myself."

Vin nodded thoughtfully and said, "When Stone gets back I want to talk to him about starting over."

"He'd love that," Josie offered. "He loves you, Vin."

The man nodded slightly and said, "I know. Sometimes, that's not enough."

Chapter Eleven

"Josie, why don't you, Tommy, and Memaw come to church with us?" Dumpling suggested at breakfast the following morning.

"No, but thank you," Josie answered kindly. "I appreciate it though."

"It's not as if we go to Pastor Skinner's church," Vin pointed out. "He takes the Bible way too literally."

"Where does he take it?" Tommy snickered.

"Don't joke about the Bible," Josie admonished. "It's a very sacred thing to a lot of people."

"You've read the Bible?" Dumpling asked hopefully.

"From cover to cover," answered Josie. "It's a good book. My father highly recommended it, along with the other Classics."

Dumpling frowned and echoed, "Classics? What do you mean?"

"I'll explain it on our way to the service," Vin said. Arching one dark brow at Josie, he asked, "What about church?"

"It's not really my thing. I don't get angry like Stone but –"

"It makes Stone *angry* to go to church?" Vin asked incredulously.

Mentally slapping herself, Josie stammered, "I – I – that's what he told me."

"Sweet Jesus in Heaven," Dumpling said with what sounded like despair in her voice. "Oh, Vin! Did *we* do that to him?"

Her husband looked away and said, "I think *I* did that to him. I've got to work this out with the boy when he gets home."

"Don't lecture him on religion," Josie advised. "I don't think lecturing of any kind would be a good idea."

"I don't intend to lecture him or to tell him he'll burn in Hell for not going to church each week. I don't believe that. It's only that I want him to be happy and not...destroy himself from the inside out."

"I'm going to be late for work," Tommy announced, obviously eager to get away from their discussion about his father. "I'll see you guys tonight for dinner."

"You have your lunch?" Josie asked, as he headed for the door.

"Yeah. Thanks. Bye!"

"Vin, we'll be late for church," Dumpling said with a sense of urgency. "We should go."

"All right. We'll be back around 12:30."

"That'll give me and Memaw time to make lunch. She said she was going to teach me how to prepare round steak or something. I think we're having rice with it."

Vin smiled and said, "You two have fun. We'll see you soon."

"He's a good man," Memaw said about her son once he and Dumpling had left for the church services. "I'm sorry his father and I weren't the best of parents. I'm thankful he's done so well in spite of us."

"You were sick," Josie told her. "It wasn't your fault any more than it was my parents' fault that they were mentally ill."

"That doesn't excuse my husband. He was just plain cruel. His family was all so wonderful. He was simply born to be a terrible man. Sad."

"For him and everyone else."

"Amen to that!" Memaw declared. "Now let me show you how to make the round steak…."

Once Vin and Dumpling returned from church, the four of them ate lunch then spent the afternoon walking the property, talking easily. When Tommy returned home, Josie prepared grilled cheese sandwiches for the family. After dinner, they lounged in the living room, watching television until Tommy excused himself to do some reading for school.

"It may be Labor Day tomorrow, but Tommy's not the only one who has to work," Vin announced. "I'll be up and out by 7:00."

"I have a women's group meeting in the afternoon," Memaw reminded them. "Perhaps Dumpling, Josie, and I can spend the morning together, and then Dumpling can drop me at my meeting on her way home. Would that be okay with you, Josie?"

"Whatever works best for everyone. The clinic is closed tomorrow because of Labor Day. The gym will also be closed, and Tommy won't get home from work until 6:00 tomorrow. I think I'll plan to read all afternoon. It'll be nice and relaxing."

Josie spent the next morning with Stone's mother and grandmother, stretching out on the bed with a pile of books beside her once they'd departed. After reading for a few hours, she decided that she should get in some physical activity. Figuring that a walk in the woods would be perfect, she marked her place in the book she was reading. It was 3:00, and she wanted to be back in time to greet Tommy, who was bringing home potato salad, cole slaw, and baked chickens from Walmart for their dinner.

Wearing a pink sundress but no shoes, Josie left the house via the kitchen door. She loved the feel of the grass and dirt beneath her feet and intended to enjoy it as often as possible. She tried not to dwell on the years she'd denied herself such a simple pleasure, all because of her father's anxieties.

Josie passed the place where she and Stone had encountered the wolves. There was a spot further down the path where one could see the river, and she thought perhaps she could sit there and relax before strolling around the area near the water. She was close to the spot when something slammed into her back, pushing her to the ground.

Stunned, Josie lay on her belly in the dirt with the breath knocked out of her lungs. Her brain directed her to rise, but her limbs refused to obey. She was confused and disoriented and wondered what had hit her so forcefully in the back. That was when a hand wrapped itself around some of her hair and jerked her head to one side.

"You stupid bitch," Cheek Romero hissed. "Did you think you could just come into our lives, break our family apart, and steal my son away from me?"

"He's not your son," she managed to say. "He's Stone's son and is very relieved about that."

She cried out as he roughly hauled her over, throwing her onto her back. Her back already hurt, and there was a searing pain in the lower right area of her abdomen. It felt as if every muscle in that vicinity had been torn, and even the most miniscule of movements brought with them great pain. She automatically moved a hand towards the spot where the pain was concentrated, but Cheek stopped her by punching her in the face. Josie saw stars.

"Stupid, fucking bitch!" he barked. "Everyone in town thinks you're so pretty, a walking, talking Barbie doll with your cute figure, pretty face, blonde hair, and blue eyes. Well, I can fix all of that. When I get done with you, you won't be pretty, walking, or talking."

"Cheek, don't –"

He hit her again, and everything began to spin in Josie's line of vision. She blindly reached for his crotch, thinking if she could grab him there and squeeze hard, then he'd become focused on that and would let her go. He punched her once more, and she instinctively drew up her arms to protect her head. The torn muscles in her abdomen burned with pain, and she moaned.

Cheek lifted her up by her shoulders then slammed her to the ground once more. Josie's arms fell to her sides, and Cheek grunted with satisfaction before proclaiming, "Not only am I going to teach you a lesson, but I'm also going to get even with my little brother for having sex with Malinda and getting her pregnant."

"Stone wasn't even fourteen," she struggled to say. "How can you possibly get even for that?"

"Like this."

Josie was amazed by how quickly what followed happened. Cheek yanked off her panties, unzipped his pants, pushed her legs apart, and prepared to drive into her. She screamed, attempting to push him away, but his big body kept her slight frame pinned to the ground. She turned her head from left to right looking for anything she could use as a weapon – a rock, a stick, anything. There was nothing but dirt and stray pine needles.

"Stone got Malinda pregnant," Cheek panted then struck Josie again in order to ensure she stayed still. As black tinged the edges of her vision, he hissed, "Let's see how he likes it when I get you pregnant. I'm going to come in you again and again to make damn sure that –"

Suddenly, Cheek wasn't talking anymore. He also wasn't on top of Josie. Dazed, she fought to understand what was happening. Cheek screamed, but snarling noises threatened to drown out his cries. The screaming and snarling went on for what seemed like hours, but Josie knew it probably only lasted a few minutes. She tried turning onto her side without success. She wanted to pull the hem of her dress down to cover herself but couldn't seem to make her hands work properly.

Eventually, Cheek's screams ceased, and Josie wondered whether or not he was dead. She continued to be unable to rise. Finally, she forced her arms to cooperate with her brain and pulled down her skirt as much as possible. At least whoever found her body wouldn't instantly see her naked below the waist and view the obvious evidence of attempted rape.

Still unable to move much at all, Josie tried not to think about what had just happened. She was hurt and covered in dirt and probably blood. A deep sense of cold pervaded her body, and she began to tremble. Then, she heard something in the distance. The something was getting closer, but Josie didn't attempt to call for help.

"Josie? My God. Josie, look at me."

She moved her head slightly and looked up at Vin with her right eye, the one that wasn't swollen shut. He was wearing his Sheriff's uniform and looked grief-stricken and grim, but he was in control. There were tears streaming down his cheeks as he looked from her to somewhere she couldn't see.

"He hurt me," Josie said quietly. "He tried to rape me. Something stopped him."

"Pepaw, did you –"

"Tommy, get out of here!" Vin ordered. "Call 911, and tell them Josie's been attacked and that your...that Cheek...appears to be dead. Wait for them at the house and lead them back to where we are."

Tommy remained rooted to where he stood, looking in disbelief between Josie and what she assumed was Cheek's body. As tears trickled down her face, she begged her stepson to do what his grandfather had instructed. He took off running through the woods back towards the house.

"I'm so sorry," Vin said hoarsely. "I can't believe my son attacked you like this."

"Thank God, Cheek didn't get the chance to rape me!" Josie cried, fighting not to babble but quickly losing the battle. "He could've gotten me pregnant! That was what he intended to do! If he'd raped me, I'd have had to take the Morning After Pill! I can't be pregnant! Not *ever*! Cheek wanted to get me pregnant as revenge against Stone, and I can't ever get pregnant!"

"What if Stone got you pregnant before he left and you took the pill and killed his baby?"

"I can never have a child, Vin!"

"But what if you accidentally got pregnant with Stone's child and –"

"It couldn't be Stone's! He had a vasectomy before we came here for Christmas."

"What?!?"

Josie felt herself mentally unraveling and cried, "You can't tell him that you know!"

"Josie –"

"Make them clean me, Vin! I feel so...so soiled. It feels...it feels...like Cheek came in me, even though I know he didn't."

"I know what it feels like to be raped, remember? Everything's going to be okay," Vin said reassuringly. "We're going to get you to a hospital; they'll clean you up; they'll treat your wounds; and we'll get you help."

"No! Stone...if he finds out...his blood pressure...and he'll never want to touch me again if he knows Cheek...what he did and...I don't understand why he wants to touch me anyway knowing what he does about me and...."

"You *will* get through this," Vin stated firmly. "But you have to have help."

"No! Vin, please! Give me your gun, and walk away!"

"What? Josie, no!"

Despite the heat, she began to shiver violently. Vin removed his shirt and covered her with it. As he quickly examined her face, head, and arms, small smudges of her blood appeared on his white undershirt.

"What if Cheek's not dead?" Josie asked, her teeth chattering. "What if he wakes up and tries to hurt me some more?"

"My son is dead," Vin said tightly. "His throat is torn up, and there's blood covering the other areas of his body I can see. Looks like wolves got to him. They most likely saved your life by killing him. They protected you."

Josie began to laugh. Her father hadn't protected her, yet a pack of wolves had. The irony of it was too much. She thought of the day she and Stone had enjoyed sex in the woods, of how they'd joked about Stone marking her with his scent. It had evidently worked.

Vin stroked her blood-streaked hair and told her he'd take care of everything. Josie lost consciousness as he reassured her that she was going to make it through her ordeal. When she woke, she was surrounded by doctors and nurses in a hospital exam room. Flynn stood beside her, wearing scrubs and looking worried.

"Flynn? What time is it?"

"8:15. They just got you here."

"But Stone will be home at 9:00 and –"

"And his mother and grandmother are waiting for him at Wolfwood."

"Tommy?"

"Insisted on coming to the hospital with Mister Vin. The Medical Examiner already took Cheek's body, and they got things squared away at the scene before it grew dark."

"Mrs. Romero, I need you to stop worrying about everyone else and concentrate on yourself," one of the male attending physicians told her. "With your permission, I'll record your explanation of what happened on a digital recorder for our sake and for the police. That way, you'll have given a statement and won't have to give it again right away. If that's okay, then I'll have you sign the release and we'll begin treating you."

Josie signed the release and reviewed what had happened before, during, and after her attack. By the time she'd relived the events, she was crying again and was acutely aware of how much pain she was experiencing. Medical personnel thoroughly examined and cleaned every wound, stitched the torn flesh of her top lip, performed an ultrasound on the area of her abdomen that was so sore, and wrote orders for an MRI and x-rays.

"The only thing we have left here is the pelvic exam," said one of the male doctors. "We have a female gynecologist who'll perform that. We need to use a rape kit and make sure no rape actually occurred."

"Cheek didn't rape me!" Josie insisted, panicked. "He tried, but he didn't!"

"You have a head injury and might not remember. We have to check."

"No! No one else is touching me there! I want to take a shower now!"

"Mrs. Romero, we have to perform the exam and use the rape kit for your own protection and as evidence for the police."

"I'll stay with you," Flynn said gently. "I won't watch, but I'll stay while they do what they have to. It's necessary. It'll be okay."

"Please, don't!" she pleaded. "*Please*, don't do it!"

"We have to," the doctor said with sympathy in his voice. "I promise we won't take any longer than we have to. Once we're done, we'll get you cleaned up, have the x-rays taken, perform that MRI, and put you in a room for observation tonight. A social worker will visit you in the morning and recommend a good therapist. Every sexual assault victim needs counseling."

Josie said nothing. She held Flynn's hand tightly as the rape kit was utilized and the exam was performed. By the time the female gynecologist finished, Josie felt violated again and wondered if she was on the edge of a breakdown.

The nurses cleaned her after the x-rays and MRI, but Josie continued to feel dirty. Thanks to the painkillers, she fell asleep before they transferred her to her hospital bed. Later, she jerked awake and stammered, "The – the wolves!"

"Shhh," Flynn said softly. "You're fine."

"Not fine," she mumbled. Fighting to stay awake, she asked, "Where is Stone?"

"Here at the hospital. He's meeting with the doctors who treated you earlier. He's understandably…upset but so relieved that you're alive. They haven't let him see you, yet. His pulse and blood pressure are pretty high right now."

"He won't want to touch me anymore. I don't want him to touch me. Nobody ever again."

She drifted back to sleep before Flynn could comment. The next time she woke, Stone was standing beside her bed, stroking her hair. He looked tense, worried, and exhausted. Josie noted he was wearing jeans and a rumpled Oxford shirt. His hair was even more disheveled on top than usual.

"How are you feeling, Josephine?" he asked softly.

"Groggy. Hurts."

"Where?"

"Back, belly, face and…everywhere."

"I'll find out if you can have more pain meds."

Once he'd pressed the button and explained his request to the nurse, Josie said, "I'm sorry."

"For what?"

"For not being able to have sex again."

"We'll have sex again."

"No, we won't. I can't. The mere thought of it makes me cringe."

"You were almost raped, Josie. I don't expect you to want to have sex anytime soon, but I *do* know that I'm your husband and love you. Sex is an integral part of our love."

"And if I can't do it?"

A nurse entered with the pain medication and quickly left after dispensing it. As Josie waited for it to take effect, she asked how the anger management retreat had gone. Stone blinked in surprise.

"My brother savagely attacked you, tried to rape you, and got killed by a pack of wolves. Daddy and Tommy found you, and Daddy and Flynn helped you at the scene and then got you to the hospital. You're in a lot of pain. And you're asking me how the anger management retreat went?" Rubbing one hand over his face, he stated, "You never fail to amaze me."

Josie repeated, "How was the retreat?"

Sighing, Stone said, "It was really good. I had all of these plans regarding how to implement what I'd learned when I got back."

"Don't change your plans," Josie insisted. "I'm so scared, and I'm scared for you. Vin is so scared for you and wanted to call you all weekend so that he could talk to you about having a better relationship. I told him that the conference was really strict about no contact, and he was so disappointed. He blames himself for your anger issues. I didn't dare tell him the truth about where you really were and the retreat, but...but I did accidentally tell him about the vasectomy when he found me in the woods. I didn't mean to say it and –"

"And it's okay. Once you're asleep again, Daddy and I are going to have the first of many long talks. I'm done with being mad at him, Mama, and Clayville. However, I doubt if my hate for Cheek will ever die. If he were still alive, I'd kill him for hurting you like this. I knew he was a sorry excuse for a man, but I never expected him to go this far and do what he did to you."

As realization dawned, Josie said quietly, "You listened to the recorded statement I gave." When he nodded, she cried, "I didn't want you to hear! I didn't want you to picture him hitting me and trying to rape me! Why did you do that?"

"Because my brother is dead, and before he died he brutalized my wife. I needed to know what I was up against in my fight to keep you from killing yourself. I'm sure that was one of your first thoughts."

"Of course it was," she said quietly. "I asked Vin to give me his gun and walk away, but he wouldn't do it. It would've been so nice to rest forever."

"No," Stone insisted. "Think of the inscription on the back of the watch you gave me. You promised to love me for *ever*. You can't break your promise. I love you, Josephine. We *will* make it through this. Trust me."

"When it comes to this, I don't think I can."

Chapter Twelve

Josie lay listless in her bed and stared at the wall across from her. It had been two weeks since Cheek's attack, and she'd only gotten up to use the bathroom, force herself to eat and drink something, take her antibiotics and pain medications, and shower once a day. The rest of her time was spent lying in whatever position was the least uncomfortable for her back. Her entire body ached, but her mind was blank most of the time. She was existing.

There was always someone in the house with her. During the daytime, Dumpling and Memaw were in attendance. In the evenings, Stone was always there. Tommy and Vin took turns sitting with her when Stone had to leave the room. Everyone spoke to her, but she didn't speak back. She'd refused to speak to the therapist at the hospital. In fact, Josie hadn't uttered a word since the day after Cheek had beaten and attempted to rape her. That didn't seem to stop the others from trying to elicit some response when they were in her presence.

"You're losing weight you can't afford to lose," Dumpling told her as they sat at the table for lunch one afternoon. "Stone, too."

Josie didn't look up at her mother-in-law, as she ate the chicken soup Memaw had made for them.

"Maybe you could talk to that therapist," continued Dumpling. "Maybe if you took some anti-depressants or anti-anxiety drugs it would help."

Josie kept eating. She wasn't about to try any of those medications. With her family history, something that was meant to help her brain chemistry might actually have disastrous results – or so she reasoned. At the moment, all she could do was survive from one second to the next and wait.

Flynn came by to visit and to talk about how much he missed her and how everyone around town was asking about her. People were worried and sent their good wishes. Miss Iris, who was quickly deteriorating, wanted to come visit Josie but couldn't because she was too weak. Josie wished she could go to the older woman but couldn't. So, she lay in her bed and stared at the wall.

Stone spent hours each night talking to her about everything going on in the world outside Wolfwood. Cheek had been buried with only his parents and grandmother in attendance, and Stone and Vin were struggling to work through what Cheek had done and to build a new and better father-son relationship. Tommy was constantly asking what else they could do to help Josie get better, but no one had an answer. Things at Carmody & Romero were suffering because of Josie's absence, but patients were understanding about delays and the doctors' efforts to do the business and administrative duties normally performed by Josie. Stone was fighting to keep his blood pressure at acceptable levels in spite of everything.

Josie felt bad that she hadn't been able to allow Stone to touch her since the attack. All he could do was stroke her hair and hold her hand. Simply trying to hug her had made her afraid, so he'd stopped trying. She wondered how long he'd be able to handle that. But the mere thought of any other physical contact terrified her.

More days passed, and Miss Iris died peacefully in her sleep. Josie wished she could do the right thing and attend the woman's funeral, but she found she still couldn't speak or get out of bed for long. Once, when they thought she was sleeping, she heard Dumpling ask Stone if perhaps Josie should be institutionalized for a while so that she could get the help they obviously couldn't provide for her. He'd vehemently dismissed this suggestion. Josie wanted to tell him to listen to his mother. She felt she was beyond help and wondered if being in a mental health facility was the answer. He could divorce her and leave her there. People would take care of her until she died. She said nothing.

One night, she woke and rose to go to the bathroom. As she washed her hands, Josie saw the bottle of Stone's blood pressure medication on the counter. It was a full bottle, one he'd gotten on his way home that day. She suddenly had an overwhelming urge to take every pill.

An image of Stone finding her lifeless body and collapsing from a heart attack or stroke flashed through her mind. Instant panic shot through her, and she called out Stone's name. He appeared in the bathroom in seconds.

"Did you call for me?" he asked, his brown eyes filled with worry.

She nodded and blinked back tears.

262

"Are you okay?' When she shook her head, Stone said, "I want to hold you, Josephine." As she took a step backward, he hastily said, "Okay. It's okay. Just talk to me. Please, let me help you! Tell me what you're feeling."

"I – I'm so scared!" she admitted, as one tear slid free. Her disused vocal cords protested as she explained, "I just thought about taking the entire bottle of your pills and ending it all. I panicked!"

"Of course you did, because you don't really want to die. If you did, then you would've downed all the pills without waking me. You wanted me to stop you."

She nodded again as another tear trickled down one cheek.

"Let me hold you. You're shaking like a leaf." When she nodded rapidly, he took her in his arms and said, "Thank you, God." As he led her from the bathroom, he asked, "Is your back all right enough to sit up on the chaise lounge for a while?"

"I can try."

"Let's do that then."

Josie leaned heavily against him, as they sat side-by-side. She was immensely relieved that she no longer seemed afraid of having Stone do more than hold her hand and stroke her hair. As a matter of fact, she wasn't afraid to have him touch her at all. Her cry for help had somehow shattered the psychological barrier that had surrounded her since Cheek's attack.

"I want to go back to work," Josie announced. "I need to be out of here, even though it scares me to think of how everyone will act."

"How do you think everyone will act?"

"They'll either kill me with kindness or whisper behind my back about what happened."

"You're probably right. However, I can tell you that most people are just plain concerned about you. I can also tell you that since your attack Flynn's had two female patients approach him and say they were raped at different times in their lives and ask for help. I had a sixteen-year-old patient do the same last week. I wish it'd never happened, but at least it's leading other people to get help. Speaking of getting help, does this mean you'll finally talk to a therapist?"

"Yes, but no meds unless I'm schizophrenic or have no control because of some other mental illness."

"I agree."

"Stone?"

"Yes?"

"I need to have sex with you."

"Before you called me into the bathroom, you wouldn't let me do anything except touch your hair and hands. Now you want to have sex?"

"Something fell back into place inside of me when I cried out for help a few minutes ago. I need to have sex and know that you still want to have sex with me."

"But...?"

"But I have to be on top and in control the whole time, at least at the beginning."

"Maybe we should talk to the therapist first."

"No. Now. I need to feel desire for you again and not just remember the violence and sickening feeling that came with the attempted rape. I need to climax. I think it will...cleanse me."

"And your back?"

"Is sore but will be all right."

For all of her certainty about her need to have sex with her husband, Josie found herself shaking as she and Stone undressed. However, the moment she was astride him and felt the familiar presence of him inside her, she became almost jubilant. What they were doing was normal and right. What Cheek had done had nothing to do with sex; it was about power and revenge. It hadn't destroyed Josie's longing for Stone or intimacy. She felt almost drunk with relief, and it didn't take either of them long to climax.

"Ow!" Josie exclaimed, as she moved off Stone.

"What's wrong?"

"My back and stomach muscles aren't happy with me. Maybe they're not ready for that position, yet. I don't care. I'm so glad we did that. It restored my hope."

The following week after two visits to the therapist and an examination by the orthopedist in a nearby town, Josie was given permission to return to work part-time. However, if she showed any signs of serious physical or mental distress then she was to stop and return for reevaluation by either or both doctors.

Despite the overwhelming enthusiasm of the clinic's patients, there was no doubt that Josie struggled as she returned to her former routine. Life with the family and Flynn was going well. Being out in public was proving harder.

Josie had been right in her assessment of how others in the community would react to her attack. Most were sympathetic to the point of smothering her with well-meaning words of encouragement, but some were either too uncomfortable to approach her and whispered behind her back or muttered things like, "She shouldn't have been walking in the woods alone." When Josie heard these comments, she wanted to engage the speakers in conversation but forced herself to say nothing. She wasn't ready. She wasn't strong enough and wondered if she ever would be. She wondered, that was, until she ran into David and Mary Ann Skinner in the pharmacy area of Walmart one afternoon on her way home from work.

At first, Josie didn't see the couple. She was standing in line waiting to pick up Stone's prescription. She'd had a good day, the best so far since her attack. Josie was feeling positive, stronger than she had in weeks, and only had a slight backache. Stone and Tommy were on their way home, and Stone was making grilled chicken, baked potatoes, and salads for dinner.

"Well, God does deal with sinners accordingly," Josie heard David Skinner say from somewhere behind her. "Look at what happened to Nelson Romero. He engaged in unnatural sexual behavior and ended up taking his own life, which is also against God's will. Cheek Romero ran that club that promoted depravity and was a habitual liar."

"And Stone and Josie Romero had intercourse before they were married," Mary Ann put in. "Perhaps the attack on Josie was God's way of teaching both of them a lesson in His vengeance for those who don't attend church or follow His word."

Josie stepped up to the counter and asked for the prescription. She didn't turn to look at the Skinners or their audience. It didn't matter. What she would say would soon be all over Clayville. She smiled as she paid for the medication and thanked the clerk.

As she turned, Josie's smile remained. She strode over to stand in front of the pastor and his wife, who were surrounded by a handful of men and women who she assumed were some of their faithful sheep.

"Hello, Pastor and Mrs. Skinner," she began sweetly. "How nice it is of you to be so charitable and concerned about my family and me. Oh, wait. You're probably two of the only residents in town who *haven't* been charitable or concerned. From what I just overheard, you're downright hateful. Your version of the Bible must have been written especially for you."

"That's blasphemy!" Skinner declared angrily. "You're a sinner who got what she deserved."

"No person ever deserves to be beaten or raped. Children get beaten and raped. What did they do to deserve it? It's like saying gay people get AIDS because it's a punishment for being gay. Yet, straight people also get AIDS. How do you explain that?"

"We don't always understand why God chooses to allow suffering. However, sinners who engage in sex outside their marital lives, lie and promote the suffering of others, or commit suicide are damned to Hell for all eternity."

"It's very tragic that you believe that, Mr. Skinner."

"And why is that so tragic? It's the truth."

"Because you just described your mother, who had an affair, lied about it and caused the death of an innocent man, and killed herself. How awful for you to think that she's in Hell for all eternity because of what she did. What she did was obviously wrong, but the God I believe in would forgive her, not damn her forever, if she were repentant or mentally disturbed. I pity you and those who follow you. Hate destroys; love strengthens."

Skinner's face paled with what Josie assumed was rage. His wife sputtered unintelligibly. One of the nearby women gasped, and a man in the small crowd cried, "Nigger-lover!"

"God loves all men and women," Josie declared. "He doesn't discriminate, and neither do I."

She walked out of the store and made it to her car before she allowed herself to begin shaking. Feeling the physical after-effects of the emotional confrontation, she closed her eyes and tried to calm herself. When someone tapped on her window, she yelped involuntarily and opened her eyes. An elderly, white woman stood next to her car door. Josie lowered the window.

"I just want to tell you how proud I was to be there to hear what you said. It took a lot of courage. You're an inspiration."

"Oh. Thank you. I just said what I felt was right."

"Well, you did a great job. Have a good night, you hear?"

Josie drove back to Wolfwood, wondering whether or not she'd overstepped some local boundaries and if there would be repercussions for her family and the medical practice. The moment she got home, she planned to tell Stone about the exchange with the Skinners and get his impressions. However, he didn't give her the chance. When she entered the house through the back door, he immediately took her in his arms and kissed her hard. She responded with equal enthusiasm then drew back and asked, "What's the occasion?"

"You are amazing! *That's* what the occasion is. I can't believe you told that bastard Skinner off in the middle of Walmart. You made quite an impression on everyone around."

"Who called you?"

"The pharmacist. He and I were in school together from kindergarten through twelfth grade. Man, Josie! He said you were fabulous and showed so much strength and composure."

"But what if what I said causes us problems or hurts business at the clinic?"

"Then we'll deal with it. That's what real change is all about, isn't it?"

"I guess it is. Where's Tommy?"

"In his room on the phone with his friends, telling them how cool his stepmom is."

She grinned and said, "Cool stepmom. I like the way that sounds."

That night, Josie and Stone made love without any reservations or hesitation on either's part for the first time since her attack. Afterwards, Josie fell asleep in her husband's arms and dreamed of a red brick house where she and Stone lived. It was located in a middle-class neighborhood and was filled with children, dogs, laughter, and love. The atmosphere in the home was chaotic but happy, and there was talk of work at a medical practice, children's school assignments, baseball games, dance lessons, and a trip to the park. Once all the children had been put to bed, she and Stone retreated to their room and made love with impressive intensity and stamina. They slept and woke to the sound of one of their youngest children proclaiming his hunger from the crib in the nursery.

The dream stayed with Josie long after she woke. It had been a beautiful dream filled with everything they wanted. Yet, it hadn't taken place at Wolfwood. Why not? Was she subconsciously wishing they would move or was her dream a premonition of things to come? Were they meant to leave Clayville? If so, why? Despite everything, they had settled there. The medical practice was thriving, and the Romero family members were all getting along wonderfully. Although Josie didn't like everything that came with living in Clayville, she loved the close-knit feeling she got from being part of a small community. Clayville was now also *her* town. Was she really meant to leave it? If so, then fate must have better things in store for her, Stone, and their family and friends.

Fate is a fickle mistress, Josie reminded herself. *We may end up somewhere else, but what will lead us there?*

Chapter Thirteen

"So, what'd you think about your first hunting trip?" Tommy asked eagerly after they'd finished their venison, potatoes, and collard greens with bacon. "Will you do it again?"

"I don't know," Josie answered honestly. "It certainly was quite an experience, and it's good to know that all those shooting lessons with you, your father, and your grandparents paid off. I hated to see the deer die though. I don't know if I want to be the cause of another deer's death in such a personal way. I *know* I never want to have to clean a carcass again. Ugh."

"Every animal we eat has to die and be cleaned," Vin pointed out.

"Yes, but I don't want to have to be the one to take care of that." Josie turned to Memaw and asked, "Did you ever hunt?"

"No. My husband abhorred hunting, and I was never too thrilled with the idea of Vin out hunting. Yet, he took to it at a young age, and I didn't want to stop him. He told me once he needed to escape into the woods, and I decided that wasn't such a bad thing with Vincent being so cruel and me being so crazy. Vin was always a very good shot, and we did eat what he killed and cleaned. Neither my husband nor I objected to that."

"It was one thing Daddy thought I could do right," Vin remarked. "At least there was one thing."

"Your father was simultaneously brilliant and dense," his mother told him. "You've done a lot of things right in your life. I'm so proud of you, Vin."

"Thanks, Mama," he said with a grin. "I'm proud of you, too. You had a lot to overcome yourself."

"I'm glad you know how to shoot a gun and a deer rifle now," Dumpling told Josie. "Every woman should know how to do those things just like any man. You may not want to shoot another deer, but you may have to someday. Our pastor was talking about the crumbling foundations of society last week. If the government and all the banks collapse, we might have to get out there with our guns to hunt for food."

"The government needs some fixing like it always has, but I don't think it's going to collapse anytime soon," muttered Vin. "I'm not going to start building a shelter underground and run from some potential threat. If it comes, then bring it on!"

Tommy beamed at his grandfather, his unabashed pride evident. Stone was grinning and nodding in agreement with his father's declaration. Josie smiled at Sheriff Vin Romero. He was a good husband, father, father-in-law, son, grandfather, friend, and neighbor. He was also a child abuse survivor, a child who'd survived living with a mentally ill parent, and a molestation survivor. Most people thought it took a brave man to be Sheriff. They were right, but they had no idea how much courage it took to be Vin Romero. Josie was full of admiration for the man.

"Thanksgiving is next week," Dumpling said uncomfortably. "What do y'all want to do for the holiday?"

Stone's smile vanished, and he excused himself from the table. Once he'd gone out the front door of his parents' home, Josie began to rise from the table in order to follow. Vin told her to stay put, that he wanted to take care of his son.

"This is all part of that getting-in-touch-with-your-anger thing that Stone and I have been working on for months. I want to help him be able to enjoy Thanksgiving again without thinking so much about Nelson's death and what happened between us afterwards. I don't know if it's possible, but I want to give it a shot."

She nodded, although she had little hope Vin would succeed. Stone had already informed her he intended to avoid spending Thanksgiving with his family. He'd said the only thing he was thankful for on that day was that the brother who'd driven his identical twin to commit suicide was now also dead.

"Stone is doing so much better with his anger," Memaw observed. "How's his blood pressure been, lately?"

"He still has to be on medication, but the upper and lower numbers are actually good. He talks more about his anger when things start to bother him, and he keeps a journal that only he reads. It seems to be helping."

"Vin started keeping journals like Stone," Dumpling admitted. "He said he never realized how much he'd kept bottled up inside since he was…a little boy." She darted a glance in Memaw's direction and said, "It's for only him to read, too. He seems more relaxed since he started writing."

"I'm glad," Memaw declared with a sad smile. "Maybe we should all start journaling."

"My journals would quickly accumulate and eventually take over the house," Josie mused. "I wouldn't care if people read mine though. They'd think my life story was fiction. No one would believe what life was like with my parents."

"Do you miss them?" asked Tommy.

"Yes."

"Even after everything they did to you?"

"They were sick. They didn't do it intentionally. They loved me. They did the best they could."

The front door opened and closed, and everyone craned their necks in order to see into the living room. Only Vin stepped into view. His eyes were red from crying, and he removed a handkerchief and blew his nose before saying, "He'll come for lunch."

Dumpling got to her feet and asked, "How did you do it?"

"I told him we'd invite Chas to join us."

"Nelson's partner?" Josie asked. "But what if he won't come?"

"He'll come," Memaw said quickly. "He needs closure himself so that he can get on with his life."

"But what about his family? What if they have plans?"

"Chas is an only child whose parents are dead. It's a shame, really. They never had a problem with his being gay, and he was very close to them. They both died of cancer a few years ago."

"Do you think he'll be able to stay at Wolfwood with us?" Josie asked. "What if it's too painful for him?"

"Then he'll stay at my house," announced Memaw. "I always did like Chas."

"You go to Stone," Vin told Josie. "Tommy, maybe you should stay here tonight. I know it's your week with your father and Josie but –"

"I think you're right, Pepaw. I'll stay."

Josie bid them all good night. After giving each one a hug, she left the house, wearing her coat and carrying Stone's. He was waiting for her in the Honda but didn't look towards her as she got in. His eyes were red like his father's.

271

"Tommy's going to stay here tonight," she told him. "Your dad thought it might be better that way, and Tommy agreed."

He nodded and started the engine. Neither of them spoke as they headed for home. When they were almost halfway there, Stone said, "I couldn't believe Daddy offered to have Chas come for Thanksgiving. I know Mama had talked about having Chas visit, but I wondered if she and Daddy would really be serious. It'll make Thanksgiving better but worse, too."

"Do you think he'll stay with us? If not, your grandmother said he could stay at her house."

"I'll ask when I talk to him. I want to call as soon as we get home."

He did, and Chas agreed to come for the holiday weekend and stay with them at Wolfwood. He and Stone discussed exact dates and times and said their goodbyes. Then Stone hung up and called Flynn and invited him to the Romeros as well. Flynn agreed to come for lunch but said he had other plans for the evening."

"Everyone in town knows he has relationships with black women!" Josie exclaimed when she heard this. "Why doesn't he just come out and openly date them?"

"Because there are still racist pricks out there who might seriously hurt or kill him and his partners if they did. At this point, Clayville's still not ready for a local white doctor openly dating black women. Maybe someday."

The next week was filled with constant activity as the Romeros planned for the upcoming holidays. Josie decided that she wanted to put up a Christmas tree at Wolfwood before Chas arrived. Stone was ecstatic, although he insisted they buy a realistic-looking artificial tree instead of a live one. They set it up the day before Thanksgiving and then decorated it with Tommy's help. Josie was happy about the tree, *her* first Christmas tree. She was thrilled that Vin, Dumpling, and Memaw all declared how beautiful it looked.

"During the Thanksgiving holidays we'll set up a live tree," Dumpling announced. "We can decorate it with the family ornaments."

Josie eyed her new tree and said, "Ours does look kind of plain with just white lights and gold bows, but I want to wait and add special ornaments over the years."

"I want to give you the first one!" exclaimed Tommy.

"That means a lot to me," Josie told him.

"And me," Stone agreed. "Our first family ornament will come from our son."

Chas arrived at Wolfwood on Thanksgiving morning. Stone went up to the main gates to let him in. Josie watched from one of the front windows as the two men embraced briefly then stood talking for thirty minutes in the freezing morning air before coming to the house. Both looked extremely sad, and she prayed that this was not a precursor of the mood that was to prevail during the holiday festivities.

Maybe it's the mood that needs to pervade the holiday festivities, she thought. *Everyone here needs to grieve for Nelson and move ahead for real.*

Chas was bald, trim, and well-groomed. He was confident and polite, and Josie could see why any man or woman would be drawn to him. He had a quiet charm that made one feel at ease from the moment he smiled. His New Orleans accent intrigued her.

The next three days turned out to be wonderful times for the Romeros, Flynn, and Chas. They shared stories about Nelson, laughed and cried, and decorated Vin and Dumpling's tree together. Everyone told stories of Christmases past with family and friends. That was the only difficult part for Josie, who had no holiday memories to share.

Chas said "goodbye" to Vin, Dumpling, Memaw, Tommy, and Flynn on Saturday; then he returned with Josie and Stone to Wolfwood. He and Stone talked all night, and Chas departed after breakfast the following morning. Once his car was out of sight, Stone climbed the stairs, fell into bed, and slept for the rest of the day. He woke as Josie slipped into bed that night.

"Are you okay?" she asked.

"Yes. It was a great farewell. We all needed that."

"You don't think you'll continue to keep in touch with Chas?"

"We agreed that it was time to let go. Nelson is gone forever, and we've dwelled on what we had with him for too long. We'll never forget, but he's not going to come back, no matter how often or long we talk. We want the best for each other, and we won't have that if we continue to hang onto the past." Draping an arm across Josie's waist, he added, "It makes it much worse for Chas that Nelson and I were identical twins. Imagine if I died, and my identical twin brother was still around. Whether he was gay or straight, it would wound you every time you looked at him. You'd see *me*, even though you'd know the difference."

"That would make the loss even more unbearable."

"Exactly."

"Don't die on me," Josie said in a small voice. "I couldn't go on without you, period."

"You could, and you would."

"No and no. So there." She kissed his neck and said, "Go back to sleep. We have a full schedule at work tomorrow."

"No can do. I have to get up and eat something so that I can take my medication. You go on to sleep. I'll be back soon."

Josie drifted off while he was gone. A high, piercing noise startled her awake during the night. Bewildered, she looked towards Stone's side of the bed. It was empty. Another high-pitched electronic wail chimed in with the first and then another. Thanks to her father's OCD and anxiety, Josie had been taught at a young age to recognize that noise. It was the sound of smoke detectors ringing.

Clark Hollingsworth had forced his wife and daughters to have practice drills off and on throughout the years. He had told Josie and Zelda that he'd see to their mother, who often didn't know where she was anyway. He'd taught his girls to grab some clothing if a fire happened during the night and to make their escape as quickly as possible. They would all meet outside at a designated location.

When Josie and Stone had first moved into Wolfwood, she'd felt silly but had suggested to Stone that they have a fire drill and a designated meeting place. To her surprise, he'd thought it was a great idea. They formulated escape routes and agreed to meet near the front gates if there was ever a fire. When Tommy began living with them, they'd reviewed their plans with him and had engaged in a family fire drill. Everything had gone flawlessly.

Now, Josie darted for the closet, hastily putting on clothing and shoes. Within a matter of seconds she'd dressed, grabbed her iPhone wallet, shoved it into one pocket, and gone to the door of the master bedroom. She felt the door handle to see if it was hot. It felt normal, so she cautiously opened the door. Smoke was billowing down the hallway, and the electronic peal of the alarms was painful to her ears. She called out Stone's name, but there was no response.

He probably can't hear me over all the other noise, she reasoned. *Get out and meet him at the gates.*

Coughing and blinking back tears from the smoke, Josie dropped to her hands and knees, crawling to the stairs. She could feel the heat from the first floor and could see flames coming from the direction of the kitchen and living room. She quickly crab-walked down the stairs and prayed that Stone was already outside. She didn't want him to do anything stupid like try to rescue her.

Half-crawling, half-running, Josie headed for the front door and unlocked it. She was enormously relieved to discover that the alarm system had been disarmed, deducing that Stone must already be outside. She yanked open the door, stumbled out, and tumbled down some of the curved steps that led to the ground. Once she'd regained some semblance of balance, she edged down the rest of the way and lurched towards the gates. To her dismay, Stone was nowhere in sight.

When she reached the gates, Josie gulped in cold, fresh night air for a few seconds before turning back towards the house. For a moment, she couldn't breathe, and it had nothing to do with the smoke she'd inhaled. The interior of Wolfwood was engulfed in flames, and the outside was slowly surrendering.

Josie fumbled in her pocket and pulled out her iPhone. She dropped it, picked it up, and called Stone's number. It went to his voicemail. She then disconnected and called 911 to report the fire. There was no hope of putting out the blaze or saving Nelson's masterpiece. Even if the place hadn't been out in the middle of nowhere and was surrounded by limitless water supplies, it would've been too late. Just like plantation homes of days gone by, the structure was vulnerable to the flames. It would be gone by the time the fire trucks and police arrived.

Josie was about to hurry back towards the house to see if Stone had left through the kitchen door when there was an explosion that knocked her backwards. She hit her backside against one of the iron bars on the fence then pitched forward. Cursing, she rubbed at her sore buttock, trying to figure out the source of the explosion.

Open the gates before all the electrical goes! she thought frantically. Punching in the security code, she prayed, *Please, let them still work.*

275

They did, and Josie heaved a sigh of relief. She stood holding onto the bars for support and watched the house burn. She knew somehow that Stone wasn't inside, but she had no idea where he might be. Josie had the urge to leave her post, but she and Stone had agreed that they would stay at the gate if they made it there in case of a fire. She wasn't about to let him down.

Stone didn't come, but a fire truck and a police car eventually arrived. Josie thought it odd that only one fire truck and one police cruiser came to the scene. Everyone in the area surrounding Clayville knew how big Wolfwood was and seemingly admired it. As a young fireman gave Josie a quick medical evaluation and some oxygen, there was another explosion. The remaining windows in the house shattered. The roof began to cave in.

"Is anyone else coming?" Josie asked the policeman. "Has the Sheriff been notified?"

The man glanced at the two firemen with what Josie thought of as a "knowing" look. Wondering what they knew that she didn't, she demanded that they tell her what was going on. One of the firemen pointed out to the others that she would have to be told sooner or later.

"Told what?"

"This isn't the only fire," the policeman said. "There are at least two other places burning right now."

"Arson?" she asked quietly.

"Has to be," remarked one of the firemen.

"Why do you say that?"

The three men exchanged glances before the policeman said, "Because one of the other two is Carmody & Romero, and the other is Sheriff Romero's house."

Josie swallowed hard and asked, "Is everyone okay? I have no idea where Stone is, but I know somehow that he wasn't in the house when it caught fire. What about Sheriff Romero, his wife, and my stepson? What about Sheriff Romero's mother? And what about Flynn Carmody?"

They admitted that they didn't know, yet. Josie quickly called Tommy's iPhone, but her call went to voicemail. The same thing happened when she tried Flynn.

"While we're here, let's search the fenced-in part of the property, the policeman suggested. "Dawn's breaking, so it won't be as hard to see. Maybe we'll find Dr. Romero somewhere nearby. If he's hurt, then we can transport him to the hospital."

Josie insisted on participating in the search. The two firemen went in one direction along the fence, while Josie and the policeman went along the other. The heat from the now-smoldering house remained intense. There were still some areas alight, although the roaring fire had ceased after the second explosion. Josie noted that both her Volvo and Stone's Honda had been destroyed by flames as well. She wondered why they hadn't exploded.

Stone was nowhere in sight. Josie and the policeman met up with the firemen at the back gates, which stood open. This was obviously how the arsonist or arsonists had escaped, most likely with Stone who would have to tell them the code. Either that or the perpetrators had somehow managed to open the gates on their own, which was doubtful.

The policeman turned to the fireman and asked, "Would you mind giving Mrs. Romero a ride to whichever location you're going or dropping her off somewhere else if she wants?"

"I don't want," Josie put in quickly. "I need to go to Sheriff Romero's first and then to the clinic. I need to see if the rest of the family's okay."

She rode in the fire truck to Vin and Dumpling Romero's home. As they approached, she saw another fire truck, two police cars, and the burnt shell of the house. She was shocked to see that Memaw's house had also been set ablaze. Josie experienced a sickening feeling in her gut, as she climbed out of the fire truck and approached the policeman who was obviously in charge of the scene.

She had met the man several times before and had thought of how much he reminded her of Vin, although this man was perhaps thirty-five and blonde. Still, they had the same temperament and were both intent on protecting and serving those in their community. The man's name escaped her at that moment.

"Mrs. Romero, I wish you hadn't come out here. It's not something I think you want to see."

"No, but I had to come." As she scanned the area, she recalled that the man's name was Officer Simon Bartels. She asked him to tell her what he knew about the fires and if any of her family members had been in the homes when they'd been burned. He told

277

her he honestly didn't know, and they would have to wait until things cooled a little more before the police could investigate.

"It's a good thing it's late November and not July," he muttered. "Even so, it'll take a while." Glancing towards Vin's truck and Dumpling, Tommy, and Memaw's cars, he said, "It doesn't look like anyone left here on their own. Still, they could've been taken before the houses were set on fire. From what the officer at your house told me while you were on your way here, it sounds like that's what happened with Dr. Romero."

"And Dr. Carmody?"

"Same story as here. We'll have to wait until it's safe for us to investigate. Carmody's truck was left at the scene of that fire. None of the vehicles were burned, except yours and Dr. Romero's. Odd."

"Is the clinic destroyed, too?"

"Pretty much. I'm real sorry."

Josie nodded sadly. Although material things meant little to her, she'd grown to love Wolfwood, her in-laws' houses, and the clinic that also served as Flynn's home. She would miss the over-sized silver bell Stone had given her the previous Christmas because of its symbolism and his intentions. Stone would be overwrought by the loss of Wolfwood. The others would be devastated that all of their lives' memorabilia and family photos were gone. The only photo Josie had of her own family was now burned to cinders.

None of it is important as long as everyone else is okay, she told herself. *But why did someone do this and why take everyone else, leaving only me?*

Just then, a shout came from one of the firemen. Josie immediately headed in his direction, but Officer Bartels ordered her to stay back. When she refused to stop, he directed one of his men to restrain her. She fought the man but didn't stand a chance of breaking free. He looked like a real-life version of the Incredible Hulk – minus the green skin and angry scowl.

Bartels disappeared around one side of the remains of the Romero household. Josie gave up struggling and strained to listen, but all she could hear was first a curse and then low voices. After a few minutes, Bartels returned, looking grim. Josie began to tremble.

"One of my men found Sheriff Romero's wife further back in the woods."

"Is she alive?" Josie asked hoarsely.

Bartels looked away and said, "She was when he found her."

"She…she's dead?"

He nodded and expressed his condolences then asked, "Did you know Miss Dumpling had heart trouble? It looks like she was running away from someone but couldn't move fast enough. She said something to our man about her chest hurting when he found her. She mumbled a few things then passed away."

In shock, Josie asked, "What kinds of things?"

"Something about ropes and about saving her family." Glancing back in that direction, he added, "I guess she asked for Pastor Skinner then lost consciousness and died."

"She requested Pastor Skinner?" Josie asked in disbelief.

Bartels shrugged then admitted, "She said 'Skinner,' so our officer thought she was asking for a preacher to bless her before she went to Jesus."

Josie suddenly felt dizzy. She'd come to love her in-laws and was going to grieve deeply for Dumpling. The woman had been like the mother she herself had never truly had. She tried not to think of Dumpling suffering a heart attack as she'd run from the arsonists.

Another shout came from somewhere else out of view. Bartels ordered his man to keep Josie where she was and hurried off again. Once more, he returned looking grim. Josie simply waited.

"Looks like Sheriff Romero's mama never made it out of her house. She didn't get burned, but she must have been trapped and died of smoke inhalation. One of the firemen found her in a fairly untouched area of the house." Shaking his head, he added, "I know you're stunned and upset by all this. So are we. We're not family, but most of us have known Miss Dumpling and Miss Gertrude our whole lives. We're going to get the bastards who did this, Ma'am. I promise you that!"

Bartels's cell phone rang, and he excused himself, walking away to take the call. Feeling numb with grief, Josie stared at Bartels and watched his body as it went from straight and expectant to deflated and sad. She waited anxiously for the next victim to be revealed. It turned out to be a young black woman who'd been found tied up in the locked room where the medications were kept at Carmody & Romero. She, too, appeared to have died of smoke inhalation. Still, none of the men or their bodies had been found at any crime scene.

"I think I need to sit down," Josie heard herself say. "Can I sit in a police car for a while?"

Bartels led her to the truck he'd driven to the Romero home. She sat, her thoughts obscured by a mental fog, as she tried to absorb the knowledge that Dumpling, Memaw, and another woman were dead and that Stone, Tommy, Vin, and Flynn were all missing. Some malevolent people had taken the men, set fire to the homes, and expected the women to die.

Thank you, Dad, Josie thought as she began to cry. *Your worry for Mom, Zelda, and me probably saved my life tonight.*

She cried for a while and then dried her tears. Getting out of the truck, she approached Deputy Bartels, asserting, "I have to go to Carmody & Romero to see what's left of the clinic. How do you intend to find Stone, Vin, Tommy, and Flynn?"

"I'll take you to the clinic for a brief look at the scene, but I honestly don't know where we're going to start looking for your family and Dr. Flynn. I'm Sheriff Vin's right-hand man and will probably be asked to lead the investigation. We'll investigate the scenes of the fires, create a timeline, and compile lists of possible enemies and motives."

"Whoever took the men obviously wanted them to know that we were all dead," Josie told Bartels, as they rode towards the clinic. "Well, they thought we'd all die. So, the kidnappers want the men to suffer with that knowledge until they…what? Kill them, too?"

"I'm not sure. There's not enough data to formulate any theories, yet. Sheriff Romero has enemies because of his job, and your husband and Flynn Carmody have enemies because they treat blacks and whites at their medical practice. Plus, everyone knows Flynn Carmody has a thing for sleeping with black women. So, there are quite a few possibilities." As he slowed his truck to a stop, he muttered, "We need more people and resources ASAP."

Flynn's castle-style home had slightly less damage than the others, but Josie suspected that it would probably be a total loss. It would have to be bulldozed and rebuilt if Flynn was still alive and so desired. Josie tried not to imagine the unnamed black woman tied up in the room, dying of smoke inhalation as the house burned around her. That led her to think of Memaw, who hadn't been tied up but had met the same end. Feeling suddenly weak, Josie put her hands on her knees and took deep breaths.

"You hanging in there?" Bartels asked. When she nodded, he added, "I need you to come back with me to the station. I want to get an official statement and figure out where you're going to stay for now."

"I'm a displaced person," Josie realized. "I lost everything in the fire except my iPhone wallet, which holds my driver's license and one credit card. I have no purse, no cash, no clothing, and no coat. I don't even have a charger for the phone."

"Our people can help you get some of the things you'll need," he assured her. "By tonight, you'll at least have cash, a charger, and some new clothing. However, someone's going to have to stay with you at all times until we catch these guys. You're supposed to be dead, and you're not."

Stone is a prisoner who thinks I've burned to death and doesn't have his medication with him, thought Josie. *If he's not found soon, they won't have to kill him. Because of his hypertension, he'll kill himself without even trying.*

Chapter Fourteen

As police officers from other parishes joined the local investigation of the fires, deaths, and disappearances, one of the Clayville policemen went with Josie so that she could get something to eat and purchase new clothing, a coat, and a purse. She also went to the bank, withdrew some cash, and requested balances for the checking and savings accounts she and Stone shared and the clinic's business account. No money had been illicitly withdrawn or transferred.

"So, whoever's responsible isn't out for money," Deputy Sheriff Bartels commented when she returned and shared the information about the accounts. "I think it's revenge, pure and simple. I'd like for you to stay at my house tonight. My wife and I have a guest room."

"But what if someone sets your house on fire to finish me off?"

"I'll have men posted outside and inside," he assured her. "I want you to be fully protected at all times until this is over."

Josie accepted his offer of accommodations for the night. Her only other option was the one motel in town, and it wasn't a very appealing prospect. Better to stay with a policeman and his wife in their home than alone in a run-down motel room.

Before going to bed that night, Josie showered for thirty minutes but couldn't seem to rid her skin and hair of the smell of smoke. She lay awake all night, praying that Stone was somehow remaining calm, that his blood pressure and pulse weren't skyrocketing, and that none of the men she cared about were being hurt. She mulled over what Bartels had told her and what she'd witnessed. Despite the fact that Bartels and his wife slept in the next room, a policeman was stationed in the living room, and another was in a cruiser outside, Josie felt utterly alone.

"I need a car," Josie said to Bartels once they were back at the station the next morning.

"Where are you going to go?"

"Wherever. I need to clear my head. Maybe if I just *drive* then something will come to me."

282

"You need protection."

"In the middle of the day in Clayville? Everyone knows everyone else's business and keeps their eyes open for juicy gossip. I won't leave town once I have a vehicle. The only problem is that all of our keys were lost in the fires."

"Sheriff Vin has an extra set in his office," a young policeman offered helpfully. "He used to lock himself out of his truck a lot after Nelson killed himself. He said he was distracted. So, he took to leaving a set of truck keys here just in case. I used to bring them to him when he'd accidentally get locked out. I know where they are."

"Good. I'll use Vin's truck for now."

Bartels eyed her suspiciously then asked, "Have you ever driven a truck?"

"You are obviously *way* behind the times," Josie said sarcastically. "Barbie owns all sorts of vehicles. For your information, I know how to drive a car, a truck, a boat, and a four-wheeler. When in Clayville...."

Josie was soon driving Vin's truck with no particular destination in mind. She noted the policeman tailing her and didn't care. She needed time to think without distraction and without being reminded every moment of the dead women and missing men and boy as the police station hummed with investigative activities. FBI agents were slated to arrive in her absence due to the nature of the case and the fact that a law enforcement agent had been kidnapped.

Around lunchtime, Josie pulled over at The Shake Shack, went to the window, and asked, "Could I have two chocolate shakes, please? Large ones."

The middle-aged, white cashier burst into tears and said, "I was *so* upset to hear about the fires! And then to hear that Sherriff Vin, Miss Dumpling, Miss Gertrude, Dr. Stone, and Dr. Flynn were all either missing or dead! It's terrible! I hope the police can catch whoever did this to the Romeros and Dr. Carmody!"

Josie felt her eyes fill with tears and thanked the woman – but not too pleasantly. The cashier hadn't mentioned the dead black woman, and Josie innately knew the omission had been deliberate.

She carried the shakes to the police car, climbed in, and handed one to the older policeman who'd been tailing her. He thanked her and offered her money for his shake.

"No," she insisted. "I want to thank you for your efforts and thought hot coffee would have been more appropriate since it's freezing, but coffee's definitely not as filling as a chocolate shake."

"Where are you headed next?"

"To buy guns and bullets."

He blinked in surprise and echoed, "Guns and bullets?"

"Yes. I have a right to protect myself just like everyone else."

And if Stone dies then I can put a bullet in my brain, she added silently. *My promise to not kill myself will be null and void if he dies.*

"You know I'm gonna have to tell Deputy Sheriff Bartels about this."

"Go right ahead. It's a free country."

After they finished their shakes, Josie returned to Vin's truck and then drove to a local gun shop. Once there, she selected a handgun and a rifle with the assistance of the owner. When she'd moved to Clayville, Josie had hated to hear that Louisiana had such lax gun laws but was now thankful for them. After a twenty-minute FBI background check performed by the shop owner on his computer, she purchased the weapons and ammunition. Since Louisiana was an "open carry" state, Josie walked out to Vin's truck with her guns clearly visible. She had no intention of applying for a permit to conceal them. She prayed she wouldn't have to use either weapon but wanted to be prepared.

Josie placed her purchases in the back seat of Vin's truck and decided to put the boxes of ammunition in the truck's large glove compartment, which was locked. She found the glovebox key on Vin's keychain. When she opened the hinged door, she was dismayed to see that there wasn't much room to add anything else. As she reached to remove the stack of papers from the front, they fell to the floor. She stared at what was tucked behind them.

Three spiral-bound, single-subject notebooks had been wedged against the back of the glove box. Josie hit the LOCK button on the truck door and then pulled out the notebooks. She opened the one that had been positioned at the bottom. It was the first of the journals Vin had begun to keep in order to help him deal with *his* anger issues.

I have to read them, Josie realized. *There may be something in them that will explain the attacks. Oh, God. Just thinking about reading these is making me sick to my stomach. I don't want to read them, but I can't give the private journals to the police and have others read these without knowing what's inside. If there isn't anything useful, then at least I'll be the only one who knows the whole truth about the awful times in Vin's past.*

Sickened but riveted, Josie read of Vin's childhood home, a place filled with a loving, unpredictable, mentally unstable woman and a hateful man who routinely beat his wife and occasionally beat his son. Vin never knew what to expect from either parent. His mother might be fun-loving and vibrant one day then so deeply depressed that she couldn't get out of bed the next. His father was given to fits of rage that ended in destruction of property or physical violence. Vin witnessed his mother being beaten many times and felt powerless to stop the abuse. At age eight, he'd taken to roaming the woods with a BB gun or a small rifle family friend Albert Skinner had given him. Albert's son, David, had the same gun.

Her hands shaking, Josie tossed down the first notebook and picked up the second. In the beginning, Vin discussed his relief at wandering alone in the woods when not in school or playing with friends. Sometimes, he and David Skinner would go hunting together. One day, David was sick and couldn't go with him on a planned outing. David's father had offered to go in his son's place so that Vin wouldn't be disappointed. Dr. Romero kept David at his house and sent Vin out into the woods with Albert. It was the first of many hunting trips involving young Vin and Albert Skinner.

The entries in the pages that followed filled Josie with revulsion. Albert had molested Vin many times over an extended period. Finally, Vin decided that he had to take matters into his own hands. While he and Albert were out hunting one afternoon, Vin waited for an opportune moment, aimed, fired his rifle, and shot Albert Skinner in the shoulder. As he stood over the injured man, the child told him he had a choice to make. Either he never touched Vin again or Vin could shoot him and finish him off right there in the woods. Skinner had come back alive, claiming that Vin had accidentally shot him when Albert had gotten careless. Vincent Romero had treated the wound, and Albert distanced himself from the Romero family. Not surprisingly, David Skinner also distanced himself, and the boys barely spoke to one another, even in school.

285

Vin fell in love with Dumpling during high school and married her after graduation. He wrote of how difficult it had been to share his secret with her. He explained how patient she'd been in the beginning of their marriage when he'd often been unable to perform sexually due to his childhood molestation. He wrote of the relief that came with his success at attaining normal relations with his wife and of their love.

The next journal was mostly about Cheek, Nelson, and Stone. Vin expressed his disappointment and disgust with Cheek, his feelings of anger towards Nelson for ending his life, and his struggle to reach Stone, whom he'd always felt was so much like him and yet so different. He wrote of how he worried he'd failed as a father and of how much he wanted to make things right with his one remaining son. Vin felt as if he'd been a good grandfather to Tommy but pondered whether or not he and Stone would ever be completely at ease in one another's presence.

Thank God for my Dumpling, Mama, and now Josie, he'd written. *The Blessed Trinity is female for me.*

Josie shut the half-filled third notebook, placed it on the seat beside her, and then drove to the police station. She locked the notebooks back in the glove compartment, got out of the truck, walked directly to the bathroom, and vomited. She experienced that sickening feeling of the old man kissing her and of the stubble above his lip rubbing against her soft skin. She heard him asking her to come into his apartment. She hesitated and –

Someone knocked on the bathroom door, and Josie jumped involuntarily. From the other side, Simon Bartels asked, "Miss Josie? Are you all right?"

She wiped her face with a damp paper towel, cupped her hand, and drank some water from the tap. It tasted bad, but it helped to mask the foul taste in her mouth.

Josie opened the bathroom door and looked into Deputy Bartels's concerned face before saying, "I'm not all right and need to talk with you in private." Glancing around, she added, "Not here at the police station."

"We can go for a drive in my cruiser," he suggested. "I promise to keep my eyes on the road while we talk."

Once they were in the car, she said, "I think you were right. I think this is about revenge, pure and simple. However, I think it's about revenge for more than one thing."

"Such as?"

"You said your man who found Dumpling Romero mentioned something about rope and said 'Skinner' to him."

"And you don't think she said 'Skinner' to my man?"

"I *do* think she said 'Skinner.' What I don't think she said was 'rope.' I think she said 'robe' instead."

"Robe? What would David Skinner and robes have in common?"

"Most people know that David Skinner preaches about a God who promotes intolerance and damnation. His father was a good friend of Sheriff Romero's father, who was also a terrible racist. They were big buddies. I think they were part of the Ku Klux Klan together. I think that when David's mother claimed Iris Freeman's husband raped her in order to cover up her affair and he was acquitted, Albert Skinner and Vincent Romero headed up a group of KKK followers and hung Miss Iris's husband. Then Albert found out along with everyone else that his wife lied and had been cheating on him. She killed herself, leaving him with baby David. I think Albert blamed his wife and blacks for his own misfortune and raised his son with the same attitudes. David Skinner grew up to be a pastor to atone for his parents' sins but was already permanently warped by his father."

"Is that why he and Sheriff Romero stopped being friends when they were boys? People still talk about how they were close and then suddenly never talked to each other again. That was around the year I was born, but folks still talked about it and wondered what happened to break their bond of friendship. Everyone in Clayville knows about it."

Josie closed her eyes and prayed for some sign that would tell her how to proceed. Nothing happened.

"You have to tell me if you know something important that might relate to this case," Bartels said abruptly. "If you want me to swear on the Bible that I won't tell another living soul, then I'll do it. I just want to find your family and Flynn alive. I'm not out to expose anything…unseemly."

287

Josie felt the old man's stubble on her face and wiped at her mouth with the side of one pointer finger before asking, "You'll swear to God that you'll never tell? Ever?"

"Never ever."

"Albert Skinner raped Vin Romero multiple times when he was a boy. Vin managed to put an end to it by shooting and threatening Albert, but that was when he and David stopped being friends. I think…I wonder if it was because Albert poisoned David's mind against Vin or if it was because he turned to his own son when he couldn't have access to Vin."

"Jesus Christ," Bartels breathed. "Sweet Jesus in Heaven! I – I'll never tell anyone about what Albert Skinner did to Sheriff Vin." Anger sharpened his voice as he exclaimed, "The Goddamned pervert! How can anyone do that to a little kid?" Glancing apologetically at Josie, he said, "I'm sorry. I know you were almost raped by Cheek. I'm not saying molestation of a child is worse than molestation of an adult. They're equally sick."

"Sort of. I was molested as a child as well, but it wasn't as bad as what happened to Vin. It was still very life-altering. A child is innocent and trusting, and when a grown-up takes that away…."

"I won't tell anyone about what happened to you when you were a child either," Bartels promised. "So, you think David Skinner is behind all of this. You think Miss Dumpling recognized his voice or something because he was wearing Klan robes and had his face covered."

"Probably."

"And David Skinner would want revenge against the Sheriff for what happened when they were boys, no matter what the story. Plus, he's a racist and condemns just about every man, woman, and child for being sinners. He doesn't believe in sex before marriage or in blacks mixing with whites, so he'd have something against Dr. Carmody and his lady friend on two counts."

"And he knows that Stone and I lived together before we got married and are good friends with Flynn," Josie pointed out. "And we recently had Nelson's former partner come for Thanksgiving. He celebrated it with the whole family and Flynn and stayed at our house, so we all associated with a man I'm sure Skinner considers a deviant because of his homosexuality. In his eyes, Stone, Flynn, and I probably also committed some big sin just by helping black

288

patients as well as whites. We'd all committed grievous sins in his opinion."

"Like murder isn't a sin!" Bartels growled. "Kidnapping would be bad enough, but to set fire to houses because you're intent on killing the women inside? How in God's name could he justify that?"

"Fanatics and psychopaths can justify anything," Josie remarked. "Setting the houses on fire was surely some symbolic gesture of how we were all going to burn in Hell."

"But why not just burn everyone together?"

"Skinner couldn't gloat and lecture to dead men. Better to get his revenge by making them suffer then kill them." She bit her lower lip then asked, "Do you think they're still alive?"

"Yes, but I wouldn't count on that lasting too long. The longer they keep them alive, the greater the likelihood that they'll be discovered."

"So, where are they? Where would they take them?"

"There are too many rural places to count. I'm going to bring you back to the station then question Mary Ann Skinner. Maybe she'll give us a clue."

"If she has any idea. She's so pompous, but she may actually be innocent."

As it turned out, Mary Ann Skinner wasn't at home. Neither was David Skinner. Bartels returned, frustrated and angry, to the station. Everyone sensed that time was running out for the four captives.

"You have to come back to my house again tonight," Bartels told Josie as dinnertime approached. "We'll eat, rest a bit, and try to figure this out."

She agreed and followed Bartels home in Vin's truck. However, as they turned into his driveway, an idea struck her. She dashed out of the truck and up to the side of the cruiser as soon as they parked.

"What about David Skinner's first wife?" she asked. "Is she still alive? Does she live in town? Maybe she'd talk to us."

"Great idea, but there is no 'us' when it comes to visiting her. I'll go alone."

"No. She doesn't know me and might be more willing to talk if I'm there. She left David, and if I tell her I think he has my husband who might die without his medication, then she may agree to help. We have to try!"

"I'll radio for back-up."

"And scare her off right away? No! Let's see what she has to say first. Then you can decide what the best approach is afterwards." When he paused to consider, she said, "Please. We have to find them very soon, and you know it."

"We're eating first. It'll be something quick, but we're going to eat. It won't do either of us any good if our brains aren't firing on all cylinders, and food is the body's fuel. Come on."

As she hastily consumed a ham and cheese sandwich, Josie thought of Stone's culinary talents and of how much he thoroughly enjoyed cooking and eating. It always pleased him greatly when others savored his creations. He'd experimented with Josie's beloved chocolate hazelnut spread and had come up with several delectable breakfast and dessert selections. One time, he'd brought a Nutella container to their bedroom and had done some experimentation outside the kitchen.

"You ready?" Bartels asked, interrupting Josie's thoughts. "Follow me in Sheriff Vin's truck. Don't bring any weapons in with you. I'll have my gun just in case there's a problem, but Debbie herself is no threat. She's afraid of her own shadow."

"Did she keep her married name when she divorced David?"

"No. She had it changed back to her maiden name of Dawson the day the divorce was final. Frankly, people were shocked that she had the guts to leave David, but she did. Things must have been pretty bad. She's very…meek."

Fifteen minutes later, Josie and Deputy Sheriff Bartels were sitting in meek, dark-haired Debbie Dawson's living room. Her house was tiny and cluttered and looked as if it could use a good cleaning. The woman herself was small and nervous but agreed to talk with them once they'd explained the situation.

"We don't have a lot of time here," Bartels told her. "Mrs. Romero's husband has a condition that requires daily medical treatment. If he doesn't get it or gets stressed, then he could die. He hasn't had any medication for a couple days and is probably pretty darn stressed right now, especially since he thinks his wife and the other important women in his life are dead." Staring at his knees, he added, "All of them except his wife *are* dead now."

290

"Please, help me save my husband, father-in-law, stepson, and friend," Josie pleaded. "If you can assist us at all, I'll be indebted to you for the rest of my life."

"I'll help you," Debbie answered slowly. "I couldn't stop David, but hopefully you can."

"Couldn't stop him from what?" Bartels asked.

"Spreading hate. Hurting innocents. He was a Grand Wizard in the KKK just like his father before him. Of course, I didn't know that when I married him. I'd been brainwashed by my parents to think of black folks as less than whites. It took David's extreme behavior with the Klan to make me realize how wrong that was. When I tried to convince him otherwise, he was shocked and told me I would burn in Hell for speaking blasphemy. I asked him where in the Bible it said that white people were better than blacks and pointed out that Jesus Christ himself was not a white man. That comment got me a broken nose. He tried to strangle me, and I knew if I didn't leave him he would eventually kill me.

"When I told David I was filing for divorce, he was shocked and begged for my forgiveness. I knew he wasn't sincere. He didn't want to lose his church was all. So, I left him. He did almost lose his church until Mary Ann swooped in to save him. She's a pretty woman with a mind as hateful as his. Her daddy had been in the Klan, and she had no problems with it. She and David were a good match for each other." Briefly closing her eyes, Debbie Dawson confided, "I was just glad to be free and live my life. I work; I have friends; and I don't live in fear like I used to. That's all I need. I'm happy."

"Did your ex-husband tell you anything about where he and his Klan buddies might go to participate in Klan activities?" Josie asked hopefully.

Debbie nodded and said, "It's a camp about an hour from here. It belonged to David's father. It's very secluded, but I can give you directions." After she'd done so, she said, "I really hope you get your family back, Mrs. Romero. I'm so sorry about Dumpling, Miss Gertrude and the black lady. David once told me that his father and Vincent Romero killed Iris Freeman's husband when they thought he'd raped David's mother. They didn't feel any remorse, even once they found out Isaiah, the man they'd hung, was innocent. Very sick of them."

Josie thanked the woman for her help and gave her a brief hug before she and Bartels left. He thanked Debbie Dawson as well and told her he would most likely have to call on her again in order to wrap up the investigation once David Skinner and the kidnap victims were located.

Debbie straightened and said, "I have to do what's right. God wouldn't want it any other way."

Chapter Fifteen

In the chaotic hour that followed their return to the police station, Deputy Sheriff Bartels and the FBI agent in charge began to plan a rescue mission relating to the camp. While Bartels was occupied, Josie slipped away and climbed into Vin's truck. She wasn't about to wait. She had a terrible feeling it was already too late, but she had to make every effort to save her husband and the others. Dressed in jeans, a sweater, and athletic shoes, Josie's only advantages would be whatever weapon she chose to carry and the element of surprise. If she got killed trying to save her family and Flynn, then so be it.

As she drove towards the secluded camp, Josie thought of the evil, violent hallucination End-of-Days. Each member of the Hollingsworth family had hated End-of-Days, who often guided Rhonda to act swiftly, maliciously, and without mercy. Now Josie wondered if she could channel some of the powerful force that had been part of End-of-Days in order to stop David Skinner and his compatriots. They had killed Dumpling, Memaw, and another woman Josie hadn't even known. They'd burned down the houses and the clinic. Now they were most likely torturing their captives. She despised David and his accomplices and would do whatever it took to end their reign of terror.

When Josie reached the turn-off for the camp road, she carefully drove the truck fifteen yards across bumpy ground through the woods and then parked. She debated about taking the handgun, the rifle or both. In the end, she pulled on a fleece jacket she'd bought after the fire, buttoned it, and then slipped the loaded handgun in its right pocket before climbing out of the truck. Then she trotted beside the edge of the narrow dirt road towards lights that were tiny specks in the distance.

As Josie got closer, she realized that what she'd seen was light escaping from the windows of a camp house. She stopped, crouched low, and listened. When there was no movement anywhere around her after five minutes had passed, she decided no one was on patrol and skulked towards the building.

Josie assumed that the men involved were arrogant and thought themselves smarter than anyone who might be looking for their hostages. Hence, there would be no need to post a guard. Hunching over, Josie edged towards a window. She peered in, instantly spotting four men dressed in white robes and pointy, white hats. One of them was David Skinner.

Hugging the wall of the building, Josie went to another window. She scanned a bedroom that proved to be empty although it appeared that someone had recently slept in the bed. A computer sat on a desk across from the mattress.

It didn't take her long to reach the next window. Josie peered inside then fought to stifle a cry of outrage and despair. Vin, Tommy, and Stone were restrained, their wrists and ankles manacled to wooden chairs with handcuffs. Vin's chair was closest to the window; Tommy sat next to him; Stone was beside Tommy; and an empty chair was to his right. It was evident that they'd all been beaten. Flynn was not in the room.

Josie focused on her husband. Wearing only pajama bottoms, Stone's head hung forward as if he were unconscious. Tommy wore pajama bottoms and a faded t-shirt, while Vin wore sweatpants and an undershirt.

None of them have shoes, she thought. Then, *Of course, they wouldn't. They were all taken at night.*

Josie studied Tommy. Despite various bruises and a busted lip, he looked relatively healthy. He seemed exhausted and sad but not in any serious physical pain. His short, brown hair stuck out in various places as if he'd just been pulled out of bed.

Vin had similar bruises on his body and a black eye. He seemed extraordinarily pale. Josie wondered whether or not he was dead and was relieved when he moved slightly, opening the eye that wasn't swollen. To her surprise, he turned towards the window. He searched with his good eye until he had it fixed directly on the corner where she was currently hiding. He paused, nodded then mouthed the words, "Get out of here, Josie."

Wondering how he could possibly know she was there, Josie moved around to the other side of the little camp house. She watched as the back door opened and a man she recognized from town stepped out to smoke a cigarette. When he wandered into the woods for a stroll, Josie cautiously crept inside, trying the doorknob that opened into the room where her family was being held. To her relief, it turned. She hurried inside and quietly closed the door behind her.

"What the *hell* do you think you're doing?" Vin whispered. "Get out of here and bring back my officers."

"They're on their way. I had a feeling I shouldn't wait for them. I thought I might already be too late. Am I?"

"For Flynn," Tommy whispered shakily. "The fucking bastards took him out yesterday and…and…." Beginning to cry, he continued, "We heard him screaming and screaming and then nothing. They said…they told us they cut off his balls for sleeping with a…a nigger and then they hung him from a tree." Josie began to tremble, as he wept harder and asked softly, "How could they even *think* of doing things like that? How could they do that to another human being?"

"I don't know," she whispered before wiping at his tears with her sleeve. "I can't think about what happened to Flynn right now or else I won't be able to act. I have to get all of you out of here before they kill you. Do you know where the keys are for the handcuffs?"

"David has them," Vin informed her. "Josie, you made it out of Wolfwood. What about Dumpling and Mama? Plus, Flynn said he had a woman friend at the house when they took him. Are the others alive?"

Josie couldn't bring herself to explain. She shook her head, wiping frantically at her own eyes. Tears streamed down Vin's cheeks, and he and Tommy choked back sobs.

I can't break down now, she reminded herself. *I have to find a way to free Stone, Vin, and Tommy and get us out of here. First, I need to make sure Stone's okay.*

"I think Stone might have had a stroke or a heart attack while Flynn was screaming," Vin offered hoarsely when she knelt in front of his son. Temporarily pushing aside his grief, he straightened in his chair and continued, "Stone had been holding his own until then, saying that he knew you were alive and had gotten out of the house when they'd set fire to it. He said he felt that his mama, Memaw, and the other woman had gotten out too and that we'd be found and freed. He seemed to be staying as calm as he possibly could until he heard Flynn screaming after those monsters hauled him outside. Then Stone started yelling and struggling to free himself even though he knew there was no chance. He got real red in the face and finally slumped over. He hasn't regained consciousness since."

"Someone's coming!" Tommy hissed. "Josie, there's a closet over there. Hide!"

Josie scrambled towards the closet, hurrying inside and leaving a crack between the edge of the door and the frame so that she could see the three men in the chairs and anyone who came close to them. She listened as the door to the room opened and closed. Then, David Skinner walked over to stand near Vin.

"I see you've been crying, Vin. Are you afraid of God's wrath? The Lord seeks retribution from all of you sinners. Which one of you should be punished next? Should it be you, Vin? You lied about my daddy and tried to turn me against him. You fathered a homosexual son who killed himself. You invited his lover to your home for Thanksgiving. You repeatedly invited a man who slept with niggers into your home. And you believed Iris Freeman when she told people that her husband was an innocent man. Isaiah Freeman *did* rape my mama, causing her to lose her mind, to say she'd made it all up because she was really a whore, and then to kill herself!"

"You're twisted, David," Vin said, his face still wet with the tears he'd shed once Josie had confirmed the deaths of the other three women. "You give white people and Southerners a bad name. Most of us are nice folks, although we all have our faults. We're not murderers or butchers or assholes like you. You make me sick."

"*You* make *me* sick," Skinner countered. "You fathered that good-for-nothing Cheek who ran that club for sinners. His whoring ex-wife slept with Stone and passed their baby off as Cheek's. Stone had intercourse with Tommy's mother when he was unmarried and then continued to have intercourse before marrying Josie Hollingsworth. And Nelson? Well, I suppose that Nelson did everyone a favor by killing himself since he was already damned by his homosexual behavior."

"My dad wasn't even fourteen when he and my mom had sex!" Tommy shouted, still crying. "How can you blame him for that when he was just a boy? And why do *you* get to decide what God wants and who lives or dies?"

"Shut up! You deserve to die as much as the other bastard children who exist in this world. The only chosen ones are those born to couples who were married when they first joined as husband and wife. The Lord will smite all the others and their parents!"

"Then let *Him* smite them!" Vin said angrily. "He didn't appoint you as judge, jury, and executioner!"

"Ah, but He did. The Lord came to me when I was a boy and told me it was going to be my duty to carry out His work here on Earth. He told me all of my own sins would be forgiven if I did His will. He talks to me and tells me His wishes."

"*Bullshit!*" Tommy roared. "You're nothing but a crazy fanatic who's trying to justify every horrible thing you've ever done and everything your horrible parents ever did! *You're* the one God will judge and send straight to Hell when you die!"

David Skinner's face turned purple with fury, and he stepped closer to Tommy. As Josie watched, Stone slowly opened his eyes and lifted his head. He looked at Skinner in his white robe, at Vin and Tommy, and at Flynn's empty chair. He seemed slightly dazed, as he slowly scanned the rest of the room. When his gaze swept in the direction of the closet, Josie pushed the door open a fraction wider. The motion caught his attention, and he looked startled for a second before nodding ever-so-slightly. She realized he'd seen the gun she currently held in her right hand.

"I'll kill you next," Skinner was telling Tommy. "Insolent child of sin!"

"No, you'll kill me next," Stone said quietly. "Just be a man and do it yourself instead of having your lackeys do it for you. If you truly believe you're killing for God, then you shouldn't be afraid of getting blood on your hands."

Enraged, Skinner lifted one foot and kicked Stone in the chest so that he fell backward, chair and all. Stone cried out as his head made contact with the hardwood floor. Skinner pulled a gun from somewhere in his robe and moved to look down at Stone, putting his back to Josie.

Forcing herself to pretend she was End-of-Days and that her only goal was to hurt and to kill, Josie took two deep breaths. She grew calm, released the safety on the gun, counted to five, pushed the door open wide, raised the muzzle, and then fired at the middle of Pastor David Skinner's back. The impact of the shot propelled him forward, and he stumbled and fell. As he did so, he raised the gun in his hand and pointed it at Josie. He pulled the trigger, and she felt a searing punch as the bullet pierced her square in the belly. She fell back into the closet and cried out with the pain as the wound began to gush blood.

Stone, Vin, and Tommy called out her name, but Josie was lying against the back wall of the closet and couldn't seem to get up. She heard others hurrying into the room and wondered if Skinners men would simply shoot them all dead and walk away. That was when she heard Simon Bartels's voice barking orders. She relaxed. She was going to die, but Stone would live.

Someone switched on the light in the closet, and Stone rushed in, crouching beside his wife. The naked bulb that hung from the ceiling blinded Josie, and she squinted in the brightness. She wanted to lift a hand to shield her eyes, but she found the effort was too great. Besides, her fingers felt wet with blood, and she'd most likely simply smear red streaks across her cheeks and forehead.

"We have to get her out of the closet!" Stone declared. "Tommy, see if you can find some towels so I can try to staunch the flow of blood!"

As men awkwardly moved Josie out of the small space, she screamed at the pain in her belly. She heard Stone thank his father then felt him put pressure on her wound. She screamed again.

"I know it hurts," Stone said before leaning forward to lightly kiss her lips. "You're losing too much blood, and I have to slow the bleeding if you're going to make it to the nearest hospital that can handle a gunshot wound like this." When she shut her eyes and didn't respond, he ordered, "You stay with me, Josephine! Remember your promise!"

"I remember," she moaned. "But it hurts so much!"

"I know. Gunshot wounds are bad in any location, but belly wounds are particularly painful and tricky. I'm just praying that nothing important got hit in there."

"Me, too. Barbie should come with all of her original parts." She groaned, as Stone repositioned his hands. Fighting not to scream again, she asked, "Did I kill David Skinner?"

"He's dead," Vin confirmed. "It was a pretty quick death. Better than he deserved."

"And the others?"

"The FBI and our men have rounded them up and have also arrested Mary Ann Skinner for her role as the arson mastermind of the operation," Bartels said. Cursing, he asked, "Why didn't you wait for us?"

"If I'd waited, then Stone would've died. Vin and Tommy might have died, too. I'm just so, so sorry that I was too late to save Flynn."

Everyone in the room was silent for several seconds. Bartels admitted that they'd found Flynn's body in the nearby woods. He didn't mention the castration. He didn't have to. Josie fought the urge to retch.

"Stone?"

"Yes, Josie?"

"I had to pretend I was End-of-Days in order to shoot David Skinner. It made me feel odd. I never want to feel that way again. I want to go away from this area forever."

"We'll leave as soon as we're able and never, ever come back."

"Will you come with us, Pepaw?" Tommy asked hopefully.

"My home is where my family is," Vin said, his voice rough with emotion. "Dumpling and Mama are gone. Flynn and his woman have also been murdered. Our homes have been destroyed. I've done all I can to make a difference in the community. It's time for me to leave."

"I want to go back to Austin," Josie said, forcing herself to speak despite the pain in her belly. "I liked it there. But I liked it here, too. I wish...I wish we could have made a real difference. I wish we could've stayed."

"We *did* make a difference," Stone assured her. "But I want to have a life for *us*, not for everyone else. Remember the kids and dogs we're supposed to have?"

"I'm not twenty-seven, yet."

"Screw twenty-seven! We'll pick out our first puppy after we buy a house in Austin. What kind do you want?"

"A Golden Retriever. A nice...normal...."

And then everything was quiet and dark.

Epilogue

Stone and Josie walked slowly around the remains of Wolfwood before heading through the back gates and along the dirt path. It was Christmas morning, and Josie wondered why Stone had asked her to come out to this place on this particular day, his first Christmas and birthday without his mother, grandmother, and Flynn.

They went to the spot where they'd encountered the wolves and then stood, waiting. Eventually, the pack appeared. Stone nodded solemnly to them, and the wolves paused then returned to the woods. Once they were out of sight, Stone took Josie's hand and slowly led her back up the path.

"How's your belly doing with all this walking?" he asked, as they neared the ruins of the house. "That's the longest walk you've taken since you were shot."

"It's a little sore but not bad." As they scanned the rubble that had once been Wolfwood, Josie asked, "Why are we here?"

"Because I had to see what's left of Nelson's masterpiece one last time before we leave Clayville forever. It's my final farewell. As long as this place stood, I think I felt as if my 'empty' half could somehow be filled by what Nelson had left behind. Now I know better. I can move on."

As Stone put an arm around her shoulders, Josie said, "Simon Bartels did a great thing when he asked residents who had any photos of your family members to make copies and donate them for an album. At least you have something you can review in order to remember the past when you want to. I wish I hadn't lost my family photo in the fire. I know I never put it on display, but it still meant something to me."

Stone stopped walking, withdrew an envelope from his coat pocket, and handed it to Josie. When she asked him what it was, he shook his head and simply told her to open it. Inside was a copy of the family photo she'd lost in the fire.

"But where did you get this?"

"Agents Katavich and Saghir of the FBI. Remember when they made a copy for their investigation? I contacted them while you were in the hospital, explained, and asked if they could send you a replacement. They said they'd be happy to do it." Kissing her on the temple, he said, "I have another present for you in the car. Come on. It's cold, and you should sit for a while anyway."

Once they'd returned to their new Honda SUV, Josie settled into the passenger seat and asked excitedly, "Where's my other surprise?"

Stone grinned and handed her a square box that had been wrapped in gold paper. Inside was an oversized silver bell that was identical to the one he'd given her the previous Christmas. The original had, of course, been lost in the fire that had destroyed their home.

Delighted, Josie exclaimed, "If it were possible for me to twist in my seat to kiss you, then I would! Thank you!"

"Save that kiss for later," he said huskily. "You got me a replacement watch and had it engraved like last Christmas. It was only fitting that I replace your silver bell so that you can put it in the house we'll buy in Austin."

"I'm happy you liked your replacement watch."

"I'll love it for *ever*," he said with a twinkle in his eye that she hadn't seen for weeks. "Let's go meet Daddy and Tommy and get the hell out of here."

As they drove back towards town, Josie asked, "What are we going to do with the property at Wolfwood? What will your father do with his land? And the clinic? Flynn left everything he had to you."

"There's a conservation group that wants to buy as much of this area as possible in order to save the wilderness and the animals that live in it. I think we should sell the properties to them. Daddy agrees. The group will work hard to preserve things and protect the animals that roam on the two rural properties and will probably build an office where the clinic used to be." After a long pause, he added, "I'm sorry."

"For what?"

"I brought you here. This was a place in which you felt secure, and then that security was taken from you, first by Cheek and then by David Skinner. We lost everything, including people we loved. You almost died saving Daddy, Tommy, and me. I don't want you to give up hope when it comes to our future happiness."

"I won't. I grew up in the Land of the Crazies, remember? This was just a different kind of bad for me."

"I don't want there to be any more bad for any of us. There's been enough insanity of varying types in our lives. It's time to start over, get settled in Austin, and find long-lasting happiness."

Resting her left hand on Stone's thigh, Josie said firmly, "I'm ready. I want a large house with a white picket fence and a big yard. That way, we'll have room for the kids and dogs we plan to adopt. We deserve a wonderful life."

"Well, Barbie has *her* Dream House, so why can't Josie have one, too? I'm fine with anything you want, as long as we're together, happy, and healthy."

"Together, happy, and healthy sounds perfect. You showed me what love really means. You helped me to heal."

"And you did the same for me. You, Daddy, Tommy, and I will be okay. It will just take time. Trust me."

Josie squeezed Stone's thigh before saying, "I trust you with my life, my body, my heart, and my soul. I *know* we'll be all right. I left my hopelessness behind the moment I opened my eyes after surgery and found you standing by my bed, holding my hand. You're my own personal guardian angel, Stone Romero."

Stone turned the SUV off the main road that led to town and drove a half mile down a dirt lane before parking. He then got out of the Honda, came around it, and opened the passenger door. Urging Josie to step out of the vehicle, he slipped one hand behind her neck and the other behind her back then said, "I may be your guardian angel, but *you're* the one who helped *me* find peace. You pushed me to discover who I really am and to let go of the anger I'd held inside for most of my life. You're the best thing that ever happened to me. You'll never know how much I love you."

"I know, because I love you just as much."

He kissed her, and Josie slipped her arms around his waist and thought, *And they lived happily ever after.*

Stone deepened the kiss and flexed his hips, being careful not to press against the tender area where she'd been shot the previous month. Josie moaned and moved one hand to rub over the bulge at the front of his jeans. Stone groaned in response and pulled back slightly, heat flashing in his hooded eyes. As he wove his fingers through her hair and leaned forward to rest his forehead against hers, he murmured, "Dance with me, Josephine."

They made love in the back of the SUV. Stone was achingly gentle with Josie, partly because of her tender belly and partly because he appeared intent on worshipping every inch of her body with his in a slow, deliberate fashion. Josie's body thrummed with pleasure, despite the limitations she was temporarily experiencing in the wake of the shooting. When Stone finally eased into her, Josie had to fight not to thrust her hips upwards and writhe underneath him. Her healing body wasn't ready for that, yet.

As Stone tilted his hips and thrust, using alternating rhythms and angles, Josie watched his muscles coil and release and felt her climax build. When he growled her name, her world exploded. She gripped his biceps and watched the beatific expression on his face as he climaxed.

Once they'd both come down, Stone automatically sagged on top of her, and Josie yelped at the discomfort. After hastily shifting his position and apologizing for inadvertently causing her pain, Stone raked his disheveled brown hair with one hand then stretched out beside Josie, stroking her cheek. She smiled up at him and shook her head.

"What?" he asked, confused but smiling back.

"I was thinking before we made love about the stereotypical phrase that ended old stories about men and women who'd triumphed over adversity and had bright futures ahead of them."

"'And they lived happily ever after?'"

"Yes. We've both had difficult times and persevered despite what many people would consider insurmountable obstacles. We're *not* a stereotypical couple in some fairy tale, so the stereotypical ending may not fit."

"Maybe not, but I think the stereotypical beginning works just fine."

Beaming up at him, Josie said, "You're right. We have years to work on the plot and will hopefully have that happily-ever-after ending anyway."

As Stone lowered his mouth to hers, he murmured, "Once upon a time...."

ABOUT THE AUTHOR

Lauren Cutrera, who also writes under the name Barbara Cutrera, has published over 20 contemporary romance, romantic suspense, paranormal romance, mystery, and fiction novels. Diverse people and plots highlight her works, drawing readers into the characters' unique journeys as they navigate their way through their struggles and triumphs. Lauren and her husband, Budge, are the proud parents of a grown son. They live in southwest Florida and have a cute and naughty Yorkie, Hadrian, who sleeps next to Lauren as she writes each day.

Explore other published works by the author at amazon.com and goodreads.com

Check out all things Lauren (and Barbara) at www.laurencutrera.com

And connect with her there or on

Facebook: https://www.facebook.com/profile.php?id=100063631654302

Instagram: https://www.instagram.com/laurencutrera/

Pinterest: https://www.pinterest.com/laurencutrera/_saved/

OTHER BOOKS BY THE AUTHOR:

The Essential Elements Series

Kindred Spirits
Scorched Creek
Spirits Corner
Memory Lane
Homeward Bound

The Limitless Series

Sight Unseen
Better Left Unsaid
Unheard Of
Under Her Skin
Brain Storm
Out On A Limb

The Seneca & Michael Duet

A Lovely Dream
A Lovely Reality

The Gift Series

The Healer's Gift
Jordan's Way
Bound by Grace
The Nameless

The Real World Series

Over, Under, Across & Through
A Good Man's Life
Mercy
Unfinished Business (Final Chapter)

Standalone Novels/Short Stories

In A Manner of Speaking
Prim & Proper
Lucky
Compromising Positions
True: 3 Short Stories

www.ingramcontent.com/pod-product-compliance
Lightning Source LLC
Chambersburg PA
CBHW070808180626
46818CB00001B/153